A SEASON OF GUNS AND DUST

MARSHAL HUNTER

FULMINE FERRI MEDIA

Paperback ISBN: 979-8-9905603-0-7
Ebook ISBN: 979-8-9905603-1-4
Hardback ISBN: 979-8-9905603-2-1
WGA Registration #: 2170879

Cover Art by Matt Ribeiro (https://www.artstation.com/mattart)

This book is dedicated to my wife Jenn, without whose encouragement I would have never started writing spicy romance. And whose unending support has allowed me to come this far.

CONTENT WARNING

A Season of Guns and Dust is a post-apocalyptic adventure that involves graphic violence and explicit sexual content. Many story elements are driven by the brute realities of living in the wastelands of a fallen world. Murder is a difficult word to quantify when the only law is survival. Killing, for good or ill, is simply part of life in the wastes. You will find slavery, child death, the threat of violence against children and the threat of rape in the pages that follow. Where there is great intensity, there is great passion. This book is about those things. It does not shy away from the harsh truths of the world it portrays.

Please keep these things in mind as you venture into this world with Adina and Asher.

Proceed gently with yourself.
~Marshal

CHAPTER ONE

Heat from the merciless afternoon sun baked into Adina Sky even under the shade at her workbench. Sweat rolled down her back as she carefully pushed needles through a freshly punched hole from opposite sides, making certain they crisscrossed as she stitched the new leather sole onto a battered boot. She didn't need to check the locking stitch; she'd been making them since she was big enough to hold needle and thread. But she checked it anyway. She didn't have much of the thick hide she used to make soles with, so she didn't want to risk a bad stitch. Satisfied, she pulled the threads, and the sole snugged up neatly against the rest of the boot.

Adina sat back and shook out her calloused fingers.

Ugh… Come on… no breeze at all?

She blew out a long breath and stood, lifting her arms to try and catch any hint of wind that might be there.

Adina pulled at her shirt to move air against her sticky body as she looked out over the rest of the camp from her rickety balcony. Being above the camp, she could take advantage of any breeze that might come along. But today the air was utterly still, and the heat just sat there, like an oppressive weight squashing everything down.

Adina leaned back until she could feel the stretch down her belly and along the front of her hips. She'd been hunched over the boots since just after dawn. She liked working in the cool of the morning before the heat set in like it had now. Her long black braid fell behind her as she reached for the hot sheet metal wall behind her. Her turmeric yellow shirt lifted to show her freckled stomach and the heavy belt that held up her faded, oft-repaired blue pants.

Her brightly colored shirt was one of Adina's most prized possessions. Last year, a caravan of cloth merchants spent a few weeks with them at their winter camp. She'd never seen so many colors of cloth at one time. It was from them that she'd learned that her shirt's bright yellow color was called turmeric. They had bolts of fabric, shirts, trousers, and coats. Most of the camp had gotten new clothes then. And there were sundries, buttons, colorful threads and yarns, even mechanical sewing machines and parts. The cloth merchants drove hard bargains for every square inch of precious fabric, each button and part.

The shirt had cost Adina a lot, but it made her happy. All the buttons even matched. Most of her other clothes were as much patches as cloth, but she loved the cheery color of the new shirt, so she was careful with it.

Adina stretched side to side, then leaned on the hot balcony railing, her eyes wandering over the scatter of ramshackle tarps, wood and sheet metal that made up the camp. Her hazel eyes were hued amber by the afternoon sun as they slid from one cluster of structures to another. People said her eyes shifted color with the light or her mood, and that they went green when she was angry or upset. A spray of freckles crossed her deeply tanned face, clustering in constellations that spanned her nose, cheeks, and forehead.

Beyond the scruffy shelters and rudimentary walls of the camp, empty, parched wastes expanded out in every direction. On days like today, heat shimmer obscured the horizon no matter what direction she looked. The wavering haze only added to the feeling that the camp was sitting in the middle of a giant hot pan -- cooking.

The camp wasn't much, twenty families plus a smattering of people like her who worked together, traded, and made things. Throughout the year they moved between locations in the yawning wastelands where there was safe water or good hunting. In some, food could even be grown. Most places where there was good soil and clean water were settled and defended.

But there were still some places where nomads like them could spend a few seasons to rest and resupply. And these meeting places sometimes brought other camps and caravans together. For nomads like Adina's camp, it was a chance to reconnect with old friends and forge new relationships. But there was always a risk. Old feuds and vendettas lived a long time in the wastes, and they could boil over into violence when camps and caravans were thrown together.

Adina had spent a long time living in the sweltering closeness at ground level. She'd wrangled her current second story living arrangement with the camp bosses five moves ago.

No, it was… six now?

The Millers who lived below her were a big family with six children and three other vagabonds like her who had become part of the extended family as if by accident over the last few years. Adina smiled and leaned over the railing, hearing it creak dangerously as she caught a glimpse of Dem Miller, the eldest son, shooing a screeching child out of the work area. The Millers were phenomenal craftspeople, making everything from thread and cloth to clothes and furnishings. Adina could see their youngest son, four-year-old Janji, twisting waste thread into useable twine. The Millers had traded almost everything they had with the fabric merchants last winter. But the results were spectacular. Adina couldn't afford to trade much with them, their skill sets were too similar. But they'd gifted her with a beautiful, brightly colored patchwork pillow made from scrap fabric. It was extravagant, comfortable, and as a gift said more about the bond between her and their family than any words could.

They'd been in this location for over four months and Adina's feet were starting to itch with wanderlust. Unless they were growing food, they didn't normally stay anywhere this long. They just weren't built to operate as a fixed settlement. But there was clean water here and the trade was good. Several established settlements were nearby. Adina had seen more strangers in the last four months than she had in the previous year.

And there was Naveer, the son of one of the first traders they'd done business with. He was wiry and strong, with long, curly black hair and smoldering brown eyes. He was pretty and there had been plenty of flirting the first day he was in camp. Since then, he'd come back every few weeks with more trade from their larger town or with some other excuse. On his third return visit, their flirting ignited, and they'd ended up hot, sweaty, and spent in her upper story room. And they'd done the same every visit afterward.

Naveer's settlement couldn't have been too far away, or he wouldn't have been able to come back so often. Adina tried to visualize it. He'd told her they had buildings of stone and mud brick, a complete defensive wall and stable power that allowed them to run machinery. Adina had seen big, powered things when they passed through large settlements, but she didn't understand what most of them did.

She knew about pumps, of course, pulleys and that sort of thing, everybody did. People in large settlements didn't share what they knew. She nearly got beaten the first time she saw a powered sewing machine. She'd been so fascinated by it that she didn't care about the swats and shoves. She had a finicky foot-pumped machine. She'd traded with the cloth merchants for some spare parts for it, but she did most of her work by hand to save the decrepit old thing for when she really needed it.

I wonder if they have powered sewing machines in Naveer's town?

Adina imagined colorful awnings swaying over merchants' booths. The fabric merchants had told them that where they came from, stalls had fabric awnings like that.

And food. Naveer said they kept livestock and grew fruits and vegetables in permanent gardens and orchards. He'd even brought her apples once.

In camp they had a few skinny goats, some chickens, rabbits, and whatever they could hunt when they were in a place with game. One of the families tended a dozen dwarf lemon and lime trees along with a few other plants that rode in baskets in their truck. Dried lemons and limes were enough to ward off the bloody gums sickness.

The lake where they were camped had some fish and snails, which were a welcome change in their diet.

Adina's heart skipped a beat at the thought of joining Naveer at his settlement. They'd talked about it. Wanderlust and the nomadic life were all Adina had known since she was eight years old, and she loved the freedom they provided. But, it was as much a curse as it was a blessing. She knew every person in camp and every bit of their business. Everyone knew hers.

As a cobbler, Adina was valuable, making shoes, doing other repairs and leather work. She could barter those same skills into a welcome someplace larger, like Naveer's town. She'd thought about leaving before, but this was the first time she'd seriously considered it.

A pang of guilt pinched. She owed the people in this camp her life. They'd found her when she was eight; a scrawny, dried out, ghost of a girl wandering the desert alone after her settlement was destroyed by raiders.

But a smile lifted the corner of Adina's mouth as she watched the sun dip lower toward the horizon. Thoughts of Naveer and joining him at a settlement where there were hundreds and hundreds of people, maybe thousands, made everything inside her light up. Adina tried to push the feelings, and more arousing images of her and Naveer, out of her head as she took up the awl again. She punched a set of fine, closely spaced holes in the leather, then passed the needles through the first hole from opposite sides, crisscrossing the threads again. She pulled the stitch tight and carefully smoothed the salvaged twine she'd spent so much time making.

I wonder what Naveer's doing right now.

Adina yanked her finger back from the sharp pain of a needle prick.

Dammit! She stuck her finger in her mouth, growling at the pain and the distraction that had caused it.

Inspecting her harpooned finger, a single dot of blood welled from the puncture. Adina threw her head back and blew out, letting her lips burble, making a disgusted sound.

Naveer was very practiced. Far more than she was.

Well, until him, when did you have the chance to get good at making love?

Before Naveer, Adina's options had been limited.

He certainly wasn't the first person she'd been with. But she was cautious. When she was sixteen, there'd been a disaster with someone in another camp that had led to violence. Since then, she'd only considered outsiders as potential lovers. As a result, it was just a night or two before a trader or wanderer moved on. Even when they'd been with other camps for months and relationships were good, the fear that something she did could end in violence again stopped her from letting things go too far. It was the same in their own camp. Expectations, hurt feelings and all the complexities of everyone knowing each other's business could create chaos. And she never wanted to be the cause of that again.

Adina pursed her lips and held pressure on her punctured finger. *Distraction is bad for quality.* She tried to focus on her work, but the guilt and embarrassment of what had happened three years ago still burned. It had been innocent enough; she and Jorge were just kids doing what kids do. But Jorge's parents had expected her to leave with them. In the end, Jorge's camp was driven off by force. One of the men in Jorge's camp died, and one of the strongest members in Adina's camp was blinded in one eye. No one in camp ever blamed her for what happened. Except her.

Once the bleeding stopped, Adina went back to sewing. She was carefully lining things up to punch a new set of holes when a call from the edge of camp brought her head up.

Naveer!

It had been three weeks since he'd visited. The corners of Adina's mouth tugged up as she visualized them together. *Perfect timing!*

Adina shaded her eyes and looked the direction Naveer always came from. There was nothing there. As she scanned the horizon, five tall dust clouds were just becoming visible from a different direction. Slow moving vehicles like trade caravans made low, wide dust clouds.

Tall ones came from fast moving vehicles. Adina's smile collapsed.

Raiders!

The thought had barely formed when the alarm whistle sounded. There were shouts and screams in camp. Adina suddenly couldn't move. What felt like a band had clamped around her chest and even her heart didn't seem to beat. All she could do was stare at the ominous dust clouds.

"ARM YOURSELVES!" someone shouted. It was Tomas, the camp leader. His shout snapped Adina out of her paralysis. His voice boomed even over the sudden cacophony in the camp. "Everyone who can, *FIGHT!*"

Adina lunged to the hinged sheet metal that served as the door to her sleeping area. Her hands shook so badly she almost couldn't grab the handle. As she stepped through, she tripped on the doorframe, crashing down onto the hard floor, every part of her trembling violently. It took everything she had to push up onto her hands and knees and crawl to her trunk. Adina threw things aside until she found the crude club she'd been given. It was just a metal pipe with blades welded to one end.

Adina heaved her chest trying to breathe. Close, dusty, air seemed to suddenly fill her lungs.

Her mother's wide, blue eyes filled Adina's eight-year-old vision as her mother's hands cradled her face. "You hide down here. You don't move or make a sound! No matter what!" Adina was smashed against the safety of her mother's chest, her mother holding her fiercely. There was a hurried, but lingering kiss on her cheek and Adina heard her mother's strangled gasp in her ear. Adina felt her mother's sob before she was pushed down into the hole under the floor. Adina watched her mother's eyes as she closed the floorboard door above her. Her mother watched her between the planks, pressing her hand against the other side of the boards for a long moment. Then she was gone.

Adina coughed at the remembered dust in her lungs as she grabbed the rough weapon. The distant howl of engines rose above the noise of the camp mobilizing for defense. The texture of the rough metal haft in Adina's hand yanked at her senses.

The sudden and distinct feeling of hands squeezing her face was there again. Adina looked for her mother as terrified tears rolled down her cheeks. There was no one there. Her small room was empty, and the world seemed suddenly off-kilter.

Adina clamped her hands over her nose and mouth to silence her cough in the claustrophobic, dust filled hole under the wooden floor. Her mother's shrieks happened between crashes of breaking furniture only inches over her head as bodies struggled. Adina hummed the song her brother had taught her to try and drown out the terrifying sounds. There were other shrieks and cries from further away, the sound of guns.

Adina stared at the weapon in her hand, humming the song her brother had taught her. Her mother's screams were so loud in her head. A gunshot made her jump. It was followed by a scream.

And then there were awful shrieks… the raider's terrifying, keening wails that filled her nightmares. The sound hacked at Adina. She recoiled from it fighting the feeling that it might chop her spirit from her bones.

Fight, hide, or die.

The words seemed to echo in a large, empty room in her head. Tomas had said them over and over when they talked about what to do if raiders attacked. Adina had always been good at hiding. Her mother's choked voice was in her ear again.

"You hide down here. You don't move or make a sound! No matter what!"

Everything was a blur as Adina sprinted from yet another hiding place trying to flee the raging fires that consumed tents and structures that had been her home only minutes before. Raiders were silhouettes against orange flames, or were highlighted by the bright sun against black, swirling smoke. She couldn't be sure if they were real, or memories thrust across her terrified vision.

Adina's lungs burned, the stench and smoke were the same as it had been when she fled into the empty wastes as a child. The cloying taste of dust mixed with bitter acidic smoke, but she didn't dare cough. Adina dodged between two structures, forcing through the narrow space. A shriek behind her made her push harder, rough metal and planks pulling at her now filthy yellow shirt, scratching her arms and shoulders. She stumbled out from between the structures and sprinted, looking back the way she'd come. Her heel caught on something, and she crashed down *hard,* her head bouncing off the rocky ground.

Everything suddenly spun. Objects sort of slid off to one side of Adina's vision as her mother's screams filled her ears again. Adina cringed from the heat of a nearby fire, the way she had in the tiny hole beneath her burning house as the searing flames threatened to consume her.

Adina kicked at what had tripped her. A body.

Adina screamed, flailing to get free of it. Her blurred vision prevented her from identifying who it was. Part of her was thankful for that. She threw herself over onto her hands and knees. Sharp gravel drove into her palms and knees as she pushed up to get her feet under her. But the world turned abruptly ninety degrees, and she hit the ground hard again.

The clash of weapons, pleading screams and the raider's keening, victorious shrieks were everywhere, overlaid on the roar of fires. Adina crawled as fast as she could, the rough gravel over what had once been asphalt gouging her hands and knees. She had no idea what direction she was going -- *Just away from the sounds.*

The back of Adina's shirt was yanked, and she shrieked. Her nails snapped against exposed asphalt, clawing to get away. Another hand grabbed her, hauling her backward. She rolled onto her back and kicked with everything she had. She'd dropped the bladed pipe somewhere. The whole world wobbled around her.

Adina could make out the outline of the raider, but he was mostly just blobs of color. She could smell his stench, axle grease, body stink and fetid, rotting death. The collar of severed fingers he wore as trinkets were unmistakable outlines among the objects that swung from his clothing.

FIGHT!

There was no other choice now. Adina screamed her terror into the raider's blurry face and grabbed it, driving her nails into his skin. Her hands were strong, and she held on with everything she had, fighting to get her nails into his eyes. The raider howled, trying to pull her hands away. Terror had become fury as she shrieked and clawed, pulling his face down to bite him.

Another raider was there, just a black outline. His hands were on her. A knee suddenly drove into her belly. The world spun violently with new, nauseating pain. It felt like their knee hit her spine -- but Adina didn't let go. Vicious instinct screamed for the feeling of skin ripping from the raider's face. But the knee drove into her belly again, and everything went white for an instant. Adina's whole body seized, curling up to try and protect her. But the knee was there, jammed into her belly with the body attached to it, pinning her. She couldn't breathe. Strong hands grabbed hers and pulled them together over her head. Adina felt rough cord around her wrists, barely able to see, her vision blurred by tears of pain and from hitting her head.

"This one will be good for trade," one of the raiders huffed, breathing hard with exertion. His stinking breath poured over her face.

"Bitch!" Adina's shirt was grabbed roughly, and she was pulled upward. She could make out the blood running from the gouges her nails had left on the raider's face. "I'm gonna fucking kill you!"

Another body pushed in, and the bloodied raider was shoved aside. "Get off! She's not yours!"

Adina hit the ground hard again. Hands pawed her breasts through her shirt. A blurred face pushed close. "Nice. And pretty too. I like freckles." The raider made an approving sound.

Hands dragged Adina to her feet, but her traumatized belly wouldn't let her straighten. She still couldn't take in more than shuddering half-breaths. The rope pulled harshly, and Adina fell forward, her tied hands skidding out in front of her. Her cheek and knees hit the ground almost simultaneously. Someone grabbed a handful of her hair and pulled her to her feet.

"Get up!"

"Not too rough, idiot! That hair's a selling point!"

Adina shrieked, trying to steady herself and find her balance to ease the pull on her hair.

Blood suddenly sprayed across Adina's face, hot and coppery tasting. She jerked back from it.

The hand holding her hair wasn't there anymore. In the strange freeze frame instant as Adina collapsed again, the bright color of blood seemed to stand out against everything else. Blood jetted from the neck of the raider who'd been holding her hair. The raider was still blurry as he staggered away. But the motion of him clawing at his slashed throat was unmistakable.

There was another body, just a silhouette, moving fast.

The awful wet whistle and choking sound the raider made trying to breathe met with a feral roar from the second. There was a gunshot. An instant later the raider whose face she'd gouged crashed down next to her. His dead, staring eyes looked past her.

And beyond him, the other figure was still moving.

The muzzle flash from their pistol pulled Adina's traumatized senses to the weapon. The crack of the pistol seemed to come a few seconds late in the disjointed time stuttering around her. The sharp outline of a saber was in their other hand.

The color drained out of Adina's vision… She could hear her sobbing breaths, her wildly hammering heartbeat. Darkness rolled in from the edges of her vision… The strange tunneling instant seemed to stretch on… and on… And echoing in that weird space were more gunshots. The raider's victorious cries became confused, then turned to shrieks of terror and agony.

Adina was falling. falling… The screams faded like the color in her vision, draining away…

Then there was nothing.

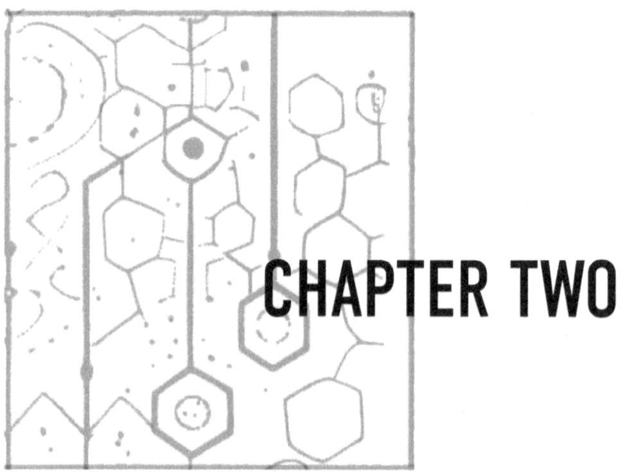

CHAPTER TWO

Bizarre, disjointed sounds, images and feelings flowed through Adina in a continuous, but madly confused stream.

Dreams? Are they dreams? They felt like dreams.

No, that's wrong... Some part of Adina's addled mind was trying to make sense of the churning mess in her head. But it felt separate, somehow disconnected. There was the distinct feeling that she was being drawn along by a strange current. At times it was tranquil. She just floated along with fleeting images that were gone before she could make sense of them. Other times she was battered against rocks in violent cataracts of gunfire and the reek of things burning... the awful sound weapons made when they struck flesh.

Adina bounced and jostled. There was sunlight; painful, angled, streaming in from -- somewhere. Things rattled and clanked around her. She was in a vehicle.

Adina screamed, lashing out in uncoordinated spasms as terror roared up with visions of raiders stealing her away. The movement stopped and there was suddenly someone there. A silhouette against the bright light.

Adina kicked and fought as hands held her. The stark outline suddenly fell out of focus, turning to swimming blobs. Then as quickly as the sunlight and jostling reality had come, they were gone.

But the sensation of movement was everywhere. Her mind and spirit seemed to move along a different path from her body.

Adina's hand bumped something. Everything *ached* in a weird, remote sort of way. She was being moved. She threw her hands at the body moving her but lifting her hands was *so hard*. They just fell against her chest. There was a *noise*… It might have been mechanical, like an engine, but it faded in and out, either so quiet she wasn't sure she'd heard it, or so loud it felt like it would split her head wide open. Then everything faded away again.

Cold… The feeling dragged Adina back to her body. She tried to swallow but her tongue stuck to the inside of her mouth and there was an intense, sour taste -- burnt things. After several painful swallows, the clotty dryness eased.

Adina blinked, trying to clear what felt like clinging fog from her vision. A blob of light floated in a sea of darkness. When she curled up against the cold, her belly spasmed painfully as if the raider's knee was driving into her all over again. She tried to raise her hands to rub her eyes, but there was resistance. Her hands were bound together.

Adina was instantly awake, terror clawing up inside her. *No, no, no, no*… She felt at her wrists, trying to force her eyes to focus.

But what met Adina's fingers made her freeze.

Where she'd expected to feel cord or roughhewn metal shackles, there was polished metal. She squinted in the dim light, trying to see clearly. Dark metal cuffs enclosed her wrists, connected by an equally polished, dark chain. When she tugged on them, they were attached to something that ran underneath her.

Adina felt desperately along the chain, still blinking.

She felt a lock. It was attached to a metal cable.

Adina's vision finally slid into focus. There was a small fire a few yards away. And around it were dark shapes. Adina froze again, her heart hammering like it was going to tear itself from her chest. It took letting her eyes adjust to the fire's brightness and more blinking before the shapes resolved into packs and bundles, not people sleeping around the fire.

Adina's relieved exhale turned to a sob as she let her head sink to the ground. Everything that had happened was suddenly pouring out in sobs. Adina clamped her mouth against her shoulder to stifle the sound, her brutalized stomach cramping as she fought to stop crying.

Images she didn't want to see suddenly thrust into her mind, so terrifying and clear. The body she'd tripped over, people she knew dead. And now she was chained; a prisoner in someone's camp.

It took painful minutes for Adina to wrestle herself under control. And when she was finally able to blink the tears from her eyes and take deeper breaths, she looked more closely at the cuffs around her wrists. They looked *manufactured,* maybe even made in a factory. Adina had heard the unbelievable tales about factories in the city-states with their farms and walls and guns. Staring at the cuffs, something in her leapt with joy, even past her pain, the cold, and her fear.

If even part of what the wandering storiers tell is true…

Adina ran her fingers over the dark metal again, fascinated by how smooth it was. It was easier to focus on the cuffs than to let what was in her mind rise to the surface again. A painful chill shuddered up her body. It wasn't until she pulled her knees up that she realized there was a blanket over her. It was impossible to tell anything about it in the firelight other than that it was thick and dark colored. Adina tucked her head and did her best to huddle into the blanket with her cuffed hands, her belly spasming as she curled up. The fire was only a yard or so away, but the warmth seemed to dissipate before it reached her. She tried to scoot closer to the fire, but the cable under her prevented it. She turned over and squinted in the darkness following the cable. It connected to a huge, ornately sculpted metal door a few yards away. The door was partly buckled, bent in the middle. She, the fire, and the extraordinary door rested under the entrance of what had once been a grand building. The worn and chipped remains of deeply carved stone designs and figures covered the façade.

A bang and clatter snapped Adina's head around.

The distinctive metal on metal sound of someone working came from beyond a corner of the building.

Cold, thirst and pain chiseled at her.

If they wanted you dead, they would have already killed you.

Adina felt her clothes under the blanket. She was still fully dressed. She kicked her numb feet. Her boots were still on. She opened the blanket a little so she could see her clothes in the firelight. Dark stains marked her once precious yellow shirt. The memory of the raider's spraying blood played in her mind again and Adina swallowed, trying to keep the other images at bay.

If they wanted... Adina didn't want to finish the thought. *They would have already done it.* The stories of what raiders did to their captives were horrific. And the stories about scavengers who'd turned cannibal were even worse. Another painful chill tore up Adina's back. She gritted her teeth, squeezed her eyes shut and called out.

"Hello... Is someone there?"

The sound of work stopped, and Adina heard boots on gravel. A tall figure appeared from around the corner of the building, just a silhouette in a long coat. Fear roared up inside her. She could make out white, short cropped hair in the firelight. He stopped, and she could feel his eyes on her even if she couldn't see them. He retrieved something from a pack, then squatted between her and the fire. He held up a canteen.

"You need to drink, you're dehydrated."

Adina's desperate thirst shouldered aside her fear. Her brutalized abdominal muscles spasmed painfully as she tried to sit up, her numb legs and feet just limp, meaty weights on the end of her torso. He put a hand under her elbow, and she flinched away violently, flopping back down on the hard earth. Adina grimaced at the fiery pain that was suddenly coursing through her legs, feet and backside as circulation returned.

He dropped his hand and sat back on his heels, just a black cutout against the fire. "Do you want me to help you?"

Adina gritted her teeth and shook her head, angry and embarrassed. She blew out a breath and kicked her uncoordinated feet to get them under her, then pushed up into a clumsy, unsteady sitting position.

She watched where his eyes should be.

He held up the canteen. As soon as she felt steady enough, she leaned forward and put her lips to the metal. Cold water flowed into her mouth. When she tried to swallow, her throat seized, and she choked. He pulled the canteen away as she coughed hard, spitting up water. It felt like strips of her parched throat were being peeled away with every hoarse cough. It took several ragged breaths before the coughing eased. She lifted her head again. He just watched her.

"Ready to try again?"

She nodded and leaned forward. He helped her drink. This time she was able to swallow, and she gulped down water as fast as he would pour it.

"Slowly."

Adina took gasping breaths between gulps feeling the water hit her stomach and her whole body relaxed incrementally. When the worst of her body's demand for water was sated, fear roared up again. She sat back, trying to see him. Whoever he was, he was big. It might have just been the way he loomed in the darkness with the fire behind him. But her impression was that he was one of the largest men she'd ever seen.

He rocked back. "You finished?" His voice was deep, not particularly threatening, but it wasn't kind, either. His tone was detached, matter-of-fact.

Adina answered breathlessly, her heart pounding.

She felt dizzy. "Yes." She couldn't be sure if it was fear, her body reacting to the water, or the fact that she was freezing cold.

He didn't answer. He screwed the top back on the canteen, set it aside and leaned forward. Adina flinched back again, but he followed until his hands were on her cuffs. Her instinct was to bite him, to force him away, but her body locked up. She was suddenly trembling violently again. Everything was spinning, terror pressing her vision into a tunnel.

She could see a bit more of him as he removed the cuffs. His coat was dark leather with armored shoulders. The curved bottom of a sword scabbard jutted out behind him. The sharp outline of his saber during the battle suddenly thrust into her mind. The raider's keens, the roar and stench of the fires, everything from that awful moment seemed to crash in on her. The wet, horrible feeling of the raider's blood spraying her face was on her skin again.

The weight of the cuffs and cable fell away from her wrists.

"You'll be warmer by the fire." His shadowed head nodded to the campfire. He extended a hand to her elbow.

Adina's legs and feet were still coming back to life. She wasn't sure she could stand, and she sure didn't want to crawl to the fire in front of him. It was so *cold*.

Adina nodded. She tried to put her arm out to him, but her body refused. Her hands and forearms were pressed so tightly against her chest that her arms were shaking with the effort. Her shoulders ached from the force of clamping her elbows protectively against her sides. She fought the instinct to jerk away as he leaned close again. He put his hand under her arm and lifted.

Adina was able to struggle to her feet and she almost burst into tears. It was all just too much. She gritted her teeth against the renewed pain of blood rushing into her lower body and the effort to force her emotions down.

He steadied her as she hissed at the fire running under her skin. "It hurts!" He waited silently, and after a few moments coaxed her toward the fire, one unsteady step at a time. He indicated a place on the ground next to the fire. "Sit down."

Adina had barely gotten her backside on the ground when the increased warmth from the fire drove a painful shiver through her. She clutched the blanket, shaking violently again for a moment before returning to the overall trembling. As he moved into the firelight, she could get a better look at him. He was as surprising as the smooth metal cuffs that had been around her wrists.

He was broad shouldered and several inches over six feet tall based on her five-feet-six. He was surprisingly well-groomed. His hair was nearly shaved around the sides and back and his beard was trimmed neatly, close to his face. He looked like he might be in his thirties, but his white hair and beard made it hard to tell. Most people in the wastes only looked well-groomed for a few hours after bathing, if that long.

Adina's leatherworker eye picked out the details of his armored long coat. It reached his ankles and was the most finely made garment she'd ever seen. It looked broken in, scuffed with wear, but well maintained. Matching-colored pauldrons were attached to the shoulders. Each was blazoned with a raised white emblem. A sword and rifle crossed each other above a stylized compass rose, all bracketed by a pair of wings.

The pauldrons added to his broadness, making him seem as much machine as man. They too were scuffed. One sported a deep gouge. His saber hung from the left side of his belt, and a big pistol was holstered on his right thigh.

Adina had never seen anyone who looked so…*uniform* before. His clothes seemed specifically made so each piece matched the rest. Even his equipment, right down to the boxes and bags that she'd thought were sleeping people, were the same color.

He had a square jaw and defined chin, both accentuated by his beard. His cheekbones stood out like rounded mountain ranges under his eyes in the flickering firelight. In a word he was -- *striking*.

He knelt next to her, and Adina felt dizzy, her neck pounding.

He nodded to where she'd been lying. "I handcuffed you so you couldn't run off or hurt yourself." His eyes fixed on hers. "You nearly threw yourself out of the truck at one point. There isn't much of anywhere for you to go out here." His voice wasn't harsh, but the matter-of-factness felt somehow alarmingly in Adina's ears.

This close in the firelight she could see several long-healed scars that marred his face. And he had the darkest blue eyes she'd ever seen. She'd seen a stone someone called Lapis. His eyes reminded her of it.

He dug into one of the packs next to the fire. When he returned, he offered her the canteen again, and a piece of dried meat.

"Eat. You need your strength."

The piece of dried meat was large. Adina eyed it suspiciously. Thoughts of cannibal scavengers rushed into her mind again. "What is it?" Words suddenly tumbled out in an unintentional stream. "Rat, lizard, and rabbit are what we usually have. Dog when we're lucky." The piece of meat was far too large for anything but a dog. And it would have had to be a *big* dog.

He nodded, extending it to her again. "It's boar."

Adina's eyes widened and she stared at it, envisioning the thousand-pound animals that roamed the wastes.

She'd heard stories of entire camps being killed and *eaten* by herds of boar. She'd only ever seen one of the truly big ones. And it had taken every man and woman with a gun to bring it down. She glanced at him to see if he was joking. He just watched her, his expression passive. She took the canteen and piece of meat.

"How did you…" she looked from the meat to him.

He stood and returned to one of the packs. "Shot him in the head." There was no pride or bravado in the way he said it, just the matter of factness again, like he was giving a report. After a moment of digging, he returned with a second blanket and handed it to her. "What do they call you?"

Adina's mind was spinning. Partially formed glimpses from right before she'd passed out flitted through her mind. Him killing the raiders… It had to have been him, there was no one else around. But the cold that bit into Adina's bones superseded any higher mental functions. She grabbed the blanket, shook it out with trembling urgency and threw it over the first, then pulled it tight around her. Another hard chill rocked her as her body heat suddenly stopped escaping. "Adina…" she answered past her shivers, rocking to try and warm up. "Adina Sky."

He squatted, watching her quietly. And again, he didn't say anything.

His fixed attention made Adina feel like she was under a spotlight. Adina took a bite of the dried meat, looking anywhere but at him, just to do something other than sit there under his steady gaze. The dried meat was salty, and concern about him watching her suddenly evaporated. Adina gulped water from the canteen between bites, but other than that, her whole attention was on eating. She hadn't finished the first piece when he handed her a second. She snatched it, ripping it into chunks barely aware of anything as she wolfed it down. When the food's spell finally released her, he was still watching her intently.

Adina pulled her legs up tight, wrapping the blanket around her, confused and uncomfortable under his silent, intense scrutiny. Her eyes traveled over the bundles and back to him.

"What... What's your name?"

"Asher." He looked up at the clear sky, the breathtaking, bright blanket of stars gleaming down at them. "It's cold tonight."

He reached out to her face. Adina shied back, but like when he'd leaned in to take off the cuffs, he just extended his hand until the back of his fingers were against her cheek. His fingers were warm, and she could see burn scars on the back of his hand. But his touch was gentle. He laid his fingers against her neck.

When he dropped his hand, he squinted at her in a way that made her feel like he hadn't really seen her until that moment. His eyes traveled from her hazel eyes under her dark, curved eyebrows, across the freckles on her forehead, down to her pointed chin. He exhaled as if he'd come to a decision. "I can try to drop you at a settlement somewhere, Adina." He gestured in a direction. "But I'm heading west. I don't know what, if any settlements are out there. You can travel with me until we find a place." He watched her for another long moment and Adina couldn't be sure if he was waiting for an answer, or if he was just observing her again. He turned and pointed to one of the bundles next to the fire. Now that Adina could see it in the firelight, it didn't look anything like the rest of the uniformly colored packs and crates. "Or if you want to leave, I've made up a backpack for you. There's seven days of food and water in it." He nodded as if checking items off a list in his head. "And a few other things you might need."

Adina's eyes flicked from him to the backpack and back again. Everything inside her was in complete turmoil. She watched his handsome, scarred features as he turned back to her. Flashes of him fighting the raiders clattered through her mind again as she took in the pistol and sword at his belt and his armored coat again.

Travel with him?

Excitement jangled at her core, playing tug-of-war with her confusion.

He sat down next to her. "You're cold as ice. Lay down."

Panic leapt up, suffocating Adina's excitement. Her neck was suddenly tight again. "Why!"

His expression changed only marginally. "You'll be warmer if you do." Again, his tone was practical, not without emotion, but not overly… anything. He unbuckled his pistol belt, freeing the sword and set them aside, then laid down behind her, keeping her between him and the fire, adjusting his belt, sword and pistol, apparently to use them as a pillow. He put a hand on her shoulder and pulled lightly. It was an invitation, not a demand.

Adina reluctantly laid down. He hooked an arm around her, pulling her against him and threw part of his coat over her, then laid his head down, resting it on his arm and weapons.

Adina's breath came in short fearful gasps. Being pulled back against his chest was like being against a warm, solid wall. As close as he was, she couldn't help but smell him -- smoke, hot engine oil, leather, sweat and a lighter oil of some kind. And under it all -- *soap*. Adina's eyebrows climbed up. She knew the smell of soap; harsh, astringent, designed to clean, not… smell nice. But he did. It wasn't a harsh perfumy smell, but a clean, fresh morning after rain sort of scent.

She waited for his hands to start wandering. But several minutes later, his arm got heavy, and his breathing turned easy.

Adina stayed still, not daring to move. He started to snore lightly. She craned her head as much as she could to see him hoping not to wake him -- if he actually was asleep. He didn't move. The intense creases between his eyebrows were gone. He looked younger.

Adina's heart skipped a beat. He was *very* handsome, with his features relaxed in the firelight.

She stayed frozen for a long time, everything inside her wrestling in fear and confusion. She pushed down the fearsome images that wanted to fill her mind. Faces wanted her to see them, they wanted her to feel for them. Adina crammed them down, like shoving them into a trunk and using her weight to force the lid closed. Right next to it was the box she was fighting to close that was filled with sudden, confused excitement. Everything in her head felt out of control, like there was a tornado raging.

But the feel of his breath on her hair, so easy and steady, and his heavy arm over her were reassuring.

He could have done anything. She turned her head as much as she could, trying to see him again. *And he didn't try anything.*

His body heat radiating through the blankets eased her clenching muscles. And as hard as Adina fought to stay awake, she was *so* tired.

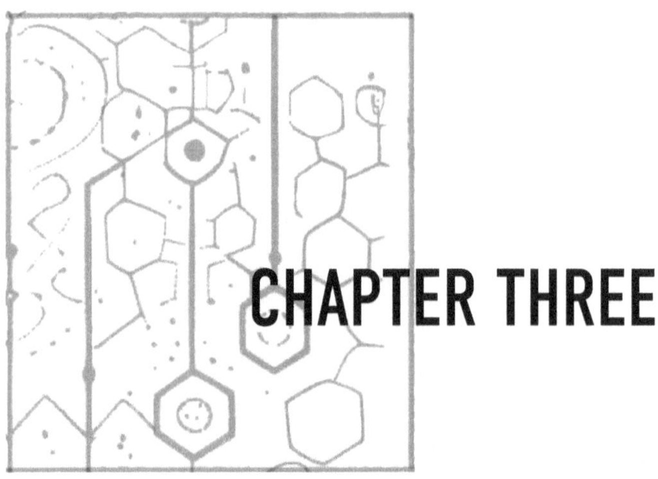

CHAPTER THREE

Adina swatted at a tickle on her cheek, brushing the offending hair away before snuggling into the warmth of Naveer's chest behind her. She loved waking up in his arms. Their time always seemed so rushed. When she got the chance to just enjoy lying with his arms around her like this, it was the best feeling in the world. She never wanted it to end. Adina tucked her hands up against the morning chill, pulling Naveer's hand up with hers and kissing his knuckle. She sighed and a small smile tugged one side of her mouth up at the feeling of his hand resting reassuringly against her breast. Her sleepy mind wondered why his hand seemed so large this morning.

Adina's eyes shot open, and she was wide awake. The realization of where she was crashed in with the thunder of her heartbeat in her chest and ears. The heat of her blush raced across her face, neck, and chest. She had Asher's big hand in hers, holding it against her breast, the way she did when she and Naveer slept together.

Adina tried not to even breathe and carefully turned her head, squinting against the bright morning light, trying to keep Asher's hand from moving. Her face went fire hot all over again as she remembered how she'd put his hand where it was. And holding his hand… *where it was* -well, that didn't really help much. Asher was watching her, his blue eyes intent on hers for a moment, then traveling over her face.

"I uhhh…" Adina stammered. "Need to go to the privy." Adina watched his expression. He looked so different in the sunlight, younger, less harsh. She moved a little to see if he would let her go, instantly regretting it as his hand shifted against her breast. "Can I?"

"Of course." He lifted his hand and Adina felt a rush of relief along with the cold air that flowed into the blanket where his warm hand and arm had been.

Adina tried to scramble to her feet but only got as far as her hands and knees before her battered stomach muscles seized, locking her body. Images and sounds crashed through her with the pain. The raider who'd kneed her in the stomach, the one who'd dragged her to her feet by her hair. Shrieking raiders were suddenly everywhere in her mind, wreaking havoc on her thoughts.

"Are you alright?"

Adina wanted to snarl at him, but she couldn't take in a breath yet, everything in her head and body a churning mess of confusion. Adina tasted blood again, the visceral memory of the raider whose throat she'd seen him cut filled her mind with other nightmare images of the attack.

Adina gritted her teeth against the painful muscle spasm and pushed her feet under her. Then with a hiss she was able to force herself upright.

He sat up and nodded to her stomach. "You should let me look at that."

Grimacing, Adina clutched one of the blankets around her. He was so maddeningly calm. And leaned up on his elbow the way he was, the dawn light played across his face making his white hair and dark blue eyes shine against his burnt tan complexion. It was… distracting.

"I'm fine!" Adina snapped the words out trying to wrestle coherence from the confusion, fear and sudden arousal whirling inside her.

He pointed in a direction. "Over there will probably be safest."

Adina marched toward the corner of the building he indicated. She did have to go to the privy -- *badly*. But more than anything else, she needed to be away from *him*.

It took a while for Adina to calm down after relieving herself. She walked in little circles, stamping on the dusty ground trying to dislodge the awful, intrusive memories and the worst of her raging confusion. The day's heat was already starting by the time she walked back to the corner of the building. She stretched her cramped belly, and it was just starting to let go as she turned the corner and stopped.

The packs were gone. The fire was out. And Asher was nowhere to be seen.

Adina stood staring at the abandoned camp, new pain twisting behind her belly button. The ground where she and Asher had lain was packed flat, the marks of their bodies still on it.

"Asher?" Her voice shook so badly she could barely hear it. *"ASHER!?"* she called more loudly.

A moment passed that seemed to stretch for hours.

Then Asher's voice came from around the far corner of the building. "Here."

Adina felt suddenly cold, and everything was spinning again, like all the blood had run from her body.

Asher stepped into view. "Feeling better?" He stopped, studying her unsteadiness. "Are you sick?"

"I…" Adina cleared her throat, trying to steady her voice. Tears rolled down her cheeks as she fought to regain her composure. "I thought you'd… left me."

Everything inside Adina was crashing and shifting again. This time it was pure terror. Dem Miller stared in her mind's eye again. His mangled jaw gaped, hanging at a sickening angle that made him look freakish and possessed, as if screaming in death. The terrified shrieks of people she knew went suddenly, horribly silent. The raiders awful, keening war cries. It all slammed into her like punches. She stared at Asher and even more confusion flared as she realized that she'd felt *safe* nestled against him as she fell asleep with his big arm thrown over her. Adina heaved a breath trying to think clearly. As she stared, trying to calm down, it made sense in a brutish way. On the other side of feeling safe in the arms of a man she didn't know was the terror of being abandoned in the empty wastes.

He continued to scrutinize her, then gestured. "You still have my blanket."

Adina looked down at the warm cloth clutched around her shoulders, then back at him. She was suddenly torn between wanting to rage at him for being so… matter of fact and wanting to feel the safety of his arms around her.

"Ye… yes. I do," was all she could get out. He nodded affirmatively and turned back, disappearing around the corner again.

Adina scrubbed the tears from her cheeks with the blanket and quick-stepped after him, not wanting to lose sight of him. As she came around the corner, she stopped dead in her tracks.

A vehicle was parked next to the leaning concrete wall of the ruined building they had sheltered in. The hulking, aggressive-looking machine reminded her of a huge, mechanized version of the bears she'd seen in a book once. It was twice the size of any normal vehicle she'd ever seen, nearly as large as the trucks that transported goods from one settlement to another. And it was armored. Just behind its broad, powerful nose, it grew tall, like the shoulders of a bear behind its hanging head, with a cupola on top. She could see it was painted a dark color under the thick coat of dust. Great gashes scarred its sides and front.

The raider vehicles that lived in Adina's nightmares, covered with their bodged-on armor and weapons, looked *fragile* compared to it. The machine looked purpose-built for war. Blazoned along the side, just below the cupola was the same crossed rifle and sword emblem that marked the armor on Asher's shoulders.

He walked to the back of the vehicle, picked up the last bag sitting on the ground and threw it inside. "We can't stay here. It's not safe. We need to move." He closed the door with a solid metal *clang!* and walked forward. He pulled the armored passenger side door open and held a hand out to her. "Come on."

Adina wanted to move, but her feet felt like they'd been nailed in place. Seeing him standing next to the war machine, her mind filled with the image of them rolling off assembly lines side by side, each made for the other. And in the bright morning light, she couldn't get over the impression that he looked more like he'd been made than born. His eyes were so intensely blue set within the frame of his white hair and beard.

When she didn't go to him, his deepest blue eyes focused on hers. He looked confused for a moment, then blew out a breath. His head fell back, and his shoulders dropped. "Right." He nodded as if her expression and what she'd said moments before finally registered. "I'm sorry if I frightened you. I can see how you might have thought I'd left you." He nodded toward the back of the truck. "I normally just pack things up first thing." He held out his hand again. "Please. We need to go."

Adina felt small under his intense gaze. It was like the heat from the sun that was starting to cut over the tops of the ruins around them. Her feet unlocked and she walked to him, then turned to the open door at his gesture.

"It's a big step up," he instructed, pointing to where she should put her foot and hands, tossing the blanket up ahead of her.

Adina stretched up to the first step and his hand was suddenly under her backside. Adina silenced a squeak as his strong hand pushed up. She got into the seat, clutching the blanket and trying to control the sudden rush of color in her face. The interior of the vehicle was as impressive as the outside. There were things stored on shelves and in cubbies. The bags she'd seen the night before were on the floor in the far back, past a short ladder up to the cupola. He hadn't been joking about the boar. Large haunches of meat hung wrapped in cloth and carefully strapped between shelves in the back. The panel in front of the driver's seat was covered with gauges and switches like nothing she'd ever seen.

He slammed the heavy door and a moment later the driver's side door opened. He levered himself into the seat, closed the door and stowed his sword in a mount behind his right shoulder in a motion that spoke of easy, bored familiarity. He threw switches and then pushed a button. The war machine chugged, like one of the large transport trucks. Then it roared to life with a ferocious howl. Adina grabbed the console next to her as the metal beast shuddered like it was waking from sleep. Lights and dials illuminated and bobbed across the console in front of him. The howl died to a deep throaty rumble.

"Buckle up."

Adina stared at him, the scare of possibly being left behind still raw inside her. And her sudden, unexpected… *feelings* didn't help either. Her breathing came in short, fast gasps and she could hear the blood rushing in her ears.

"You know what a seat belt is, right?" When she didn't move, he leaned across. The vehicle was large enough that he had to all but lay across the console between them to reach her, which meant his face was nearly pressed against her chest when he reached past her, pulled the belt around her and secured it.

"I… I know what a seatbelt is." Adina nodded, leaning as far away from him as the belt would allow.

He settled on his elbow for a moment, the corner of his mouth coming up. Adina couldn't tell, but it might have been the beginning of a smile. He leaned close and sniffed, then settled back into his seat and buckled his own belt. He handed her the canteen she'd drank from before, taking a long swig from his own.

Adina took a drink, unsure what else to do.

"You're pretty ripe. We need to fix that."

Adina spat water, feeling it burn up inside her sinuses, leaving her coughing as the big vehicle pulled away with a thundering rumble.

CHAPTER FOUR

Adina wasn't sure what to say as they drove, or how to even start talking to him. Hours passed without more than a few words passing between them. He was stoic, only asking simple questions or giving instructions.

As the day wore on, they moved from well-traveled areas with remains of roads, onto open ground, heading steadily west. All the stories Adina knew said there was nothing to the west. It was supposed to be a poisoned landscape filled with mad, cannibal scavengers and creatures as dangerous and toxic as the land itself.

No one went west.

Adina felt more relaxed but was as confused -- *more* confused than ever. Asher had taken off his long coat in the heat, revealing square, burly shoulders. Adina's eyes kept being drawn to him. His muscular arms stretched the sleeves of his shirt and as the truck bounced and rattled along, his shirt tugged and pulled giving tantalizing hints about his torso beneath.

Adina had been infatuated plenty of times, usually with men who showed her there was more to the world than what existed within the confines of camp. But even knowing that, the intensity of her attraction surprised her. She felt drunk with his proximity.

Of course, you're attracted to him! He's handsome and exciting. He's like no one you've ever met before. And he saved your life!

Pangs of guilt stabbed at her from odd angles. There were so many thoughts – *feelings* she felt like she should be having. Everything she knew… every one she knew was gone. Dead, burned up or lost to the wastes.

I should be sad, or angry, or… something.

Adina knew she was pushing some of it down, maybe all of it. But guilt and confusion battered her. The grief, love, and loyalty she should feel for her friends was completely buried, supplanted by an overwhelming fixation with this man she'd only just met. How he'd felt pressed against her during the night was like a distracting itch on her skin. Adina turned when she thought he was looking at her. But his eyes were on what was in front of them. If he was stealing glances at her when he thought she wasn't looking, he was frustratingly good at the game. It was hot, so Adina had tied her shirt up to expose her midriff trying to stay cool. The fact that it wasn't a way she ever wore a shirt set off an all-new tug-of-war in her head.

Well, it's hot!

Really? You're just wanting to show off for him.

I am not!

The afternoon sun highlighted the scars on his face and neck, adding to his fierce, rugged appearance. But the brute scars seemed to jostle against the civility of his neatly trimmed hair and beard.

In the distance, a line of huge, ancient signs drew Adina's attention. She sat up and leaned forward, squinting. They ran like a boundary around the sagging skyline of what had once been part of a city.

"Here." Asher handed her a pair of binoculars from a cubby in the center console.

Adina couldn't help but admire them. They were dusty, but otherwise looked brand new. She raised them and leaned forward watching the signs grow larger through the windshield. She'd seen signs like these before. Years ago, the camp investigated a new area and they'd skirted the remains of a bombed-out city. It had been surrounded by signs like these, their attention-grabbing red paint faded to rusty brown, but still visible. It was the first time she'd seen the symbol for radiation. The signs were from the old world; when there were still governments to construct such things.

Most of the signs she and Asher drove past were just wilted metal heaps. But as they got closer, she could make out patches of distinctive green, the warning color for disease. And on one sign that was still standing, the pointed triangular symbol for biological danger was still faintly visible.

Asher turned toward the signs and Adina's stomach dropped.

"What are you doing!? You're not going into a quarantine, are you?"

He nodded, scanning the line of buildings half a mile away as if looking for something.

"But it's not safe in there!"

Asher continued to watch the buildings as they breached the line of signs, the city skyline looming larger by the moment. He nodded. "That's the point."

Adina sat back and pulled her knees up, wrapping her arms around them, her heart suddenly racing. She watched the imposing ruins loom larger, glancing at Asher to see if maybe this was some kind of joke.

Everyone knew to stay away from quarantines. It didn't matter why the old world quarantined them -- No one went *into* quarantines. All too graphic stories told of things still living in them and so-called 'survivors' who made cannibal scavengers sound tame by comparison.

Asher turned the vehicle more right, almost heading back the way they'd come, watching the buildings. "There it is." He seemed to be talking to himself, concentrating.

Adina looked from him to the buildings. "There what is?"

He turned the truck toward the ruins, his eyes fixed ahead of them.

Adina shrank back in her seat as the shadows of the ruin fell over them with a feeling like they were being swallowed as they passed from open wasteland into it.

Everything but the sky directly overhead was suddenly replaced by towering structures. But Asher drove confidently as if he knew exactly where he was going, navigating the war machine between crumbling buildings and along increasingly narrow, rubble strewn streets.

"Asher, where are we going?" Adina tried to keep her voice from shaking.

"You'll see." Again, his response was utterly deadpan.

If Adina wasn't so anxious, she might have wanted to reach across the console and throttle him.

Asher turned them into an alley, just barely wide enough for the machine to pass, and as they approached the end, it looked like a dead end.

"What are..." Adina's question was cut off as Asher turned the vehicle sharply right, into what had looked like a shadow between sections of the building. Adina suddenly had to hold on, leaning back as the front of the vehicle tipped down onto a steep incline.

"Just wait." Unlike Asher's normally stoic, not quite emotionless tone, there was an edge of what might have been amusement in his voice. And when Adina glanced at him, gripping the door and arm of her seat to steady herself that lift at the corner of his mouth that could have been the beginning of a smile was back.

Dark, scarred concrete suddenly fell away to reveal a wide,

breathtaking panorama. A jagged valley spread out, encompassed on all sides by red sandstone cliffs that erosion had faded to pink and even white in places.

Reflections from shiny surfaces on buildings on the rim above the canyon played across the rough walls in shapes and bars of sunlight.

Adina heaved in a huge breath, her eyes going wide as she came forward out of her seat, gawking at the extraordinary landscape. The canyon walls were hundreds of feet high, and the skyline above stood like teeth between the canyon and the sky. Some buildings had crumbled and crashed down into what Adina now realized was a massive rift in the earth.

Lush grasses and other plants carpeted most of the valley floor with strange stone formations that thrust up throughout. The whole place looked as if it had been created by some titanic artist's hand.

Adina had heard stories of places like this. They were supposed to be rare and extremely dangerous. The gigantic bombs used during the wars caused catastrophic earthquakes that opened rifts like this one. And even centuries after the last bombs fell, rifts could sometimes just open without warning -- or collapse.

But nothing in the stories had said anything about them being *beautiful.*

Asher turned them onto another dangerously steep path and pools of water along the bottom of the valley came into view. Adina gasped at their extraordinary colors.

Many were cloudy jade green, the earth around them brightly hued in iridescent oranges, reds, yellows and whites. Other pools were crystal clear, the deepest blue. A wide, clear lake lay adjacent to the brightly colored pools like some idealized view of what the natural world had once been like.

Adina could only stare in amazement.

Asher chuckled and she tore her eyes from the pools.

The corner of his mouth had come up into a grin. He had dimples under his closely trimmed beard. "You should see your face."

"What is this place?" Adina turned back, drinking in the natural beauty as they reached the bottom of the slope.

"Safe."

"But, how can it be safe? This is a quarantine zone."

"The biological agents that this place was quarantined for died off a long time ago. There are probably still some dangerous spots, but overall, it's as safe as anywhere else. Mostly because no one comes here." He nodded out the windows. "I found this years ago on a patrol." He gestured upward. "Damn near drove off the edge up there." He pulled the truck up onto a rocky spit next to a set of clear pools, tucking the vehicle in against a towering red stone pillar. The lake was only a few yards away. "We're here." He shut the engine off and climbed out.

Adina had been so overwhelmed that she hadn't even noticed the birds. With the truck turned off she heard ducks. Other bird sounds filled in and as she looked up, some soared on thermals, while others flitted and played on the breezes that moved the grasses and plants.

Her door was pulled open, and Asher reached up for her. "Come on."

Adina set the blanket aside and put her foot on the first step down, facing him and letting him help her down. Her belly twinged as her body lengthened with his hands under her arms. Adina's whole body slid against his, smearing them together as he lowered her to the ground. Adina's face, neck and chest were on fire again.

Adina stammered, "Thank you," blushing harder at the way his blue eyes watched hers.

"You're welcome." He turned and walked to the back of the truck. "When was the last time you had a bath?"

Adina wrinkled her face. She couldn't be sure if he was joking, being mean, or just checking facts. "Uhhh… About a week ago?" She followed, hearing him pull the rear doors of truck open. By the time she got there, he had his pistol belt off. His sweat-soaked shirt clung to his muscular torso.

Adina was used to men being thin, even if they were strong, not *big* the way he was. He pointed to the terraces of pools. "Start in the lowest ones. The flow from the springs pushes the water out over the sides into the lower pools. Use the lower pools to get clean, so you don't contaminate the other ones, and move to the higher ones once you're clean. And they get hotter." He pointed, "Until you get to that one." He pointed to the large, broad basin that stood above the others. "It's too hot for anyone, I think." He kicked off his boots and grabbed some bags from a storage bin.

"The water's warm?" Adina turned in a circle taking in the wonderous place. "How?"

Asher nodded to the lake. "The lake is cold, but these are heated by geothermal activity. The water gets pushed up from volcanic vents below." He gestured absent-mindedly toward his feet. "It also picks up trace elements that are good for healing in the process." He walked to the water and dropped the bags a few yards from the edge, then shook out a tarp and weighed the corners down with rocks and set his pistol belt on it.

Adina was still trying to wrap her mind around the amazing place when Asher suddenly picked her up and threw her over his shoulder like a sack of grain.

Adina flailed, her belly twinging as she tried to push herself off his shoulder. "Wait! Stop! What are you doing!"

He waded into the nearest pool.

"Put me DOWN!"

He was about waist deep when he answered, "Okay," and dumped her unceremoniously into the warm water.

Adina's backside bumped onto the sandy bottom, and it took more flailing to get her feet under her. She pushed up, splashing to keep her balance, sputtering and spitting water. "What is wrong with you!" Adina dragged her hair out of her face. When she finally blinked the water out of her eyes, he was smiling. It was an honest, joyful expression. The creases between his eyebrows were gone. He looked years younger. Adina staggered on the uneven bottom and her mind was just registering how pleasantly warm the water was when she saw his eyes travel down from her face. She looked down. Her bright yellow shirt was all but transparent, clinging to her breasts. She crossed her arms and dunked down into the water. "Well, don't look!"

But his grin, so out of character, tickled her and a nervous laugh suddenly sprang up with the feeling of blood rushing up into her chest, neck and face.

He cocked his head playful. "They're kinda hard to miss." He smiled again and pushed through the water to her then held out a piece of soap. "Wash." He indicated her clothes. "You can wash your clothes while they're on you."

Adina took the soap, still ducked down. Everything inside her felt like it was on fire now. A crooked grin of her own was now stuck to her face like her sopping hair.

He stepped away and pulled another piece of soap out of his pocket. Then, smiling at her, he let himself fall over backward into the water with a splash. Adina couldn't help but laugh at the boyish action. He stayed under for a moment then pulled himself back up, tossing his head to throw his hair back out of his face. Then he started scrubbing his shirt.

Adina lifted the bar of soap to her nose. It smelled like him. Clean, a nice smell, not harsh or astringent. She turned her back to him and rubbed soap over her clothes. It lathered nicely in the warm water. She kept looking over her shoulder. He was concentrating on an oil stain on his shirt, then dunked down again. When he stood up, he peeled off his shirt, rinsed it and threw it over a rock.

Adina nearly dropped the soap.

Scars, large and small crossed his torso. Adina had seen bullet scars before. There were two right next to each other under his left arm. She was so focused on the terrible scars that she barely noticed the black, abstract, curvilinear tattoos on his chest and shoulders. They were fierce, with what looked like stylized talons interwoven with curving, concentric whiplash curves. He was bruised almost black on his right side. More tattoos ran from his wrists to his elbows, precise flowing patterns made up of repeating geometric shapes. The burn scar on his left hand was part of a larger burn that marred the tattoo right up to his elbow.

Confusion tore through Adina like a thousand-pound boar through a tent. Under the scars was hard muscle.

She'd seen very few men as strongly built as Asher was. And none of them had been as handsome or… *exciting* as he was. Every part of Adina *wanted* him.

But his scars told a story of pain and brutality that stabbed into her like hooks in her heart. Their painful tug battled with the hungry ache at her center. She looked at the massive machine and the scars on it, then back to Asher again. The image of them rolling side-by-side off some mythical assembly line returned.

Machines of war.

He turned back with a grin and saw her staring.

His expression stuck for a moment as he watched her expression, then his smile faded. Following her gaze, he looked down. "You've seen scars before, haven't you?" There was an unapologetic edge to his voice. The matter of factness had crept back in. Adina's heart fell at its return.

The creases reappeared between his eyebrows.

Then he raised his arms as if to say, "This is me," and turned slowly, so she could see the roadmap of pain scribed across his skin.

Adina could hardly breathe as she counted the bullet wounds, burns, cuts and gashes. Thirteen significant scars in all. When he finished his circle, his smile was entirely gone.

Everything inside Adina was tumbling like she was falling down a hill. And before a thought dawned, she'd waded to him and wrapped her arms around him. She pulled herself tight against his chest, terror and awful memories suddenly flooding through her.

"Thank you…" It took everything Adina had to keep from bawling, but tears rolled down her cheeks and she had to swallow before she could say, "Thank you for saving my life."

Adina just held onto him, her eyes closed, her breath catching as she tried not to sob. Her hands gripped him hard, feeling the muscles under his skin and the irregularities of the scars on it.

He didn't move. He didn't even breathe for a long moment. Fear climbed up in Adina.

Is he going to push me away?

Then his arms wrapped around her, heavy, but gentle. "You're welcome." The matter of fact edge was there, but it was softer than a moment before.

Adina opened her mouth and tried to say something several times, but she knew if she did, she'd just cry.

Images and feelings that she'd been holding at bay battered at her. Things she didn't want to remember.

He gave her a reassuring squeeze. "Do your people shave?"

His question was so nonsensical it completely derailed the images and feelings. Adina wasn't sure she'd heard him correctly. "What?"

"Do your people shave?" When she looked up, the creases between his eyebrows were still there, but a corner of his mouth had come up again. He raised an arm indicating his armpit; his were shaved. Then he pointed down significantly, watching her eyes with his amazingly blue ones, one eyebrow raised playfully. "You know, to help against parasites and the like?"

Pressed against him, his smell and the soap were intoxicating. Adina stood up on her toes and pushed her lips toward his, her fingers exploring his skin. He stopped her, leaning his head back and gently laying his fingers against her lips.

But his other arm still held her firmly against him. "Not yet."

"What?" Every part of Adina ached for him. She could feel his arousal too, pressing against her.

He dropped his lips onto her soaking hair and kissed her head, then scooped her up. As confused as she might have been before, his rebuff left her feeling like she was spinning as he carried her out of the water. He took her to the tarp and set her on her feet where water squished out of her sopping boots. He knelt at one of the packs. When he stood and turned back to her, his smile had returned. The creases between his now playfully arched eyebrows were gone. He held up a razor. It was shiny, dark metal, and like everything else he had, it looked brand new and manufactured. It was beautiful.

Adina couldn't help the laugh that tickled its way out at his expression, her anxiety falling off. She put a hand out for the razor, cocking her head at him. "You want me to shave for you?"

He pulled the razor back, his own smile widening. "You won't be the one doing the shaving."

A corner of Adina's mouth turned up so hard it almost hurt as she arched a black eyebrow at him. "*You* want to shave *me?*"

He stepped close and pushed hair back out of her face with a finger. "If you'll let me." He took her right hand and laid her fingers on a ropey scar on his left breast. "If you trust me."

Adina bent tentatively to kiss the scar waiting to see if he would stop her. When he didn't, she kissed it gently, then looked back into his lapis blue eyes and just watched them for a moment. His right cheek dimpled with his smile. It made him look like a naughty little boy. "I do, I trust you." She let her hands trail over his shoulders, her eyes taking in the details of his wet skin. The feeling of it under fingers made everything inside her tingle.

"Good."

He put the razor in his back pocket, his eyes traveling to her breasts, her erect nipples pushing through her wet shirt. He undid the first button, and her heart skipped a beat at his touch. Adina took a startled breath.

He smiled, his eyes moving to hers. "Is this alright?"

"Uh huh…" It was about all she could get out as she felt the warm sun on her wet shirt.

He slowly unbuttoned her shirt. She gripped his arms to steady herself. He finished unbuttoning it but didn't pull it open. He left it hanging, still covering her and ran his fingers lightly down from her neck between her breasts and down her stomach. Adina's breath caught again when his hand touched her waistband. She bit her lip, trying not to squirm at the sudden fire between her legs. He grabbed a small canvas pail from one of the packs, filled it with water and returned. He pulled the soap from his pocket, then lifted her left arm and ran the soap over her armpit through her shirt, lightly massaging it through the soaking fabric. Adina took deep breaths to combat her excited dizziness. He put her arm over his shoulder. As he changed to her other arm, he let the hard bar of soap run across her nipples, each in turn. Adina bit her lip hard and sighed. Her whole body shuddered with each touch. Then he raised her other arm and soaped her armpit through her shirt.

After it lathered, his eyes traveled over her face again. "Put your arms down."

She lowered her arms, and he pushed her shirt off her shoulders, letting the wet cloth slip down, hanging on her nipples until the weight of the fabric pulled it off. He tossed her shirt into the shallow water at the edge of the pool. Adina was shaking head to toe now. She smiled at him, her nipples standing erect in the center of dark pink areolas. "I… I think I need to sit down."

He pulled her against him. Adina's head fell forward against his shoulder, and she bit her lip hard, a groan slipping out as her naked breasts finally made skin to skin contact with his bare chest. He lowered her onto the tarp and just held her against him for a moment. Adina was breathing hard and fast.

"Are you alright?"

Adina nodded, swallowing hard, a small laugh escaping before her breathless answer. "More… More than fine." She pushed him back so she could see his face, smiling and staring into his eyes. She leaned close but stopped before he had to raise a hand to stop her kiss. "When?"

He smiled at her. "Soon."

He sat next to her and raised her right arm, putting it behind her head. His eyes traveled over her womanly, handful sized breasts shining damp in the sun. She was dark tan where her skin was exposed, her arms tan to where her sleeves ended, as well as her chest where her shirt opened. But the rest of her was pale and freckled. His eyes lingered on her naked upper body, then shifted to her hazel eyes as he worked soap into the short light brown hair under her arm. Adina's chest lifted and her belly pushed out trying to breathe evenly, but her body kept twitching. He picked up the razor and put it against her skin.

"Ready?"

Adina nodded. "Uh huh…"

He drew the sharp safety razor up from the bottom of her armpit carefully and confidently, using small strokes and flushing the razor often.

Adina couldn't help the catching breaths that kept happening. She bit her lip and squeezed her eyes shut.

He's done this before…

"Ticklish?"

Adina nodded. "Mmm hmmm." She tried to not move.

"I'll try not to tickle you."

Adina had never imagined how wildly arousing it would be to have someone else shave her.

He used a wet cloth to wash the last bit of soap from her armpit, the warm water running down her side. Then he gave her clean armpit a kiss.

Adina shied away from the tickle of his whiskers, laughing. "Stop! That tickles…" Then he gave her a quick peck on her right nipple and Adina's whole body seized. He sat back watching her as she covered her nipple, blushing hard and laughing. "That was just mean!"

He moved to her other side with the bucket and gave her a thoroughly naughty smile. "I'm just getting started." He shaved her other armpit, and like the first one, gave her clean armpit a kiss when he was finished. And as she'd hoped, her left nipple a kiss. That left her laughing hard, holding her hands over her breasts, him smiling widely at her.

Then he twirled the razor in his hand. "Now for more dangerous territory."

Adina just held her hands over herself drinking in what he looked like. The mischievous expression, the bright sun beating on his broad shoulders, his scars that just didn't seem to matter suddenly, all set against the background of brightly colored pools, the moving water glinting in the sun.

He set the razor aside and pointed to one of her sopping boots. "May I?"

Adina grinned and held up her foot. "Please."

He pulled off her soaking boots and socks. She laid back on the tarp, her arms over her head displaying herself for him. Her pants hung low on her hips. He ran a hand up her leg until it was on her waistband. "Would you like some help with these?" He bent and put a kiss on her abdomen.

Adina curled up at the tickle of his kiss, a giggle bubbling out. Then she watched his eyes and laid back, displaying herself for him again. "I would love it if you took my pants off, Asher."

He unbuttoned the top, his eyes still on hers. "It would be my pleasure."

Adina wriggled, helping him pull her wet, clinging pants down. He was careful to leave her underwear in place. As he got her pants just past her hips, he slid his hands inside the waistband, trailing his fingers over her bare legs as he drew them down. He tossed her pants in the shallow water next to her shirt.

He smiled at her, lathering soap between his hands. "Nice legs."

Adina was about to answer when he put his soapy hands around her upper thigh, and she suddenly couldn't get the words out -- whatever they had been. He slowly soaped her right leg. At the top, he made sure to soap just to the edge of her panties. Adina squeezed her eyes shut, biting her lip hard again at his proximity to her center. He shaved her leg from bottom to top making sure to shave as close to her panties as possible without quite touching them. He repeated the process on her other leg. Adina was more in control by the time he finished, but still trembled when he touched her in certain ways.

With a smile of purest naughtiness, he slid his fingers in the waistband of her panties. Adina lifted her hips, biting her lip as he slowly pulled them down. She always kept her pubic hair fairly short, but a lack of sharp and appropriate blades made shaving hard. His hands pulled her panties down, his strong fingers exploring as they went again. When her panties were off, he wadded them up and tossed them into the pool with the rest of her clothes. He looked at her slightly unruly pubic hair, then lightly stroked it. Adina's head rolled back against the tarp and a moan pushed its way out. Adina sat up and pulled herself to him.

"I want you."

He stroked her face, pushing her hair back. "I want you too. But not yet." He smiled, his hand on her pubic hair again. His smile was mischievous. "Would you like me to shave," he stroked the hair lightly and her legs tightened. "down here?"

Adina was biting her lip again, her forehead against his shoulder. "Yes. I'd like that very much."

He laid her on her back. Sitting on his knees he put one of her legs on each side of his hips. He lathered soap in his hands. "Ready?"

She nodded, lying back and watching him, her chest rising and falling rapidly. He rubbed soapy water over the top of her pubic hair first and worked down, warm water running between her legs. He was careful with the soapy water -- frustratingly careful, avoiding her clitoris and labia. Warm soapy water ran over her anus, and Adina shuddered.

He put the razor against the skin at the top of her mound and made the first stroke, watching her face.

Adina put her hands over her mouth, her whole body trembled.

"Doing alright?"

Adina nodded. He shaved her front and she managed to keep from twitching, holding herself to just a whole-body tremble. She hadn't realized she was holding her breath until she sucked in a deep belly breath. He lifted her left leg and shaved, so close to her labia that she twitched at the tickle. He was careful not to cut her, then he did the other side, and she was managing to breathe more evenly as he finished.

Then he ran soapy fingers on her mound, down over her clit and along her labia. Adina's whole body spasmed at the feeling of his slippery fingers on her utterly smooth skin. Her hips rose to meet his touch as she pulled in a gasping breath. Then his hands were off her. Adina groaned and when she looked down, he was smiling, cleaning the razor.

"That was…"

"Mean. I know." The dimple appeared on his right cheek again. "Turn over if you want me to finish the rest."

Adina pulled her legs up and rolled over onto all fours. Asher scooted forward, his knees between her feet, pushing her legs open, exposing everything to him from the back.

"Still doing alright?"

She looked back at him past her lifted ass. "Yes… Please."

Her whole backside was already soapy, it just took some quick, slippery rubs of his fingers to make it lather. Adina fought to hold still, pressing her forehead against the tarp, breathing in gasps. He carefully shaved everything, again, avoiding her most sensitive spots.

"There." He set the razor aside. And as she was easing forward, a slippery finger ran over her anus. Adina twitched hard at the excruciatingly intimate touch and fell forward. Her whole body felt like it had lit up.

And when she looked back over her shoulder, he was, as expected, smiling at her. "You should wash off now." He grinned with the naughty little boy look again. "Can you get to the pool by yourself, or do you need a hand?"

Adina narrowed her eyes at him but couldn't help the smile that pulled her cheeks wide. "I can get there by myself. But I might need a hand up." He helped her to stand and as she leaned against him, he took one of her hands and put it between her legs, her hand completely encompassed by his larger one. Using her hand in his, he cupped her mound. "Smooth now?" He slid her fingers lightly onto her clit.

The contact nearly took Adina's legs out from under her. She squeezed her legs together and tried to stay standing. "That's… *mean!*"

He moved his hand, leaving hers between her legs and looped his arm under her knees, then picked her up, walking into the water. "Mean? I'm never mean."

Once he was waist deep in the water again, he let go of her legs so Adina's feet could find the bottom. The warm water felt *so* good.

He stood behind her to keep her steady. Adina's skin prickled as he rinsed her armpits with handfuls of water. Her head fell back against him as he splashed water onto her and ran his hands down her arms and sides to make sure there was no soap left. His hands slid slowly around her body following the outside of her breasts, then under them until he was cupping them in his hands. Adina pushed back against him and arched her back, groaning as his fingers played lightly over her nipples, each touch making her twitch. She reached over her shoulder and grabbed around his neck as her other hand guided one of his down, between her legs.

"Is… it smooth now?" she panted.

He let his hand slide over her clit, then along her labia until they were almost touching her anus.

"Very smooth."

She moaned, gripping his neck and pressing herself against his hand. She reached back and grabbed his waistband with her other hand, but he stopped her. His fingers lightly stroked her labia. "Not yet."

Adina's hips pivoted back at his touch; her body demanded to have him inside her. "I want you now."

He picked her up and carried her to the tarp. He settled down onto it, holding her seated in front of him. She could feel how hard he was through his pants, pressing into her back.

His hand glided down between her legs again. His lips were at her ear. "Not yet for some things." His fingers parted her labia, playing lightly before slipping forward onto her swollen clitoris. "Not for others." His other hand wrapped around her onto her breast, brushing her nipple again.

Adina threw herself back against his bare chest, paralyzed by his touch, a moan escaping from some primordial place within her. She grabbed his hand between her legs guiding his fingers while her other snaked around the back of his neck as she thrust her breasts out. She shuddered with every brush of her nipple. Her whole body was on fire now.

Adina's orgasm struck so quickly that she wasn't prepared for it. Her mouth opened and she squeezed her eyes shut, her hand on his between her legs gripping hard, the nails of her other hand digging into the back of his neck. A few strangled groans escaped as she arched and tensed.

Days of fear and anxiety and the cramping tension of her arousal for him suddenly exploded from inside her. Adina screamed and her legs clamped around his hand, her hips rolling. Her whole body felt like it was trying to collapse in on itself. All she could do was gasp between the tightening convulsions, clinging to his arm as her whole body jerked, tensing and then unleashing. Another spasm threw her head back and her legs out. She went rigid, shuddering, held in his strong embrace riding the ecstatic spasms.

Her straining trembles eased, but he moved his fingers on her clit just a little, and her orgasm reignited, throwing her into a whole new set of hard spasms. Adina writhed, clawing at his hand and neck.

Adina's orgasms were always wonderful, but this was… so much. There were no thoughts that went with it, but when the spasms finally released her, Adina felt like she'd been lost to some other place. She was panting, collapsed against him. His fingers played lightly over her clit, her body twitching with each gentle caress. She hadn't caught her breath when another orgasm began to build.

Earth and sky!

But she was ready for it this time.

"Yes… Yes… There…" Adina caressed his neck pushing her hips to work his fingers into her most sensitive spot, arching her back to push her breast into his strong hand. As the orgasm built, she let go of his neck and grabbed his hand on her breast. She squeezed her breast with his hand, putting his fingers on her nipple. As her hips squirmed and trembled, she squeezed his fingers on her nipple. "Like that.. ha… hard…" then Adina didn't have a voice again, just shaking gasps and moans as she shuddered against his strong arms and the ground, her orgasm crashing through her. She could hear his excited breathing in her ear and feel him pulling her back against the hard bulge in his pants. Adina pitched forward as her muscles clenched hard, cramping and then in a shattering release, she was thrown back against him. Everything spun.

When Adina could finally make sense of the world again, her pumping hips were slowing, the other spasms easing. Adina released her fierce grip on his hands and collapsed in his arms, her body slack, legs and arms shaking.

"Feel better?" he whispered into her ear.

Adina smiled and nodded. It took a several gasping breaths before she felt like she had enough air in her lungs to say, "Yes." The release of fear and tension was like being bashed over the head with a mallet. Asher laid them down on the tarp, pulling her close against him.

Adina just basked in the sun in Asher's strong arms.

She felt him roll over and heard him digging in one of the packs next to where they lay. He kissed her ear to get her attention. Adina was losing the battle against sleep.

"Adina, I'd like to inoculate you."

Adina opened her eyes, and he was holding a squarish yellow and white medical injector where she could see it. She'd seen things like it, always expended. Because of their bright colors, they got used as decorations sometimes.

"Inoculate me?" she panted.

"Do you know what vaccinations are?"

She nodded sleepily. "My mother told me about them when I was little. People got stuck with pins or needles to keep from getting sick."

"That's it, in a nutshell. This works best when you are relaxed."

"Okay…" Adina swallowed, still trying to catch her breath, her eyes closing again.

Adina felt him turn her to face him. "It's going to make you sick, Adina. *Really* sick. Maybe sicker than you've ever been -- for about twenty-four hours."

Adina opened her eyes at the sudden seriousness in his voice. She turned more fully to him.

The open concern in his expression as he watched her made her already racing heart thump harder. She wanted to kiss him so badly she could barely stand it. "That's why you made us wait?"

He nodded, holding up the injector for her to look at. "Yes. We'll be able to do anything we want afterward. And it will help keep you from getting sick in the future." He pushed wet black hair out of her face. The furrows between his eyebrows had returned. "But it will be *bad*, Adina. It takes about twenty-four hours to purge any toxins from your system. I'll be right here with you. But I want this to be your choice."

Adina watched his eyes. The way he said it, *I want this to be your choice*, made everything inside her warm. A smile grew on her face. She stroked his scarred cheek. "I trust you." She took his hand with the injector and put it against her neck, still holding his eyes. "I *trust* you." The relief that flooded his expression made her chest ache.

He nodded. "I'm glad." Adina felt the sting in her neck. Asher set the injector aside and dropped his face against her damp hair and pulled her close.

Adina held his arms tightly and curled up against him. She pulled his hand around to cup her breast and let herself slip into sleep.

--

It was still light when Adina woke. She lifted her head and Asher was a few yards away removing things from a crate. She could see her clothes hanging in the sun on a makeshift clothesline. She rolled over and stretched just watching the way Asher's shirt pulled across his broad back. He'd changed clothes; both his shirt and pants were different. His other clothes were laid out on rocks. Adina smiled thinking about his hands on her and the tremendous orgasms they caused. Her smile turned into a happily embarrassed grin. She couldn't remember ever cumming that hard. It had almost knocked her out.

"Asher?"

He turned and smiled, setting things down and coming to her. "How do you feel?"

Adina stretched, making sure her breasts appeared from beneath the blanket for him as she did, smiling. "Good. Tired."

He smiled at her showing off for him and settled down on the tarp next to her. He was barefoot. He put a hand on her face, feeling her skin, then her neck.

"You feel alright?"

Adina nodded. "Mmm hmm." She stretched again and reached up putting a hand on his chest. "Thank you. That was… amazing." She turned and looked at the water. "I better clean up."

He trailed his fingers through the hair on the side of her neck. "Okay."

Adina wrapped the blanket around her and headed for the water. She'd only taken a few steps when blinding pain suddenly split her skull.

Everything was spinning.

Asher's arm slid around her.

"I don't feel very good."

He picked her up and when he laid her down it was on something springy -- a cot. At her curious look, he answered. "It's only big enough for one." Adina laid her head down and there was a pillow, then squeezed her eyes shut against the dagger stabbing behind them. "It's the inoculant." He lifted her head. "Drink this. It will help."

Even trying to drink was suddenly overwhelming. All Adina's strength felt like it had fallen straight out of her body. The broth was salty, tangy, and bitter. Adina made a face.

"I know. Drink it all. You're going to need the electrolytes."

Adina did as he asked, but it was only through sheer will. As soon as she finished, her whole body seemed to succumb to gravity as if each bone was being pulled down individually.

"You'll be alright. It's just going to be a rough day or so." Adina opened her eyes at his fingers running over her brow. "I'm going to be right here, Adina."

She put her hand on his and smiled weakly. "I know. I trust you."

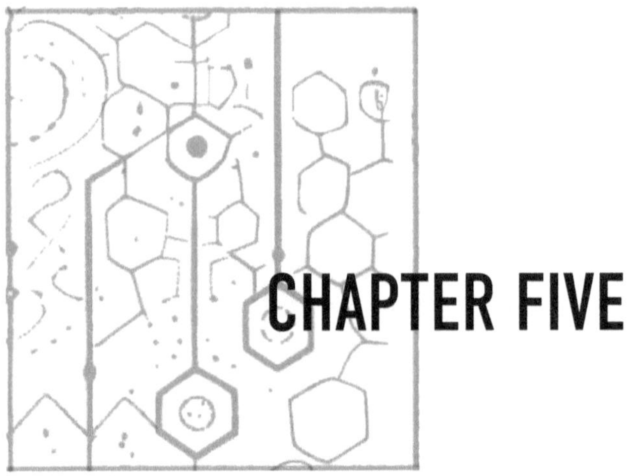

CHAPTER FIVE

Adina threw her hands out, screaming and fighting against the searing claws tearing at her. She could see the ramshackle house she'd grown up in from the dusty road where she lay in the twisting, searing sun. Water rolled over her skin. Adina screamed again and looked down, kicking at the agony in her guts. Her belly writhed. She could feel the worms of ice and fire squirming inside her.

Fever dreams -- sometimes she knew they were just dreams…

Raiders shrieked in her ears, their eyes nothing but hellish, soulless pits burnt into their grotesquely painted faces.

Awful screaming… Terrified, shrill, then suddenly silent. So much worse that the nightmares… The things she knew weren't nightmares.

She threw up.

"Adina. It's alright…" Asher's voice seemed so far away. It was gentle and reassuring. He was holding her arm to keep her on her side. There was a pan. "You're safe…"

Everything disappeared again.

Her mother screamed and screamed. In the night, in the day…

It was dark out when Adina opened her eyes. Her mind was filled with flashes -- pain, vomiting. Asher's face grew freakishly large and then small again in her pulsing vision as raiders danced in and out of focus, howling their inhuman battle cries. She could see the pools she lay next to, the agonizingly cold sheet over her. Asher's eyes burned away to become black pits. He was a raider too. Adina shrieked and clawed, trying to fight, but she was too weak. His burning face twisted, and every millimeter of Adina's skin felt like it was under a blowtorch, being struck with a hammer. His hands, gentle on her face felt like they were peeling her skin off.

"It's alright Adina. It's just the fever. You're hallucinating. They're not real. They're not..."

Real...

Adina's eyelids hurt as she slowly opened them. Everything hurt. Long shadows stretched that might have been from a lantern, or the sun cutting through the buildings above the rift. *Day or night?* When she moved, laces of fire raced through her muscles. She was on the cot again. Consciousness filled in as if she was a cup it was pouring into. It was night. A fire was burning a few yards away with pots and a kettle on stands over the coals. Adina turned her head.

Asher lay on the ground next to her, his right arm propped on the edge of the cot, his hand closed around hers, snoring lightly. Adina just watched him, emotions filling her until they overflowed as tears that ran down her cheeks. She closed her hand around his.

Asher jerked awake. When he saw her looking at him, he became still as a statue, his lapis blue eyes traveling over her face.

Adina thought her heart might explode at the worry in his eyes.

His hand closed around hers and he pushed to his knees. His other hand moved to her face, then her neck feeling for her fever. A relieved smile split his face.

"There you are."

Adina shifted her head to see him more easily with a grimace and small hiss of pain. "Here I am." She drew his hand to her lips and kissed his fingers.

He pushed hair out of her face, lightly trailing his fingers over her brow and temple. "You had me worried." He gently kissed her forehead.

"Why?" She let her eyes close and shifted over onto her back. Even now she could feel strength returning to her muscles.

"You've been sick for over three days." He lifted a cloth and ran it around her lips, wetting them, then squeezed it. Cool water flowed into her mouth. "Do you think you can drink some more?"

Adina nodded. Her throat was raw, but now that she'd had something, she was parched. He helped her sit up, tucking the blanket around her naked body. Adina's hands shook, but steadied as he helped her hold the canteen, watching her eyes. "I was afraid I was going to lose you."

She drank carefully, but it only took a few swallows for things to feel more normal. When she'd finished, she rested against him feeling strength flow back into her. "You said it would only be a day."

Adina felt him nod. "It should have been. A day, maybe a day and a half. Whatever the inoculant was trying to get rid of had a real hold on you."

Adina was suddenly *starving*. She stayed tucked up against him, just resting. "I don't want to do that again."

She felt his lips on her forehead. "I bet. I wouldn't want you to either."

Adina smiled. "I'm hungry."

When she looked up, he was smiling at her. "Good. I was hoping you'd say that." He sat back steadying her. "You okay to sit up on your own?"

Adina adjusted herself. "Mmm hmm."

He stepped away and returned with a steaming cup. "It's not very interesting, but it's what you need. Careful, it's hot." He handed her the cup and Adina passed it from hand to hand, blowing on it until it was cool enough to drink. It was strong and salty; she could taste fat in it. She took a few drinks, the heat from it seeming to help spread strength back through her battered body. "It's good. What is it?"

"Boar marrow broth. I threw in extra salt because you need it." He smiled again and sat on the cot next to her. She leaned against him again, tucking the blanket up and hugging the cup to her. Adina suddenly shivered. It was cold. "What now?"

He put his arm around her. "We let you rest for a day or so, see how you feel and then I'll start training you."

Adina lifted her face. "Training me?"

His expression was serious, but the creases between his eyebrows weren't there. "If we're going to be together, you need to be able to protect yourself. You need to know how to fight, how to shoot," he nodded to the truck. "And how to drive the Bearcat."

"Bearcat?"

"That's what we call them."

Adina looked at the Bearcat and back to him. "You're going to teach me to drive that? And to fight?"

He nodded. "And a lot of other things." His expression softened. He watched her eyes, then leaned down and gave her a soft kiss on the lips.

Adina's body felt like it caught fire. She wanted to grab him, but her hands were occupied with the broth and holding the blanket around her. She pressed her lips hard against his. The kiss was long and lingering and when he pulled back, she was still leaning forward wanting more.

He smiled again, a wide, playful thing. "You need to get some rest before we go much further down that road." He ran his thumb lightly over her lips. "I just wanted you to know what I'm thinking."

"I like what you're thinking," Adina answered breathlessly, having to concentrate to not dump hot soup all over herself.

He got up and when he came back, he was carrying a stack of clothes and a pair of boots. He set the clothes on the cot next to her, the boots on the ground. "I grabbed some things that I thought should fit you." He pointed to the boots. "They seemed to be about the right size." He pointed back to the truck. "There are more things in the bearcat, but I washed these since they seemed like the closest fit."

Adina's heart sank as she looked at the trousers, shirts, and underwear. There were even a couple of jackets. The way Asher's expression closed up when she turned to him told her everything. She didn't need to ask where they'd come from.

He was watching her expression. She could feel the sympathy behind his eyes. He'd acted out of pragmatic, brute necessity, but images of people Adina had known flashed through her mind. Adina swallowed the lump in her throat. "One of my friends could have been wearing these…" She couldn't say the rest.

He nodded. "I'm sorry for that."

There was so much control in Asher's exterior. But Adina could see the emotions beneath as plainly as the sun in the sky. That she could read him so easily took her breath away. She'd never been able to see into Naveer so clearly. Every other man she'd ever 'loved' had been opaque compared to Asher.

He pointed to a rock. "Your clothes are over there if you'd be more comfortable in those. But you'll need…" He hesitated. "extras."

Adina's heart was racing. Asher scared her. And aroused her. And there were so many other feelings that suddenly crashed through. And with them came a realization. She looked around the small camp.

"You didn't take anything from the camp?" She looked around again, seeking anything that looked out of place among his orderly equipment. Something that had been scavenged would have. "You didn't salvage anything from the camp." She paused, glancing at the pile next to her on the cot. "Other than clothes for me?"

Adina's thoughts were now spinning as things connected, her mind finally seeming to come up to speed after feeling addled for the last few days.

"I try not to. I salvage if I have to, but unless I really need something, it just feels wrong. I know it's normal out here. It's survival. But for me, it feels like robbing the dead."

Where does he come from that he doesn't need to salvage things?

Adina finished the broth just for something to fill in her confusion. "I'd like to clean up."

He nodded. "The towel is on the rock with the soap."

Adina got up, holding the blanket around her and gave him another glance before walking to the pool. Her confusion only deepened when he didn't follow or say anything.

Adina wanted some space to sit with her feelings. Seeing the stack of clothes churned up memories of people she'd lost. She felt steadier to deal with them. She also wanted his attention, his touch. He stayed away. Maybe he could sense her desire to be alone. He didn't even look at her when she dropped the blanket and stepped into the pool.

Adina couldn't help the deep sigh that escaped as she let herself slip down into the warm, enfolding waters. She looked back and he was doing something at the fire. His body language felt forced; he didn't even look in her direction. She dunked her head and washed. Her skin's soreness seemed to wash away with the soap. Lathering her long black hair, she kept peeking at him. He never looked at her. When she finally felt clean, she set the soap on a rock and climbed carefully into one of the higher pools. It was *hot.* The mineral tasting water seemed to seep between her fever-battered muscles and bones. And it made her buoyant, the mineral rich waters holding her up. After she'd adjusted to the temperature, she let herself float on her back, goosebumps rising across her breasts, her nipples hardening in the thrill of the cold night air as the rest of her relaxed in the penetrating heat.

The stars filled in beyond the teeth of the buildings atop the cliffs. It was like looking out of a giant mouth. The bright pinpoints were blue-white or turned different colors. The fabric of stars seemed so solid Adina felt like she should be able to reach out and touch its creases and folds. A satellite streaked across. As Adina watched it, stories people told about them and the other wonders of the world that was rolled through her mind. And as they did, the memories of the people she'd lost in camp were pushed aside.

Best to not dwell on the past, an old woman's voice said in her mind. The memory rose as Adina watched a shooting star cross the sky, bright and fluorescing green in the darkness. She'd been watching a similar one the night the old woman had said it. Adina hadn't been with the camp very long, and she was crying, missing her mother and her friends. That was the night when she first understood what death truly meant. Her mother and friends were gone-forever.

The wastes have no time for the past, child, the old woman had told her. *It takes and then forgets. And so should you. The past is a weight that holds you down. Only the present matters out here. That's where we live.*

And that old woman had been lost too. So many years ago, that Adina couldn't remember her name. She was buried in a grave that had long since been consumed by the desert.

Adina realized she had dozed only when her breasts ached from the cold, and she pushed down into the water again.

She turned, looking for Asher.

He wants to teach me to fight?

He had one of the side panels of the bearcat open, doing something. The idea of learning to fight was both frightening and exciting.

There it was again, fear and arousal.

If I'd known how to fight when the raiders attacked… Terrifying images of raiders silhouetted against burning structures or cut outs in the smoke flashed through her mind. Adina pushed down under the water again.

That's the past.

The image of Asher bare chested, his arms thrown out, displaying himself to her was suddenly there again. And the ache inside her blossomed suddenly. She climbed out of the hot pool and slid down into the lower pool. The cooler water was a shock and thrill.

Adina ducked down and watched Asher, sliding her hand between her legs. His broad back was to her as he worked, his pants pulling tight over his handsome ass.

Adina squeezed her eyes shut, holding herself rigid as she moved her fingers. She felt like she was on fire.

Adina stood up and waded out of the water, not bothering with the towel. She walked to him, barely noticing the rocky sand under her feet.

He turned as she reached him, and Adina threw her arms around his neck, putting her lips to his, smashing her body against his. "I want you. I can't take it anymore."

He returned her kiss, their tongues playing. His lips moved onto her neck and down her chest as she arched her back, her mouth opening as his lips found her inflamed nipple. Adina sighed, and her body twitched as he kissed it, her hips pressed hard against him, moaning as he began to suck on it.

Adina's head was spinning. She felt hot and cold.

She lifted his face and kissed him again, her fingers fumbling with his shirt. He helped her, pulling off his shirt and pulling her hard against him. Adina's breath came in short gasps as he picked her up and carried her to the tarp again. She felt like a toy in his strong arms as he lowered her to the ground. She tore at his belt and pants and when she felt his penis, she looked down. It was bigger than she'd expected, thick and hard in her hand, Adina smiled at him and put it against her wet folds, slowly slipping it up and down. Then she carefully slid the head into her.

Adina's vision tunneled at the thick penetration. She couldn't catch her breath. She threw her head back as she pushed it further inside. She clawed at his back, pulling his mouth onto hers. Asher pushed into her, just a little and Adina bit her arm, curling her body and wrapping her legs around him. She didn't dare bite him. Everything was spinning faster.

Adina felt more of him slip inside, stretching her. He was bigger than Naveer. Or anyone she'd ever been with.

Suddenly, she was falling.

"Adina?"

Then there was nothing.

Adina woke to Asher's face close to hers. He was smiling, still breathing a little heavily. She blinked, trying to sort out what happened. Then it all suddenly came back, and Adina blushed furiously. She put her hands over her mouth, her eyes huge, watching his. Her face felt like it caught fire. "I passed out, didn't I?"

He nodded.

Adina hid her face in her hands and pushed against him. "Oh, Earth and Sky!"

Asher chuckled, holding her close. "I'd like to say that was me, but that would be a lie. I don't think you were up to it after being so sick."

"While we were…" She couldn't look at him, her embarrassment tickling her belly and making her laugh.

"Mmm hmm…" he acknowledged, still chuckling.

"Stop laughing!" she laughed into her hands against his neck.

"You first."

Adina dropped her hands and pulled him into a kiss. "It was still… Wonderful." She was smiling so wide it made her cheeks hurt. She raised an eyebrow. "What I remember of it." She pulled back watching his playful expression. "Did you?"

He shook his head. "No. Your eyes rolling back in your head kind of spoiled the mood." His crooked good-natured smile took any potential sting out of the teasing. He got behind her and pulled her against him, then drug the blanket over them. "You should sleep." He looked up and around. "It will be light in a few hours." He kissed her ear and nuzzled her hair. "We've got plenty of time to get to know each other." She pulled his hand around and put it on her breast and then let her head relax onto his warm, burly arm. Her grin only eased a little as she wiggled back into his strong chest, feeling his still semi-erect penis against her backside. She kissed his hand.

"I like that."

The sun was high above the buildings when Adina woke. She squinted against the brightness. When she rolled over Asher wasn't behind her, his arm had been replaced by a pillow under her head, but she was still on the tarp, naked under the blanket. Adina rolled onto her back and stretched, looking for him.

He was back to doing whatever she'd interrupted, working on something in the open side hatch of the Bearcat.

"Good morning."

He turned at her voice and smiled. "Good morning." He shielded his eyes and looked up at the sky as he walked to the fire. "Or should I say afternoon."

"Hi." Adina felt like herself again. But as she arched into a long, whole body stretch she realized there was more to it than that. She felt *really* good; sort of stronger than she could remember in a long time. She pulled the blanket around her and sat up. Everything seemed a little brighter, more focused.

Asher dished some food onto a plate.

"What was in that shot you gave me? I feel… great."

He walked to her with the plate and a canteen and handed them to her.

"The inoculant's working then." He settled cross-legged in front of her. "I'm not surprised you feel better. You must have been carrying around something nasty for the inoculant to knock you down the way it did. You've probably been sick for a long time."

Adina didn't realize she'd been wolfing food down until the raised corner of his mouth caught her attention.

"Well, you've got an appetite, that's a good sign."

Adina blushed again, putting a hand over her mouth. "Sorry, I'm just *really* hungry."

His grin turned to a smile. "Nothing to apologize for. You should be. Don't let me stop you." Adina went back to eating. "There are a few things you need to know about the inoculant. You're likely to feel a little up and down for the next few days, while it figures you out."

"Figures me out?" Adina asked between mouthfuls of the porridge mixed with boar meat.

He nodded. "The inoculant is artificial; it learns about you and adjusts things to help you."

Adina narrowed her eyes at him, not sure if he was making a joke. She knew what vaccines were. Her mother had talked about them when she was a child. And like everyone else, she knew what medications did. But how they worked? That was a different matter. "How does medicine know how to 'figure me out?'"

"Tiny machines; robots. Like me, you now have millions of tiny robots running around inside you just looking for things to fix, to make better."

Adina stopped eating. "You put robots *inside* me?"

Based on his laugh and smile, her expression must have been something to see. "That's the easiest way to describe them. They bolster your normal immune system; help fight off diseases. But they do a whole host of other things too."

Adina furrowed her eyebrows.

Is he making fun of me? People can't do that... But even as the thought formed, what she'd already seen contradicted it. Adina's eyes traveled over the bearcat and all his equipment, then back to him.

"What else do they do?"

"Well, for one, you can't get pregnant. At least not for a while."

Adina stopped eating again. "What? What do you mean I can't get pregnant?" It wasn't like she'd ever wanted to have a child, and she'd been lucky enough to not end up pregnant, but him being so blunt about it was still... unsettling.

"The inoculant sterilizes us. It depends on the person, of course." He waggled a hand. "But it only lasts about a year before we have to immunize again."

"You do this every year?" Adina couldn't imagine going through it again.

"No, not the full inoculation. It's a lower order immunization. It reinforces what's already there."

The idea of having a baby had never been in the forefront of Adina's mind. But being told so bluntly that she suddenly couldn't, even if she wanted to, threw yet another wrench into her internal workings. "What if I wanted to have a baby?"

"You'd be able to after the inoculant's effects wear off. Like I said, for most people, it takes about a year. 'We take nothing from the wastes and leave nothing of ourselves behind.'" He sounded like he was quoting something.

"Who is we? You keep talking like there are more of you out there. But I've never seen or even heard of anyone like you before."

"You shouldn't." Asher raised his eyebrows. "At least not if we're doing our jobs correctly." He took her empty plate. "Are you still hungry?"

Adina nodded. "Yes."

He went back to the fire, talking over his shoulder. "We try not to be seen. We're called Longhunters. We look for secrets from the old world and try to learn about what may still be out there."

"Why?" The idea of spending resources to just wander the wastes felt far-fetched, if not outright sun-mad. But the bearcat, the inoculant, even his clothes were concrete, real.

He returned with the plate and handed it to her. "Because we believe there are things still hidden out in the wastes that can help us to turn the world back the way it was; green, growing, full of life." He sat again.

Adina's insides felt like a sheet flapping in the wind. He sounded like he was out of his mind. "How do you *turn the world back?*" Adina tried not to sound like she was scoffing.

"In small pieces. Around the city states, the growing zones expand every year. But it is slow."

Adina's stomach flip-flopped. "The city states are real?"

He nodded, and to her relief, he didn't look at her like she was an idiot for asking. "They are. They're just a long way from here." He smiled and put a hand on her leg, his expression playful and disarming again. "And they are as beautiful as you've probably been told. More beautiful probably. The walls of Cosanti, where I come from, are of faded yellow stone. They are topped with gardens. The most amazing green growing things trail down from the towers and walls all over the city like water."

Adina could see him looking back in his mind, his expression softening, becoming joyful at the memory. Again, he looked so… different. So open.

"Windmills, sails and turbines move the breeze into the city, some create power. And every rooftop and balcony is covered with gardens." He looked her straight in the eyes. "And not just food, but flowers. People grow things just because they are pretty or smell good." He gave her a kiss on her bare leg. "And outside the walls, there are miles and miles of farmland, apiaries and…"

"Apiaries?"

"Groups of beehives," he explained, another kiss falling further up her thigh. She set the plate aside, her breath suddenly coming fast again.

"Tell me more…"

"Markets filled with fruit and vegetables, bright woven cloth." He pushed the blanket out of the way so he could kiss the top of her leg, his beard brushing her sensitive skin. "Houses and apartments filled with light and growing things, with baths of hot and cold running water." His lips touched her stomach as she laid back, letting the blanket fall away.

Thrills ran through her skin as his lips and hands moved lightly over her legs and stomach. Adina laid back, her hands caressing his hair.

"And there are people who don't have to fight." He kissed her mound lightly and Adina twitched. He kissed down along the inside of her legs. She arched her back letting her head hang back as his beard brushed her labia. He kissed her inner thighs, so close to her center, but not quite touching. Adina gripped his hair, her belly pulling in hard as she tried to breathe.

"Yesss… Tell me more…" she groaned.

"Spices you've probably never heard of, flavors you can't imagine."

Adina moaned, a sudden, sharp sound, as his lips fell onto her sensitive folds. Her whole body contracted, then released as his tongue touched, gliding along it. She squirmed, pulling his hair with one hand, her other grabbing the blanket as his tongue found her clitoris.

He stopped talking, his tongue playing there, his fingers slipping along her wet center. She let go of his hair and grabbed his other hand pulling it up onto her breast, her body shuddering.

"Yes… Asher…"

His fingers slipped inside her. She moaned loudly, her whole body shaking. She couldn't move, paralyzed by the sensation of his tongue on her clit, his fingers inside her and on her nipple. He pushed his fingers deeper, running the tips along her clitoral ridges. She spasmed, curling around the sensation as he sucked her clit. Her fingernails scratched his scalp and she clung to his hand on her breast, only able to take catching breaths. He slid his fingers in and out of her slowly, stopping every few motions to stroke her ridges again. Fire was building inside her as she clung to his hand and his hair, her abdominal muscles clenching in preparation.

Then he lifted his head, "Enjoying yourself?"

Adina's paralysis was broken, but she could barely speak. "Uhhh huhh…" She grabbed his shoulders, pulled him up and dragged his shirt off over his head, then unbuckled his belt. He sat up and kicked off his boots as she kissed his scarred chest and worked to open his pants. As soon as they were down, she pulled him on top of her. He kissed her hard, running the tip of his phallus along her outer lips, then pushed inside.

Adina froze again for a moment. She couldn't even moan, all her attention stolen by the feeling of him entering her again and his mouth on hers. He pushed into her, but only a little at a time, teasing her. She wrapped her legs around him and pulled herself onto him.

Adina had never felt anything so deep. He stretched everything inside her… it was maddening, piercing, agonizing -- *amazing*. And he still wasn't all the way in.

She pulled him against her, pressing her bare breasts to his chest.

Adina took a catching breath as her vagina relaxed around him. "You're so… big," she whispered in his ear breathlessly.

"Are you alright?"

She nodded, kissing his neck fiercely. "Yes…" She put her lips to his mouth. "Yes. I want to feel all of you." She clamped her legs around him for emphasis.

He slowly and rhythmically slid in and out of her, not penetrating any deeper for what felt like a long time. She had no idea how long it might have been; she was lost in the feeling of him inside her. Adina was shuddering again, sweating, her whole body a tight spring ready to break free.

"Oh yes… Yes… I'm going to…" He kissed her nipples lightly and her voice failed, the muscles of her abdomen contracting ecstatically. Adina arched her back, pushing her breasts up to meet his lips. He pulled her nipple into his mouth; his tongue playing over it. Then he pushed himself all the way into her.

Adina yelped, a surprised, ecstatic cry as his pelvis met hers. The feeling of him plunged so far inside her shocked her pending orgasm to a pause. She couldn't move or breathe. Then he pulled back.

The next minutes were a blur. The sound of their sweaty bodies slapping together mixed with their cries as he drove into places she'd never imagined being touched. "Yes… I want you so bad, Asher!"

There was nothing blurry about her orgasm. She grabbed at him and the tarp as her body shook, her climax roaring through her like a tempest. She heard her voice echo off the nearby canyon walls as she screamed with release. It was overwhelming. Her whole body felt like it had been clamped in a vise, then exploded out of it, leaving everything spinning.

But he was still filling her, his strong body against hers, his hard cock driving into her.

In the aftermath, her body relaxed and as her spasms subsided, she was able to luxuriate in the feeling of him inside her. She joined his rhythm instead of being tensed and paralyzed by the intensity of the sensation.

Asher pushed hair out of her face, watching her expression as it relaxed. "You're beautiful." He smiled and kissed her, his rhythm slow and certain. His expression turned playful. "This is a good look for you."

She ran her fingertips over his scarred chest and let her eyes travel brazenly over him between her legs. "I like the way you look there too."

His thrusts turned faster and harder along with his breath. She curled up, holding his face and kissing him. "Yes… I want you to cum so hard in me."

"You feel so good, Adina," he told her breathlessly, his eyes closed with pleasure.

Adina laid back watching his expression. Her body suddenly arched hard, another orgasm roaring up. Her hips thrust to meet his as he slammed against her. Her moan was all but a scream. "Yesss! Your gonna make me cum again!"

He grimaced ecstatically and tensed, his body coiling as he growled animalistically. His pelvis crashed against hers in hard spasms, her abdominal muscles clenching as he drove her into the tarp and ground. He groaned loudly and she felt the heat of his ejaculation.

Adina responding orgasm blasted through her. She pressed her face against his hard chest, kissing his scars frantically as she rode the ecstatic spasms of their fiery mutual release, his fierce passion transmitted to her through his pelvis crushed against hers.

Adina finally collapsed back onto the ground, the hard contractions in her stomach becoming sensual twitches. Asher's weight was on her a moment later. She ran her fingers through his hair and down onto his neck, just relishing the feeling of him on her and his sweaty skin under her hands as they lay panting together.

Asher slid an arm under her, holding her firmly against him, still inside her, and rolled over pulling her on top of him.

Adina smiled as she came up on top. He was still semi-erect inside her. She watched his expression as she pushed back, taking a sighing breath as she slid as much of him into her as possible.

He lifted his hips to meet hers, his expression momentarily fierce, then pushed her cascading hair back and returned her smile as she relaxed down onto him. He kissed her gently. "I didn't want to smash you," he told her breathlessly.

"I liked it." Adina laid her sweaty cheek on his equally sweaty shoulder, her long hair streaming across him. She traced the curving line of one of his tattoos with a finger, running it over the raised skin of a scar and closed her eyes feeling like her whole body was melting down onto him.

He strained, reaching for the blanket on the cot, but she put a hand on his arm and shook her head. "It's too hot."

Adina's head was still cradled against Asher's shoulder when she woke up. He was watching her with his intensely blue eyes, a finger brushing strands of hair out of her face, running lightly over her brow.

Adina smiled and pulled against him, loving the feeling of her naked skin against his. She turned and kissed his arm. He strained to reach for something.

"We don't need the blanket." She rolled on her back, using his bicep as a pillow, and looked up. It was late afternoon as far as she could tell from the way the shadows were cast by the buildings surrounding the canyon.

When he turned back, he had his pistol in his hand.

He smiled and gave her a kiss on the cheek. "I wasn't reaching for that."

The pistol was shiny black, new looking, and like nothing she'd ever seen before. Its blocky frame was fearsome and strangely handsome in the same way Asher and the bearcat were. Its cleanly perfect, manufactured lines made it feel sort of *permanent* in a way that so few things in the wastes felt.

Adina cocked her head trying to figure out how the thing worked, snuggling the back of her head against his burly arm. When he slid the magazine out of the handle, Adina wrinkled her brow at it.

"It's supposed to do that? I mean… Come *apart* like that?" Revolvers were engineering wonders to her with the way their cylinders aligned perfectly when they were fired. The complex mechanisms and small, fine parts reminded her of the innards of her sewing machine. But revolvers didn't… *come apart*. At least not unless you were cleaning them.

"Yup." He turned and watched her eyes, then carefully placed the magazine on her naked belly. It was a little cold, but she didn't move, returning his playful smile.

"This is a very good friend of mine." He pulled on the upper part of the pistol and the whole top of it slid back, ejecting a cartridge into his waiting palm.

"What…" Adina sat up a little, careful of the magazine on her stomach, fascinated by the complex weapon. "How does that work?"

Asher just smiled and carefully tried to stand the cartridge upright next to the magazine on her rising and falling stomach. It tickled.

Adina laughed and it toppled.

He raised an eyebrow. "I guess that won't work." He poked the base of the cartridge lightly into her belly button. Adina laughed and wiggled, but he held it in place until she stopped. "Don't move."

Adina couldn't help the grin the pulled her cheeks at his playfulness. She stayed still, concentrating on keeping the cartridge from toppling again. He finished checking the weapon and then held it up for her. "You're going to need to get familiar with this."

Adina freed her arm from against his body, careful of the cartridge and magazine, then took the pistol, hefting it. It wasn't as heavy as she'd expected. Revolvers were always heavy. "Show me."

He lifted the magazine and indicated the opening at the base of the grip. "This goes in there. It can only go one way. But you need to make sure it seats all the way in. Until it clicks."

Adina took the magazine. Unlike the pistol, it was heavier than she expected, like a dense, blocky stone in her hand. Asher plucked the cartridge from her belly button and ran the polished metal casing lightly around the sensitive perimeter. She bit her lip and squinted an eye.

"I can't concentrate when you do that."

He sat up and kissed her stomach, then her belly button. "Good. That's the point."

After a moment to focus, Adina turned the magazine to align it, then pushed it into the pistol until it clicked.

It was so different from any pistol she'd ever handled. It was sort of square in her hand, but at the same time felt like it fit better. Asher kissed her belly again.

"That's not fair."

"Now, you're going to pull the slide back. That's the top of the pistol." He pointed to the part that moved and put her hand on it. "You need to watch your fingers. It has a very strong spring, and it can pinch you. When you pull the slide back it will load a round from the magazine."

"Magazine?"

"The box with the ammunition that you put into the grip."

Adina pulled tentatively. The slide only moved a little.

"You need to pull harder."

She did, yanking the slide all the way back. It snapped forward.

"Good, now it's loaded." He leaned on an elbow. "Take the magazine out." He pointed to a button on the side of the handle. "That's the magazine release. Just push it."

She did and the magazine popped out. Adina set the magazine on her stomach again.

"Now pull the slide back again to eject the cartridge." When she did, the cartridge spun out, reflecting in the sunlight. It bounced on the dusty ground and Asher retrieved it.

He blew the dust off the cartridge and wiped it clean. He handed her the two cartridges. "Put these in the magazine. Then load the pistol again." Asher took the pistol so she had both hands free. "You push it down and back into the magazine, base first."

It took a couple of tries to get it, but she got the cartridges in.

Asher nodded approvingly, then handed her the pistol again. "You've got strong hands. That's good."

Holding the pistol and magazine Adina sat up enough to give him a kiss. "I used to make shoes." Adina shook the hair out of her face and slid the magazine into the pistol, then pulled the slide back. It was much easier this time, the pistol didn't feel as foreign in her hands.

Asher pointed to the side of the pistol. "That's the safety."

Adina looked at the little lever. "Safety?"

"So it can't go off accidentally."

"That's a smart idea." She flicked the lever. "There."

Asher took the pistol and gave her a long kiss. His kiss was like a wrench that tumbled, clanging through every part of her, turning her organized internal workings to chaos. She was still leaning forward, wanting more when he pulled back. His playful eyes watched hers.

"Let's see if you're as good at shooting as you are at other things." He bent and kissed her stomach again, then pushed up to his feet.

Adina watched him, confused, her spinning insides thrown

completely out of whack by their intimate luxury being so suddenly interrupted. Her eyes lingered on his naked, muscular legs and backside as he turned to where his clothes were.

"Wait…. What? You mean *now?*"

CHAPTER SIX

Adina groaned sleepily as she rolled over on the tarp. Her whole body was complaining after three solid days of training. Every day there was hand to hand combat, knife fighting, pistol and rifle drills. Asher was careful not to hurt her, and strong enough that he could control her body weight when he threw her, but she still hit the hard, dusty ground a *lot*. It was exhausting and exhilarating; a mix of thrill, frustration, and to Adina's surprise, fun. She'd never felt much like a fighter. She knew enough to keep people's hands off her, and how to use a gun, but beyond that, fighting wasn't something she ever thought she'd be good at. But Asher made it so easy. He was relaxed and confident. He made jokes, and constantly encouraged her, even when she got frustrated. And he seemed to know exactly how to tap into a competitive side that Adina didn't even know she had. She still wouldn't say she was any good at fighting, but the small amount of training they'd done made her confidence swell.

Adina grimaced at the sudden pain in her bruised shoulder as she pulled the blanket up, then fell back asleep, a smile stuck to her sleepy face. Part of her soreness had nothing to do with training. Their sex was as physical as their training. They were fucking at least twice a day, napping, and just lying together for long hours in between. And as they lay sweating together or tucked up against each other under the blanket against the night's chill, he'd told her more about Cosanti and other city states. Images of Cosanti played through Adina's mind like the movies she'd heard about as she drifted back to sleep. Asher's descriptions of the vibrant city crept in often when she wasn't thinking of something else. The lush gardens that topped the faded and sunburned yellow stone of the outer walls, the expanses of green that spread out for miles in every direction were sensuous fantasies of abundance. He said hundreds of thousands of people lived in and around Cosanti. Adina saw them walking down the lanes and streets he described. There were so many different colors and styles of clothing, newly manufactured, of hemp, bamboo, wool and even silk. And there were market stalls and cafes. Adina's mouth watered at his description of the foods and exotic spices. She could almost feel the cool breezes that sighed through the streets, moved by the giant windmills and turbines that dotted the rooftops and walls. Some of the turbines even hung mid-air, held aloft by huge balloons he'd described as *sky fish*, their long, brightly colored trailing tails and fins helping to keep them aligned to the wind.

Adina knew about honey. When she was young there had been a town where they would stop every year on their meandering annual route. They had raised bees. It was gone now, destroyed by raiders years ago, but she remembered the honey, even though she could barely remember the taste.

When Asher produced a straw of the amber liquid, Adina thought it was a trick. Until he'd cut the end off and put a dot on her tongue. They'd spent the rest of that evening reveling in the honey's sticky sweetness, enjoying it one drop at a time. He'd put a drop on her nipples, licking and sucking them until they weren't sticky anymore. He'd kissed down her belly and followed suit, putting a drop on her clitoris. She'd cum once as he licked and sucked her to clean it off, then again, her legs trembling, her hips bucking as his tongue played inside her, following where the honey might have gone.

The scene was replaying happily in her mind when she felt him press against her, pulling her body against him through the blanket.

"Come on sleepy." Adina leaned into the contact as he kissed her ear. "Time to get up, we've got work to do." He gave her a peck on the cheek then pushed up giving her a light swat on the backside as he stood up. "We're running today."

Adina grinned, her cheeks pulling hard as she rolled and stretched.

Their makeshift bed was still in the shade, but the sun was already cresting over the ruined buildings that towered above the bleached red stone walls of the rift. She got up and grabbed her clothes then went around the corner to where their latrine was. When she came back, Asher was sitting in the bearcat's open side hatch with a plate of food. There was another full plate sitting next to him.

He'd surprised her when he showed her the small crate of honey he had hidden in the bearcat. There were more than two hundred straws of it.

"I like honey," he'd told her. "And it's got a lot of uses." He held up the small box filled with straws. "For trade if nothing else." He nodded to her. "Your reaction is pretty typical."

"You're not testing it out on all the other the girls the way you did with me, are you?" She asked, watching him with narrowed eyes and a grin.

He cocked his head. "Do you think I go through all of this…" He gestured to the canyon, bearcat and their camp. "With every girl I run into in the wastes?"

"I don't know. Maybe you're just, *industrious.*" She leaned in and gave him a long kiss, their lips and tongues playing lightly.

"Too much of a pain in the neck." He eyed her. "Like you."

She feigned offense. "My delicate sensibilities!"

He sat back and closed the box. "If you had delicate sensibilities, I'd have left you behind."

Adina picked up the bowl he'd made up for her, a corner of her mouth up, stuck in a half smile at the memory of their honey play. She sat against the other side of the hatch, putting one of her booted feet on top of his.

"Running? Isn't that a bad idea?" She took a bite. It was the same thing they ate every morning. It wasn't very interesting, but she wasn't complaining. They ate three times a day, every day. And none of it had the skunky, spoiled flavor of things she'd eaten so often in the past.

"What do you mean?"

"Running is bad for you. You burn energy you don't have to, you breath harder, take in more toxins, and if it's cold, you can get pneumonia because of it."

Asher stopped eating, just watching her. His eyebrows came together, and Adina got the impression he was trying to figure out if she was joking. "Are you serious? People say that?"

His look of unvarnished shock and disbelief drove into Adina like a boot heel. For the first time since she'd met Asher, she felt *stupid;* like a little girl making pronouncements in front of a room of adults who all clearly knew she was wrong.

"Yes. Well, it's…" she stammered. "It makes sense, right?"

He opened his mouth to answer, stopped, and just watched her. He closed his mouth again.

Now everything inside Adina was whirling. She could feel her cheeks redden as her embarrassment grew. And with it came anger. "What were you going to say?"

"I'm just surprised is all." He picked up his plate and took a bite without looking at her.

"What were you going to say?" Adina's emotions were rising to a storm inside her.

He lowered his plate, looking uncomfortable. "What I was going to say would have hurt your feelings even if I wasn't talking about you, but whoever told you that."

"What were you going to say!" Angry tears now welled in Adina's eyes.

"I was going to say, 'That's the stupidest thing I've ever heard!'" He spat the words out. "But I wasn't thinking about you, Adina. That's why I didn't say it. I didn't want you to think I was talking about you. The people who say things like that are just so…"

Adina knew his expression wasn't aimed at her, but it felt like he'd kicked her in the guts just the same.

Adina fiercely wiped the tears that were now rolling down her cheeks. "So what?!"

He sighed. "Ignorant. Uneducated." He set his plate aside, then looked at her, his eyes on hers. They followed the tears on her cheeks. "I don't think you're stupid, Adina. You know that right?"

Adina set her food aside. She suddenly wasn't hungry. Where anger had been a moment ago, now she just felt… *small.* And when she answered, "Yes," it felt like that smallness was speaking. Even as she fought them, more tears flowed.

She saw Asher's jaw clench. "People in the wastes just don't know some things. It's not their fault. They don't have access… They're not taught things."

"We know plenty of things!" Adina snapped, trying to recapture her anger so she didn't just sit there and bawl like a pathetic child.

Asher held up his hands. "I know that. I'm not saying anyone is stupid." He reached out and took her hands. "Especially not you." He lifted her chin, locking her eyes with his. "I do not think you are stupid, Adina." He enunciated every word clearly, squeezing her hands. "Alright? You believe me?"

"Yes. It's just…" Her words petered out.

Adina couldn't say anything. It took everything she had to try and control the storm inside her.

Asher just watched her, waiting for her to continue.

He finally gave her hands a reassuring squeeze. "Tell me."

She lifted her eyes, then glanced at the interior of the bearcat, the camp, his equipment.

"You're just so…" Adina shrugged, the smallness battering against the emotions she was fighting to control. "You have all *this*. You know things… Cosanti, everything you talk about, what you show me. I just feel so… *stupid.*" She looked at him, words and emotions suddenly tumbling out. "I feel like I'm playing a game and I don't know the rules… and as soon as I…" Tears were rolling again. "…as soon as you see how stupid I am…" Her voice caught on her tears, shearing up and she started to cry. "…you're going to leave me behind." All the fear she'd been holding at bay suddenly roared up, flooding out in an avalanche of tears and body-shaking sobs.

He slid across the open door and pulled her into his arms. "Shhh…"

Adina clung to him pressing her face against his scarred neck, shaking and sobbing.

For one of the few times in her life, she felt *safe.*

Really safe. And with the realization, the terror she lived with every day roared up inside her.

"I'm so scared!" she wailed. The terrified little girl who'd hidden under the floorboards of her house had found her voice and Adina couldn't silence her. Adina couldn't remember when, or if, she'd ever acknowledged her all-encompassing terror.

Asher just held her close and rocked her.

It took a long time before Adina's sobs began to slow.

"Shhh… It's alright," he said through her dark, tear-wet hair.

When the worst had passed, he kissed her hair and pushed it out of her face, then lifted her chin. She could see the concern in his lapis blue eyes as they watched hers. "I want to show you something."

Adina followed his hands as he pulled an amulet from around his neck. It was so nondescript that she'd never given it any thought, barely realizing he was wearing it until he took it off. Hanging from the steel chain was a thick gray metal disk with a domed garnet-red stone set into a recess at the center of it. He put it into her hand. "If anything ever happens to me and you need help, press the stone." He indicated it with a calloused finger. "You'll have to press it hard, but you'll feel it click. Or just smash it with something, a rock, whatever, either way, it will activate it." He held it up for her to look at, watching her eyes. "They may not come quickly, but they will come."

Adina took it, running the back of her hand over her nose and looking at the nondescript piece of jewelry. She wiped her cheeks. "Who… who will come?"

He pushed strands of hair out of her face. "Other Longhunters. A rescue team." He put the chain around her neck and settled the amulet against her chest. She ran the smooth, manufactured metal and polished stone between her fingers. He took her face in his hands, watching her eyes. "I will *not* leave you behind, Adina."

His words penetrated like the warmth of the sun, easing the fearful ache inside. Adina threw her arms around his neck, hugging him fiercely, wishing she could press herself through his skin and into his body. Tears came again, but they weren't from fear now. She whispered, "Thank you."

His burly arms pulled her tight. It felt like he might squeeze the air right out of her lungs. Then he released her and leaned back, his strangely blue eyes on hers again. He gave her a confident, reassuring smile. "Feel better?"

Adina leaned against him, nodded and sniffled.

"Yes."

He gave her a gentle kiss on the head and they just sat, his safe arms around her before he gave her another squeeze and leaned away. He grabbed his plate and pointed at hers. "Finish your breakfast. Then we're going for a run." When she looked up, he was giving her a dazzling, playful smile. "You'll probably think it's going to kill you, or maybe wish you'd died. But I promise you, it won't."

"That sounds like what you said about the medicine."

He grinned. "It won't be that bad, I promise."

__

Adina collapsed to the broken ground unsure if she was going to throw up, pass out or if her body was going to literally fall apart. In her mind's eye, her arms and legs just kind of dropped off, hitting the baked beige earth and lying there, useless as she tried to pull in air. Asher jogged to a stop a few yards away and looked back. He was stripped to the waist, the sun beating on the tan skin of his muscular, scarred, tattooed torso. Sweat was rolling from his gray-white hair, down the nearly shaved sides of his head and through his short-cropped beard.

Adina's diaphragm seemed to have completely forgotten its duty to the rest of her body. She was sweat-soaked through and through wearing just the light t-shirt and knee length trousers that left her calves bare above her dusty boots. She collapsed completely onto the ground, not caring about the rough stones that poked her as she rolled onto her back, staring at the burning blue sky, trying to breathe.

Part of Adina hated Asher at that moment as he stood there, only huffing lightly, breathing far too easily compared to her.

Adina's guts cramped and her stomach felt like it pushed up. She pitched over onto her front. "I'm gonna be sick!"

"Don't!" Asher took the few steps to her. "Take deep breaths. You need to learn to control it. You lose moisture and calories by throwing up. Deep breaths, Adina. You can do it."

No, she couldn't. Adina threw up long and hard, everything they'd eaten an hour ago splashing the beige rocks around her.

She felt his hand on her back. "It's alright, you're…"

Adina threw his hand off, angry and frustrated with herself. "Don't! Do that!"

He backed off and she moved away from the puddle of bile and fell back against a rock, then pointed at him. "You said it wouldn't be…" she had to take another breath. "… be as bad."

He smiled at her and squatted down, his trousers pulling tight across his burly thighs and backside, his sculpted belly moving in and out as he breathed. "You'll be alright in a few minutes."

Adina narrowed her eyes hatefully at him. "Provided I don't die first!" She spat sour tasting bile onto the ground.

He handed her his canteen. She nodded to thank him but couldn't talk. She rinsed her mouth and drank.

"Not too much. We might have run too soon after you ate."

Adina shook her head. "I don't think it has anything to do with…" She heaved her chest up to get a breath before she could continue. "… when I ate."

He smiled again. "You're probably right."

She closed the canteen and threw it at his head, then let hers fall back onto the rock. She was already feeling better, the nausea fading.

Bastard.

Half an hour later they'd nearly run up and out of the rift. They were among the concrete foundations of some of the buildings that topped the walls. Adina's legs felt shaky, but strangely stronger than she expected. She was in some pain, heaving to breathe, but felt... good.

As they rested, Asher studied her eyes intently, a smile growing, pulling his cheeks up.

"What?"

He grinned playfully. "Nothing. Come on."

"We just sat down!"

He pulled her to her feet and then walked to a wall, double his height. He smiled at her again and set his feet facing the wall a few meters away. Then he sprinted at it. With a leap and some quick clambering, he was suddenly on top. Adina's mouth hung open. He'd all but run up the vertical face, then sat on top straddling it. "Alright, your turn."

Adina looked at the wall, then back to him. "I can't climb that! I'm not half cat or whatever under earth and sky you are!"

He grinned, brushed his hands off and then leaned down. "Just grab my hand."

Adina glared at him and his hand, nine feet off the ground. "I can't reach that!"

He opened his hand emphatically. "Just try." He nodded behind her. "Get a good run and focus on my hand. Like there's nothing else in the world. Just look at my hand. Let your body do the rest."

Adina put her hands on her hips and paced back and forth, still glaring. He didn't move. She shook her head. "This is stupid." She walked back a few paces.

"Adina, only my hand." He sounded like he was trying to hypnotize her. "Take a deep breath, close your eyes and when you open them, just focus on my hand." Adina shook her head, then closed her eyes.

"Only my hand. Deep breaths. Focus," he repeated.

Adina took a deep, slow breath, the way he'd been teaching her. She pulled the breath in, feeling her ribs push out, filling into her back, down into her belly. She felt her heart slow.

He was still talking, his voice calming her. And as she listened and took a second breath, it was like diving underwater. Everything suddenly felt a little… *fuzzy*.

When she opened her eyes, everything was slightly out of focus. Everything except his hand. It was crystal clear, like it was the only thing that existed in the world.

Adina dug the ball of her back foot into the gravel, her heart suddenly the only thing in her ears. Her whole body had felt like a shaking, shuddering mess a moment ago. Now it felt taught, like a twisted rope, desperate to spin loose and release its energy. Adina pushed off, running as hard as she could, her eyes locked on his hand. She leapt up, her body acting on its own as her foot hit the concrete wall and she pushed off.

There was a loud *Slap!*

Adina's hand was clasped around Asher's wrist and his around hers. His vise-like grip was certain, unwavering. The rest of the world came back into focus. It didn't snap back, but neither did it fade back in. It eased into focus, like a muscle relaxing. She looked down. She hung from Asher's grip, the soles of her boots several feet off the ground.

Adina's heart raced with accomplishment as what had happened sank in. "How…?"

She climbed as he heaved her up, smiling.

"You remember me telling you there are tiny robots inside you, making things better?"

Adina threw her leg over the wall, the new thrill crashing through her as she looked down at the vertical distance she'd cleared. "Yes."

"You're getting stronger. And you'll continue to get stronger. Faster too." He pulled a shiny metal box out of one of his pockets and held it up for her. "See for yourself."

Adina raised an eyebrow and looked at herself in the reflective surface. She didn't see anything. "What?"

"Look closer. At your eyes." He grinned; his eyes focused on hers.

When Adina looked closer, she could see flecks of deepest lapis blue, tinged with green in her hazel eyes. Similar to the color of Asher's eyes. She just stared from one eye to the other. "But… What does it mean?" Adina finally tore her eyes from her reflection.

He was smiling. "It means you're becoming like me." Adina looked back at her eyes, marveling at the alien blue green. "Why didn't you tell me?"

"It doesn't happen to everyone. Like I said, the inoculant works differently for each person. But you're… *special.*"

The look in his eyes was hard to describe. It was joyous, but also proud, open, and fiercely excited. It was the most living, passionate, all-encompassing expression she'd ever seen. "What does it mean?"

"It depends on the person. But you're never going to be the same." His expression softened. "I hope that's alright."

Adina scooted across the top of the wall and pulled him into a hard kiss, pressing herself against him as they balanced on the rough twelve-inch shelf. She kissed him and kissed him, her tongue playing in his mouth and his in hers. Adina finally pulled back, staring into his lapis blue eyes. "I want that more than anything." She kissed him hard again.

He smiled broadly, brushing his beard against her cheek. "I think we should get down off this wall, don't you?"

Adina nodded, grinning.

He dropped off the opposite side and she levered over the edge, sliding down until she was within the safe cordon of his arms.

"Exciting?"

Adina kissed him, her hands running over his sweaty skin as he let her down. She smiled, her lips at his. "Hot as hell." She pushed him against the concrete wall kissing down his chest and grabbed his belt, pulling him down to the ground. "You stay right there and don't move." Adina unfastened his belt and pulled his pants down, leaving his hard eight-inch cock standing out at her. She laid down between his legs propped up on her elbows. "I just want to watch you." She kissed his cock, watching his expression, running her lips and tongue up and down the shaft, feeling it getting harder. He tasted like salty sweat. She held it in both hands running them up and down as he sighed. She kissed the tip again and pushed her mouth down onto it. Adina had given head plenty of times, but she'd never been as aroused by it as she was now. It was like everything else with Asher, she couldn't get enough.

She pushed him deep into her mouth, lifting her head and pushing down again, then she pushed down farther. He was so much bigger than anyone she'd ever been with.

She coughed as his cock hit the back of her throat. She could tell how much it turned him on when she gagged and backed away, catching her breath. Her juices were flowing freely between her legs.

Earth and Sky!

Adina squeezed her legs together. She felt like she might cum, just playing with his penis. She pushed her mouth down onto it again, gulping the head in further, deeper than she ever had. She felt his hips pump at her strangled gulp but put her hands on his muscular thighs and pushed down even further. Her eyes watered as she felt wetness flowing between her legs. Adina pulled back and caught her breath again, looking up at him as she stroked and sucked him. His hips thrust as she used her mouth all over it, cupping his balls and pulling lightly.

Asher's head fell back, and he moaned with excitement, his hips pushing up into her face. And she pushed her mouth down to meet them. Gulping and feeling her throat stretch, she pushed all of him into her, until her lips were at the base of his penis. Adina held herself down as long as she could before pulling back again. She panted, stroking and kissing his cock. Asher's entire body was trembling. "Yes, Asher, I want it. I want it so bad!"

She worked her fingers up along the shaft, stroking, her thumbs playing with the sensitive tip as she sucked his balls into her mouth, rolling them with her tongue. His whole body bucked.

"Yesss… Yess… don't stop…" he gasped, and she pushed her mouth down onto his cock again, pumping up and down, holding it with her hand. She was moaning too, her belly tensing, squeezing her thighs together and squirming, her hot fluids flowing over her mound. She felt him tense as she ran her mouth up and down the whole length again, faster and faster. His hips pushed up and she concentrated on the sensitive head. She tasted the salty precursor, leaking into her mouth.

He groaned, his whole body shaking. Then he exploded in her mouth. Her eyes went wide as she drank his hot sperm. There was so much of it! And the salty, nutty taste was so arousing that Adina's belly cramped with a sudden, squirming orgasm. Trying to keep her mouth on his penis as her hips spasmed was an ecstatic, confusing, almost debilitating sensation. She moaned around his penis continuing to gulp until the flood stopped. Asher's hips relaxed to the rough ground. Her belly contracted and released, her legs shaking in the aftermath of her own ecstatic release. He finally eased and she licked his shaft, sucking the last of his sticky semen clean.

Adina finally laid her head on his naked groin, panting, his penis near her lips as she stroked it gently, every touch making him twitch. "Earth and sky…" She had to catch her breath before she could go on. "I've never felt anything like that before."

She closed her eyes as his fingers lightly caressed her temple, pushing her dark hair away from her face. He was panting too.

"Neither have I…" His belly contracted with a laugh. "That was amazing, Adina."

She kissed his penis and balls, then his belly. "I'm so glad." She reached down to feel how sticky she was, her clit was so sensitive it felt like it was on fire when she touched it. "I've never cum giving someone head before."

His head came up. "You came?"

She grinned up at him. "Hard too." She blew out a breath.

He smiled at her and let his head fall back. "I guess I was a little preoccupied to notice."

Adina kissed his belly again. "I hope so." She laid her head on his pelvis and let her eyes close, a smile pulling her cheeks until they ached.

Wow!

_

Two more days of hard training passed. While Adina's muscles still complained, she felt stronger and more confident each day. But Asher was *relentless* today, pushing her from one grueling task to the next. They'd run the canyon right after breakfast, then spent hours climbing through the ruins, practicing falls and quick climbs. She'd fallen hard three times, but he didn't let up. He kept pushing her, giving her no space to quit. She'd barely been able to eat at lunch. She fell asleep as soon as she stopped moving. It was only Asher nudging her that kept her eating. After lunch it was hand to hand training. In their first pass, he'd bloodied her nose; a warning of what was to come. He landed controlled punches and threw her again and again, never really doing more that hurting her pride, but forcing her to use everything she'd learned to keep from getting hurt. By mid-afternoon she felt like a boneless, wobbling doll. Then when she was barely able to drink from a canteen because her hands were shaking so badly, it was time for pistol training.

Adina's ears were ringing from the echoing gunfire in the canyon as she ran to her left, her eyes fixed on the piece of debris standing up on the broken dirt mound. She threw her wrist the way Asher had shown her, pitching the empty magazine out of the pistol and trying to get a new one in.

"Watch your footing!"

But his warning was too late. The toe of Adina's left boot hooked on a piece of concrete. Adina twisted her hips and shoulders to break her fall while keeping the pistol and magazine up away from the ground. The uncoordinated result was that she barely got her left elbow down before landing on her face. But neither the pistol nor magazine touched the ground. She blinked and spat dirt, getting the magazine in while Asher's constant admonition rang in her mind.

"Focus!"

Adina braced her shoulder against the hard ground, aimed and pulled the trigger -- and missed completely. She breathed out, ignoring the taste of dirt and blood and concentrated on *squeezing* the trigger this time. She hit the target, fired twice more, hitting each time.

"Up! Kneel and finish the magazine!" Asher instructed.

Adina rolled up onto a knee, the pistol still locked onto the target and emptied the magazine in a series of systematic squeezes. She only missed once. Adina pulled the empty magazine and checked the pistol for dirt, holding pistol and magazine up in her hands as she pushed to her feet and turned to him.

Asher was smiling as he walked to her. "Excellent!" He narrowed an eye looking at her lip, then reached out and wiped gently. There was blood on his fingers when he pulled them back and showed them to her. "Now *that's* focus."

Adina let her hands drop, smiling at his compliment.

Her lip suddenly hurt, and her shoulder, and her hands from

repeatedly pulling the pistol's slide back against the heavy spring.

He stepped close and rolled her lip out gently with a finger to see inside. "It looks like you bit your lip." He was still smiling widely -- *beaming,* she thought. He looked so proud of her. "It's nothing serious." He gave her a light kiss and brushed dirt from the side of her face, his eyes on hers. She put her arms around him and pressed against him, pistol and magazine still in her hands, their sweaty bodies pressing against each other through their shirts. "Can we be done now?" She looked up; the sun was starting to disappear behind the buildings at the top of the canyon.

He smiled at her. "Do you think we've done enough for today?"

Adina narrowed her eyes at him. "If we do anymore, I think I'll fall apart."

He kissed her lightly again, cautious of her lip. "Alright." He nodded to the magazine on the ground. "Get that, clean the pistol and magazines, and I'll get some food started, what do you think?"

She kissed him again. Her lip hurt, but not enough to deter her from satisfying herself with kisses before she let him go. "Alright."

Adina had finished cleaning the magazines and had the pistol disassembled, carefully cleaning the components when Asher came back from the fire and set a canteen next to her on the makeshift work bench they'd set up. "Here." He pushed dark hair out of her face, his eyes taking in her slightly swollen nose and lip. "You did *really* well today, Adina." He caressed her cheek. "I'm sorry if I was hard on you."

She smiled at him and wiped her hands on a rag. "I understood what you were doing." She stood and pulled herself against him, watching his eyes. "And thank you." She gave him another careful kiss.

He watched her eyes. "We're leaving tomorrow." He glanced around their idyllic hideaway. "And we probably won't be back here this patrol."

Adina leaned back. "What does that mean?"

"We should enjoy it tonight. There won't be any place like this for a while." He smiled. "Provided you're planning on sticking with me."

Adina gave him a dazzling smile. "There's no place I'd rather be." But she felt a pang of uncertainty. "Where are we going tomorrow?"

"Out into the wastes."

The uncertainty turned to a sharp stab of fear. She did her best to hide it. "And when we finish the patrol?"

He smiled at her. "I'll show you Cosanti."

The fear fell back, and Adina couldn't help the huge smile that pulled her cheeks. Everything inside her felt like it swelled up. The fear was still there, but it was shot through with excitement. She pulled herself tightly against him and stood on her tip toes, so her lips were almost touching his. "I would like that." She gave him another long kiss.

Adina was naked, tucked up against Asher when she woke up. It was still dark. They'd fallen asleep still entwined after their last round of love making. She pulled his arm around her and onto her breast, looking out over the gurgling springs and up to the cutout of stars above. She just drank it all in, her senses filled with Asher's smell and that of the hot springs, the cool of the air on her face, the sound of the moving water.

She couldn't remember when she'd been so happy. She wanted to draw the moment into her, everything about it, right down to the tawny rocks she couldn't see under the tarp that pushed up into her back. She never wanted to forget this place and all that had happened here.

Adina smiled and closed her eyes, taking a deep breath of the cool night air and its scents.

This is where my whole life changed… She looked up at the thick blanket of stars between the shattered buildings. *No. This is where my whole life began.*

CHAPTER SEVEN

Hot afternoon wind swirled loose strands of Adina's hair as she stared out the window of the bearcat. The air had that distinct, hot, dry afternoon odor, not just dust, but the baked smell and taste of merciless sun on Earth. She pulled the errant locks away from her face and shifted the holstered pistol on her belt to try and make it more comfortable. Every time she moved the holster, the handle of the knife on the other side of her belt invariably found a way to jab her in the side. Adina grinned as she wriggled the knife into a position that didn't press against her ribs. Asher had given her the belt with the holstered pistol and knife just before they'd left their secret paradise in the rift.

He'd just said, "Here," and handed over the leather bundle. "It's the best of what the raiders were carrying." His tone was matter of fact, and he seemed to think nothing of it.

But she'd nearly broken down in tears. Like the beautiful pillow the Millers had made for her, it said so much about how he thought of her. He trusted her. He thought she was capable.

Adina smiled, letting her fingers run over the dried-out leather.

I'll fix it when I have materials.

She thought about how she might make something better, but immediately decided against it. At least not immediately. This belt – old, warped, with its cracked leather holster, and decrepit knife sheath, were special. Adina sat back and stared out the window, letting the imperfections in the leather run under her fingertips.

There was a feeling... it was hard to pin down. Maybe satisfaction or happiness. Under it all a sense of confidence she'd never felt before. It seemed to fill her up like she was a cup. Asher's belief in her, and the physicality of carrying the pistol and knife, and knowing how to use them, were like keys that had opened something in her, letting possibilities she'd never considered flow out.

Adina had finally gone through the things Asher had brought from camp that morning. And it had taken half the day afterward to recover from it. Underneath the new feeling of confidence, her heart... her *soul* was bruised.

She'd recognized more things than she didn't. It wasn't like she hadn't seen every article of clothing people in camp had, day in and day out, for years. And of course, the things that Asher grabbed were the things in the best condition. Which meant someone had spent time and effort to keep them that way, like her yellow shirt. So, she recognized them. And each item she touched was like a barb that hooked at her insides as people she'd known appeared in her mind. Her last memories of some were... things she'd been working hard to block out. Adina had been able to keep her emotions in check until she recognized a warm vest the Millers had made. It was too much. She'd broken down, holding the worn garment between her hands as Dem Miller's torn and distorted face forced itself up in her mind again. And with his face came the image of her house, sitting atop the Miller's, burning. She couldn't even see the outline of it. There was just a pillar of fire where she and the Millers had lived. And where most of them had died.

Everything she had -- everything she *was,* was gone.

Asher had given her space. Adina knew he was watching her. He stayed where she could see him, like he was offering support from a distance, but he didn't approach. And that was confusing too. Part of her ached for him to come and comfort her, while another part recognized that by letting her deal with it in her own way, he was showing her that he knew she didn't *need* his help. He was there if she wanted it. All she had to do was call out. He let the choice be hers. She'd sat, staring at the vest for a long time, taking in the stitching. She could see Carina Miller, the mother, making each with the ease of long practice and the care of someone who took pride in what she did.

She would have wanted me to live...

The Millers knew -- everyone in camp knew the harsh realities of living in the wastes. Fury burned in Adina over the base cruelty of it all, the brute necessity of it. But the Millers wouldn't have wanted her to lie down and die because they had. Carina and her son Dem wouldn't have wanted her to just survive -- they would have wanted her to *live.*

Adina had held that thought in her mind as she sorted out what Asher had salvaged for her. She chose what she could use, then she'd burned the rest.

Somehow, sending it all up in smoke and ashes to join the rest of their burnt camp felt like the right thing to do.

Another day passed with nothing but yawning wastes stretching in every direction. Adina had rarely been this alone amidst the desolation of emptiness. The squeak and rumble of other vehicles in the caravan were a constant companion that she'd never noticed until they were gone. Echoes seemed to try and find her in the hot wind. Shouts and calls of other people; singing, the clammer of children. It felt like they were searching for her. Adina eyes wandered instinctively, watching for the little ones who could quickly get into trouble among the big moving vehicles.

Last night was their first in the open desert after the rift and Asher seemed to sense her clinging grief.

"You're a shoemaker, right?" he'd asked after they'd finished eating.

Adina's mind had been elsewhere. Today she couldn't remember where. "I am."

Asher had cocked his head and given her a smile. "Show me how you make shoes."

They'd spent the evening talking about shoes, leather, stitching, and how to make thread. Adina knew he was just trying to take her mind off the friends and family she'd lost. But she appreciated it, nonetheless. He was good at making her feel smart and valuable. He seemed genuinely interested in what she said and took time to let her teach him things. He paid attention, got frustrated trying to twine thread with his thick strong fingers, and laughed at his failings. His laughter and dimples drew her into laughter with him.

"I don't think I'd be much of a shoemaker," he'd told her. It was such a simple thing. Acknowledging that she was better at something than he was. And like everything he'd done, it made her heart ache. He valued what she knew -- he valued her. His willingness to let her lead made other parts of her warm too. Their session ended with them naked again, reveling in each other's bodies.

A bump woke Adina and the dreams faded away. She blinked the sensual images out of her eyes as the whole bearcat swung side to side. They were thumping slowly over uneven terrain. The flat ground had turned rocky, parts of the landscape now littered with giant boulder-like hills divided by small canyons and washes.

"You'd better hold on."

Adina sat up and wiped her mouth in case she'd been drooling. Her eyes were pulled to Asher as he looked out, picking a path for the bearcat. She smiled, the image of him holding her breasts and watching her as she rode him the night before filled her mind. Things lower in Adina's body started to warm all over again. Her skin remembered the cool night air and the way the open wasteland spread out around them as she plunged down on his hard phallus, crying out in ecstasy.

"I love you, you know," Adina told him loudly.

He only glanced at her, then turned his attention to the ground outside. "I know that." He smiled.

Adina waited. And when he didn't go on, she did. "Well, that usually means there's supposed to be an answer." She grabbed the canteen from its safe storage spot and lifted it to her lips. They hit a bump *hard* and she spilled water all over herself. Adina turned and narrowed her eyes at him.

"You did that on purpose."

"Don't look at me, I'm just over here driving." But she could see the barest smirk on his face.

Adina watched the ground ahead and drank carefully, so he couldn't make her spill, then stowed the canteen again. "Well?"

"Well, what?"

She clambered over the console between them and squeezed in between him and the steering wheel.

"Adina! I…" He tried to look around her. "I can't see."

Adina settled down until she was straddling him. "Well, I think I'm a lot more interesting to look at than what's outside. Don't you?"

He stopped the bearcat, then turned his attention to her with a smile as he set the brake. "That's for sure."

"Well?"

He glanced at her chest and grinned. "You're all wet."

Adina sandwiched his white-bearded face between her hands, watching his lapis blue eyes and squeezed his cheeks together, forcing him to make pursed lips face.

"Do-you-love-me?"

He watched her eyes, but his gaze suddenly shifted past her shoulder. The crease between his eyebrows deepened and his eyes narrowed.

"Well?" Adina bent to kiss him, but he stopped her, his eyes focused past her. The stony expression he'd had when they first met was back. Adina turned, following his gaze. "What is…"

In the distance she could see a line of dust rising in the sky. Vehicles, moving fast. Moving in their direction.

"You said there wasn't anyone out here."

"There isn't supposed to be." He lifted her hips. "Move."

Adina slid back across to her seat as he maneuvered the bearcat into the canyons. "Who is it?"

His tone was deadpan cold. "I don't know." He pulled them up behind rocks on a slight rise that hid most of the bearcat's silhouette, then climbed up into the cupola and pushed open the hatch, binoculars in hand.

"What are we doing?"

Asher didn't answer. He stepped up just enough that his head and shoulders were outside.

Adina slid out of her seat. He was very still, watching what she couldn't see from inside.

"It's an attack, but it doesn't concern us," he finally answered. "We'll let them pass and then keep moving."

Adina climbed up the step, squeezing into the cupola with him. "What do you mean it's an attack?" She grabbed the binoculars. Through the red amber lenses, she could see a small group of vehicles in the thick dust clouds racing at what looked like top speed. And three other vehicles were chasing them -- raiders.

"Two scouts and an assault truck." Asher's tone was cold. "It's already over, they just don't know it yet."

Adina's heart felt like a vise suddenly clamped around it. Even at this distance she could almost feel the terror of the people as they pushed their vehicles to the breaking point trying to escape. The awful helpless feeling that had torn through her when the raiders attacked was there again. The terrifying understanding of what was going to happen to her... Adina heard their panicked calls to one another in her mind. One of the fleeing vehicles suddenly careened sideways, flipped and rolled, shedding parts, equipment and to Adina's horror, at least one passenger. Adina grimaced, horror stabbing her in the chest like a dagger. She couldn't take a full breath. "We have to help them."

"This isn't our fight." The finality in Asher's voice was almost more damning than his utterly cold pronouncement of their fate a moment before.

Adina turned and punched him in the chest. "You have to help them! We can't just stand here and watch while the raiders..." Adina's words fell off abruptly. "We have to help them!"

Asher watched her eyes. His expression was hard. The lapis of his eyes had never felt so cold. She could tell her hit had surprised him, but his expression hadn't changed.

"We can't save them, Adina. We have limited resources that are now being shared by two people. Anything we expend now we can't recover. This isn't our mission. Those people aren't our problem."

Adina punched him again -- hard. "*BASTARD!* Do something! Those people are going to die!"

"People die out here, Adina. That's the wasteland."

The horror of what was happening, and her own terror tore through Adina like a fire, destroying everything in its path.

"Is this what the people in the city states do?! Just let people be taken as slaves, raped, and killed?" She punched him again. "What's the matter with you!"

He just watched her eyes. Everything that she loved about him seemed to have vanished, locked away behind the cold curtain in his eyes.

Adina lifted the binoculars and her horror turned to tears as she watched helplessly. She lowered the binoculars and turned to him again.

"We don't have to save everyone," she choked, tears rolling down her cheeks as she grabbed his shirt, sobbing. "Just these people. Asher - *Please*. I... *can't* just watch and do nothing. Not after..." She couldn't finish the sentence. *"Please."*

He watched her eyes for a long moment as she listened to the distant sound of roaring motors and echoed shrieks from the raiders.

Asher suddenly climbed down out of the cupola. Adina followed him, but he didn't move for the driver's seat.

"What are you doing? Aren't you going to help them?!"

He opened a compartment in the ceiling of the bay and withdrew the largest rifle she'd ever seen.

Adina gawked at the huge weapon. "What is that?"

Again, he didn't answer. He pushed past her and climbed back up into the cupola, disappearing onto the top of the bearcat. Adina climbed after him.

He threw a side of his coat out of the way and dropped to his knees on the bearcat's sloping top and popped the bipod out on the front of the big gun, then laid down behind it. He pinched dirt from the top of the bearcat and watched it as he released it into the breeze.

"What are you going to do?"

He adjusted the rifle's scope without answering. "Cover your ear."

"What?"

"Your ear closest to me, cover it."

He was blowing out a long, slow breath. She covered her ear and raised the binoculars. Almost as soon as she'd covered her ear, Adina was hit in the side by a shockwave as the giant weapon discharged. Adina yelped in surprise as a dust cloud was thrown up from the top of the bearcat by the concussion of the shot. Her uncovered ear rang painfully in the aftermath.

She watched the raider vehicles, but nothing happened. She expected to see at least one of the raiders fall.

"You missed."

Then the large assault vehicle careened suddenly, slewing wildly back and forth. The front of the truck dove down as if one of the front tires had disintegrated. The truck was suddenly tumbling violently, hurling raiders and equipment skyward as it came apart.

"You... You shot the *truck?*"

He was breathing out slowly again. Adina took the hint and covered both ears this time.

BOOM! Dust that hadn't fully settled was thrown into the air again. Adina coughed. It wasn't just from the suddenly airborne dust, but the pressure wave hitting her in the chest.

She pulled up the binoculars just in time to see one of the scout vehicles suddenly decelerate, flames erupting from it as it skidded to a stop.

Asher abruptly snapped the covers over the scope, folded the bipod and got up, then marched to the cupola, stepping down through it.

"But there's still another vehicle out there!" He didn't answer.

Adina looked back through the binoculars. The other raider vehicle didn't seem to realize that the others weren't with them. Another of the fleeing survivor vehicles was belching smoke. It rapidly slowed, falling away from the rest.

She climbed down through the hatch after him. "Close the hatch," he instructed, stepping from where he'd stored the big rifle again, digging in a box. He tossed her a mask, goggles and gloves. "Put those on and don't take them off until I tell you to, then strap in."

He slid into the driver's seat and the bearcat roared to life. They were already in motion by the time she got into her seat.

"There's a five-point harness connection on your belt. Put it on." Adina looked over her shoulders, searching for the other belts. Asher seemed almost unaware of her as the bearcat rolled out from the rocky ground. They hit open ground and she was thrown back in her seat as they accelerated powerfully, tearing up the ground between them and the fleeing convoy.

"You do exactly what I say, when I say and don't ask questions until this is done," he hollered over the motor. "And you don't take off the mask, gloves and goggles until I tell you. Do you understand?" His tone was harsh, harsher than it had ever been.

Adina felt tiny against the fierce energy that rolled off him like heat from a fire. "Yes."

They spent minutes with the only sound the bearcat's motor and the crashes and rattles of them barreling over the baked desert. She watched the convoy and the raider get bigger. One of the convoy vehicles suddenly caught fire.

"Fuel bomb," Asher told her.

The burning vehicle skidded, and Adina could see people jumping off it to escape the flames. They tumbled like sacks, raising small dust clouds of their own.

The raider vehicle suddenly turned -- toward them.

Asher pulled a lever on the center console. Loud hydraulic groans and the clunk and rattle of metal suddenly filled the cab. Heavy louvers slid down over the windshield and the side windows. She heard and felt metallic clangs as armor plates dropped over the wheels.

Asher drove straight at the raider. It grew bigger with terrifying speed.

"You're going to ram them!?" she hollered over the noise. The scars on the bearcat's side and nose suddenly filled her mind. He didn't answer.

The bearcat's motor roared with fury as he accelerated again, driving straight at the other vehicle. He pulled a lever over his head and a terrifying, demonic howl split the air. The air siren filled Adina's ears as the bearcat's powerful roar shook her body. The giant machine seemed to have suddenly become alive, charging down on the raider like a relentless predator. The thought of Asher and the bearcat coming off the assembly line next to each other was in her mind again. He and the machine were like one being now.

Adina could see details of the raider vehicle. Skulls and bones decorated the pitted, rusting hulk, splashes of paint adorned its brute armored nose with the raider's arcane looking symbols scrawled across the exterior. The markings were different than any she'd ever seen. Most were usually animalistic totems, something the raiders seemed to try and emulate.

But these were stylized, misshapen, terrifying human faces and skulls with freakishly large white eyes that glared from the front of the vehicle like ghastly specters.

And she could see the raiders, painted red, black, and white with their terrifying masks and headdresses. Their faces and masks were painted with the misshapen, oversized white eyes too. They looked like demons spat out from some holocaust underworld.

"Hold on."

Adina looked from the raider to him and back, gripping the arms of her seat and pushed herself as far back as she could. Asher's face was nothing but a grim mask.

Adina shrieked at the instant she was sure they were going to hit, but the raider turned. But not quickly enough. The bearcat crashed into the rear corner of the vehicle. The bearcat's great weight sent the raider spinning, all but ripping the smaller vehicle in half. Adina was thrown forward against the straps as Asher stomped on the brakes, then left as he spun the wheel, the air siren's pitch dropping as they decelerated. The bearcat skidded over the hard ground with far more grace than she would have believed the brutal machine capable of. The engine shrieked again as Asher stepped on the accelerator, fishtailing the bearcat's back end around. The shattered raider was stopped in a cloud of dust. Adina could see the left rear wheel had been folded completely under the back half of the torn vehicle.

Asher brought the bearcat to a stop and reached into a storage bay behind his left shoulder. He pulled on a hood, tucking it into the collar of his coat.

Adina jumped at the sound of bullets bouncing off the bearcat, but Asher continued calmly, seating a helmet and mask combination over the hood. Like everything else he had, it was well made, but a large gouge had been taken out of one side of the helmet and mask along with several other cuts and dings. It made him look more machine than man. He pulled his saber from its storage place and attached it to his belt, then turned his masked face to her. "You stay in the bearcat no matter what happens. And you don't open the doors for anything unless you hear my voice, or I bang three times. Three times, got it?"

Adina wasn't sure if she should be terrified, grateful or if she was just in shock. He seemed otherworldly in his mask as he watched her, intense, but otherwise, utterly calm.

"Say it," he demanded.

"I'll stay in the truck no matter what happens and won't open the doors unless I hear your voice or three bangs."

Then he turned back forward and drove head-on at the five raiders who had abandoned their wrecked vehicle.

Adina could hear their war shrieks as they leapt out of the way. She was thrown against the straps again as Asher brought them to a skidding halt once more. The vehicle had barely stopped before he was out the door and had slammed it shut behind him.

Adina clambered out of her seat and went to his door, trying to see out through the armored louvers, but there was nothing there. There were gunshots and the feral shrieks from outside, then an agonized screech. She climbed up into the cupola looking through the small ports trying to see what was happening. She caught a glimpse of Asher; he was near the back of the bearcat.

A raider appeared from where he was, crawling and holding his throat, then collapsed. Another ran and Asher stepped into the open. Asher's left arm came up, he aimed for a moment then shot the fleeing raider. He turned and walked to the fallen raider and stood over him for a moment.

Adina suddenly felt sick. *He's making sure he's dead.*

Asher walked to the wrecked vehicle. He looked inside. Adina could hear someone screaming. Asher raised his sword and thrust into the interior. As he walked back to the bearcat, he flicked his saber and Adina saw blood fly from the blade. She was shaking. Fear or adrenaline, she couldn't tell which. Asher walked around the bearcat, as if searching for something.

"No, please! We was…" she heard from outside. Then there was an awful animalistic cry and a terrible whistling, choking gag. Adina covered her ears, but the awful sound seemed to go on and on.

Adina jumped at the three loud bangs from the driver's door. It was pulled open, and Asher climbed in.

He looked for her, craning his neck to follow her legs up into the cupola. His mask looked ghoulish now. Blood carved little snail trails down through the thick dust that covered his mask and helmet. "Get back in your seat. We're not finished."

Adina was shaking so badly as she climbed down that she had to concentrate on each step so she didn't fall down. She'd never *watched* violence like this. In the raider attack, and when she was a little girl, she'd been hiding.

She'd always covered her eyes. She didn't want to see. Adina could barely buckle her belt. The pistol and knife at her waist felt suddenly heavy against her sides, hot with their meaning. Asher spun the bearcat back the way the caravan had come with a powerful roar of the engine.

They drove past the surviving vehicles that had fallen out of the convoy. Adina watched the survivors. Some waved for help, others hid.

"We need to stop and help them."

Asher just kept driving. "We need to finish what we started."

There had been time for the intensity of Adina's emotions to lessen. The awful fear she'd felt for the people in the convoy had fallen away and a cold stone had grown at her center, pressing against her heart, lungs and stomach. There was no passion in what was happening now, no racing to help people who were in danger. Asher drove straight to the second scout vehicle. Three raiders huddled in the shade of the vehicle while two more gestured fiercely at them. He took the binoculars and scanned them. "No guns, three of them are wounded," he catalogued, handing her the binoculars and driving directly to the two who were ready to fight. Adina turned the binoculars to the three in the shade. They were wounded, burned black from the fire Asher's bullet had caused.

Asher brought the bearcat in fast, but in a strange arcing course. It wasn't until he skidded sideways in front of them that she realized he'd maneuvered upwind, his skid creating a dust cloud that blinded the raiders as he once again leapt from his seat.

This time it happened right in front of the windows. By the time the dust cloud thinned enough for Adina to see, one of the raiders was down, kicking and thrashing, his guts spilled red and wet onto the parched ground.

Asher stood waiting, bloody saber in his hand. The second raider seemed uncertain what to do. Asher said something to him, but she couldn't make it out. The raider charged. It happened so quickly that Adina wasn't sure what happened. The raider joined the first, thrashing and kicking, blood spraying from his neck, staining the ground red. Asher walked to the three cowering in the sun. Adina wanted to turn away, to cover her eyes, but she couldn't. He killed each in turn with an efficient thrust of his sword.

The whole world was tunneling as Asher climbed back into the truck again. He turned to her, watching her violent tremors. "You're in shock. You'll be alright."

He turned the bearcat back along the convoy's route again. Adina's belly spasmed tighter and tighter as they approached the black smoke pillar from the crashed assault vehicle. As it grew larger, visions of what was about to happen roared up in Adina's mind.

"I… I'm going to be sick!"

Asher stopped the bearcat and Adina nearly fell from her door in her hurry to get out. She hung onto the side of the giant machine, bent over, her body see-sawing with nausea. Asher stepped around the front of the bearcat, his head moving side to side as he scanned the area around them. "We're not safe here."

All Adina could see was the blood glistening on his gloves and sleeves. She ripped off her mask and threw up. The stench of the burning assault vehicle filled her lungs when she inhaled and she vomited harder at its sickly smell — and it's meaning. The violence of the expulsion brought her to her knees. She retched again and again, her body heaving, soaked in sick sweat.

Adina jumped at a gunshot. When she turned, a raider was collapsing to the ground twenty yards away. She wiped vomit from her chin scrubbed her hand on the gritty earth.

"We need to go." Asher's pistol was still trained on the fallen raider.

Adina turned to him, trying to see the man she loved in the blood splattered killer standing there. The image of him killing the three cowering raiders wouldn't go away. The ruthless sword thrust that killed each played over again and again.

Confusion swept up everything in her like a whirlwind. He stood like a statue, an inhuman presence, his mask giving nothing away. She wiped her mouth. "Don't you feel *anything?*"

"This isn't the time, Adina. It's not safe here. Put your mask back on and get in the cat."

She shakily climbed to her feet and pulled her mask back on, staring at the man he'd just shot.

You begged him to do this.

He offered a hand to help her in, but she pulled away. "Don't touch me."

He slowly lowered his hand and stepped back.

Confusion howled in Adina. She couldn't hear anything but her hammering heart. She was shocked by his ruthlessness, loved him, was afraid of him, and so many other things. All she wanted was space away from him.

And for the first time, Adina felt like a prisoner.

What did you think all that training was for?

The schism between the man she loved and the machine of war that she'd set in motion refused to mesh in her heart and mind. Back in her seat, she caught a glimpse of her eyes in her reflection. She could see the blue green flecks there.

You're becoming like me...

He drove to where the assault truck had crashed, its scattered remains strewn recklessly over a wide area.

The truck itself was engulfed in flames, billowing thick black smoke. Armor, pieces shed from the truck, bodies and parts of bodies lay all around. As they circled the wrecked vehicle, a corpse appeared and disappeared in the flames, melted to the vehicle's structure.

Asher didn't say anything as he drove the perimeter. Half a dozen battered raiders were still standing, ready to fight. He pulled the truck away as bullets pinged off the armor then turned back running straight toward the densest group of them.

"Are you just going to run them down?"

He didn't answer. Again, turning the bearcat at the last moment and sliding sideways, he kicked up a huge cloud of dust and rocks amidst the black smoke. And once again, he was out of the truck the instant it stopped moving.

Adina couldn't see anything. Thick smoke billowed over the bearcat blacking out everything, including the sun.

When the smoke blew away four bodies lay dead or writhed on the ground. Asher was fighting the last two remaining raiders.

Five yards from the bearcat, a burned and bloodied raider was propped up against a chunk of debris. Adina thought he was dead -- until he moved.

He rolled over with a rifle, and carefully took aim at Asher's back.

Adina had snatched her pistol from its holster and pushed open her door before a thought formed. Her boots hit the ground before she realized she'd jumped from the bearcat.

"HEY!" Her pistol was fixed on the raider.

He turned and Adina saw his eyes. Even through the filth and blood, she could see he was young. There was fear in his eyes -- and pain. She'd seen that look so many times...

Part of Adina wanted to yell, to beg him not to move. But he brought the rifle around. Adina squeezed the trigger. There was no thought -- just three loud pops. They sounded so different in the open air than they had in the rift. *Pop! Pop! Pop!* Like something being dropped onto a metal plate.

The raider slumped against the debris, the rifle falling.

Everything suddenly turned crystal clear with the strange out of body feeling she'd had in the rift when she'd climbed the seemingly impossible wall. Adina pivoted to where Asher and the two raiders were fighting. The lost, confused feeling that she'd had since she'd set the terrible sequence of events in motion was gone.

Asher turned at the sound of her pistol shots. And before Adina could do anything, one of the raiders brought a heavy bladed club down across his back. The blow nearly knocked Asher off his feet. He staggered forward but didn't fall. Adina raised the pistol, but Asher was in the way. The other raider shrieked victoriously and charged at him.

Like when she'd climbed the wall, things suddenly went fuzzy. Things had gone slightly out of focus, but she was completely aware of it all this time. The charging raider was clear; a cut-out standing against a faded background, the only thing that existed in the world.

Even as she aimed her pistol, Asher turned back to the man who'd hit him, and relief washed over Adina. The pistol went off in her hand.

Pop! It was like watching something happen in slow motion. She saw the bullet hit the raider in the left shoulder. Pop! A bullet struck him in the belly. *Pop!* His head jerked oddly as the bullet tore through his neck. Then he fell like a marionette that had its strings cut, his arms and legs flailing as he crashed to the ground.

Everything snapped back into focus. It didn't ease back in the way it had at the wall. It was like a switch inside her had flipped, and the world was in real-time again.

Asher smashed his helmet into the raider's face.

The raider staggered back and before he could recover, Asher's saber slash all but cut his head from his body. The raider's head tipped strangely onto his left shoulder at a sickening angle as blood sprayed from his opened arteries. Then the raider dropped, making a small cloud of dust when it hit the scorched earth.

Adina was still staring at him when she felt Asher's solid grip on her arm. It pulled her attention away from the dead man.

"Adina! Are you alright?" The unforgiving mask covering Asher's face couldn't hide the concern in his voice. "I told you to stay in the cat!"

"He…" Adina had to swallow before she could talk.

"What!?"

"He was going to shoot you!" she said more loudly to be heard through her mask. She nodded to the dead raider with the rifle. She was gripping his bloody sleeve hard, but she wasn't shaking the way she had been. "He was going to kill you."

Asher's masked and helmeted head turned to the dead man, but only for a moment. Then he pulled her tight against him. His armored coat was hot from the sun, and she felt the blood on it, but she didn't care. He crushed her against him. "I told you to stay in the damn cat! No matter what!"

Adina felt out of body, encircled in his violent, bloody embrace, her arms wrapped around him, the pistol in her hand. She closed her eyes and took deep breaths, confused by the reassurance she felt in his arms. "I'm alright," she said into his armored shoulder.

Asher pulled back, holding her at arm's length, she could see his eyes searching hers through his mask. "Are you sure?" He ran a bloody glove over her masked cheek.

There was blood on her hands when she drew them back -- Asher's blood. The raider hitting Asher in the back with the bladed club suddenly rushed up in Adina's mind. "Earth and Sky, you're hurt!"

As she tried to see his back, he held her arms. "You can look at it when we're finished here."

Adina watched his eyes, the lapis of his irises seemed a deeper, more penetrating blue than before. She took a deep, shuddering breath. "We need to finish what we started." The words seemed to fall out as if she hadn't said them at all.

What we started…

He nodded, holding her arms. "That's right." He nodded to the wreckage around them. "We don't leave the wounded to suffer and die out here."

His words hit Adina like a kick in the guts. Her assumption of cruelty and brute necessity slammed into her like the bearcat nearly tearing the raider vehicle in half. "*That's* why you killed the wounded?"

She could see the understanding in his eyes. "Giving them a quick death is the only mercy we can offer. We don't leave the wounded for rats or whatever else might find them out here. It will only take a few minutes."

He let go of her arms and turned to walk away. She grabbed his coat. "I…" She hesitated, watching him, her eyes drawn to the scattered debris and bodies around them. "I want to help."

He stuck his sword point-down into the hard-baked ground and held her masked face between his gloved hands. "Not this time, Adina." He ran gloved fingers over her masked cheeks and nodded to the man she'd shot. "You can help by gathering weapons and ammunition from them." He nodded to the six fighters they'd killed. "The survivors will need anything we can find for them. And there may be things we can use."

Adina held onto his armored shoulders, not wanting to let go of him, then forced her hands to open and nodded.

Asher pulled his sword from the ground and walked away, his heavy coat swaying as he went, a line of blood running down the back from the rent left by the raider's weapon.

We don't leave the wounded to die out here.

Adina knelt and took the rifle from the dead man's clutching hands, looking at his burned, warpainted face.

More kindness than you would have shown anyone.

She searched his bloody and scorched clothes. There was a strangled cry from the smoke. The ache in her chest for Asher was sharp, like her heart wanted to tear itself in half as what he'd said, and more importantly -- what he hadn't, took root. Asher wasn't hard because he was cruel. He was hard because he *cared*. She could see it clearly now in his seeming indifference when they'd come upon the fleeing caravan. The cold, harsh way he'd talked wasn't *without* emotion. He was *controlling* his emotions.

Adina couldn't wipe the tears that ran inside her goggles as her hot, angry, confused words echoed. *Don't you feel anything?!*

When he got back to the bearcat Adina didn't know what to say, or how to even begin. He just went to work, salvaging anything they or the survivors might be able to use. And every time he bent; he groaned in pain.

--

Asher finally spoke as they rolled up to where the survivors had gathered. "Do you still want to help them?" he asked through his mask.

Most of the survivors hid as Asher pulled the bearcat up thirty or so yards from them.

As Adina stared at the battered survivors, the minutes that had transpired since she'd begged Asher to act flew through her mind. They had been some of the most awful of her life. And the sum of the storm raging inside her stood before her in the form of the filthy, traumatized people. No matter what happened, Adina *knew* she would be safe. And that knowledge twisted in her guts like a knife.

They will probably never have any idea what that feels like.

Adina nodded trying to find words, swallowing hard. "We've come this far."

"Alright. Stay here till I call for you." He opened the door and slid down out of the seat, hitting the ground with a pained grunt.

Adina opened her door and stood in the open door, her pistol in her hand as he walked toward the group. A few who stood in front pointed weapons at him, but most backed away, their hands raised.

The fact that any stood their ground was testament to their bravery -- or their desperation. Adina's first response to seeing the bearcat in the dark had been awe and intimidation. But it hadn't been rigged for battle like it was now. She hadn't seen the awful fury of it, or its occupant. As she stood in the passenger door, she heard the snap of the banner that had been deployed with the louvers and wheel covers. The large blood-red pennant blazed with the crossed rifle, sword and wings of the Longhunters. The same emblem on Asher's shoulders. And after what Asher had done to the raiders, seeing him step out of the bearcat like some force of war personified must have been terrifying.

Asher stopped; his hands raised. "We're not here to hurt you." He announced loudly through his mask. He gestured back to the bearcat. "We've recovered some things from the raiders that might help you."

One of the men in front, who was holding an ancient looking rifle, kept it pointed. "Who are you?" He looked past Asher at her and the bearcat.

"LOOK!" one of the survivors suddenly shouted, pointing.

Adina turned and in the heat haze she could see a narrow line of dust rising. It was a single vehicle, tearing across the baked landscape, closing fast. She grabbed the binoculars from the cab.

"Who is that!" the man with the rifle barked, aiming at Asher.

"Whoever it is, they aren't with us," Asher answered calmly. "What is it?!" he hollered over his shoulder at her.

It was someone on a motorcycle. But from what she could see, the motorcycle was like nothing she'd ever seen before. It was *big*. It slowed, then came to a stop, over a quarter of a mile away.

"It's someone on a motorcycle!"

"It's Haro!" one of the survivors shrieked and there was suddenly fear, near panic among them.

Adina could see the rider, they sat up and there was a flash of reflected light.

"He's just looking!" Adina called again. "He's got binoculars!"

"Calm down!" a woman among the survivors called.

Adina turned to the voice. The woman was *old*, she looked to be in her seventies -- at least. But it was hard to tell in the wastes. The hard life of privation and sun aged everyone prematurely. The woman stood slowly from where she'd been sitting and lifted a gun that seemed to be as old as she was. "If it is Haro, or any of his Ghost Eyes, we will fight!" But there was nothing decrepit in the old woman's powerful voice. It was a voice that was used to being listened to.

Adina watched the man in front of Asher, he cocked his head, listening to her. She was obviously a leader among the survivors if not their headwoman.

Then there was a distant *bang!* and Adina spun. An arcing trail rose from where the rider was. A bright white flare rose in the sky, hot and dazzling even in the searing daylight. Then there was a second bang and a black flare followed it.

Adina turned back to Asher. "They fired a..." He was already marching back to the bearcat. "flare..." His body language was intense and purposeful as he strode past her open door. "What is it?"

He didn't answer, throwing open the side hatch of the Bearcat. He grabbed something from behind her seat and then stepped away from the bearcat. He raised the flare gun and fired. A black flare. Then he loaded a second and fired. A crimson smoke trail rose into the air.

Adina turned back to the rider. As she watched, the rider raised a pennant above the back of the mammoth motorcycle. "What in Earth and Sky…" She climbed down from her door and met Asher as he returned to the truck. He unbuckled his sword and pistol belt and stowed them behind his seat.

Adina watched the intensity of his movement. "What is it? What's going on?"

He reached above the door and opened a panel. "A formal challenge. Whoever that is, is from one of the city states."

"A challenge? For what?"

Like the big rifle that she'd never known was inside the bearcat, Asher withdrew a huge sword from the discrete panel. Adina stared at the giant two-handed weapon as he stepped down again, pulled the scabbard off and set it on the decking. The shining blade alone was four feet long. With the long handle it would have reached his chin if the point were on the ground.

"What… What is that?"

"Be ready to leave if something happens."

"Wait, what?" She grabbed his shoulder and turned his masked face to hers. "Asher, talk to me! I don't understand!"

He rested the blade of the big sword on his shoulder like it was the beam of a building. "The challenge is for possession."

Adina didn't like the sound of that. "Possession? Possession of what?"

Asher nodded to the vehicles around them, then to her and the survivors. "Everything."

All of Adina's feelings of certainty and safety shattered into a million pieces and her emotions see-sawed again. "Do you know them?" Her voice was shaking. "Who are they?"

Asher shook his head, his eyes narrowed in his mask. "I don't know." He nodded to the rider. "But whoever that is, is probably in charge of this group of raiders."

"The Ghost Eyes, the old woman called them."

He nodded affirmatively and then into the bearcat. "Get inside and if anything happens to me, you get away from here."

"I'm not going anywhere."

He snapped, "Just do it!" and Adina recoiled at his uncharacteristic harshness. "Slavery is common in some city states. And that is not a life you want, Adina." He jerked his head toward the rider. "My guess is that they were probably banished. And that is no one you want to meet." He turned and focused on her eyes through his mask. "If anything happens. You get out of here. Promise me."

Everything inside Adina was in disarray. "But you're already hurt."

He gripped her shoulder hard. "Promise me."

Adina nodded, watching his eyes, and holding his hand against her shoulder. "I promise."

He pulled her against him and squeezed her hard. She wrapped her arms around him again, holding him desperately for a moment. Then he turned and walked away from the bearcat into the empty plain.

"I love you!" she called after him. But he didn't seem to hear.

"What's he doing!" one of the survivors called. "He can't fight Haro!"

Adina spun to the voice. The survivors stared as Asher walked purposefully onto open ground. "You saw what he did to the raiders who attacked you!" Adina shouted at them through her mask. "Are you just going to stand there?!" She threw her hand out at the old woman. "She said it. Get ready to fight!"

Adina's heart was in her throat as she checked Asher's pistol and then hers. If anything happened to Asher, she wasn't going to run. There was nowhere to run *to*. Adina took a deep breath, and her hand found the pendant at her throat. Her fingers ran over the polished metal and smooth stone. Then she dropped her hand.

Nothing's going to happen to him…

She watched as he continued to walk. He raised the giant sword, gleaming in the intense sunlight, signaling to the rider. Adina heard the distant roar of the motorcycle's engine, and the rider brought it up onto the back wheel, pulling it in tight circles throwing up dust as if the bike were a rearing horse. Then it streaked across the barren earth, straight at Asher.

Wait! That's not fair!

Asher raised his sword and settled into an easy stance, his right foot back, the blade horizontal across his body at the level of his chin. It flashed and glinted in the bright sunlight as he moved. Adina watched the rider. The glints from Asher's blade weren't random. As the rider barreled down on him, Adina could see Asher adjusting the blade, then as the rider drew near striking distance, his own sword a glinting arc against the dust cloud behind him, a bright bar of reflected sunlight suddenly flashed onto the rider's face. The rider continued to bear down on Asher, but Asher moved. He walked steadily to his left, keeping the flash of sunlight fixed on the rider's face. At the last instant the rider pitched the motorcycle on its side into a skid, putting it between Asher and himself. There was a flash of blades and movement. Then everything was obscured by a thick cloud of dust.

Adina heard the roar of the motorcycle engine again. The bike suddenly appeared from the dust cloud, streaking away. Her heart hammered, looking for Asher in the swirling dust. Agonizing seconds passed before he appeared, the big sword on his shoulder again, but he was limping. The motorcycle stopped again, the rider appearing to assess Asher. Asher walked toward the rider and raised his sword then stopped again. The rider raised his sword and the engine roared, tearing up the ground and raising a huge cloud of dust as he held the bike in place. Then the motorcycle appeared from the dust again, shrieking down onto Asher. This time, Asher didn't move. The glint of the blade was on the rider's body again. Again, Asher blinded the rider and sprinted forward closing the distance with the screaming motorcycle. Asher turned the sword point on like a spear. As the bike passed, he lunged. Adina couldn't tell if Asher hit the bike, the bike hit him, or if his tumble across the ground was intentional. But the motorcycle whipsawed wildly back and forth, then slid to one side, disappearing in a thick cloud of dust again.

Asher pushed up painfully, the sword tip resting on the ground. He was too far away to see clearly, but she could tell he was hurt. He hefted the big sword up onto his shoulder again and waited.

The sound of the motorcycle's engine came from the cloud and the machine suddenly appeared, seeming to leap from the dust, straight at Asher. It happened so fast Adina could hardly keep track of what occurred. Asher rolled out of the way and as he finished his roll, his sword was high above his left shoulder as if he'd completed a rising cut. Adina suddenly remembered the binoculars and grabbed them. She found the rider in all the dust.

He was holding a wound on his left leg. As she watched, he pulled a gun from a holster behind the handlebars.

Oh no you don't!

Adina climbed into the bearcat and pulled the big rifle from its storage bay. She could barely lift the heavy barrel as she half-stepped, and half-fell down from the open side door of the truck. Watching the rider as he swung around out of the corner of her eye, she popped out the bipod, mimicking what Asher had done, finally chambering a round and then laid down behind the big gun. The rider was much closer than the gun's scope was designed for, and Adina had a hard time finding him. Then, there he was. Adina aimed as best she could with the huge, unfamiliar weapon and pulled it tight against her shoulder knowing it was going to kick hard. She breathed out the way Asher had and squeezed the trigger.

Adina thought she'd blacked out.

The pain in her shoulder took her breath away and she realized the reason she couldn't see was because of the huge dust cloud thrown up from the ground when the gun went off. Adina's ears *hurt*. She bit her lip and clumsily cycled the action, her right hand weak and uncoordinated. Then she looked for the rider again. Her whole arm was numb, electric shocks of pain shooting through her fingers.

Where are you…

Adina stopped and closed her eyes, taking a long breath. The world went fuzzy again. She opened her eyes and looked for the rider. He was just appearing from another dust cloud. She'd missed completely. But he'd turned and was racing laterally, trying to see who was shooting.

From some distant place, she could hear Asher yelling. His voice was muddy through the painful post-shot ringing in her ears. Then the rider saw her. As she lined up on him, he all but laid the motorcycle down again and vanished in a billowing cloud of dust. She heard the motorcycle's engine scream. She looked up from the scope and tried to find him. She could just make out the flying banner in the dust as he raced straight away from her, the dust cloud concealing him.

"ADINA!"

Asher was limping toward her. Fiery, shooting pain tore through Adina's shoulder when she put her hands down to get up. Then her right arm failed. She shrieked in pain as she collapsed across the hard stock of the rifle. Adina rolled onto her left side, holding her useless, agonized limb. She heard Asher's boots and the clunk of the big sword hitting the ground next to her. But she couldn't see anything past her tears of pain.

"What did you do!?" She felt his hands on her shoulder. "Hold on. This is going to hurt." He put his knee against her ribs and grabbed her upper arm with one hand and her lower arm with the other.

Adina felt tension. When he pulled and twisted, she screamed. Everything winked out at the excruciating pain. Then there was a loud, popping sort of crunch -- and the pain was suddenly gone. "Don't move."

Adina's shriek of pain died in her throat. She blinked in surprise, suddenly able to breathe again.

"Is that better?"

Adina stared in amazement at him and then her arm. She raised her hand and made a fist. "What...What did you do?"

"You dislocated your damn shoulder!" Asher snapped. "And you violated the laws of challenge! He has every right..."

"He was pulling a gun!" Adina snarled back at him as she levered herself up to sitting. She ripped off her mask and goggles. Part of her instantly regretted it because of the thick dust lingering in the air. "And..." She coughed hard. "What rules! Him on a motorcycle and you on foot! What kind of rules are those!"

Asher pulled off his helmet and mask, his eyes on her. The crease between his brows had deepened to a canyon. Adina couldn't tell if it was anger, pain, consternation, or all of them. After watching her eyes for a moment, he turned over his shoulder, looking where the rider had gone. "We haven't seen the last of him."

"You... You drove him away!" a voice cried. Adina didn't realize the pistol was in her hand, pointing, until Asher put his hand on hers. "Easy." She dropped her hand, the pistol suddenly too heavy for her burning shoulder.

The man raised his hands, the barrel of his rifle up to the sky and

took a step back. But his eyes were wide, looking between them. "You…
you fought Haro and made him run away!" Others were gathering. "Who
are you?"

CHAPTER EIGHT

It had been more than an hour since the fight with the man the survivors called Haro, and Adina could tell Asher was anxious to be on the move again. Although his armored coat had saved him from a much more serious injury, the raider's bladed club had ripped loose a six-inch chunk of skin from Asher's right shoulder blade, right through the heart of one of his tattoos.

He hissed in pain as Adina carefully lifted his shirt off. Everything spun when Adina saw the large, ragged flap of hanging skin. Grimacing and hissing herself, Adina had to put a hand down to steady herself against swaying nausea.

"Oh Asher… He tore a big hunk of skin loose!" She pushed her long dark hair back behind her ears and tied it to keep it out of the way, then leaned unsteadily for the first aid kit and grabbed the big bottle of sterile water. Adina had seen plenty of wounds in her nineteen years, but she wasn't usually the first one to treat serious ones. She wasn't a healer. As part of the training days in the rift, Asher asked her what she knew about treating wounds. Adina knew about using pressure to stop bleeding, how to stitch things and keep them clean, boiling water for sanitizing, the signs of infection and poisoning, even some medicinal plants. But as far as she knew, those were things everyone in large camps and caravans knew. He'd shown her where what he called 'trauma' supplies were and had given her quick lessons in how to use the ones she was unfamiliar with. Adina was grateful for that. But it took everything she had to keep her hands steady while what felt like ants crawled under her skin.

Locked in the bearcat, Adina could hear the activity outside. The chaos was surprisingly organized. There wasn't the panic or debilitating grief and helplessness she'd seen in some groups after they'd taken such losses. The headwoman gave orders, cajoling, and consoling in equal measure.

Adina grabbed the stitching kit looking away from the wound and taking a deep breath to steady her nerves. They'd retreated into the bearcat so she could look at his wound after they'd helped gather the remaining survivors together. Lookouts were posted in case Haro or any of the other Ghost Eyes returned.

Asher turned over his shoulder trying to see. He indicated the first aid kit with his eyes. "There's a mirror in there. Slim left side internal pocket. Let me see."

Adina grabbed the polished metal mirror and spent several distracted seconds just running her fingers over it. She'd never seen a *brand-new* mirror before. Then she handed it shakily to him. He peered at the reflection of the wound. His lapis blue eyes were particularly bright in the angled light inside the bearcat. Adina's eyes were drawn to the way his burly, tattooed forearms cabled and flexed as he handled the fine mirror.

"Yeah, he really did a number on me. One of his eyebrows came up. "I guess I'm lucky I'm with someone who's so good at stitching." He grinned, his cheek dimpling which made him suddenly look younger than his thirty-something years. "Otherwise, my tattoo's going to be a mess."

Adina stared at him dumbfounded for a moment before a barking sort of laugh erupted from her. She just watched his expression, her mouth hanging open. "You're joking? You've got a big chunk of…" she gestured at the flap, then threw her hands in the air, "*skin* hanging off your back like some kind of… I don't know what. And you're joking!?"

Asher smiled at her. "It's not the first time I've been hurt, Adina." He pointed to some of the numerous scars on his bare chest. "And it probably won't be the last." His expression softened. "Thank you for being so concerned."

Adina let the stitching kit fall into her lap with her hands, his easy humor undermining her anxiety. "Well, this is all new to me!" She pointed to the hanging flap, a shudder racing through her. "I'm used to stitching skin -- after -- it's off the animal!"

He laughed, then grimaced. "Okay, that hurts." He leaned toward her. "Come here."

Adina grinned stupidly caught between revulsion at his wound and his sudden charm and gave him a kiss.

"Do you think you can put it back?" He smiled again, looking at the wound in the mirror.

"I think so." She pointed to the bearcat's decking. "Lay down."

He did, grimacing at the strain as he put weight on his arm and the skin stretched. He glanced at her shoulder. "Once you're done, we need to immobilize your shoulder so that things knit back together."

Once he was settled, Adina flushed the wound. He hissed as the bloody water flowed over the raw meat where the skin should be and onto the metal floor. She carefully laid the skin flap back in place. "We're going to be the most attractive couple around," she quipped, able to breathe a little easier. The wound wasn't as frightening with the skin flap back in place. "Me trussed up and you stitched up like a pair of old shoes."

"Who's old?"

Adina grinned again and opened what Asher had called the suture kit. She'd always worked with whatever they had, her sewing needles or things the makers put together. The purpose-made needle was so small and smooth that it seemed to almost glide through the skin when she made the first stitch.

"Use the forceps in the kit," he commented, watching her work in the mirror. "It makes working with such a small needle easier."

"Forceps?"

"The bent jawed things that kind of look like scissors. They help hold the needle."

Adina looked in the kit and pulled out what he described. "These?" They were brightly polished and moved with amazing ease, then locked in place with little teeth between the handles.

He nodded. "Use those to hold the needle. It also helps to keep your hands away from the wound so that it doesn't get contaminated."

She gingerly grabbed the needle with the forceps and ran the next stitch. He was right, it was much easier.

There were local anesthetics in the kit, but he'd told her not to use them unless he told her to. It only took a few minutes to finish the job, carefully lining up the tattoo so that when it healed it the lines would be minimally broken.

"There, have a look." She held the mirror so he could see clearly.

"Looks great." He grinned at her. "Thanks."

Adina flushed it again and dressed the wound. The bright white medical tape was *really* neat. She'd heard of it and had seen some examples. But there were whole rolls of the bright white adhesive-sided cloth in the trauma kits. She could think of a-million-and-one uses for it. Adina kissed his shoulder. "Okay, all done."

He grabbed a fresh shirt from his locker and pulled it on with a grimace, then nodded to his torn one as he hung it up, then his coat. "You'll have to show me how best to fix those." He smiled and sat down cross-legged in front of her. "Okay, your turn." He put her right arm in a sling and tied a long strip of cloth over the sling and under her other arm. "That's to keep you from using it. You should only have to wear it for a day or so. The nanos will take care of the rest."

"Nanos?"

He was closing up the kit. "Sorry, that's what we call the little robots running around inside us. "Nano" just means really tiny." Asher leaned forward and put his forehead against hers. "Hey." He waited for her to look up so he could see her eyes. "Thank you for saving my life today."

Adina just wanted to stay there, lingering in that look forever. Her heart felt like it suddenly ballooned to twice its normal size. She couldn't think of anything to say, so she just pulled him into a kiss, cautious of the dressing on his back and frustrated by her bound right arm. He pulled her against him and when their lips finally parted, he ran a filthy hand over her cheek.

"We need to get going."

--

Adina stood at Asher's shoulder as the headwoman looked them over through narrowed eyes, sitting on a crate in the shade again with the ancient, but well-maintained lever-action rifle across her lap. The old woman's skin was dark, the color of red clay – baked and lined by the harsh sun. Her hair was long and gray, braided into thick ropey dreadlocks. Most of it was hidden by a head wrap that looked like it was made up of brightly colored scraps. She wore a long, light colored, now scorched, sleeveless coat over a homespun shirt that was dyed orangey red. A wide belt with charms and pouches filled the space between her shirt and the dark, narrow-legged trousers that tucked into the top of her moccasin-like boots.

Survivors stood and sat around her. Many were injured, hollow-eyed with loss and grief. Most were blackened by soot, if not from the fires, then from recovering things from burning vehicles. Some stood watch for the Ghost Eyes or Haro. Others who were too badly injured to move or grieved over friends and loved ones were scattered in the shade of the other vehicles.

But the headwoman seemed as hard as the baked ground they stood on. Adina had seen the deep compassion she showed to her grieving tribemates, even as she kept them moving.

"I've seen your kind before," the headwoman said, her eyes on Asher. "Since I was a little girl. Just never so close." She nodded to the bearcat. "Seen your hunchbacked machines in the distance, watching us. Sometimes just driving past." She leaned forward putting her ancient elbows on her knees, the rifle cradled like it was part of her withered frame. "Never seen your kind fight before." She watched him for a long time, then shifted her gaze to her. Adina could feel her assessing her with faded brown eyes. Then the old woman turned her attention back to Asher. "I have a bargain for you."

Asher stood easily; his thumbs hooked in his pistol belt. "We've done what we can for you. We've given you what aid we can."

"You're looking for something." The headwoman interrupted. "All your kind are." She pointed a wizened finger at him. "Seen you from far in the east when I was little, then out here -- again and again." She made a gesture left and right. "Like ants crisscrossing the desert looking for the trail of something sweet. Myrmidons…" She sat back. "That's what I'll call you." She waved her hand dismissively. "You won't tell me the truth of who you are or what you're doing out here. Not like that matters anyhow." She raised a thick white eyebrow at them. "Myrmidon means *ant* in one of the ancient tongues. I always liked that word." She eyed him, her wrinkled features closing up. Adina couldn't tell if it was suspicion or respect. "And there was supposed to be great heroes called Myrmidons in the ancient world."

"We're not here to be anyone's heroes," Asher dismissed. Adina picked up on the shift in his posture, it was slight, almost imperceptible, but it was there. He was uncomfortable.

The old woman cast a glance significantly around her. "I think some folks'd disagree."

Asher cocked his head slightly. "What's your name?"

His tone was pleasant enough, but there was an edge to it that Adina could only think of as grudging respect, like he might have for a potential adversary. Or it might have been curiosity. But he was wary of this woman; Adina could feel the tension coming off him.

Adina looked at the old woman again, trying to understand what it was that he saw, what set off his instincts. There was *something*. It was hard to pin down. It could have simply been that she'd never seen anyone as old as this woman be so powerful, so in control, especially after what had happened to her and her caravan. And there was something *extra*, hiding beyond her ancient, hooded eyelids, behind her eyes. She *knew* something.

"I'm Priav." The old woman twisted her head slightly, watching Asher more with one eye than the other. "Or you can call me old woman or mother. Just don't call me late for supper. It takes me a while to get anywhere anymore." She gestured at them with a pursed lip sort of point of her chin. "And who are you?" She eyed Asher. "Or should I just call you Myrmidon?"

Asher pointed to his chest. "I'm Asher," then to her. "This is Adina."

As the old woman watched them, one thing stood out that made Priav seem so unusual. She was utterly unafraid of Asher. It wasn't a bravado sense of 'you can kill me, but I won't back down.' It was something that emanated from the old woman, a sense of certainty as if she were rooted to the earth beneath her and it to her.

Asher inclined his head to her. "Priav, we have a mission that we must return to. You are correct, we are looking for some…"

"Two days," Priav interrupted again. "It'll take us about two days, no more than four, to get to our camp. You help us get there, and I will tell you about the lights in the sky and the haze city in the west."

What she said didn't mean anything to Adina, but its effect on Asher was clear. He stood stock still for almost a minute, his eyes never leaving the old woman. "You've *seen* the city?" He emphasized the word. His tone wasn't disbelief but seeking clarity.

"Of course not." Priav gestured to their remaining battered vehicles. "We look like we could navigate the sandsea? We look like we been showered with riches?" She leaned forward again. "But I've seen the way to it. Least the beginning of it. Two great pillars, like a gateway, glowering black, shiny things, maybe from the old world…" Priav's tone turned ominous. "But probably not."

Adina cocked her head at a shift in Priav's tone.

"And the lights in the sky to the west…." There was something like wonder in the old woman's pragmatic voice, or maybe awe. "Always to the west."

"When was this?"

Priav sat back. Whatever had overtaken her in the strange moment had vanished. "Years and years ago when I was young. But I know where it is. Can't never forget that. Find that, then somewheres beyond it, the sandsea and your city with its strange lights in the sky."

"Black Pillars?"

Priav scoffed with a sharp "Ha!" then pointed at him. "Two days and I'll give you your answer. 'Sides, once you're at our camp you can trade. We got clean water and maybe things you need." She gestured to the bearcat. "Things to repay what you used helping us."

"We didn't help you for pay," Adina interjected. She was thoroughly confused by the exchange. But Priav seemed to know exactly what to say to get Asher's attention.

Haze city in the west? The sandsea? Lights in the sky?

There were occasional storms of strange lights in the sky. Sometimes they were meteor showers, other times sheets of blue and green light shimmered from horizon to horizon, but they were always short lived, maybe two or three nights.

Priav turned to her, and her eyes narrowed to slits. "You're a fool, or naïve, girl. Nothing comes without payment." She nodded to Asher without looking away from her. "He knows that. There's a cost to everything." She looked her up and down again. "But you should know that. You're not one of them. You're like us -- spent your life scratching dirt to live. How you come to be with him? Captive, slave? I've heard of these, or some like them taking slaves."

Her question struck Adina like a punch and the accusation of her being naïve made heat rise in her face and neck. Confusion kicked up again like the dust cloud from the big rifle.

"I'm not his slave, or his captive," she challenged back, her tone prouder and haughtier than she'd intended.

"Ahhh…" Priav sat back. Adina didn't like what her look said.

"We helped you because it was the right thing to do!" Adina riposted, feeling small and stupid in the old woman's gaze.

"We will be glad to trade," Asher interrupted, breaking the momentum the conversation seemed to be building. His voice was even, but Adina could hear the harsh edge creep into it. "We will help you for your information. But we can't expend more resources to assist you that we can't replace. If we fight again while we are escorting you, we will need to be compensated. What we did here. We did on our own." He nodded to the aftermath of the battle around them, then turned his gaze to Adina, keeping his eyes on her. "Because it was the right thing to do."

Adina's chest tightened at his unequivocal support.

Asher turned his attention back to Priav. "Now you are asking us for a service; one that must be paid for."

Priav's ancient eyes traveled between them. Then she barked, "Done!" without hesitation.

Getting the caravan moving took hours and it was dark before they were finally underway. And they didn't get very far. Priav wanted the caravan away from the battle site.

"Battle sites always attract predators and scavengers, some on four legs, some on two," she'd said.

They'd made camp when the stars were almost halfway through their nightly rotation and the camp fell quiet quickly after people stopped moving. Adina followed Asher when he climbed up onto the top of the bearcat. He helped her up. With her right arm tied against her in a sling, getting off the top of the ladder was challenging. Adina sat next to him as he took a fine-looking instrument from the box he'd brought up and raised it to the stars. "That's a sextant, isn't it?"

He nodded, adjusting the instrument. His look told her he was surprised. "You've seen one before?"

"Not as nice as that one. One of the caravan leaders used to use one. What are you doing with it?"

"The same thing he probably was, trying to figure out where we are." He looked at the side of the sextant and jotted down some numbers. He put the sextant back into its case and then sat cross legged in front of her, making quick calculations. He set the little notebook aside and watched her in the light spilling from the bearcat's open hatch. "You're very pretty, do you know that?" He pushed a strand of hair back behind her ear, his finger caressing her cheek and ear as he did.

The compliment and his touch made Adina grin stupidly again, everything inside her feeling like it had been knocked sideways. "Thank you."

Their lovemaking that night was a gentle, quieter sort of thing. There was very little privacy in camps and Adina was used to everyone knowing each other's business. Groans and ecstatic moans, the slapping sound of bodies against each other were normal. But even inside the bearcat she felt awkward about having the kind of passionate sex they normally did when so many people around them had suffered so much. And there was, of course, the issue of them both being injured. The torn skin on Asher's back was his worst *injury,* but Haro had sideswiped him with his motorcycle during the fight.

There was all-new purple red added to the yellow of the fading black bruise he'd been sporting the first time he took his shirt off. His left elbow and shoulder looked like he'd been dragged across the hard ground. Even with his coat's protection, he had wide, raw abrasions. But both the bruises and abrasions already looked like they'd been healing for days. Rationally, Adina understood what the nanos did from Asher's description. But seeing how quickly he healed was an entirely different matter. It was comforting to know he healed so fast, but she couldn't shake the gnaw inside her at how *unnatural* it was.

Adina's shoulder *ached.* Now that everything had calmed down, the ache she'd barely been aware of seemed to be all she could think of. And as Asher lay on top of her, her hips pitched up to meet his pelvis as they made love, he kept pushing her arm back down.

"Do I have to tie it down?" He grinned at her as their bodies rocked against each other, his cock exploring inside her again.

Adina wanted to grab and hold him, but he kept pushing her injured arm back down when she tried to reach up.

"Are you saying you want to tie me up?" Adina asked playfully, distracting herself from her frustration and ache in her shoulder.

Asher smiled back at her, drawing his cock almost all the way out of her and then driving in, slamming against her, making her take a quick, catching breath. "If you'd like?"

Adina moaned, squeezing her legs around him. "Maybe when we're not both about to fall apart.

The following day passed, largely uneventfully.

They'd had to stop for several hours to work on one of the caravan vehicles which suddenly started belching smoke and steam just before midday. Then they were moving again, heading almost due east based on the track Asher was making on his map.

As they made camp that night, Priav approached them, her ever-present rifle cradled absent-mindedly in the crook of her left arm.

"It was a good day. We didn't bury anyone," she began.

Asher stood up, his coat off, wearing his freshly stitched shirt.

We really need to wash and shave… Adina thought, her mind suddenly back in the rift, images of Asher naked, dripping wet, washing himself filled her mind. Then her helping him, her hands on his stiff cock, stroking it until they were once again fucking hard on the edge of the water.

Priav looked Asher up and down. "I want you to seed some of our girls."

Asher was wiping his hands. The motion slowed and then stopped as he watched the old woman. But his expression gave nothing away.

Priav pointed to a young dark-skinned woman with a short braid of smooth black hair who was helping settle injured survivors under a shade. "Mirin just finished bleeding a few days ago. It should be a good time for her." Priav turned back. "And there are other women in our main camp who would also be good candidates. We are a small community, and we have to be careful about who makes babies with who." The old woman shrugged.

Having conversations like this was common enough in camps, but Priav's... bluntness was unsettling.

Adina stammered out. "We are..."

What are we? Adina suddenly had no idea. It's not like there had been anyone else around, but the whole 'are we going to be having sex with other people?' thing just hadn't really come up.

Adina just stood there and stared at Priav, then turned back to Asher. Words wouldn't come out.

Asher pulled himself up straight. "I understand your need, Priav." He glanced at her and then back to Priav. "I'm afraid I can't help you."

Priav made a dismissive gesture with her free hand. "If you two are together, I understand that, but this isn't about that. This is a transaction. We need you to impregnate as many of our women who are willing as you can." She made a sour face and gestured back toward the battle site. "The other ways our women become pregnant by those outside our camp are... problematic."

Rape... She's talking about women who are raped by raiders.

Adina felt ill.

"Priav, I'm afraid I can't help you. I have radiation injury. I can't father children."

Adina swiveled her head to him. The ease... the practiced way he said it.

He's answered this question before.

"What about you?"

Adina turned to Priav's voice.

Priav held her in a fixed stare. "If he can't." Priav gestured to a strapping man who was manhandling a big piece of equipment from one of trucks. He was burned tan with an unruly shock of red hair sticking out at all angles, some braids with charms hung down the left side of his face. He was taller than Asher, but not anywhere near as broad shouldered. "Aaron can put a baby in you. He's very fertile. He's had seven children, four strong ones who've survived." Priav's eyes returned to her. "Or if he's not to your liking." The old woman was looking her up and down as if she were a livestock animal she was trying to sell. "I'm sure there are many other men at home in the camp that would be happy to impregnate you."

Adina felt faint. Again, it wasn't like these kinds of conversations didn't happen, they just weren't usually so -- direct.

"Don't be shy girl. You are pretty and have good bones for making babies. How many have you had? Not that many by the look of you."

"Adina and I were involved in the same accident," Asher interjected. "She can't get pregnant." He eyed her. "We've tried."

Priav narrowed her eyes at him. "That could just be your seed."

"I uhhh… I don't bleed… anymore." Adina stammered, trying to fend off Priav's all-too-direct intentions.

Priav's expression closed up and she seemed to be deeply in thought. Then she sighed and looked between them. "That's a pity." She walked to Asher and regarded him for a long time. She watched his eyes, seeming to react to their stark lapis color, then gently patted him on the cheek in a grandmotherly gesture and then approached her. Priav's ancient eyes traveled over her face. Priav watched her eyes too. There was a look of deep, remembered happiness in her expression. She gently put bony fingers under Adina's chin and turned her face left and right, then gave her a wizened smile. "Such a shame," Priav said with a wistful sigh as she turned to walk away. "You both would have made such *beautiful* babies."

_-

The following day passed without anything interesting happening. It felt strange to Adina to stay isolated from the rest of the caravan the way they did when they camped. Asher parked them upwind at least thirty yards from the nearest camp.

"We have to keep a buffer between them and us," he'd told her. They'd washed up after they set camp, so they were finally able to get the worst of the filth from the fight off. Adina *loved* the little brush that Asher had for getting the dirt and grit from around her finger and toenails. She scrubbed and scrubbed and scrubbed until her nails and beds were pink and clean. It was such a novel feeling. And she'd taken to stealing the mirror from the first aid kit so she could really see what she looked like. The blue green in her eyes had grown from flecks of lapis to streaks among the rest of the hazel.

About an hour after they'd set camp, Asher made an unusual sound, like he was clearing his throat. After the second time he did it, Adina turned to him. He was smirking and made a subtle gesture with his right hand, pointing to his left as he squatted at the fire. Adina followed where he pointed. A little girl, maybe four or five years old, in grubby clothes was peering out from behind one of the bearcat's tires, her brown eyes like saucers as she looked at the equipment they had laid out. Her skin was on the light side of Priav's red ochre, her features broad with a cutely flattened, wide nose, which made her eyes look even larger in her dark face. She seemed to think they didn't know she was there. She scooted out from the wheel well and peeked into the bearcat's open side hatch, staring in wonder.

Adina's hand came to her mouth to stop from laughing, her cheeks aching with the width of her smile. Asher went about what he was doing, then looked over his shoulder. "If you want to have a look around, you just have to ask."

The little girl started and banged her head hard on the door.

Adina grimaced and sucked in a sympathetic breath, but the little girl just made a pained face, put both hands on her head and ran away.

Asher turned where she'd gone, his face pinched with sympathy as well. "Ouch. That must have hurt. I hope she's alright."

Adina walked to him watching the girl's distinctive hands-on-her-head silhouette disappear. He absent-mindedly made sure her injured arm was held against her body, still watching where the little girl had gone. "Keep an eye out and make sure that everything gets stowed as soon as you're done using it. We don't want anything to walk away."

"They're not thieves," Adina commented, her left arm running up his back, feeling the dressing under his shirt.

He nodded. "Locks exist to keep honest people honest." He looked where the little girl had gone. "The temptation is just too strong, even for adults sometimes." He gave her a quick kiss. "Think what it would have been like for you if you were just a part of this caravan."

Adina leaned into him and nodded against his chest, a pang twisting in her belly. "We have so much they've never seen. So much they probably never will."

Adina leaned into his hand as he ran it down her back. She could hear sympathy in his voice. "Exactly. That doesn't make them thieves, it just makes them human. But we still can't afford to have things walk off." He turned his face to hers again. "How's your shoulder? Still hurts?"

"Aches, but not like it was. When can I be out of shoulder prison?"

"When it stops hurting."

_

As darkness was falling, a small group approached them and stood at a respectful distance. Adina could see the little girl with them.

A woman gestured toward the fire. "Can we… talk to you?"

Asher waved them in. "Of course." He squatted down and looked at the little girl, his white hair and beard shining in the fire light. "How is your head?"

The little girl hid behind the woman. The way she did made Adina assume the woman was her mother, or at least her adopted mother. The woman was very fair skinned, the child wasn't. It was common for orphans to be adopted by whatever family had resources to care for them. Or the child could have just favored her father.

The little girl peered around her leg.

"You hit it pretty hard," Asher mimicked her holding her head, watching the little girl as they drew closer.

There were five in the group. The mother, daughter, a girl a few years younger than Adina, and two young men. The younger of the men, more an older boy, lanky in oversized clothes that were belted and tied up to keep them on, stared around at the camp, his eyes running over the bearcat in open-mouthed wonder.

The little girl nodded, both hands holding a tail of her mother's coat, chewing on it uncertainly.

"I'm sorry you hurt yourself," Asher told her.

The mother coaxed her daughter forward. "Go ahead."

The little girl looked from her mom to Asher. Adina could see her struggling. "I'm sorry… I…" she looked at her mother for guidance.

"Came into your camp without permission," her mother mouthed.

The little girl made a face, started to mumble with her mother's coat tail still in her mouth. Her mother pushed it out of the way.

"Came to your camp without asking."

Adina couldn't help the grin that pulled her cheeks wide. "It's alright."

Asher winked at the little girl. "I was going to offer to let you to look around when you bumped your head." He stood again.

The woman brought the little girl in front of her and seemed to be trying to gather her courage while not to gawking at everything around her. Her eyes traveled up and down Asher uncertainly. Adina remembered her first impression of him and how intimidated she was.

"We're not thieves and we don't press in on people's privacy. I'm sorry for what Shella did." She looked down at her daughter. "She knows it's rude."

"Thank you," Asher answered.

"I'm Devon. These are my children." She blew out a breath. "They were so curious about you. I didn't want you to think… So, I thought I would ask… if it wasn't a bother…"

To Adina's surprise, Asher just said, "Of course." He stepped around the fire and squatted down in front of Shella. "Do you want to look inside?" The little girl's eyes were huge, locked onto his. Her fist, with part of her mother's coat tail in it, was stuck in her mouth. She just nodded.

The next hour went by with Devon and her children exploring the bearcat and Asher telling them bits and pieces. He was open, but Adina could feel the careful practice in each explanation, every word he spoke. He never mentioned the Longhunters, the city states, or what they did. Everything was conversational. He didn't give anything away but explained what they could see with their own eyes.

Asher was on top of the bearcat with the boys when Devon stepped close to Adina, holding Shella next to her.

"I don't want to be… rude. But Priav said he can't make children? But he's so healthy." Then, Devon looked suddenly chagrined. "I'm sorry. I… If you two are… together and don't want to." She nodded. "I understand. It's just he's so… I mean he's someone who isn't…" She seemed to run out of words. "He's not like anyone I've ever met before."

Adina had no idea what to say. Having someone walk up to her and basically say she wanted to fuck the man she was in love with to make a baby wasn't something she was really prepared for.

Devon turned to her watching her eyes. "And you don't want to have a baby?"

Adina kept from sputtering out nonsense, but not by much. "We were… in an accident. We can't have children," she got out.

Devon suddenly looked horrified. "Rotted ground. I'm so sorry." Devon flushed, her expression turning to compassion. "I'm so sorry for you."

Adina felt like her mind was stuck, trying to get in gear. *She thinks we were trying for a baby and…* Adina's uncertainty had apparently come across as anguish. She nodded, trying to catch up, playing to the fiction.

"It was… is… hard. She put a hand on Devon's arm. "Thank you for understanding." The wave of relief almost came out as a laugh at Devon's concern.

Devon laid a hand on hers. "I'm so sorry to have brought up something painful." After a moment, her expression changed again and Devon cocked her head, her eyes searching. She squeezed Adina's hand. "Even if we can't make a baby… I could come back later. After my smallest are asleep. My eldest can watch them." Devon smiled. "You are so pretty. And Asher." She breathed wistfully.

"Uhhh…" Adina once again had no idea what to say.

"Do you have people want to fuck you all the time?!" Adina asked, pulling her hair back with her left hand, her right arm still trapped against her side. It kept her from gesturing with satisfyingly large motions. They were safely locked in the bearcat again after she'd declined Devon's invitation and she and her family had left. Adina paced in the tiny space.

"I mean, I've had lots of men interested in me like that, but this… It's like…"

"Being treated like a breeding stud?" Asher filled in flatly.

Adina stopped her manic pacing and turned to him, his deadpan tone feeling like it hit her in the chest. She stood reading his expression. He wasn't any happier about it than she was.

"To answer your question, yes, it happens." His tone wasn't angry, but his words were clipped. "It's one of the reasons we stay away from people. It's also not safe. Like with you, we have no idea what illnesses or contamination these people may be carrying. They treat us like studs at a fair or something, but it's worse for the women in our ranks…"

"There are *women* longhunters?" Adina blurted the words out. She was already off balance from the encounter with Devon, but the idea of women doing what Asher did had never crossed her mind. It didn't even make sense.

He sat back; his expression surprised. The furrow between his eyebrows had become canyon deep again. "Of course, there are. Why wouldn't there be?"

Adina could only stare at him. "But… But…" Words were just coming out in a babble, a direct stream from her currently undirected thoughts. "How? You're so strong and… All alone, aren't they at risk. You know… of."

Asher's look of disbelief was unrestrained. But even as confused as Adina was, she didn't feel stupid under his gaze.

"Rape?" He crossed his arms. It wasn't *quite* annoyance, but it certainly wasn't his normal, easy way. "First of all, all longhunters aren't the same. We have different strengths and weaknesses. There are things women in our ranks can do that I'm simply no good at. Second, women aren't the only ones who get raped." He leaned forward, putting his elbows on his knees. "But you know that." He eyed her intently. "What's really going on, Adina?"

Adina could only gawk at him. "I just..." She knew that men and boys were raped by raiders. The fact that there were women longhunters was a surprise, and as she thought about it, she should have been happy about it.

But instead, she was confused and angry.

"Did Priav tell everyone in the caravan that we can't make babies? What else has she said? And what are we? Are we together? Are we just riding around together and fucking?"

"That's it, isn't it?" Asher asked.

"What? What is?" Adina was so wound up that she had to think back to remember what she'd said.

"The question about what we're doing, what we are." Everything was a churning mess inside Adina.

"Well... yes. I just... I don't know."

Asher got up and walked to her, putting his hands on her arms. "We, you and I, are together." His tone was firm, reassuring. "Things out here are uncertain. You and I are one thing I'm certain of." He put a hand on her cheek, a calloused thumb running lightly over her skin.

Adina was still confused but felt better.

He smiled, and his smile turned to a mischievous grin. "I'm going to make some hot water. It's been a while; someone needs a shave." He ran a hand down her body over her clothes.

Adina pressed herself against him, her anxiety suddenly turning to arousal. She put her face against his neck. "I'd like that."

Adina was shivering as Asher finished shaving her right armpit. It had nothing to do with cold. It was warm and stuffy in the bearcat now. The warm pan of water made it humid. He kissed her left nipple, then her right, then down onto her stomach, her mound and then ran his tongue over her clit. His tongue slipped inside her. Adina shivered again, opening her legs as he ran warm water over her mound and her vulva. He shaved her clean again, pushing her legs wide and carefully working around her anus. When he was finished, her ran soapy fingers over her anus and then slipped one inside. Adina shuddered as he played with her ass, the thumb of his other hand running over her slippery clit. Adina could only take quick sighing breaths, her hips pumping at the alternating hard pressure on her clit and then him pushing his finger deep in her ass. She leaned back against the cargo net on the side of the bearcat grasping the heavy webbing and moaning as he increased the pace on her clit. He pushed a second finger into her ass. Adina bit her arm, moaning and arching her back feeling the fire in her ass spread through her pelvis into her belly, her hips spasming forward. She was taking hard, catching breaths, her eyes closed when his lips touched her nipple. He bit lightly and pulled. Adina's orgasm crashed through her, and she shook hard, but he held her firmly, keeping his fingers inside her. She couldn't escape them or the fingers on her clit. She bit down on her arm to keep from screaming as her whole body spasmed harder, her orgasm rolling through her like lightning striking her nervous system, throwing her into wild quivers. She wasn't sitting up anymore but was on her back on their bedding as her hips eased, their spasms becoming less straining. He turned her over and as her body was finally starting to relax, she felt the head of his cock running over her slippery, swollen clit. He lifted her hips and pushed himself inside slowly, his thumb playing at her ass. She moaned as he penetrated her sensitive depths. And when his thumb pushed into her asshole, she pushed back hard with a groan. She pushed up, careful of her injured arm, her breasts hanging as she thrust back onto him.

"Oh… yes.."

Adina was already shuddering again. Her body felt confused by the dual penetration and the erotic feeling of her arm strapped down, her breasts bouncing as their bodies slapped together. She collapsed back onto the bedding, unable to hold herself up on just one arm as he rhythmically drove into her. She clawed at their bedding, her whole body on fire with the feeling of his cock deep inside her. She sighed with disappointment when he pulled his thumb out of her ass, then two fingers took its place, plunging deep into her. Adina went stiff, everything in her seeming to lock up. She just quivered, trapped in a spasm as his pelvis crashed against her, a long, ecstatic moment. A long groan stifled her short, gasping breaths, seeming to rise up from deep in her belly and the paralysis was broken. She came hard, nonstop, every inch of her shuddering hard.

Adina thought she might have passed out. There seemed to be an ecstatic blank spot, just crashing emotions and sensations until he collapsed on top of her. Her legs were trembling, and her breathing was more gasps than anything else. As she came back to her body, she could feel his hot semen leaking out around his softening cock.

"Ooohhh…" she panted. "That was… amazing. I think I might have passed out." She reached behind her to grab any part of him she could.

He was panting too. "Uh huh… It was…"

He rolled them so she was on her left side, taking the pressure off her shoulder, then leaned over and gave her a long kiss on the neck as she tried to catch her breath.

Adina pulled his arm up onto her breast again, letting herself slide toward sleep.

__

Adina had already cleaned most of the back of the bearcat by the time Asher rolled over, blinking awake. She'd used their shaving water to wipe most of the dust off the interior surfaces and had finally gotten to clean up the dried blood and other filth from parts of the decking. The back of the bearcat was anything but clean, but it was *cleaner*.

Adina smiled at him as he turned and looked at her. "Don't move. You're in a good position for me to change your dressing."

He relaxed back onto the bedding, one eye squinting at the light coming in through the small cupola windows.

Adina settled down with the medical kit and carefully removed the dressing. She cleaned the wound again and patted it dry. The skin was healing nicely. What would have been over week of healing had only taken a day. She kissed the healing skin, covered and dressed it again.

"How does it look?" he asked, his face smashed up from the blankets he was laying on.

"It looks good."

He rolled over, smiling and pulled her against him. "How do you feel this morning?"

Adina grinned. "A little sore." She took his hand and put it on her ass, squeezing his fingers on her backside. "But good." The remembered feeling of her whole body tensing and releasing in a new way with his fingers in her ass, made her stomach pull tight. "That was -- amazing."

He kissed her. "I'm glad." She just lay against him for a few minutes. "How's your shoulder?"

Adina hadn't thought about it this morning. "It doesn't hurt," she answered, surprised. "Can I take off the stupid sling and sash now?"

"Give it another day. Just for safety." He squeezed her tightly. "Besides, you need to get used to being tied up."

"Is that a promise?" Adina leaned up on an elbow smiling at him.

"Count on it."

A loud bang on the side of the bearcat made Adina jump. Asher rolled to his knees and moved up to the passenger seat, looking out the window.

"Do you hunt?" came a muffled voice from the other side of the armor.

"Yes," Asher answered, wiping a hand over his face.

"One of the lookouts saw a big herd of boar."

"Big herd?"

"I know!" came the voice from outside. The surprise was clear even through the bearcat's thick armor. "The big ones don't normally herd."

"How many?" Asher asked.

"Not sure, at least thirty."

"Alright, we'll get rolling."

"We're stripping everything off one of the fast trucks for a chase vehicle."

"We'll be ready to go in twenty minutes."

"Okay!"

When Asher turned back, naked in the early morning light, a wide, boyish smile drew his features up into an expression like nothing Adina had ever seen on him before. "Ready to go hunting?"

CHAPTER NINE

Adina's hazel eyes followed Asher as he made rapid preparations for the hunt. He seemed manic in what was obvious, unrestrained excitement. He'd pulled on his pants and boots but hadn't even bothered with a shirt, his grin now a sudden, permanent feature on his face.

Adina couldn't help her own smile watching his expression as she sat on the ground brushing her hair. She pulled her long, dark hair back behind her ears and tied it into a loose ponytail. "You really like hunting."

Asher stopped what he was doing, neatly stowing the last of their camp supplies. "We train by hunting from the time we're little." He hopped down out of the side hatch and stood up fully, the morning sun shining on his short gray-white hair and close-cropped beard. The light's angle and color were particularly suited to show off his hard-muscled torso, scars, and tattoos.

He seemed to have entirely forgotten the wound on his back and the scabbing abrasions on his shoulder and elbow.

He gestured around them. "Out here, we only hunt out of necessity -- alone. We never get to hunt with a group like this." The boyish smile split his face again. "It's like being back home." He pulled what Adina had thought were stowed awning poles from where they were strapped to the outside of the bearcat. After leaning the half dozen eight-foot poles against the bearcat's exterior, he pulled a box from one of the storage compartments and withdrew a spear point. It was over a foot long and had barbs at the base that would prevent it from being pulled out. He held it up for her to see and winked with a devilish grin and glint in his eye.

Adina stopped mid-motion as she was standing up, staring from the poles to the spearpoints and back to his expression. Boars were feared by caravans and small communities alike -- and anyone else with common sense as far as she was concerned. Large boars weighed more than a thousand pounds; massive, angry, four-legged mounds of muscle that didn't see people as anything more than another mobile protein source in the landscape. They were terrors. Even small herds could destroy an entire camp, killing and maiming large numbers of people. And this herd was larger than any she'd ever heard of.

"You're going to hunt boars with a *spear?*" Adina couldn't help the way her voice sheared up.

He fixed the point to one of the shafts, smiled and nodded. "You're going to drive." He didn't even seem to have heard her.

Adina finished standing, her joy at his boyish excitement suddenly shot through with anxiety. "Drive?" She glanced at the bearcat and the spears. "What are you talking about?"

"It'll be simple. You drive close, get alongside one, keep us steady and I'll lance him."

Adina stared at him open-mouthed. "Lance him? But wha…"

Asher stepped to the heavy passenger door of the bearcat and pulled pins from the hinges. Then with a groan and strain of effort, lifted the heavy door off the hinges, leaving the passenger seat open. His back and shoulder muscles bulged under the weight of the armored door, each clearly defined, right down to the striations as he hefted it into a set of storage brackets aft of the now wide-open door.

He's out of his sun-touched mind!

After securing the door in place he pointed to the passenger seat. "See. All you have to do is get us close." He grabbed the lance and climbed up into the passenger door well, hanging onto the door frame and raised the lance. "It's easy."

Adina just gawked at him.

"What... what if you fall..." Where he stood wasn't too high for one of the big boars to reach with its eighteen-inch-long dagger tusks. "Or if the boar turns back... or..." Now she was just sputtering words.

"Wow!" a voice cried, and Adina turned. Devon's younger son, whose name they'd learned was Nat, stood frozen at the front of the bearcat where he'd just come around the corner. He stared at Asher with wide-eyed adoration painted across his face.

Adina could understand his reaction. Asher stood in the open passenger door like some kind of golden god, the morning sun streaming on his scarred, tattooed skin, his unintentional pose with the spear like he was one of the statues she'd seen faded pictures of.

"Are we ready to go?" Asher asked, dropping out of the door and onto the ground, his boots raising a small dust cloud. He leaned the spear next to the rest and fixed a point to the next one.

Nat just stood there for a moment before collecting himself enough to answer. "Yes, five men will be on the chase truck." He stared at the spears. "You're going to hunt... with those?"

Asher tossed a completed one to Nat, who barely caught it. It almost smacked him in the face. Nat ran his twelve-year-old fingers over the smooth weapon, then the lethally pointed head. "It's so sharp!"

Asher finished affixing the rest of the heads. "It has to be to get through their hide," he explained confidently.

Adina was still trying to figure out a way to express how… *mad* the entire concept was. "But you have the big rifle… You could just shoot them. You wouldn't have to get anywhere near them."

Asher took the spear from Nat, set it with the others and then turned to her. His grin and expression now had a slightly maniacal, testosterone driven glint to it. He stepped close and untied the sash that held her arm to her side. "Now where would be the fun in that?" Then he undid the sling, freeing her arm and clambered into the back of the bearcat. "I guess you're out of shoulder prison now." He tossed both sash and sling inside. When he came back out, he was carrying the smaller bolt-action hunting rifle she'd trained with in the rift along with a bandolier of rifle cartridges. He handed her the rifle and bandolier.

Nat whistled at the finely made rifle.

"But you should keep this at hand in case of emergencies."

Adina looked at the rifle and bandolier in her hands, to Asher, then Nat, and back to Asher again, unsure if he was making some kind of elaborate joke.

"You're serious? You're going to hunt boars with… spears." She threw her hand with the bandolier out toward the spears. The bandolier swung heavily from the motion. "While you're hanging out of the side of the bearcat like some kind of raider?"

"Wicked," Nat breathed.

Adina turned and narrowed her eyes at Nat. "Nobody asked you."

Asher gave her a distracted kiss on the cheek. "It'll be fine. It'll be fun!" Then he turned to Nat. "How long before we're ready to go?"

"Uhh… half an hour or so. They're still getting the truck rigged."

Asher nodded. "Alright, tell them we'll be ready."

Nat didn't move, still staring at Asher, the spears, and the bearcat.

"Go on," Asher coaxed.

Nat turned and bolted for the rest of the caravan. Thirty seconds later Adina heard Nat hollering. "Asher's going to hunt the boars with a SPEAR!"

_

As they rolled across the desert, hot, dusty wind whipped in through the open door of the bearcat. Adina was going through the sequence of events trying to make sense of what they were doing. It had all happened so fast. She'd cleaned up the inside of the bearcat right after waking up. It had been anything but thorough, but still… She glanced at the thick cloud of dust now billowing inside and sighed. Then she'd changed Asher's dressing. It and he were now coated with dust, like everything else. Adina raked stray, windblown strands of dark hair out of her face and focused on the parched landscape in front of them.

This is insane!

But Asher's excitement hadn't ebbed in the slightest and it was hard to not be swept up by his frenetic energy. Her heart was pounding.

Excitement… or sensible terror?

The whole camp was in an uproar as they left. Adina couldn't be sure how much excitement there normally would have been for a hunt, especially after the caravan's losses. But Nat's town crier performance had brought everyone out to stare. Asher stood in the open passenger door of the bearcat; a spear gripped in his hand as she drove them to where the preparations on the chase truck were being finalized. He was still bare-chested, the rest of the spears standing neatly trapped between the dismounted door and armored exterior of the bearcat.

Asher had never seemed the sort to want to draw attention, but she could tell he was thoroughly enjoying himself as they rolled through camp. He called to the other hunters, cajoling them, and shouted to the rest of the caravan, working them up for the hunt. It was like he'd become a completely different person. He projected fierce, unbridled joy, and raucous, easy confidence.

Adina couldn't help the smile that kept tugging her cheeks as her emotions pulled to and fro. Even Priav was excited. It was more than matronly leadership, motivating the caravan for the dangerous hunt to come. She stood on top of one of the vehicles, leading a stomping, clattering chant, seeming caught up in Asher's energy too. It could have been normal for them; Adina had no idea. But for long minutes, people banged on metal holding the rhythm, others clapped and used their voices, some people danced. It was a stomping circular dance where the participants thrust their arms down and then up again every few beats, spinning and throwing their arms wide.

Adina had never seen anything like it. Asher howled and banged the exterior of the bearcat along with everyone else. The celebratory atmosphere felt strange, given all that had happened.

But that was yesterday. We don't live in yesterdays — only today.

The old woman's voice echoed in Adina's mind as she watched Priav dance. The rest of the caravan would follow along their route. Then Priav threw her rifle high over her head and led a howling, yelping cry, and ululation as they drove away.

Adina had her rifle safely stowed just to the left of the steering wheel. She'd made sure she checked every part of it and the eight rounds in the magazine before storing it. If she needed to use it, there wouldn't be time for anything to go wrong.

What if Haro, or the Ghost Eyes are out there?

That thought seemed to have been completely forgotten by Asher and the rest of the caravan -- at least on the surface.

"Stay on this line!" Asher called down from the cupola. He was standing up in it, scanning the horizon for the herd. Adina looked right. The other chase truck was roaring across the desert twenty yards away, their hunters hanging all over it. They too had stripped off their shirts following Asher's example. The energy of the whole thing felt disconcertingly like how she perceived raiders might feel. But this time, she was a part of it.

Adina's heart was pounding, and she felt *alive* in a way she could never remember being. Everything was sharper, more in focus, every sensation more intense.

There was a blast of noise from the chase truck, and they veered away. Adina looked and the hunters were gesturing and pointing.

"They see them! Follow them!" Asher hollered.

He clambered down out of the cupola and grabbed the back of her seat as she turned the bearcat. He gave her a rough kiss on the cheek, smiling like some kind of fiend and climbed over the console to the passenger seat. "Here we go!" He pulled the lever on the center console and a moment later the air siren howled to life. He suddenly pointed. "There!"

Adina could just make out the dark dots against the beige landscape. The entire herd broke into a run, away from the sound of their vehicles. The thought suddenly crashed through her head again. *This is insane!*

"Swing left! We want to keep them between us and the chase truck!"

Adina stepped on the accelerator. As they passed the chase truck Asher gestured and hollered. "TAKE THE RIGHT SIDE! WE'LL HOLD THEM BETWEEN US!"

The driver waved and they pulled away.

It was hard for Adina to tell how large the boars were as they closed rapidly on herd's dust cloud. Asher was standing outside the door now, his left hand hooked on the handle above the passenger seat. She heard the clatter as he grabbed a lance.

The herd was less than a hundred yards ahead of them. She heard the first report of a rifle from the chase truck.

"They'll never hit anything from this far away in all this dust!" Asher yelled back into the cab.

Fifty yards. Adina had never seen, or even heard of a herd this size. There were more than thirty animals -- a lot more. Most were smaller, maybe one or two hundred pounds. Then as they got closer, the big males appeared from the dust. Half a dozen hulking monsters running at the head of the herd. Nothing about this herd made sense. Big males kept harems of females and drove off rival males. They certainly didn't work together.

"There they are! Look at 'em!" Asher hollered triumphantly. "They're magnificent!" He turned to her, smiling fiercely. "Put us right on top of them!"

The whole herd suddenly swerved away from them, the chase truck had fallen behind, the herd turning ahead of it.

"Stay with 'em, Adie!"

Adina smiled widely at his shortening of her name. This was a different Asher than she'd ever seen. More just… *him*. All the constructs and rules that seemed to define him had fallen away. The crease between his eyebrows had vanished completely again. Everything about him pulsed with unbridled self-expression, no governors, no restrictions, just pure joy, and life.

"Get 'em!" he encouraged.

As she turned the bearcat, it tore up the hard packed, hoof-turned earth beneath them. Asher leaned out, into the motion, part of the machine's movement.

Something felt like it broke loose inside Adina. Fierce joy suddenly surged up through her, hot and primal. She threw her head back and a loud ululation erupted from somewhere deep as she leaned into the turn, swinging the bearcat wide, her eyes fixed on the leading edge of the herd.

"Perfect! Bring us in!" Adina glanced right, she could just see the chase truck, a huge cloud of dust rising as they skidded sideways, turning hard to keep the head of the herd from getting around them. She heard gunshots, three in rapid succession.

"That's one!" Asher shouted, his head swiveling to the chase truck then to the head of the herd again, leaning all the way out. He adjusted the spear in his hand. "Closer!"

Adina focused on one of the big males, chasing him, edging closer and closer, the other boars turned away.

You're mine… She brought the bearcat up behind him. He tried to turn across her path, but she stepped on the accelerator, and he faded back to her right.

"Almost there!" Asher hollered. "Steady…!

Steady….!"

Asher rose up, his arm with the lance disappearing above the door frame.

The boar disappeared, falling back along the right side, in front of Asher.

"WHOAH!" Asher dodged back into the door and Adina saw the boar's massive head through the open door as it hooked its wicked tusks up, trying to reach him. "Slow!" he shouted. "Ease right!" She couldn't see the boar at all now. She had to rely on Asher's directions.

The boar reappeared suddenly in front of them on her right again. Adina lined up on him, bringing him down the right side.

"That's it! You're right on him!" Asher shouted. The boar disappeared again. Even craning her neck, Adina couldn't see him.

With a loud shout, Asher threw his body down, plunging the spear downward.

Adina decelerated trying to see the boar again. "Did you get him!?"

"He's a strong one! He needs another lance! Right! Turn right!"

Adina turned and the whole rig suddenly leapt up from the back.

Adina fought for control as the back slammed down again, everything inside rattling and crashing from the impact. "What was that!"

Asher was still leaning out the open passenger door, swaying from the violent motion as if he was welded to the rig. He looked back. "It's alright! You hit one of the smaller ones, it went under the back wheels!" He pointed as she held the turn, the back of the bearcat skidding around.

In the rising dust, she could see the big boar again, the lance jutting out of its back. It was still running.

"He's a strong one!" Asher hollered, his voice ringing with fierce approval.

Adina heard more gunshots as she lined up on the boar again. It was slowing. She heard the clatter as Asher grabbed another lance. She pulled up behind the boar, carefully adjusting her speed. Now that she'd done it once and knew what to expect, it was easy to pull left, drawing the animal down the right side, in front of Asher. Asher rose up once more and with a shout, hurled the lance downward. He turned, watching behind them as she maneuvered into open space again. "That got him!"

Another ululation tore from Adina as if it had a life of its own as her heart thudded loudly, her hands and arms shaking with adrenaline as she gripped the big steering wheel. The hurtling armored machine felt like nothing more than a part of her now.

"Hard right, back into the herd!"

She turned, skidding the bearcat as Asher grabbed another lance. Seconds passed as she chased another big boar through the thick dust clouds raised by the herd and the trucks.

"GOOD! Right on him!" Asher rose up again and hurled another lance.

Adina stood on top of the stopped bearcat, heat waves rolling off the barrel of her rifle as she ejected the last spent casing. It tinkled onto the metal where the other seven spent casings glittered in the blazing sun. Her excited breaths were slowing, but her heart still pounded in her ears. The dust was clearing as the rest of the herd trotted away. There were ecstatic whoops and hollers from the chase vehicle, stopped a hundred yards away.

Between them and scattered along the path they'd come; more than a dozen boars lay dead.

Adina squeaked in surprise when Asher grabbed her from behind and picked her up, planting a kiss on her neck.

"You were amazing!"

Adina leaned into his kiss and when he put her feet back on the bearcat, she turned and smashed her lips against his, pulling his dust-caked, sweaty chest against her. She was smiling so fiercely when they finally parted that her cheeks ached. She hadn't stopped smiling since he'd thrown the first lance. "You killed three boars with spears! You're not so bad yourself!"

He smiled and gave her another kiss, his gaze moving to the fallen animals. "I guess the fun's over. Time to get to work."

Adina ran a hand over his sweaty chest, feeling the dust and grit stuck to it. "I guess so."

Half an hour later the rest of the caravan caught up. The hunting group was well into slaughtering the boars by then. All the hunters, both in small groups and individually, had come to compliment Asher on his prowess. While he clearly enjoyed it, he was self-effacing. Each time, he pointed to her and told them, "Adina killed more of them than I did. I was just having fun. Besides, the big males aren't much good for eating." It was true. Adina had killed four boars with the rifle. It had taken all eight rounds to do it, but him making such a point of giving her credit made everything inside her swell with pride.

Asher looked like he'd been bathing in blood when Priav finally caught up to them. Adina pushed stray hair back out of her face with the back of a filthy hand as Priav approached where they were skinning one of the large kills. The thick hide would be excellent for all manner of uses, from armor to boot soles. Priav's expression was approving as she scanned the field where everyone was busily working.

"You are… and are not… a surprise, Myrmidon," Priav announced, squinting at him in the glaring sun. She approached him and patted his burly shoulder. "You are a good man. I am glad we have met."

Adina could see the curiosity working behind the old woman's brown eyes when Priav approached her. Priav leaned forward and gave her a long, affectionate kiss on her blood-streaked cheek, then leaned back with a sigh.

Priav just looked at her for a long time. "You would have made such beautiful babies." Then there was a particular twinkle in her eye, and she leaned close. "But if you don't have to worry about being pregnant," she glanced wryly at Asher. "You are lucky. I wish you all the joy you can have." She made another knowing face, an eyebrow slowly climbing up. "I had nine children. Sex isn't so much fun after a while." Priav leaned back again and scanned the work around them. "They said you took four. What will you do with them?"

Adina was still recovering from the old woman's affectionate kiss and direct sexual comment about Asher. "Well, I… We… certainly don't need four." She picked up some dirt and scrubbed her hands and bare arms to knock off the worst of blood-sticky boar hair. She'd stripped down to a sleeveless shirt for the bloody work of skinning and butchering. She nodded to everyone who was now working. "I hunted them for you."

Priav narrowed an eye, and after a beat, a corner of her mouth came up again. "Not naïve maybe… or stupid. We will have to find something to trade for such a fine gift." Priav glanced at Asher again and laid a hand on Adina's arm, giving it an affectionate little shake. "Just kinder than we're used to." Then she walked away without another word.

Adina watched her go, pride brimming in her chest.

It wasn't that she was unused to being recognized for things she'd done. She was very good at making shoes. But this was… *different*. She couldn't help the smile that pulled her cheeks again.

"You've made an impression," Asher called, shoulder deep in the boar carcass.

Adina turned to him and cocked her head, then threw her hip out, putting a dusty, slightly less sticky hand on it. "Me? I'm not the one running around with his shirt off killing boars with spears!"

Asher pulled out a big bloody organ with a satisfied sigh, looking it over as he rolled it between his hands. He blew out through his nose trying to knock loose boar hairs sticking there. "I was just having fun." He wiped a forearm across his nose leaving a smear and looked at her, taking in her posture and grinned. "You helped people you didn't have to, Adina. People you didn't know. It feels pretty good, doesn't it?"

It did feel good. Adina felt powerful, and Priav had recognized it.

Asher held up the organ. "I hope you like liver."

--

Adina was meat drunk. She couldn't eat any more.

They'd feasted wandering from one group to another until she almost couldn't walk. They'd eaten more meat than she would have consumed in months in her previous life. It was mostly organ meat; fresh, rich and often bloody. It wouldn't keep the way other meat would. It wasn't something Adina was used to. Organ meat rarely made it back to camp. It was a privilege reserved for hunters. And now she was one. Anything that they couldn't preserve with just heat and the sun had to be eaten or go to waste. So tonight, and the next days, they would gorge themselves on the rich meat until it was gone or went bad.

There were still those among the survivors who were badly injured and people who isolated themselves in their grief, but the mood of the rest of the caravan was celebratory. It took all day to harvest the boars, begin drying the meat and processing the hides and other things that were useful. Guards were posted to watch for scavengers as much as for Haro or his Ghost Eyes. If a fifty-strong herd of boar could live out here, then other things certainly could too.

As they wandered back to the bearcat, she leaned against Asher. He was back in his shirt and long coat.

They'd washed off when the worst of the work was done, rinsing away blood, sticky boar hair and dust, but they picked the dust up again as soon as they touched anything.

She gazed up past Asher's face to the blanket of stars above them. "I've never seen a caravan or community hunt like this. The caravans and communities I've been in had small groups or families whose work was hunting." She turned, listening to the creak of his leather coat and the happy bustle of the camp around them. She gestured back to the rest of the camp. "I've never seen a whole group shift over to hunting the way they do."

"The whole community didn't share work?" he asked, his head turning as he scanned the landscape around them.

"Well yes, but not quite like this."

They reached the bearcat, and he pulled open the side hatch. The smell of fresh meat wafted out. Every surface that could support it was hung with drying strips of meat, along with racks outside made from the spear shafts and anything else handy. The big hides were laid out on top of the rig, packed with dry earth until they could be properly tanned.

Adina pulled Asher's arm, so he faced her, smiling. He was the hero of the day; everyone had come to talk to them at one time or another.

Devon visited several times on various excuses, her top loosened 'from the heat,' showing off her big breasts, her invitation obvious. Adina couldn't blame her or anyone else who stared at him shirtless or complimented his prowess.

Adina's eyes traveling over his handsome face and strong body, admiring him.

He's ruined me.

Adina couldn't look at other men the same way anymore. No one could possibly measure up to him. Everything below Adina's belly button felt like it squeezed, making her chew the inside of her lip and squirm.

It's only been… two weeks? It was hard for her to imagine how so little time had passed and how much everything had changed.

It wasn't just that Asher was heart-stoppingly handsome. He listened to her, made her laugh, and of course the sex was *amazing*. He was so confident… He didn't do things to prove he was strong, or masculine, or anything else. Instead, he went out of his way to make her feel capable, smart, *powerful.* And, of course, pretty.

Adina pulled herself against him in the open hatch of the bearcat. "Every woman in camp wants you," she told him as she unbuckled his belt and pants. "I want you more."

He smiled at her. "I'm not interested in any other woman in camp." He pulled her into a kiss, unbuckling her belt and lifting her shirt up. She was trying to get his pants open when his lips were suddenly on her nipple, kissing and sucking.

"Ohhh… Asher…" Adina ran the nails of one hand through his hair, holding his head to her breast, her other still working on his pants. She abandoned the thought and shoved her hand inside grabbing his cock. "Mmm… this is what I want."

He pulled her shirt off and she was able to get his pants down. She pushed him down on the step into the bearcat, throwing his shirt up and kissing his naked chest. He threw off his coat as she kissed and licked down his chest onto his belly. He was pulling his shirt off when she cupped his balls and pushed her mouth down on his rigid cock.

His hiss of pleasure was met by Adina's excited moan as she tasted his saltiness, working her mouth up and down lightly squeezing his balls with one hand, her other exploring the feeling of his muscular abs.

He sat up and pushed her pants down while she worked on his cock. Adina stood up and wiggled her pants down, shoving off her boots as he did the same. Then she pushed up against him, her breasts at his face. He wrapped his strong hands around her ass, pulling her cheeks apart, a finger playing at her anus while his other hand slid around to her already soaking pussy.

"Should we go inside?" He asked.

"No," Adina breathed, bending, and kissing him hard. "I don't care who sees or hears us."

She felt his smile as she kissed him. "Feeling territorial?"

Adina smiled fiercely. "Fuck yes I am." She put a knee on the bearcat's hard metal step, and he adjusted up onto the deck properly. She followed, pressing her stomach against his, then straddling him. She reached down and grabbed his hard shaft and put it against her opening. "I don't want you thinking about Devon or anyone else." Adina pushed him inside her.

He groaned as she slid down onto him. "You don't have to worry about that, Adina." He grabbed her hips and thrust up into her. Adina's breath caught as he filled her. "You're the only one I want."

Adina pushed him onto his back, putting her hands on the deck on either side of him, then lifted up to draw his cock most of the way out of her, then slid back down on it. "Good." He cupped her breasts, fondling her nipples as she rode him. Adina bit her lip, her senses filling with the stimulation of him playing with her nipples, his cock slipping inside her and the satisfying pressure as she ground her clit against him at the bottom of each stroke. She rolled her hips with him buried in her, pumping her clit against the base of his shaft, then leaned back. "Should I just call you Myrmidon? A great hero of the ancient world."

He sat up, a hand under her ass, his other wrapped around her back to hold her steady as he kissed her neck and ear, her long dark hair cascading over her shoulders. She shivered at the light prickling of his beard against her neck. "You can call me whatever you want."

Adina wrapped her arms around his neck, riding in ecstatic joy, her body twitching and shuddering at his touches, his kissing and sucking her nipple, his finger playing on her anus.

Asher hooked his arms under her legs and before she realized what he was doing, he'd stood up, letting her body weight drive his cock up into her. She was all but sitting on her clit. Her stomach curled instinctively as she moaned and bit his shoulder, words forgotten. He lifted her and dropped her again, his cock seeming to be the only thing holding her up as she rolled her hips to keep him inside her.

"You like that?"

She could only moan, 'Uhh huhh…" and nod, biting his shoulder, trying not to bite too hard.

Adina wasn't sure if it was him suddenly and sharply starting to drive into her rapidly, or just the constant pressure on her clit that made her cum. But she was sure that being held off the ground, helpless to do anything but hold onto him as the orgasm clenched her muscles into trembling cords was what made it last so long. She tried to hook her feet behind him to get some control, some purchase, but her legs wouldn't work as her orgasm rolled through her again and again turning her legs into shaking, useless appendages. When her spasming finally eased, he laid her down on the deck of the bearcat.

Adina kissed his neck, and successfully hooked her feet around his waist, panting. "You're not done, are you?"

He pulled back so she could see his face. "Are you?"

She smiled, all of her flushed, watching his lapis blue eyes. She shook her head, "No."

Adina was standing barefoot on the dirt, holding onto the hatch of the bearcat when her next orgasm nearly took her off her feet. The intense sensation of two of Asher's fingers pushed deep into her ass as he took her from behind was just too much. It was only him pulling his fingers out and grabbing her by the hips that kept her from collapsing as her legs turned to shuddering noodles again.

She was still cumming when she felt his fingers wipe slippery lubricant around her anus. It was so erotic she couldn't help but push her hips back against the sensation.

"What is that?" It was almost a moan.

"Fat from the boars."

Adina felt the head of his penis at her ass. All her senses were jumbled, overwhelmed as he penetrated. She bit her lip hard at the stretching pain, still in the final trembles of her waning orgasm. She felt her fingernails snap against the hard metal of the hatch as her anus stretched to accept him.

"Are you alright? Do you want me to stop?"

She shook her head and nodded in a confused motion, unsure how to answer the opposed questions.

"No…" she panted; her voice pitched high as she tried to talk. "Don't stop."

Asher pushed in deeper, and Adina groaned. It hurt and excited her so much at the same time. And as always, how badly Asher wanted her was one of the most arousing things she could imagine. She scooted a foot up to get more firm footing putting a hand between her legs, slipping her fingers along her swollen clit. "Earth and sky!" She held her hips rolled back to accept him, but everything felt like it was going to spasm. "Yes… I want to feel…"

He pushed in further and she yelped in pain, squeezing her eyes shut. "Wait!" She grabbed his hand. "Too much!"

He held still, just letting her relax. She was trembling and couldn't catch her breath. His other hand reached around, pushing her hand aside, his fingers finding her clit, stroking it lightly. Then he rolled it again. He knew just how to touch her. She sucked in a deep breath as her back arched. And with his cock partly in her ass, hanging onto the bearcat's hatch and his fingers playing on her clit, she came again. This time there was no standing, she collapsed down onto her knees, his arm around her stomach keeping her from falling hard. Her palms hit the dirt, then her cheek as her clenching muscles forced him out of her.

Her legs were still trembling, and she was taking shuddering breaths when he asked, "You don't really want to lay in the dirt do you?"

Adina could almost see his smirk. She would have given him a withering look if she'd been able to. She waved an uncoordinated hand at him as he helped her back up onto the deck of the bearcat. "Shut… shut up…"

Ecstatic minutes later, he lay panting next to her after his own climax. He'd driven her across the deck of the bearcat in his passion until she was smashed against the wall when she finally felt his hot release, his sperm filling her. After they'd finished, Adina pushed away from the wall. The ribs on her right side were tender. She smirked to herself as she looked at the shelf she'd been pressed up against. *I'm going to have a bruise from that.*

"We'll have to go slow with my ass," Adina said into his chest after they'd caught their breath and were just lying under the blanket, staring out the hatch at the stars. Her knees were a little raw from riding him on the hard deck and hitting the dirt, but everything inside her was so blissfully calm now.

"Alright." He kissed her sweaty hair.

"I want to do it." She blew out a breath. "It really excites me." She was a little shocked she could even say it. "It's just… new."

Asher kissed her again. "We'll go at whatever pace you're comfortable with. You're alright?"

Adina smiled and an embarrassed giggle boiled up. "I'm going to have a bruise." She rolled so he could see her ribs. "From the shelf."

He kissed her ribs, which were already darkening red. "I'm sorry."

"And I'm going to walk funny tomorrow." She pulled him to her so she could kiss him. "Part of that is just how hard you make me cum."

He kissed her deeply and then smiled, watching her eyes. "Glad I can be of service."

Adina narrowed her eyes and stuck out her tongue at him. "Did you enjoy yourself?"

He gave her another kiss. "Always." He held her eyes intently. *"Always."*

Adina cuddled up against him again and let her eyes close.

--

The next morning was all work, packing up, finishing processing the boars for transport to Priav's larger camp. And Adina was sore, as she expected. Priav eyed her at one point with a smirk.

How much noise did we make last night?

Adina and Asher had joked, calling the bearcat the *meat truck,* because of all the drying meat hanging everywhere as the caravan moved slowly back along the route they'd been on. The slower pace was so that the vehicles, which were laden with drying meat and parts of carcasses, could keep their hard-earned rewards intact.

It was a long day of driving, and it was far past dark when Adina finally saw a glow on the horizon. The camp was larger than she'd expected with a watch tower and a perimeter wall under construction. There were probably two or three hundred people in it. As they got closer, she could see it was perched on the side of what had once been a Quarry. The bluff at the far end of the Quarry was warmed by firelight from the camp.

"It looks like they're building a permanent settlement."

Asher nodded from the passenger seat. "If there's a permanent water source, then there's a good reason to. But if Haro and the Ghost Eyes find it, there won't be much left, unless they have a lot better resources in that camp than the caravan had."

The caravan stopped when the lead vehicle reached what appeared to be a large gate under construction.

Asher opened the passenger door and stood in it. He watched the caravan and camp, then leaned back in. "Don't shut down, keep us angled in case we need to break away."

Adina looked out, she couldn't see much, the rest of the caravan was in front of them, in the way. "Is there trouble?"

Asher attached his sword to his pistol belt and climbed into the back, locking the hatches. "I don't know but stay here." He stopped before stepping out. "I don't think it's anything, they're probably just being careful, but you never know."

He stepped down, closed the door and she heard it lock.

Adina watched as best she could, but most of what was happening was in front of the lead vehicle where she couldn't see. She could see Priav and some people from inside the camp. The bearcat's rumble made it impossible for her to hear anything. Uneasy minutes passed, then she saw Asher again, walking back. She unlocked his door, and he climbed up inside. By the time he was in his seat, the front vehicle was already moving.

"We're alright," he told her. "We're just strangers and they're rightfully wary." He patted the door. "They saw the bearcat and thought we might have seized the caravan."

"But it's okay now?"

He nodded with a skeptically raised eyebrow. "As good as it can be. They still aren't going to trust us, but Priav was singing our praises when I got there. And apparently, she carries some weight. At least with the people who were there."

Adina followed the truck ahead of them when it started moving. "This is a lot bigger place than I thought it was going to be."

"Yeah, it is." Asher peered up at the guard tower as they passed. "But they still aren't very well defended." He shook his head. "I wouldn't put money on this camp being here in a year." There was something in the way he said it. It wasn't disappointment. Maybe weariness?

"What is it?"

"I've just seen this before." He scanned the encampment as they followed the other vehicles. "It ends badly so often."

"You don't sound very confident of these people."

He nodded. "Yeah… It's prejudice. It's hard to see something like this as permanent after living in the city states."

Adina looked at the encampment and what they were building. She'd been in much larger towns, walled settlements that were well defended. Some of those had been razed by raiders. These few hundred people with their cobbled together tower and defenses looked paper thin by comparison. "Hope builds…" she said.

Asher turned to her. "What was that?"

"Hope builds, despair destroys. It was something someone used to say."

"Hope isn't a plan…" he countered. "Is something we say."

Adina felt a sudden tickle down deep. "But what you do is based on hope, isn't it?" She found herself grinning for some reason. "Going out into the wastes looking for things to try and rebuild a world from nothing?"

He narrowed an eye at her and cocked his head, then looked out again. "Yeah, I guess so." He gestured at the camp around them. "This… just isn't what we're trying to build."

"It's not yours." Adina nodded outward. "It's theirs."

--

Adina felt strangely good when she woke the next morning. She peered out through the bearcat's windows and from the portholes in the cupola. She could see the glow of fires and smoke rising from camps. It was just before dawn and a few people were moving around, starting their days. Her chest tightened as she watched them. She remembered her own morning routine in camp before the attack. Before everything changed. The tedious, repetitious, menial daily tasks… She suddenly missed them. And her own people. Her emotions flip-flopped between heartache and happiness. She'd been in communities like this one, or smaller her whole life. Her first memories were of people all around her. In the burning hot, freezing cold, joy and terror. Adina felt suddenly -- lonely… and *excited* all at the same time.

It had been utterly quiet last night. They'd been shown where to park on the edge of camp and Priav had joined them briefly after they'd parked. A larger group of townspeople had followed her but hung back. Some were armed and Adina could sense Asher's unease. She made sure her pistol was easily accessible at her hip.

Priav had nodded to them, her rifle resting in the crook of her elbow as always. "The council needs to talk about what happened. That doesn't involve you." She glanced over her shoulder then back to them again, an eyebrow raised. "We also need to talk about you. I trust you. Those who were with us trust you. But others don't." She smiled; her eyes wrinkling with the expression. "They don't know you yet, Myrmidon." Her eyes flicked to Adina. "Or you." She leaned forward with a merry sort of expression and winked at her. "I will send someone to fetch you in the morning. For now, good night."

"Are you alright?"

Adina turned to Asher's voice. He was lying on the deck, the blanket at his waist, his big arms flexed, hands behind his head. Adina nodded. "It's just… strange, being in a camp again." She blew out a breath. "I… don't know how to feel." She climbed under the blanket again, pulling it up and snuggling against him, laying her head on his shoulder, and pulling his arm over her. The feel of him was so reassuring. "I'm really happy to be around people again, it feels more normal, but it reminds me of *my* people." Her words trailed off.

"And they're all gone now," Asher offered. Adina nodded against his chest. He stroked her hair. "I'm sorry that you lost people you cared about."

Adina kissed his chest. "It's alright. It wasn't your fault." She felt odd. Now that they were talking about it, why didn't she feel more? Loss or anger? She missed them, and her heart ached. But the terrible loss; what felt like it should have been there -- wasn't.

"Is something wrong with me? Or does the inoculant… I don't know… lessen what you feel?"

Asher craned his head so he could see her eyes. "Why would you say there was something wrong with you?" He held her eyes. "There is *nothing* wrong with you, Adina." His tone was firm, certain, assuring. He kissed her hair, adjusting his other arm further under his head to prop it up. "And no, the inoculant shouldn't affect your emotions. At least not that I've ever heard of."

Adina tucked her hand up under her cheek, her fingers and palm just feeling the skin of his chest. "I feel like I should… I don't know. Be more upset. Most everyone I know, people I've known for years were killed, and I don't feel -- what I should."

Asher didn't say anything for a long time. Adina could tell he was thinking. "And what *should* you be feeling?"

"Sad, angry. I feel like I should be crying, or…" She shrugged. "I don't know."

He was quiet again, maybe waiting to see if she was going to continue. "Maybe you're not ready yet. Maybe it's too much." He ran his hand up and down her arm, then gave it a reassuring squeeze. "There's nothing wrong with you, Adina. I can't imagine what it would be like to lose everyone close to me. I don't know how anyone comes to terms with that."

There was a bang on the side of the bearcat. Asher gave her a kiss and rolled up to his feet then moved to the passenger door and looked out. He smiled in recognition. "Good morning, Nat."

Adina heard the young man's voice from the other side of the armor. "Priav wants to see you."

"Did you sleep at all?" Asher asked.

Adina could almost see the younger man shrug from outside. "People wanted to hear about you."

Asher snorted. "Alright, we'll be out in a few minutes."

--

Adina felt the eyes on them as they followed Nat. Most of the camp was just waking up, but there were a lot of people out. Adina got the impression it was because of them. A few who watched them seemed suspicious, but most of the expressions were curious. And they had an escort. Two children, Adina guessed about five and seven, followed them being led a boy who couldn't have been more than ten. He followed, tugging the seven-year-old boy along, who in turn tugged the five-year-old girl in a daisy chain. They looked like they might be siblings. All were wide-eyed, staring at Asher and barely sparing her a look.

They reached a largish open-sided, octagonal structure that might have been a communal meeting hall. Nat led them inside. At one end a small group of people gathered. And right at the center was Priav, along with a man who appeared to be about the same age.

Asher scanned the way the group sat and stood together, then leaned over. "I think this is the leadership council." He eyed Priav significantly. "And I think Priav is the headwoman of the camp, not just the caravan." He nodded to a few of the people behind her. "They were at the gate last night and took their cues from her. The big guy there is the guard captain, I think. The woman next to him, the shorter one, is in charge of camp operations."

Priav waved them to her, simultaneously shooing Nat out. Nat herded the children with him as he went, their little faces turned back even as he pushed them ahead of him. Priav stood up and waited for them to reach her. Once they got close, Priav extended a hand toward Asher, then her, introducing them. "This is Asher, the one I spoke of as being like a Myrmidon, and Adina.

She is a…" She turned a conspiratorial eye to her. "Shoemaker." Then she turned to the old man at her left. "This is my husband, Rafi."

Adina was taken aback. Somehow, she'd imagined Priav to be the fiercely independent old woman, not beholden to any man. A husband hadn't fit into her expectations.

The old man stood up, the movement strong and smooth for his apparent age. And when he reached out with a long cane, Adina realized he was blind. She hadn't been able to see his eyes clearly in the dimness and angled light, but they were clouded. He stepped confidently to where Asher was, the cane stopping expertly against Asher's boot.

"Priav says good things about you, Asher. Others have too." He held up his hands and gestured to Asher's face. "If you don't mind. It is the only way for me to know what you look like."

"Of course."

Rafi stepped close and lightly brought a hand down on the top of Asher's head as if to find a point of reference. "You are tall," the old man said approvingly. Rafi carefully worked his hands down over the sides of Asher's face, feeling his features. "What color are your eyes, Myrmidon?" Rafi asked with a smile. Priav and he obviously shared enjoyment of the word.

"Dark blue."

Rafi nodded. "Unusually dark blue from what Priav tells me. And what color are your hair and beard?" His hands followed the edges of Asher's beard as if making a mental map.

"Gray, or white, depending on who you ask." The corner of Adina's mouth crinkled at the patient look in Asher's eyes as he submitted to the inspection.

Rafi's hands traveled onto Asher's neck, feeling the scars there, then onto his coat and armored shoulders. "You're a big fella, aren't you?"

At that, Asher laughed and smiled. "So, I've been told."

Rafi laughed with him; it was an open, unabashed sort of thing.

And there it was again. The same sense of fearlessness that she'd sensed from Priav.

"I imagine so." Rafi grabbed Asher's shoulders firmly and squeezed, giving him a bit of a shake as if to see how solid he was. "You are everything Priav has said you are." Rafi cocked his head. "And much more than you appear, she also says." Then he turned confidently to her, extending a hand, one still on Asher's shoulder, apparently for spatial reference. "If it is alright with you, Adina?"

She looked at Asher, then nodded. "Sure."

Rafi stepped to her. Again, the confidence in the way he moved made him seem almost sighted.

"How long have you been blind?" she asked. "You don't move like anyone I've ever met who is blind."

Rafi reached up again and found the top of her head. "Most of my life. I lost my sight when I was a young man." He smiled, his hands following her hair to get a sense of how long it was. "As you can see, that was a long time ago." His hands lightly touched the sides of her head and felt her ears. "And what color are your eyes, Adina."

"Hazel."

He felt her eyebrows, following them onto her cheekbones, then her temples, her nose. "You are pretty." His head cocked slightly. "And your eyes have some of the same blue that Asher's do?"

Adina glanced at Asher. "Yes. And a little green.

It's… from the accident we had."

Rafi straightened his head, his expression easy. "It doesn't take sight to see the lie in that." There was no accusation in it. He felt her chin and back along her jaw. "Your secrets are yours to keep." He felt her neck, collarbones and out onto her shoulders. "And my wife says your hair is dark?"

"Black," Adina replied.

Rafi nodded and again squeezed her shoulders and gave her a bit of a shake. A grin wrinkled a corner of his mouth. He nodded back toward Priav. "I can see why she was so disappointed that you can't have children. You are quite lovely." Like Priav, he put a palm gently on her cheek for a moment, then turned and walked confidently back to his seat.

As Adina watched him take his place again, she couldn't help but feel there was something… regal about the two of them. So self-possessed, unflinching, open and honest, utterly unafraid.

Rafi nodded to Priav.

Priav pointed to a pair of chairs. "Please, sit."

After they did, she extended a hand as if to indicate the whole camp, then to the others in the group. "You have done us a service we can't repay and asked nothing in return." She inclined her head to Adina. "Because you said it was the right thing to do." She turned her attention to Asher. "We bargained with you for help to get us home, but you helped us hunt, spending your resources and then gave away most of what you took." Priav turned her palms upward and opened her fingers in a gesture of giving something to the air, then set her hands in her lap again. "We have agreed that you are welcome here to trade, resupply from our stores within reason, stay and rest for as long as you like."

"And should you wish," Rafi added, cocking his head to the rest of the group as if listening for any sound of dissent. "We would be glad for you to join our community." He waited for several seconds, listening.

Hearing nothing from the others, he smiled knowingly and turned back to them fully. "Although we know you will not. A Myrmidon must always return to the nest." He placed his hand lightly on Priav's and she wrapped her fingers around his. "And we respect that. We all must be what we are. But you will always be welcome here." He lifted his hand with Priav's in it. "Thank you for returning my wife to me and so many others who would have met terrible fates had you not intervened."

Priav gestured to one of the men behind her, then smiled at Adina. "I said I would have to find an appropriate gift to repay you." The man hefted a large roll and brought it forward. Adina blushed furiously.

Priav was smiling, her eyes twinkling as the man set the rolled mattress between she and Asher. "I think you will find this a comfort."

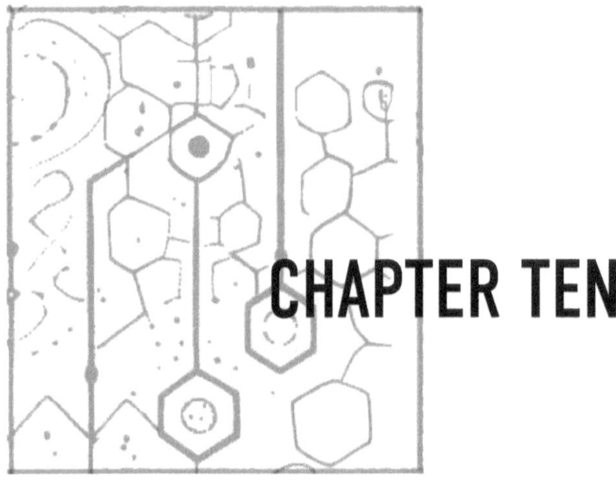

CHAPTER TEN

Adina kicked hard, holding her breath trying to reach the bottom as she swam down into the Quarry's clear water. Her loose pants and sleeveless shirt flowed around her as she passed through the boundary between the sun warmed upper layer of water into the colder water below. The sharp, squeezing pain in her ears that had stopped her from going deeper on her three previous attempts disappeared when she pinched her nose and blew out the way Asher had shown her. The relief was amazing. She *would* reach the bottom this time… Adina kicked harder; feeling the pressure build as the previously unattainable sandy bottom loomed closer. She pinched her nose and blew another two times before she was finally able to reach down and grab a handful of sand in a victorious fist. Hovering there, she smiled. Adina's dark hair flowed around her, and she felt the sand push through her fingers as Asher's words rang in her ears. "You can do it, Adina. I know you can."

Adina equalized her ears again and squinted, looking for her target, opening her fist and releasing the sand into a little cloud. The heavy, squarish, brick-sized stone with a piece of cloth tied around it sat on its side a few yards away. The long cloth streamer waved lazily in the

Quarry's subtle current. The cloth had been red on the surface, but here on the bottom, the changed light turned it black. She swam to it and blew out enough air to let herself sink, touching down and feeling the sand crunch between her toes. Her head ached a little from the pressure, but she couldn't help the giant smile that split her face. Adina looked up, grinning at the way the bubbles zigzagged toward the surface. It looked so far away, but it wasn't frightening. It was an all-new thrill that rushed through her as she stood there and took in the strangely beautiful, blue-hued world around her. Adina had never been in deep water like this before. She picked up the rock and kicked to the edge of the cut stone ramp she stood on. Beyond the edge, the quarry plunged down more than two hundred feet below.

The water's so clear!

Adina's lungs burned with the demand to breathe. She pushed off the bottom. The pressure on her ears and sinuses lessened as she rose. She passed through the thermocline again into the warmer water and relaxed letting her buoyancy pull her toward the surface like she was being born upward by her exhilaration.

It was so quiet -- *peaceful.*

All she could hear was her own heartbeat and the sounds her body made as the pressure changed, things she would have never heard on the surface. Dully, further away she could make out sounds from the surface and metallic clunks through the water, but if she didn't think about them, they faded away, leaving just her and her heartbeat.

Adina could see legs and bodies at the surface. The faces of the half dozen children who had become she and Asher's constant companions now peered down as she glided up in the silence. Devon's twelve-year-old son Nat was there, treading water with his face down. He waved at her. Adina broke the surface to the children squealing and cheering in delight. She held up the stone, kick-turning toward the edge where Asher sat, the sun once again gleaming against his scarred, tattooed chest.

The gray-white stone of the edge was a nearly a perfect match to his hair and beard, the stone's gray veins and striations catching the same tones and highlights in the bright sunlight. He was nearly dry from his own dive, wearing pants he'd traded for and then cut off into shorts. They were *ugly;* a dreadful mishmash patchwork of brightly colored pieces stitched together. At least as shorts there was less of them to see. He applauded, then repeated what had been going on since before Adina had done her first dive. He put his hand carefully under a little girl's rear end and launched her upward, off the stone and into the water. She squealed in ecstatic joy as she hit the water.

Asher hollered over the splashing and hollering children around them. "How did it feel this time?"

Nat climbed out of the water a little way from Asher and helped a smaller boy up onto the rocky edge.

"Better!" Adina panted, side stroking to the edge, then put the rock up on the side. She grabbed Asher's arm, and he hauled her up out of the water. She turned and dropped her soaking backside onto the hot stone, water running off her onto the sunbaked white stone.

The boy ran up next to Asher for his turn to be thrown out into the water. Asher pointed away from them. "Later, alright?"

The child looked crestfallen, and Nat stepped close, water streaming off him, his expression entreating. "He was really wanting to have another chance."

Asher smiled at the little boy and then called loudly to all the children. "Last one, alright! We have work to do!" He put his hand under the little boy's butt. "Ready?"

The boy all but jumped in place with excitement, nodding. Nat grinned and hurled himself into the water, then popped up watching. Asher launched the boy high, the child flailing in the air and shrieking with joy before hitting the water. Nat was there a moment later pulling the boy to the surface, smiling widely.

Behind them, Adina could hear a gaggle of women, some of whose children were part of their new retinue. But there were others as well, both men and women whose only reason was obvious in the way they watched she and Asher. Devon wasn't there, she had work of some kind.

Adina wrung her long black hair and pushed it back, the water making a wide puddle. "It didn't hurt this time." She inhaled deeply to catch her breath, her shirt clinging to her. She'd worn two shirts for their swimming excursion. Wearing only one was about the same as wearing no shirt at all once it was wet. Normally, she didn't think about it. She wasn't immodest, there wasn't a lot of privacy in camps for the most part. People had bodies, and sometimes other people saw them. But they were both getting a lot more sexual interest since they'd arrived at the quarry than she was used to. And with the looks came echoes of the conflict that had erupted between her camp and the other when she was sixteen.

"Pinching my nose really helped."

Asher nodded and smiled, his lapis blue eyes on hers. "That's over forty feet down, Adina. You may not know it, but what you did is really hard. Most people can't do that. Not without a lot of training." He bent and gave her a kiss.

Adina kissed him back, aware of the eyes on them, grinning. "And it's fun!" She shivered once hard. "But wow, it's cold once you get down there!" She appreciated the sun beating down on them in that moment in a way she rarely did.

He nodded again. "That's the thermocline I was talking about. Colder water is heavier. If there isn't sufficient current or another force to stir it up, it just sits down there like a block."

"You can really feel it when you pass through it. I never thought it would be so clear."

Asher started drawing on the dry stone with a wet finger. It was a square sort of design. "Ramps run down the sides of the Quarry." He drew two long rectangles inside the square, one along its bottom, the other on the right side. "They used them to move heavy equipment around and get the stone out. The ramps give us an opportunity to do controlled dives." He looked at her. "It's not likely we'll ever have to do dives like this, but diving puts different stresses on the body. That's good. And swimming is great for you."

Adina knew how to swim but was flatly shocked by how easily Asher moved through the water. Then again, she'd only ever swum in relatively small bodies of water, never vast ones like this. She'd been amazed when Priav showed them the Quarry and instantly understood why they wanted to build a permanent settlement here.

The Quarry was full of fish and there were even fresh-water clams. Shallow areas around the perimeter were thick with reeds and grasses that were home to ducks and other birds. The water was clean and clear, being fed into the deep pit from underwater springs.

Adina could see right to the bottom in some places. The rusting remains of pumps and other equipment still lurked in the depths; vague, dark shapes visible from the surface. The metallic clunks she'd heard under the water were the sounds of work being done to clear the machinery. A dismounted vehicle engine, drive train and axle were being used as a winch with a makeshift crane arm to haul up the sunken wreckage. According to Priav, one of the young men was able to hold their breath long enough that they could reach the bottom on a weight.

Then they hooked the crane to things or filled baskets with debris before returning to the surface. And others were training to do the same. Adina couldn't imagine how frightening and exhilarating working in the cold dimness down there had to be.

Rafi said there were entrances down at the bottom of the Quarry that led into mines beneath. No one had any idea of how deep they might go, or what might be hidden down there. Priav told them they planned to completely clear the old machinery from the Quarry and build something called fish warrens that would increase fish productivity. Large garden beds were being prepared with silt and mud dredged from the Quarry and surrounding ponds. With all the fish and birds, they had fertilizer. And there were plans to chisel out channels to divert water from the Quarry for irrigation. For now, they were using a pully and weight system to pump water into the beds.

Adina had never been to a community that sat next to a lake like this. It was amazing. Especially considering the camp had only been established four months ago.

Rafi said it would be the following year before they would know if the gardens would work.

The other thing about the Quarry was that it was *beautiful*. The white stone; limestone, Rafi called it, shone brightly, stained dark orangy-red in patches. Asher said that was from iron deposits. And the water was blue-blue-blue, ranging from light, clear turquoise, almost the color of the sky, to intense clear blue, then plunging to deepest blue, almost black, depending on how the light caught it. There were secondary, smaller pits around the perimeter of the bluff, where the water was the color of jade. Something about sediments, Rafi said. They reminded Adina of the pools in the rift.

The main pit was an enormous, a roughly trapezoid shape. Its longest side was where the stone bluff was, opposite the camp. That side was almost a quarter of a mile long. The white bluff itself was over two hundred feet high in places, splashed red brown from iron. From the bluff to the camp was more than four hundred feet. And the side of the Quarry where the camp lay was five hundred feet long.

Asher seemed to be thoroughly enjoying himself, just relaxing.

"What's the city of haze?" Adina asked, squinting at him against the bright sun. "And what was it Priav was saying about lights in the sky?"

Asher raked his short hair back with burly fingers. Adina couldn't help but admire the way the sun gleamed off the raised markings of his scars and the smooth curve of his strong shoulders.

"There are stories about a city far in the west. Some say it's a ruin, others say it's large and advanced. It's all rumors right now. No one has ever found it." He nodded toward the rest of the camp. "Except maybe Priav. We've been trying to find it for years. If it is a ruin, it could be a treasure trove of information that we might be able to use to help recover the world. If it's a living city and it's advanced." He just looked at her and raised an eyebrow. "Who knows what it could mean."

"And the lights in the sky?"

He shrugged. "Since no one's ever seemed to actually *see* it; it's always second hand 'my brothers third wife's cousin said…' that sort of thing. It's hard to say. But the stories are consistent, 'lights in the sky,' or 'a glow on the horizon.' That could be good, or bad. If it's a living city, then obviously that's good. But if it's a ruin, the glow could be from radiation. That would be bad."

"Radiation would mean everyone's dead, right?"

Asher nodded and let his head fall back, seeming to just be reveling in the sun beating down on him. He was all but dry now. "They should be by now. Radiation doesn't necessarily kill people immediately. It can take years for the effects to destroy the body. But it only ends one way." He turned his head and squinted at her. "But you're going to be better protected from it than most people. The inoculant helps protect us. We don't hold onto radiation the way most people do." He grinned at her and leaned close. "It's nothing you have to worry about. If we can see it, we're staying away from it."

Adina bent and gave him a kiss. This time the children squealed and made rude noises at their display.

"Nobody asked your opinion!" Asher called after finishing the kiss, playfully kicking water at the closest children.

Adina turned to the crunch of feet approaching and shaded her eyes. A big man, over six feet tall and broad shouldered with the kind of belly that spoke of heavy muscles underneath stopped a few feet away. His dark, unruly hair was loosely braided back. Omar was the captain of the guard. His eyes surveyed the scene from under thick, dark eyebrows. He grinned lopsidedly. A large scar that cleft the right side of his face clearly hadn't healed properly so he had a droop on that side of his face. But he was a pleasant enough, tough-demeanored fighter in his forties.

"Priav and Rafi want to see you." He eyed the children. "I can put them to work if they're bothering you." He eyed Nat in particular crossing his burly arms. "Aren't you supposed to be helping sort scrap metal for the wall?"

"I helped this morning." Nat tread water, squinting at Omar. "They said to come back tonight."

Omar grunted, seeming unconvinced by Nat's answer. Adina could see the big man's deep affection in the good-natured smirk that lifted the good side of his mouth.

Asher squinted at the children. They became still and quiet, treading water and staring at Omar as he cast his baleful gaze over them. Asher shook his head, smirking at their wide-eyed awe of the scarred, good-natured warrior. "No, they're just being kids." He rolled his head back around to Omar again. "We'll get changed and head over."

Omar nodded. "I'll let them know." He turned and left, eyeing Nat as he went.

Asher pushed to his feet and held out a hand to help her up. "Well, maybe now we can get some answers."

Adina was surprised by how casual he'd been about getting the information from Priav. He seemed to just be relaxing. They passed the gaggle of people that were apparently only there to stare at Asher. He nodded to them as they passed.

"You like it here," he said as he pulled her against him.

Adina nodded and tucked up against him, recognizing the clear signal he was sending to anyone watching. "It's nice to be around people again. It feels more… normal."

He nodded. "I'm glad. We're going to be on our own for a long time, so take advantage of it while we're here." He gave her a kiss on the hair.

"When are we leaving?"

"Maybe tomorrow?" he answered noncommittally. "We've got a lot of ground to cover, and depending on what Priav says, a long way to travel. If she's seen this landmark only once as old as she is, it's either a long way away, or in a place people just don't go."

Adina nodded. "That soon?" She looked up at him. "I can tell you like it here too." She ran a hand over his chest. "You've been so relaxed since the hunt. It's like you're a completely different person." She kissed his shoulder. "I like this different you."

"We'll see what Priav says. But we need to get moving." He gave her an understanding look. "I still have a job to do."

Adina squeezed him. "I know that. But a few days here aren't going to wreck things, especially if you've been looking for this place for so long. A few days certainly won't make that much of a difference."

He looked down at her. "We'll see."

__

"What are you even doing out here?" Asher asked from his place across the table from Priav and Rafi.

They'd been through the hellos and pleasantries and Asher's relaxed demeanor had quickly faded. There was no furrow between his eyebrows, but his energy had changed. His tone wasn't interrogation, it was more good-natured curiosity. But it was so… *pointed* compared to how he'd been since they'd gotten into camp. Adina already missed the relaxed Asher; smiling and launching children into the water at the edge of the quarry. "There isn't supposed to be anyone out in these areas."

Priav half-snorted, half-huffed at him, one of her eyebrows coming up. "In case you hadn't noticed, there's lots of empty space out here." She gestured widely with an arm. "Even you myrmidons scurrying around in your fancy trucks can't cover it all."

Priav's clay red skin shone clean and bright now. She wasn't caked with road dust anymore. Without that coating of dust, Adina could see her hair was almost uniformly grey, silver in places, a cascade of braids and dreadlocks around her narrow, burnt red-brown shoulders. She wore a different, lighter homespun sleeveless tunic. Like the faded one she had been wearing when they first met, it was red orange, as if designed to be a shade off her own skin color. It was held against her narrow frame by the same wide, charm-festooned belt which had been divested of the travel pouches that had weighed it down before. Clean, dark blue, narrow-legged trousers covered her to her moccasin-like shoes.

Asher nodded. "Fair enough. But you have to understand, you are the first people, or even evidence of living people, we've ever found out here. Up to now we haven't found so much as the remains of camps. Now I suddenly find not just you, but an established raider presence. To say it was a surprise is an understatement."

Rafi watched where Asher's voice came from, his whitened eyes searching from the dark complexion of his face as if they still had sight. "Nine months ago, we crossed into the western wastes. We wanted to find someplace new, far from the established trade routes, raiders, static camps, and villages that seemed to come and go at the whims of the winds. We wanted someplace we could build, start something new."

Priav picked up for him. "The last thing we expected was to meet the Ghost Eyes. Raiders are scavengers, they need others to prey on. We thought that being so far out, there would be no raiders." She flicked her eyes between them. "We were wrong."

"It was chance that brought us here." Rafi tapped the table with a finger. "One of our scouts followed a flock of birds, hoping to find their water source. They led us here. But once we found it, we knew this was what was meant to be."

"Until the Ghost Eyes find you," Asher countered.

Priav and Rafi went quiet. Adina could feel the tension in that silence, thick and caustic, eating away at them.

Priav took a deep breath seeming to breathe in acceptance with the air. "We have avoided them up to now and have been able to keep them from following us back here."

Adina remembered the winding, confusing, circuitous route they'd used to mask their path back. But a talented scout might be able to follow that trail.

Asher completed the thought for her. "But every time you venture out there's a risk they will find you." He nodded over his shoulder as if to the camp at large. "And then all of this will be theirs."

Rafi's normally peaceful expression closed up, his jaw cabling as Adina watched. "We will fight to keep our home. This is the best chance we've ever had for something… better."

Adina saw Asher's attention shift to Rafi. Asher gauged Rafi's expression, then turned back to Priav. Her expression was as firm and certain as ever, but there was also something else there. To Adina, it looked like acceptance. They would fight, but according to Priav's expression, she didn't believe they would win.

"We will not give up what we've found," she finally replied. We have our solar generators up now, so we can power all of our vehicles, we're getting the wall built." She shrugged. "We can't know what's going to happen in the future. We can only go from where we are now."

Asher sat back and crossed his arms. There was a long, lingering silence.

"I can't help you fight the Ghost Eyes," he finally stated. "That isn't why we're out here."

Rafi nodded. His quiet, sagely manner had returned.

"We understand that," Priav replied. "We are not asking you to. We have an agreement for what you have *already* done for us."

Adina could feel the pull to and fro inside Asher. It was clear from the way his fingers clenched and unclenched his crossed arm, out of view of Priav and Rafi. Part of him clearly wanted to help them. But she could hear the argument in his head without having to ask. *They aren't our mission,* part of him was saying.

"I promised to tell you about the city of haze, the black pillars, and the glow in the sky. I was just a girl when we found it, but I remember it as clearly as if it was yesterday." She breathed out, as if her child's view of the world from so long ago was filling her up. "Unforgettable."

Asher listened intently as Priav recounted the story of how her caravan had found the black pillars and seen the glow of the city in the distance.

Adina had never heard anything like it; a caravan venturing widely, exploring deep into dangerous and unexplored lands, throwing all safety to the winds. The caravans Adina grew up in after her home settlement was destroyed depended on mobility for survival, never stopping for long. The attack that brought she and Asher together only reinforced what Adina had known; they'd stayed in the same place for too long. But what Priav was talking about sounded like suicide. No established water sources, no guaranteed game, even as sparse as it was at times, no ability to grow crops, or any of a dozen other reasonable assurances. It was mad beyond belief.

"And you never created settlements? Anything like this?" Adina gestured around them.

"It was just the way we lived," Priav answered with a shrug. She turned her old, brown eyes to her. "Did you ever question why you lived in walled towns?" Priav turned back to Asher. "That's when we saw the Pillars."

She narrowed her eyes at Asher and pointed a finger at him. "That's why I said it was a landmark you can't miss!" She waved her hand as if denoting the passage of time. "Those will be there in a thousand years, or ten thousand. There was a glow on the horizon. It came and went. Some nights it was bright, others dim. Beyond the Sea of Sand. And one time… only *once*." Priav raised a wizened finger. "The haze appeared, and the towers of a city. But they were there, solid, real." Priav closed her fingers into a fist and shook it for emphasis. "It was no mirage."

Asher turned to Rafi. "You saw it too?"

Rafi turned his head and placed the chipped, ancient teacup in his fingers neatly in the center of the matching saucer with the certainty of long practice. "No. Priav saw it before we met."

"And where are these pillars?" Asher asked, folding his hands in his lap. "We've been all over the western wastes and have never seen anything like you describe."

"I've seen you use your sun instrument to navigate.

Can you navigate by the stars?" Priav asked.

Asher nodded. "Of course."

"It was a long time ago, but I remember some things because people talked about marking where it was." Priav got up and moved into the center of the space where the earth was bare. Asher followed her. She used her stick and drew a slightly canted trapezoid in the dirt. The top of the trapezoid was shorter than the bottom or the sides, then she drew a line down from the bottom right point of the trapezoid and tapped the end of it with the stick. "That is the center star you are looking for. It is not as bright as the rest of the stars in the crow." Asher turned his head to see the drawing from her angle, standing behind her. Adina joined them, staring at the scratched marks in the dirt. She'd seen people navigate by the stars and knew some of the constellations, but most of it was inscrutable to her.

Asher pointed right of the figure. "South is that way?" Then he pointed left. "And that's north?"

Priav nodded. "Yes." She drew a circle to the left. "That is the North Star." Then she drew a shape to the right of the trapezoid. "Higher above the crow to the south are the stars we called the chalice. She pointed to one of the stars. "That's the brightest star in the chalice." Then she held up her stick. "But the most important stars to help you find the crow… and to guide you to the pillars, are the stars we called the virgin -- to the north." Priav drew what looked like a headless stick figure lying at an angle, above and to the left of the stars of the crow. She pointed to the star that made up one of the 'feet' of the figure. "That's the Virgin's Ear. It's one of the brightest stars in that part of the sky." Priav canted her head looking at the figure. "I'm not sure why they called it the ear. It always seemed more like a foot to me." She shrugged, then after a moment of considering the image, pointed to the crow again. "The crow is below and between the virgin's ear in the north and the brightest star in the chalice in the south." She turned to Asher." Do you know these stars?"

Asher nodded, appearing to burn the image into his mind. Adina could sense him calculating. "Yes, I think I do."

He indicated the stick in Priav's hand. "Do you mind?"

Priav handed it to him.

Asher added lines to what Priav had drawn as the Virgin. "That's the constellation Virgo." He pointed to the 'legs' of the constellation. "Her legs are made up of these stars." He pointed to the star Priav called the ear. "According to star charts, that's Spica. It's called the ear because she's represented as holding an ear of wheat." Priav nodded, watching closely as he pointed to the crow. "That's the Corvus constellation. Corvus is another name for crow or raven." He pointed to the other significant star she indicated. "I don't know the name of that star. But you're right. It's very low on the horizon."

Priav made a noncommittal sound of acceptance, cocking her head to look at the patterns anew. "You need to find the place where these stars," she pointed. "Make a triangle in the sky. She held her hands up over her head, touching the tips of her index fingers and her thumbs creating a triangle. She angled it to the left as if aligning it with the stars in the night sky. "Find that, and you will find the pillars."

Adina could almost feel Asher soaking up the information like a sponge. He looked at the scratched outline and went to his bag. He took out a small notebook and pencil, copying what Priav had drawn. Priav looked at the paper and pencil enviously.

"Then what?" Asher asked, adjusting his drawing, and adding notes about the celestial positions.

"Then you wait."

Asher gave her a sidelong look as he finished up his notes. "And what are we waiting for?"

Priav canted her head a few degrees. "When you find the pillars, the city will probably be obscured. It was to us. It just appeared one day when we were there. When the sun was rising." Priav made a hand opening gesture like something coming into being from thin air. "It shimmered. The way heat haze does that makes things look closer or farther away. But when the light was right, we saw it. It was so clear -- like you could reach out and touch it."

Asher set his notebook and pencil on the table. "How long were you near it?"

"Several days, I think. I wasn't very big, but I remember there was a lot of talk about what to do. Everyone was excited. I remember the adults talking about whether we could go that direction."

As Adina listened, the thought of driving deep into the wastes based only on Priav's word, some vague star alignments, and how the sun interacted with a nefarious phenomenon felt crazy.

A few weeks ago, it would have felt like suicide.

A feeling, like a tickle, moved through Adina. It was a new, different, kind of excitement. The thrill of discovery surged through her; something she was a part of. She wasn't just a captive or passenger along for the ride. She was a *partner* in it. Adina took Asher's hand and watched his expression as he considered what Priav was saying.

He turned to her. "What is it?"

Adina couldn't help the grin that pulled up the side of her mouth. "Nothing. I'm just glad to be here."

Asher squeezed her hand, then turned his attention back to Priav, who was watching her with a twinkle in her old eyes. "How far along that bearing, Priav?"

Priav returned to her seat and took a long moment, her hand resting absent-mindedly on Rafi's, thinking. "It would have to be at least a month from here." She raised a gray eyebrow to Asher. "A lot of time and distance have passed since I saw that place. It could be forty or sixty days." She shrugged. "I can't say." She leaned forward again, putting her old forearms on her knees and pointing at him with the stick. "But if you find the pillars, where the stars align, you *will* find it, Myrmidon. If anyone could," she poked her stick at him again. "You will."

"That's a long way out there," Asher acknowledged with a nod, then raised an eyebrow to match Priav's. "For something that as far as we know is just empty desert.

No one has found even foundations of ruins beyond this point." He pointed west. "I don't think anyone's been out that far; not more than thirty days west."

"But there is a lot of empty space out there," Rafi reminded him, his blind eyes fixed on where Asher's voice had come from. Then he smiled, seeming to play off Priav's emotional state. "A lot of *unexplored* space."

Asher's expression shifted between what seemed like excitement at the challenge and resignation. He nodded. "Yeah…"

Priav sat up, peering at Asher with sudden matriarchal authority. "You supply yourself with whatever you need from our stores." She made a negative gesture, crossing her hand in front of her. "But it's not free." She pointed at him. "You have to return to us with the story of what you find." She narrowed an eye at him, and her eyebrow curved into a conspiratorial arch. "And you just have to return to us, Myrmidon." The affection in Priav's otherwise matronly tone pulled the side of Adina's mouth up and made her heart ache with its sound.

Asher stood up and inclined his head to her and Rafi.

Adina's heart heated up even further at the open and honest smile he gave them. "I would like that. But I can't make any promises."

"Bah!" Priav lifted the stick again and gave a good-natured, dismissive wave. "Promises-schmomises. I'm too old for promises from pretty men! Now go! And let us know when you are ready to leave."

__

"That's sixty to a hundred and twenty days out in the wastes," Adina said as they walked away from the communal structure. Her excitement about the exploration wrestled with anxiety about the far off, unexplored reaches. She'd heard the stories of the wastes since she was a child. Some were fantastical, others straightforward. But the common theme in them all was that the western wastes were a barren, hellish landscape of lethal radiation and toxins left after the wars.

Asher nodded, then turned to her, his eyes squinting against bright sunlight. "It will be a long run, but if we're careful, we should be fine." He watched her eyes. "Are you afraid?"

Adina shrugged, her chest tightening at his concerned gaze. "Of course, I'm afraid." But she smiled at the confidence in his lapis blue eyes. "But I'm also excited. I've never done anything like this before. It's so far out there without... Anything."

Asher's expression turned boyish again, his eyes twinkling with the same fierce joy she'd seen before the hunt. "Exactly."

Parts of Adina low in her stomach flip-flopped at that look. Everything below her navel suddenly squeezed and she was breathing fast. She pulled herself against his arm, her fingers running over his strong forearm as she pressed a suddenly hard nipple against his bicep. "I'll take promises from a pretty man." She put his hand on her ass and smiled, stepping in front of him and pressing against him.

"And what can I promise you right now?" he asked with a smirk, watching her eyes, his expression as gentle as it was aroused.

Adina took his hand and pulled him along the path, smiling back over her shoulder. "I'll show you." She marched them through the camp ignoring the people that stared on her mission to get him back to the bearcat.

Adina's back arched as Asher's mouth completely consumed her mound, his tongue playing inside her and up, running over her clit.

"Uhhh... Don't stop..." Adina moaned, her head thrown back, her legs spreading wide, pushing her bare mound against his tongue.

His hands slid up her body, over her breasts, cupping them and rolling her nipples, then up onto her arms, pushing them up over her head as he kissed up her stomach. "Don't stop what?" he asked playfully, holding her wrists together as his lips found her aching nipples.

Adina wiggled down, lifting her hips to press against the bulge in his ugly shorts. But he held her hands firmly together, one of his large strong hands easily encompassing her wrists. He took one of the packing straps from the shelf and wound it around her wrists.

Adina looked up at her hands as he pulled the strap tight. "What are you doing?" she asked breathlessly, her heart suddenly hammering in arousal as she tried to move her wrists. But they were firmly bound.

"Tying you up." Still holding her bound wrists, he kissed her rock-hard nipple again. Adina squirmed; the feeling almost overwhelming knowing she couldn't protect her sensitive nipples. "Is that alright?"

Adina felt the flow from between her legs, her body answering for her even if all she could get out was a breathless, "mhmm…" as she lifted her head and tried to kiss him.

Asher held her down, smiling mischievously and she turned her head to watch him fix the strap to one of the shelves. Then his mouth was on her neck again and worked its way down her body, lingering on her breasts and nipples, his fingers lightly playing along her armpits, and down her ribs.

Adina immediately squeaked, thrashing against his tickling and suckling on her nipples. "Nooo!!! No… tickling!" she begged, thrashing, her eyes shut, biting her lip. Her whole body felt out of control.

Asher's fingers stopped moving. "Are you sure?" He kissed her ribs on both sides and up onto her armpits, specifically not tickling her.

Adina's mind felt like it had slipped between gears, not into neutral but certainly not in any gear that worked. "I…." She leaned into his kisses as his fingers moved, just a little, the sensation sending her into whole body convulsions. "… don't know!"

Asher kept moving his fingers and his kisses, tickling her again. "If you want me to stop, you just have to tell me." The fingers of one hand were now trailing along the inside of her thigh.

"I don't know!"

She saw his wide grin and her legs were pushed open. She felt his mouth on her mound again. And he started tickling her in earnest, his fingers on her sides and armpits.

Adina's mind felt like it had fallen off a shelf and shattered under the sensory overload. She grabbed the strap around her wrist for something to hold onto. She cried out making nonsense noises as both 'yes' and 'no' tried to come out at the same time. Fire was roaring up inside her and she trembled, sweating from head to toe as Asher held her legs open with his forearms, his fingers on her defenseless sides.

"Please…." She panted. "Just… don't stop…"

He moved his mouth off her mound again, kissing her spasming stomach, his hands now holding her ribs, no longer tickling. "Don't stop what?" he asked, a devilish edge to his voice.

"Bastard!" She squirmed trying to get her aching mound back up to his mouth.

"Don't stop… this?" He plunged his tongue inside her and as he pulled back, sucked her swollen clit, his fingers lightly, mercilessly tickling her armpits and ribs.

Adina arched hard as all the tension in her belly tore loose is a fierce, fiery orgasmic spasm that threw her forward against the strap holding her wrists, her knees trying to clamp closed. Asher's strong forearms held her legs open as she struggled, her hot fluids pouring down between her legs. Adina kicked and fought as the orgasm seized her, overwhelming her senses. Her hips were bucking when she realized Asher was holding them. Then she felt him penetrate her. Adina was clamped so tightly in her orgasm that Asher forcing his penis into her was like him taking her the very first time all over again. Her whole body locked in a paralytic spasm as he pushed inside. Adina thrashed spasmodically as her cramping belly muscles unlocked, gripping him as he pumped into her.

Adina fought against the strap around her wrists helplessly as her hips rolled to meet his hard thrusts. She wanted to touch him, to pull him against her. She couldn't tell if she was still in the middle of her orgasm when Asher pushed her legs up high. As her feet bumped the shelf behind her, a new orgasm hit her like a freight train. Everything was spinning. She was dizzy and out of control, unable to escape him penetrating her. Adina's whole body quaked uncontrollably, tense as a spring.

Then everything inside felt like it shattered and collapsed inward. Adina screamed with the cataclysmic release of the new orgasm, convulsing in uncoordinated spasms. She was so lost in the whole-body overload that she barely felt him cum. She felt his hot semen pump deep into her and then his weight collapsed onto her.

Adina was lost in the aftermath of her orgasm for a few minutes, them both just breathing, spent. Her body felt like it had been drained of all its strength.

"I guess I'll have to tie you up more often," Asher panted, his hot breath against her neck. Adina felt him free her wrists, but she didn't have the strength to do more than pull her arms down as he rolled, pulling her against his side.

She barely had the strength to turn her head to kiss his hard, sweating muscled arm as her noodle arms flopped against his chest.

"Oh fuck…" she sighed into his shoulder. His skin tasted sweat salty and like the minerals in the Quarry waters. She took deep breaths between panting ones, his smell filling her nose. "I never… thought being tied up would be like that." She kissed his neck. "I think it's you.

Everything you do to me…" She took another sighing breath. "Does… *things* to me." Adina moaned as the muscles in her belly cramped for a moment then released again. She blew out a breath, pulling her knees up, feeling her muscles still twitching in confusion. "I think I'm broken."

__

The feeling of Asher kissing her wrists woke Adina with a smile as she lay with her head against his chest. Her wrists were still a little red from her struggling against the strap even after their nap.

Asher looked up from her wrists, watching her hazel eyes. He gave each wrist another kiss and then pulled them against him, putting her hands on his chest. "Why don't we stay a few more days?"

Adina grinned widely. "What?" She smiled at him, her heart jumping. "Are you sure?"

He smiled at her. "I have some ideas about the defenses that I want to share with Priav and Rafi." He bent and kissed her hair. "And I know how much you like it here." He heaved a huge breath, his chest lifting her head and shoulder. He looked up at the ceiling of the bearcat. "And you're right. Another day or two won't make a difference in the overall scheme of things."

Adina kissed his chest. "You like it here too," she chided. "Don't pretend like you don't." Adina shifted so she could see him more easily and rested her chin on his chest, her fingers tracing the large scar on his left side, feeling the bunched skin run under her touch. "But thank you. I do like it here."

He raised a corner of his mouth as his eyes settled on her again. "I like the way you are here too." Asher pushed sweaty hair from her face. "I like you happy."

Adina kissed his chest again and then laid her head on it. Nothing felt better than this. She closed her eyes, letting the feeling of his scarred skin and his strong fingers running through her hair pull her into sleep.

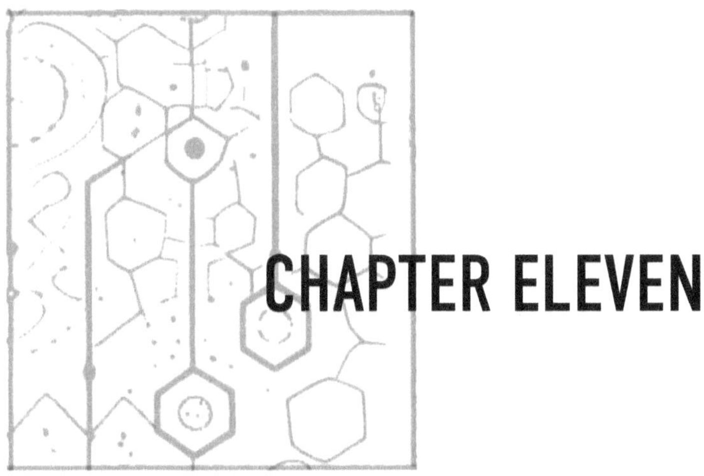

CHAPTER ELEVEN

It was *hot*, hotter than it had been since they got to the camp as Adina followed Asher along the side of the quarry toward the towering bluff. Priav, Rafi, Omar and a half dozen others trailed behind them. All Adina wanted to do was throw herself off the side of the quarry into the welcoming water as the heat blazed down on them.

Her eyes watered from the fierce sunlight reflecting off the white-gray limestone and water. She shielded her eyes feeling the sweat run down her back.

"You can either use limestone from the bluff or take it from the shallow areas of the Quarry," Asher was saying, pointing toward a particular rust-stained section of the bluff. "It will be slow, but you have all this stone just waiting to be used." He turned back shielding his eyes as he looked at Priav, Rafi, Omar and the others. "Even if you only use it to build a foundation for the wall, you are going to be ten times more defensible than you would be otherwise."

"That's a lot of manpower," Omar countered and several of the other council members nodded in agreement.

Asher nodded in return. "I understand that, but in the long run, it's a good investment. Since you aren't using people for farming right now, it seems like a good use for anyone that's strong and capable."

Priav's eyes were slits in the blazing sunlight. She stared at the bluff and then the water below them as they walked. She had put a blindfold on Rafi. Since he couldn't see, he had no instinct to squint against the blinding light. Priav pointed to the stone around them. "We'll have to make tools specifically for cutting stone."

They finally reached the bluff and Asher put a hand on the hot white wall. "You already harden tools. I might be able to give some advice on how to improve that a little." He made a scales gesture with his hands. "Maybe, maybe not. I don't know what you've got. You just may not have the components for a hardening compound. But even without that, people have been cutting limestone with everything from wood to copper for centuries." He squinted and looked back at Priav. "It just takes work."

Omar crossed his burly arms, squinting beneath his wide brimmed hat. "I like the idea of a stone wall, even a stone foundation to start with." He blew out a long breath. "But it is going to be a *lot* of work. And we'll have to use the same steel we would otherwise use for weapons to make tools." He let a deep rumble roll out from his belly. "But long term, it's the best option." He nodded his head back the way they'd come. "We're already cutting the walls to channel water. The more we do it, the better we'll get at it."

Rafi made his way to the bluff with Priav's help and put his hand on the stone, running his fingers and palm over the rough, white-gray surface, nodding. "We are not afraid of hard work. And this." He patted the stone. "Is ours, just waiting to be used. To help us make our home here a permanent one." Rafi held his hand against the stone for spatial reference and turned back to the group. "This is wise. But it is a challenge." He scanned the group again as if he was sighted. "We have chosen to be here." He patted the wall again. "With this, we prove our commitment." Rafi gestured toward where he'd heard Asher's voice. Asher walked to him and put Rafi's hand on him. Rafi gripped his shoulder firmly. "I think you may believe in us more than we do, Myrmidon."

Asher put a hand over Rafi's. "I'm not the one who wandered into the wastes to create something new, Rafi. I think your people have plenty of faith. I just want to see you succeed."

Adina's heart squeezed at the heartfelt expression on Asher's face as he stood there, holding the blind man's hand. *It's like he was made for this.* She suddenly had a hard time breathing.

"So then!" Priav pronounced loudly. "We become stone cutters!" It was a statement filled with resolve and certainty. She looked across the Quarry to the engine and drive train being used as a crane. "We have other scrapped vehicles that could, with some modification, be turned into large cutting machines, could they not?" She turned to one of the others with them.

The woman she was looking at cast her eyes across the glistening water and shrugged. "It won't be easy..." The woman stopped herself and looked back to Priav, then Rafi and Asher. She pulled herself upright as if casting off the doubt of her words. "We didn't come here for easy. Of course, we can do it."

"Good!" Priav called strongly. "Then it is settled."

One of the young men that Adina had seen on patrol near the wall suddenly raced up the quarry path to them, his cap and rifle gripped in his hands. He skidded to a halt, panting, his face dripping with sweat. "Nat's gone!" he blurted out to Priav and Omar between heaved breaths.

"What!?" Priav demanded.

The young man pointed to one side of the camp. "No one's seen him since he was helping at the wall last night! Devon's in a panic."

Adina's heart climbed into her throat as her mind filled with Nat's awestruck expression before the hunt, when he'd come around the front of the bearcat and saw Asher standing in the open door. The boy's excited, "Asher's going to hunt the boars with a SPEAR!" was suddenly in her ears again along with his happy laughter as he splashed in the quarry's waters.

Omar stepped to the young man who couldn't have been more than sixteen or eighteen and put a thick hand on his shoulder. "Slow down. Tell me what happened, Teppi."

The young man nodded and took a breath. "Devon came to the gate a little while ago; said she'd been looking for him since first light. We started searching. Just figured he'd wandered off somewhere." He pointed again. "I think there's tracks leading away from camp. Looks like somebody might have been dragging something."

Adina's heart dropped into the pit of her stomach, fear and concern churning up inside her.

"You show us where," Asher suddenly said. The commanding rumble in his voice brought everyone's heads around to him. The open, hopeful expression that had been there seconds before had evaporated and the canyon deep furrow between his eyebrows was back. "Show us where you saw the tracks."

CHAPTER TWELVE

Adina climbed onto the top of the bearcat where Asher was scanning the horizon with binoculars. He looked like a black clad statue silhouetted against the burning bright landscape and blue sky.

"Anything?"

Asher dropped his hands but continued to stare out across the dusty, empty expanse. "Nothing." His voice was hollow, and Adina could feel the suppressed fear and pain beneath it as she stepped next to him. He didn't turn to her. His face was a hard, chiseled mask of controlled concern as he glared out over the sun blasted landscape. His expression had barely changed since they'd left the camp to search for Nat two days ago.

An hour after Teppi had found them at the bluff, they'd discovered the abandoned camp in a ravine half a mile from the quarry. It was empty save for the remains of a small fire and tire tracks heading west. It had taken Priav interceding before Omar agreed that they were the best choice to go after Nat. If Nat had been taken by the Ghost Eyes, the camp would need every available body to defend it if they attacked.

Omar's fury still rang in Adina's ears, barely checked when he'd clamped Asher's arm and leaned close. "Find him Myrmidon." The intensity in Omar's eyes burned in Adina's mind. "And punish the ones who took him."

Adina wrapped a hand around Asher's leather clad sleeve. "We'll find him."

Asher finally turned his eyes to her. They were so hard it hurt Adina's heart. The severe cut of his short white hair and beard, normally so handsome, now only intensified the harshness of his demeanor. He'd been so different at the quarry. And now he was different again. Angrier, locked down -- like a machine. He just watched her eyes, then put a hand gently on her cheek. "I hope so. But you need to be prepared. Even if we do find him." He looked in the direction they had been heading. "It could be bad."

Adina kissed his dusty sleeve. "But we're going to find him. No matter what," she told him with absolute certainty. He didn't look back at her and she could hear his emotion in the way he swallowed hard. He nodded.

Adina hadn't realized how fond Asher was of Nat until the boy went missing. It might have just been that Nat was a child. The image of Asher's joyous face as he played with the children at the water's edge was a bitter irony compared to the harshness of his expression now. But Asher's reaction had been so sudden and extreme. He was genuinely fond of Nat.

He'd barely talked to her since they'd left.

Adina tugged on his arm to try and get him to look at her. When he didn't, she reached up and put a hand on his cheek and turned his face to hers.

"Please don't shut me out, Asher." Adina watched his eyes. "I can feel how upset you are. But we're in this together." She leaned up and gave him a kiss. Then just watched his eyes. "Alright?"

He swallowed again and nodded. "We should get moving. They have at least a whole night's head start on us." He climbed down into the cupola leaving her standing alone on top of the bearcat staring out across the sun scorched plains.

They drove for another day, and it was fully dark when Adina turned to him from the passenger seat. "We need to stop, Asher." She leaned across the console and put a hand on his arm. We haven't stopped to rest in three days."

The only sleep they'd gotten was napping in the passenger seat as the other person drove and she could barely move from exhaustion. "We need to stop and rest." She pointed out the windows. "You're not going to see anything in this."

Adina wasn't sure exactly what he was following. She couldn't see a thing. But Asher seemed certain. Every now and then they stopped and he got out, looking at some clue or standing and gazing into the distance at some other inscrutable sign.

Asher didn't answer her. She squeezed his arm, more insistently. "We need to sleep -- real sleep, if only for a few hours." He didn't look at her, but the bearcat slowed. His head sagged and he nodded in agreement.

Adina's heart twisted at the anguished gesture. Of everything she'd seen of his many emotional states up to now, this was new. She stepped around the console and wrapped her arms around him, leaning her head against his. "Shhh... It's alright." Tears rolled from her eyes, her heart feeling like it wanted to tear itself from her chest.

Asher put a hand on her arm and squeezed. "He's just a kid."

Adina kissed his hair and pulled herself tightly against him. "I know."

They settled down on the mattress, Asher's heavy, armored coat hanging from one of the shelves. Adina's head rose and fell with his breathing, and she pulled herself tightly to him, everything inside her was a confused tumult of fear for Nat, anxiety, and helplessness. She kissed Asher's chest and climbed on top of him.

Her lapis and green flecked hazel eyes watched his as her long dark hair streamed over one shoulder in her loose ponytail. Adina ran her hands across his strong chest, leaned down and put her lips on his. It was like kissing a stone at first as she lightly laid her lips on his. Then she kissed him with more urgency and his hands moved, his arms wrapping around her. He kissed her back and she put her hands on the sides of his face, her elbows on his chest, stroking his white bearded cheeks.

"I love you, Asher." Adina whispered it, kissing him more and caressing his cheeks. "I love how strong you are." She stopped and watched his eyes. "And how much you care." The more Adina kissed him, the more the heat low in her abdomen grew.

Asher took hold of her shirt and tugged it up, not hard, but insistently. Adina sat up and let him pull her shirt off over her head, holding her arms up and displaying herself for him. As he set her shirt aside, Adina took his hands and put them on her breasts. He cupped them, squeezing gently, his fingers playing over her nipples. The thrill that ran through Adina arched her back, pressing her breasts into his hands.

"Ohhh… yes, Asher."

Part of Adina wanted to find a way to help ease his pain, but another part simply missed his hands on her. Since they'd met, this was the longest they'd gone without having sex and her body ached for him.

Adina pulled his shirt up and as soon as it was off, kissed his chest. He pushed her upright, his mouth finding her breasts, sucking each nipple. She hissed at the feel of his tongue and lips on her hard, sensitive buds.

Her breath caught and her legs clenched closed a little as the smoldering ache inside her blew into sudden flames. He pulled her long, dark hair out of the ponytail so it fell loosely around her shoulders and ran a hand over her hair and where it lay over her breasts. Adina's breath came fast as she reached down and opened his pants, then slid her hand inside and wrapped her fingers around his hard penis.

"Ohhh... yes..." Adina whispered.

Adina hung onto the shelf with one hand, her head thrown back, breathing hard, the tail of Asher's coat brushing her face as he thrust into her from behind. She was on her knees on the mattress, lost in the ecstatic sensation of him inside her. The ache of her wanting him had turned to building tension. Adina groaned at him filling her so completely. She could feel every sensation as he slowly pushed in and then withdrew, their lovemaking slow and intense.

"It's so deep!" she moaned, already so tight inside, each push of his cock a thrill that drove her closer and closer to the edge as she pushed back against it. Her other hand was on his, holding it firmly, his thumb pushed into her ass. Adina bit her lip, her hips rolling as everything inside her stomach clenched. She gripped his hand hard, feeling her nails on his skin, squeezing her eyes shut.

"Keep going! Just like that!"

He kept his movements rhythmic and certain, and the slow build was tormenting. Adina's legs shook, and her hand on the shelf failed. She fell face down onto the mattress, clinging to his hand, her other hand grasping at the shelf with no coordination as he continued the inexorable, slow driving rhythm. The sudden, sharp pleasure pain of her body giving way made her yelp as her orgasm tore through her. Her feet kicked in uncontrolled spasms, everything inside her feeling like it was clenched around his cock. Even as her body shuddered and bucked, he held her tightly, his thumb still in her ass, driving into her, pushing her through her orgasm. Her whole body locked, and she felt the sudden flood down her legs. Everything was spinning.

Adina was twitching and trembling helplessly, sagged onto the mattress when she felt him pull out of her. A relaxed moan rose up from somewhere deep inside her. "I've missed you," she panted into the mattress.

Asher wrapped an arm around her, and the strong arm pulled her easily against him. Adina turned and settled her head on his chest, luxuriating in how relaxed she felt after her shaking orgasm.

Once her breathing had slowed, Asher carefully rolled her onto her back and got between her legs, looking down at her. His expression had softened, but the crease between his eyebrows was still there. She ran a hand over his scarred, tattooed chest as he pushed his cock along her labia and clit, making her twitch all over again. Adina smiled, watching him watch her, arching her back and rolling her hips to meet his movement. He stroked strands of her long dark hair out of her face, then bent and kissed her. It was a long, gentle thing.

Adina wrapped her arms around his neck and her legs around his back pulling herself up against him, smashing her breasts against his chest. "I want you so bad," she whispered in his ear.

Asher started gently, but their lovemaking quickly grew into violent, animalistic mating. Adina was streaming with sweat, her body arching and collapsing, nothing but a rag doll in his powerful arms as he mercilessly drove his phallus into her. He only rested for a moment after his first climax before rolling her onto all fours and taking her again. Adina was so exhausted, she'd come over and over, thrown into fits of primal ecstasy by his wildness, taking what he wanted from her as she moaned and cried, her body responding instinctively.

She'd felt his hot rush of semen a third time before he finally collapsed down on top of her, sweat soaked and panting. Adina had no idea how many times she'd cum or if she'd just been in a constant ebb and flow of one for… however long it had been.

Adina didn't care. She just lay there feeling him on top of her, both of them heaving in ecstatic exhaustion.

Asher finally rolled off her and pulled her against his chest again. Adina watched his belly rise and fall as he caught his breath. She was *sore*. She had to let her breathing calm again before she could say anything. She kissed his chest, tasting his salty sweat again.

"Are you alright?" Adina asked between deep breaths. "You've never… done anything like that to me before." She glanced up at his face.

He nodded, still breathing hard as he rolled his head to kiss her sweat matted hair. He turned lapis blue eyes to hers. "I didn't hurt you, did I?"

Adina shook her head and kissed his chest again. "No. You've just never been that way before." A shadow seemed to pass over his expression. She set her chin on his chest, holding his eyes firmly. "You did *not* hurt me, Asher. I'm fine." Adina raised an eyebrow at him and kissed his chest playfully again to ease what felt like sudden tension. "I'm going to be sore… I'm already sore. And I'm going to walk funny," she grinned. "But you didn't hurt me." She slid up and took his face between her hands kissing him deeply. He drew her onto his sweaty chest returning her kisses. Adina pulled back and watched his expression. "You're never going to hurt me, Asher." She ran a hand over a stubbly side of his head, taking in his white hair, the curve of his beard. She ran a finger lightly over his lips. "I've never been able to say that about anyone else in my life." She kissed him again. "That's why I love you."

Adina grimaced at a sudden muscle spasm in her stomach, dropping her head against his chest and laughing. "But I think I need a break!"

—

Hours later, Adina was still having aches from their intense sex. She just grinned when it happened. It brought her right back to the feelings and his amazing expression of release when he finished the last time. It was only in looking back that she realized how amazing it was. She was too caught in the sensations of the moment to understand what was happening. A blush suddenly ran up her neck as she thought about being so completely lost in it. Adina was watching the unending sameness, images of their hard sex running through her mind when a long vertical line drew her attention. She sat up and turned in the passenger seat, squinting. Thoughts of she and Asher faded. It wasn't a dust devil. It was too dark. Adina grabbed the binoculars.

"What do you see?" Asher asked from the driver's seat.

Adina pointed. "What's that? Is that smoke?"

The bearcat rolled to a stop and Asher looked across her. "Yeah, it sure looks like it." He climbed out of the driver's seat and pushed hanging things out of the way to pull the big sniper rifle from its storage place, then climbed up the ladder to the top of the bearcat. As Adina put her head up through the cupola, Asher was on his belly on the top of the truck. "Stay low. We don't know what they might be able to see. We already stick up pretty high." Adina laid down next to him looking through the binoculars as he popped out the bipod on the rifle and looked down the large scope.

It was a streamer of smoke, but it looked like it was a long way away. In the glaring sun it was hard to tell. It came and went in the heat shimmers.

"Yeah, that's smoke," Asher confirmed, watching carefully. "But it's a long way away -- miles." His cheek was laying against the rifle stock as he glanced away from the scope to get a good look around, then looked through the scope again. "With the heat haze it's hard to tell how far it is." Asher got up on his knees and folded the bipod closed, snapping the covers over the scope. "But that's got to be it, a camp of some kind. That much smoke isn't from just a few people." He settled onto his knees. "Now we just need to figure out how to approach it."

Adina stared at the smoke through the binoculars. She'd envisioned catching up to the single vehicle. The idea they would encounter a whole camp hadn't crossed her mind. She rolled to look up at him. "What are we going to do?"

Asher let out a long breath, watching the streamer for a moment before answering. "I don't know yet. We need to see what we're dealing with." He looked down at her. "But no matter what, we're in for a fight. Do you feel ready for that?"

Adina's heart climbed into her throat. The feeling of rough cord being tied around her wrists was suddenly there again, raw, and terrifying. The pain of the punches, the kicks in the stomach, being dragged when she couldn't breathe, when she could barely stand. And their leering eyes, their laughter...

Suddenly Nat was in her mind's eye. His small wrists red and raw from the rough cord. He was so small compared to them as they punched, kicked, laughed and leered at him. The image clattered against the memory of him at the edge of the Quarry; so joyous as he helped the little girl out of the water.

And another kind of heat suddenly blossomed in Adina.

Not again...

Adina's teeth clamped together so hard it made her head hurt. She nodded at Asher, unsure if she could get words out past the sudden fierce emotions. She swallowed the lump in her throat. "We're..." Adina ground her teeth together and looked straight into his eyes, swallowing again. "We're going to get him home."

Asher nodded, watching her intense expression.

CHAPTER THIRTEEN

The camp was much further away than Adina had imagined. It took them more than three hours of cautious driving to reach a place where they could safely see it and remain hidden. The sun was just setting as she and Asher crawled up to the top of a rocky hill. They'd left the bearcat in a low depression not far away. As soon as Adina pushed her head up enough to see the camp, a spasm of fear jabbed her in the chest and her heartbeat suddenly thundered in her ears. The camp was *much* larger than she'd expected.

There were the typical shade shelters, just cloth strung up between poles, or over shoddy structures. But there were also rows of metal cages with dozens of people in them. And half a dozen vehicles were parked around the camp's perimeter.

Adina whispered fiercely. "I thought you said there was no one out here!"

Asher shook his head, carefully bringing the sniper rifle up. "Well, there aren't supposed to be!" He settled the big rifle, scanning the camp through the scope. "Priav and Rafi were right. There's a lot of empty space out here. We must have just missed whatever is out here on our patrols." He was quiet for a moment, observing the camp half a mile away. "It isn't surprising, I guess. We like to think we're more efficient than this. Obviously, we're not."

Adina searched the camp through the binoculars, but they were too far away for her to see any real details. "Can you see Nat?"

"No, we're too far away. But those are Ghost Eyes, that's certain." He pointed to a tattered banner flying and other rotting hangings that showed two stylized white eyes within a pair of joined circles, like figure eights laid on their side.

"There has to be a large community or communities somewhere nearby for there to be that many prisoners."

Adina tried to get an idea of how many people were packed into the cages. "How many Ghost Eyes do you think are down there?"

"Based on vehicles, I'm guessing no more than twenty." He pointed to what looked like a structure. "That's two large vehicles with shades thrown over them." He slid away from the rifle stock and held it so she could look through the much more powerful scope. "Probably some kind of flatbeds that those cages are carried on." Asher scanned the camp with the binoculars. "This looks like some kind of satellite camp. Those cages had to be built somewhere and they had to be brought out here. This is part of a much bigger operation."

As Adina scanned the cages through the rifle scope, she couldn't count the people in them. "There have to be fifty or sixty people in those cages." She counted raiders. "I only count eight Ghost Eyes down there."

Asher took the rifle back, assessing the camp. "I counted ten, the rest are probably inside the tents." He blew out a breath. Adina couldn't tell if it was frustration or resignation. "This is a *much* bigger fight than we're geared for. If we can figure out where Nat is, we can probably sneak in and grab him."

"What about all the people in those cages?"

Asher made a growling sort of noise in his throat.

"Yeah, I thought you were going to ask…" He looked at her, lowering the rifle stock to the dirt. "Freeing those people means having to fight every raider down there." He nodded toward the camp. "That's a *lot* of fighting. Even if we could do it and not get killed, it means using a lot of resources -- *bullets* that we can't necessarily replace."

Adina acknowledged him with a nod of her own.

The thought of fighting an unknown number of Ghost Eyes was terrifying. But the dagger stabbed her in the heart again as she imagined Nat, tied, bruised, and left to their mercy. "One of those Ghost Eyes took Nat. That means they know where the Quarry is."

Asher blew out another breath, his expression turning hard. Adina could feel the decision he'd made in his expression as he watched her eyes. He turned back to watch the camp through the scope. "We need to wait until everyone is asleep and grab one of their sentries."

It was pitch dark, the sky a blanket of stars beyond the brightness of the half-moon as Adina crept behind Asher following him into the camp. They'd been able to move the bearcat to within fifty yards of the camp by running only on the batteries and carefully maneuvering along the bottom of a gully. They'd spent long, tense hours waiting for the camp's activity to quiet. Adina felt the cold of the night air as she followed Asher's black silhouette under the cloudless sky. But the feeling didn't penetrate the adrenaline heat coursing through her. At this range the stench of the camp was overwhelming.

Adina kept swallowing bile as the stink of unwashed bodies, the open sewer smell of human waste and other odors engulfed her.

From their hidden place they couldn't see much of the slave cages. If Nat was there, they couldn't see him.

Asher was in his helmet and mask again and Adina wore her makeshift equivalent as they settled next to a draped awning that hid them from the rest of the camp.

Asher turned to her and whispered just loudly enough to be heard through his mask. "Are you sure you want to do this?"

Adina's heart was hammering, and she was having to consciously take slower breaths. She just nodded and adjusted her grip on Asher's small, secondary pistol with the silencer on it. Asher had taught her how a silencer worked, but she hadn't trained with it.

"It's going to make it barrel heavy and throw off your accuracy," he'd told her, making sure she took time to get used to the unbalanced weight. "Only use it if you have to. And you'll want to be close." He was carrying his short semiautomatic rifle, also silenced, but had it slung, leaving his hands free.

As they'd watched the camp, he'd pointed out the sentry's patterns. There were only four on watch, three on the perimeter and one that wandered through it, specifically checking the slave cages. The plan was to grab that sentry and learn about the rest of the camp from him.

Asher moved from the shadows, quietly sliding around the awning. Like everything else about him, Adina was surprised how quietly he moved for such a big man. They slipped from one shadow to another along the back of some of the slave cages. The slaves were asleep or remained unmoving as they quietly passed.

Suddenly the flap of a tent a few yards away was pulled open. Asher pushed them back into the shadows, the length of thick cord he intended to use to capture the sentry held between his hands. A tall Ghost Eye stepped out of the tent, silhouetted by the lantern from inside.

Adina could hear snores from the other side of the fabric of the tent they were backed up against.

The white paint around the raider's eyes made him look wide-eyed and insane. He was tall, not as tall as Asher, nor as broad. But his scars and the rough, ugly tattoos on his arms and chest were intimidating. Light colored body paint was smeared across his torso to look like ribs. He stretched and approached the slave cages.

The Ghost Eye looked into the cages, eyeing the slaves inside, then stopped. He took out a set of keys. The slaves in the cage and those adjacent to it were instantly awake. Their anguished sound was awful as they reacted to him unlocking the cage, a mix of pitiful moans, crying and fearful pleading.

The Ghost Eye pulled the cage open and stepped inside, grabbing a young woman in a dirty dress. She shrieked and fought, the other slaves cowering in fear. Adina felt Asher's hand on her and turned to him.

His eyes were intense behind the lenses of his mask. He held up his hand and whispered, "Wait."

The young woman was Adina's age. As she struggled against the much larger raider's hands, everything inside Adina was suddenly tumbling. The feeling of rough cord wrapped around her wrists was there again. Adina shuddered at the memory of the raider's hands pawing her.

A voice suddenly rang out from one of the adjacent cages. A black woman threw herself against the bars. "Takin' a girl 'cause you're afraid anyone else would laugh at your tiny little limp dick!?" The woman barked fiercely. Even filthy in the stinking cage, she was ferocious. She pressed her face against the bars. "A tiny little limp dick dirt fucker," she taunted. "That's what you are! Can't get it up for a real woman, huh!?" She let out a harsh barking laugh. "You pathetic, clown painted, half man!" She snarled and threw herself at the bars, rattling the cage.

The snores on the other side of the cloth next to Adina stopped. There were grunts and complaints and she could hear bodies moving. Asher put his hand up again, mimicking shushing her, then pointed.

Adina followed his finger and saw eyes. A pair of wide, terrified eyes stared from inside one of the cages. Adina put a finger to where her lips were inside the mask, watching the slave. The slave stayed silent, but suddenly there were other faces turned to them.

She heard Asher's quiet, "Shit."

Adina listened carefully over the roar of her heartbeat for the sound of people getting up in the tent next to them as the Ghost Eye dragged the screaming girl from the cage. The girl kicked and fought, but he was so much bigger and stronger than she was. It was useless.

Adina heard a quiet hiss from the adjacent cage.

One of the slaves drew the fierce black woman's attention, pointing to she and Asher with her chin. Without turning her head, the black woman glanced in their direction. She watched them for a moment. The black woman's jaw cabled and her hands clenched into fists. She moved back from the bars to one side of the cage and squatted, watching them for only an instant longer then looked back to the Ghost Eye. The fierce black woman grabbed the other woman's face and turned it away from them to not give away their location.

The Ghost Eye closed the cage door and locked it. "Decided to have some fun, Bulla?" a voice asked from somewhere. Adina froze. The sound was from the opposite side of the tent. She heard boots on gravel.

"Shut the fuck up!" came from inside the tent. The black woman craned her neck and pointed in the direction the voice had come from. She raised a single finger indicating one person and mouthed the word 'sword' and put her hand on her left hip. She then made subtle pistol shape with her fingers and put them at her back where a belt would be.

"Don't make me come in there and crack your skull," the big Ghost Eye, Bulla snarled, lifting the thrashing girl, and dragging her toward a tent. She clawed at his face, but he just leaned back and pushed her hands out of the way. The sentry Ghost Eye appeared where the slave had pointed.

The sentry leered at the screaming girl. She was crying and pleading, beating uselessly at Bulla. "She'll be fun." He turned and smacked the cage with a long, thick stick he was carrying and pointed it at the black woman who was now huddled quietly with all the others. "I'm looking forward to seeing you chained for breeding, bitch!" The black woman didn't move, she just glared at him from the dimness inside the cage.

Anger that had been a quiet undercurrent in Adina suddenly ignited with a feeling like fire roaring up inside her, burning away her fear. She shifted her feet, readying herself. Asher shook his head 'no' and put his hand on her. "Wait until I take down the sentry," he whispered, then nodded to her belt. "Take him with the knife -- *quietly.*" Asher's eyes bored into hers, harsh and demanding.

Adina heard another grunt from inside the tent. Her heart felt like it was going to explode when Bulla disappeared into his tent with the girl. The girl started screaming again.

Asher kept his hand on her, holding her there, waiting, watching the sentry.

Adina felt tears of fury and anguish roll down her cheeks inside her mask. Her whole body was shaking as she drew her knife, straining against Asher's hand. She shoved the pistol with its long silencer into the back of her belt.

The sentry turned to the sounds of the struggle going on inside the tent. Asher gripped her arm to get her attention. "Wait until he's on the ground." Then he let her go and slipped along the back of the slave cage. He only paused for a moment at the end of the cage before lunging out. In a single fluid motion, he threw the cord over the sentry's head and drove his knee into the sentry's back. The sentry toppled back, and Asher dragged him into the shadows, twisting the cord tight around the sentry's throat. The sentry kicked and struggled unable to make any other sound; the noise of his kicking feet masked by the girl's screaming.

Hands reached out of the slave cage and grabbed the sentry, holding him fast, faces filled with rage and hate moving in and out of the shadows as the sentry fought.

Adina raced from the shadows, the knife gripped in her hand. She paused only long enough to peak past the tent flap where the Ghost Eye Bulla had disappeared with the girl and make sure no one else was there. The young woman was naked on her back on a filthy mattress, trying to cover herself, her torn dress thrown aside. The Ghost Eye was on his knees forcing her legs open.

Everything went foggy around Adina, except the girl's panicked, terrified expression and the Ghost Eye called Bulla. He was crystal clear, like a snapshot cut out from everything around him.

Adina lunged forward and planted her left foot outside his left leg, her other between his feet as she grabbed his forehead and pulled his head back hard against her chest. His eyes had barely registered she was there, staring into her mask when she drove the point of her knife into the side of his throat the way Asher had shown her, paralyzing his vocal cords. Adina glared into his eyes watching the panic register there before she slashed away from herself. Her blade cut veins, arteries and his windpipe in a single vicious motion, opening his neck completely from his spine forward.

The young woman screamed anew as the Ghost Eye's blood sprayed her naked body. Adina held him with grim strength born of her fury. He tried to rise but she pulled him back, her knee in his back and forced him back onto his knees. He clawed at his cut throat while the whistling, gurgling sound of his attempts to breathe were covered by the girl's screams. Adina watched the color drain from his face as the blood poured from his neck. It took only seconds for his arms to drop and his eyes to go static, staring at her. Adina stepped back, letting his body fall. Adina stared down at him, her bloody knife a strange artifact at the edge of her vision. She couldn't really feel it in her hand. She knelt and picked up the young woman's torn dress and handed it to her. The motion felt mechanical. The young woman's eyes were wide. She'd stopped screaming, staring from Adina to the corpse and back again in confusion and shock.

"Keep screaming," Adina instructed her quietly as she stood again. Adina's heart was still hammering, but now she was shot through with a strange sense of calm.

The young woman just stared at her. Adina drew her pistol with her other hand. "Scream to cover the noise."

The young woman looked at the pistol and through her fear, Adina saw understanding. The young woman began screaming again.

Adina knelt at the body and took his keys, then stepped out of the tent. Asher was trussing the unconscious sentry, whispering quietly to the slaves holding him. A million emotions seemed to crash through Adina in a confusing rush as she walked to him. She put the keys into one of the slave's hands and turned to the tent she and Asher had hidden against.

She quietly pushed the flap open. There were six Ghost Eyes sleeping inside. She stepped carefully between them, everything suddenly, utterly crystal clear. There was no fear. The pistol jumped in Adina's hand; the strange little pop of the silencer sounded odd, somehow unsatisfying as she put a bullet into each of their heads. The last raider roused, only a bit, enough to open his eyes and look at her before she shot him.

Adina stepped out of the tent and Asher was watching her. He glanced past her into the tent as the slaves opened their cage and passed the keys to the slaves in the next cage. The fierce, tall, dark-skinned woman appeared and looked from Asher to Adina, then to the bloody knife and pistol in Adina's hands. She didn't say a word. She just stepped past Adina into the tent and emerged a moment later carrying weapons from the Ghost Eyes.

Asher watched the woman hand weapons to other able-bodied slaves, then turned and watched Adina's eyes for a moment, registering the grim set of her mouth. "Alright then." He turned back to the black woman. "We're looking for a little boy. Twelve years old, dark hair. He should have arrived yesterday."

The woman shook her head. "I don't know. We don't see much."

Another of the slaves, a young woman, stepped to Adina. "Crida?" Adina pointed into the tent and leaned close, whispering. "She's alright. I stopped him before it happened. Keep her screaming to cover the noise. The young woman disappeared into the tent.

Asher looked at the tall black woman. "How many raiders?"

"Twenty or twenty-five." She crouched and led them toward the center of the camp. "This way." Adina heard the shuffle and scrape of many feet following them and the creak and groan of metal hinges as cages were opened.

The air around Adina was filled with hoarse shouts, the clatter of weapons and claps of gunfire. Many of the Ghost Eyes died in their sleep, completely unaware of what was happening. But now the whole camp was awake and a dozen slaves were with them, led by the fierce black woman. Slaves both freed and still in cages roared, their arms and bodies creating silhouettes in the light of burning structures as the fighting raged.

Adina was trying to see one of the Ghost Eyes who was tucked in against a vehicle when quick movement drew her attention. A vehicle suddenly appeared from behind a set of tents, accelerating away from the camp.

Adina pointed to where the man was. "He's right there!"

The tall black woman looked where she pointed, and Adina turned and sprinted for the bearcat. Faces of Ghost Eyes she'd killed before they had a chance to wake up swam in Adina's mind with those of fierce slaves, whose rage matched her own. When she turned back over her shoulder, the raider vehicle had disappeared into the darkness.

Adina slid down the embankment on a hip, ignoring the scrape of rough rocks and gravel through her pants, then clambered up into the bearcat. She could see the flashes where Asher and the slaves were fighting in her peripheral vision, but her attention was fixed on dust cloud left by the other vehicle.

She'd barely gotten the door closed before she threw the bearcat in motion, turning the heavy vehicle to climb up the gully's sloped side. She stomped on the accelerator and felt the wheels claw the parched, rocky soil as she roared up it. The bearcat came off the slope like a ramp, airborne for a moment, the engine howling as the wheels freed themselves from the ground. Then it slammed down hard, the impact nearly throwing her out of her seat. She jammed the accelerator to the floor again and the bearcat tore up the parched earth, hurling rocks and gravel skyward. Even if Adina couldn't see the raider vehicle, its dust cloud was easy to see in the dim moonlight. Adina plowed over one or the Ghost Eye's tents as she turned to follow it.

The helpless naked girl, screaming as the Ghost Eye was about to rape her filled Adina's mind. The remembered pain in her ribs from being kicked and punched were there again.

No more!

Adina pulled the lever on the central console as she broke onto open ground. The demonic howl of the air siren pitched high as she gained speed, matching the howl inside her. She threw a second lever. She heard and felt the loud metallic clang as the armored wheel covers came down.

Not again…

Adina caught a glimpse of the other vehicle. It was lighter and faster than the bearcat, opening distance away from her. She would never catch it. Adina slammed on the brakes and jumped out of the driver's seat. She grabbed the sniper rifle from its storage bay and hauled it up onto the bearcat's top. After the last time, she'd had Asher show her how to use it without hurting herself.

She laid down behind it and yanked back the bolt, chambering one of the huge rounds. She pulled it tightly against her shoulder and braced herself. Even with the rifle's optics she could barely make out the vehicle in the dust cloud and the darkness. Adina took a deep breath, slowly letting it out, every part of her feeling like it was reaching out through the scope. The raider appeared from the dust for an instant and the rifle went off as if someone else had squeezed the trigger. The recoil was a whole-body shock, and the concussion wave threw up a dust cloud from the top of the bearcat. But she knew how to absorb the blow this time. The raider vehicle veered, suddenly visible as it swung, struggling, dragging. Adina had no idea what she'd hit. It didn't matter.

She climbed back down and stowed the rifle, then leapt into the driver's seat again.

There was no way for them to get away now.

The air siren howled again as she tore through the dark after the wounded vehicle. It felt like only seconds passed before she heard the snap and ping of bullets ricocheting off the bearcat's thick skin. Two of the Ghost Eyes were hanging from the outside of the vehicle, firing at her. The vehicle turned, suddenly obscured by a thick dust cloud, made bright in the moonlight.

It's just like chasing the boars.

Adina controlled her skidding turn, following them. The bearcat bounced heavily over the hard ground, but its weight bit into the baked earth, helping her hold traction.

The Ghost Eyes hanging from the outside of the other vehicle were shouting to the driver, pointing urgently. The raider tried to turn tighter, but unlike her, the lighter vehicle lost traction, starting to skid.

Adina bore down on it watching the face of one of the raiders as he grew larger in the windshield. She watched his expression. His eyes went suddenly wide, an instant before she plowed into the right rear corner of the vehicle.

The crash threw her hard against the wheel. Adina watched the raider bounce off the front of the bearcat. He was there for a moment before being dragged underneath as the bearcat clawed partly on top of the other vehicle. The damaged vehicle spun away, scattering parts and debris in all directions. Adina turned and accelerated to put distance between her and the Ghost Eyes. When she turned back, she could see the spun-out vehicle through the dust cloud. Its whole right rear side was collapsed, and Ghost Eyes were struggling to get out of it. Adina stomped the accelerator to the floor again, staring at one of the raiders fighting to get out of the vehicle.

Adina watched his expression too, seeing it turn to panic in the instant before she drove, full speed, into the center of the truck. The raider truck all but exploded from the impact. Adina was thrown forward so hard that her face hit the top end of the large steering wheel and she tasted blood. There was an awful grind and screech of metal and the bearcat slowed, bogged down for an instant, then was free and she accelerated away again.

When she turned back again, the Ghost Eye vehicle was torn apart, pieces of it still tumbling across the dark desert.

And she could see one of the Ghost Eyes thrashing, on fire, trapped in the burning vehicle.

The girl screaming and fighting against her rapist filled her mind once more.

Not again…

Adina stopped the bearcat, grabbed her lighter hunting rifle, and climbed up into the cupola, just enough so she could see. One of the Ghost Eyes, it looked like a woman was limping away. Adina put the front sight blade of the rifle on the woman's back and pulled the trigger. Adina didn't feel the kick of the rifle. The woman pitched forward as Adina chambering another round, the motion as automatic as breathing. Another Ghost Eye was running, looking this way and that as if trying to find someplace to hide in the broad empty landscape. Adina's first shot took him low in the body. He fell, clawing over the hard earth, leaving a bloody trail. Adina climbed up further so she could get a clean shot.

And she killed him.

Adina climbed back down and drove in a careful circle around the burning wreckage to see who was left. When she stopped, Adina didn't bother with her rifle. Or the pistol with the silencer on it, or even her knife. She pulled the big wrench they used to secure the lugs of the wheels from its storage rack, letting the heavy head hang low as she approached the vehicle. One of the Ghost Eyes stared blankly, blood streaming from an open wound in his belly.

Adina cocked her head, just watching him for a moment. She kicked his obviously broken leg. "Look at me." The pain brought him around. He looked up at her. And Adina brought the heavy, three-foot wrench down on his skull before he had a chance to say anything. His blood sprayed across the lenses of her mask. Adina slammed the wrench down on him again and again.

Through the hiss and crackle of the burning wreckage Adina heard movement. She squatted down and looked around the edge of the vehicle. Another of the Ghost Eyes was stumbling away, a pistol in his hand. He fell face first into the hard, rocky ground.

"I see you!" Adina called.

He turned back and Adina could see the fear in his expression. The fear in the girl's face was there again. He fired. Adina ducked behind the vehicle hearing the hollow smack of bullets against metal, feeling the searing heat from the fire inside. When she peaked back around, he was squeezing the trigger, but the gun was empty.

The noise in Adina's mind and heart had gone suddenly, utterly quiet. And there was calm… Complete, crystalline, and perfect, as clear as the stars above her.

She stepped out with the gore covered wrench hanging from her hand.

The raider realized his gun was empty. He tried to stumble to his feet but fell again. One of his ankles was twisted at an odd angle.

"Haro sees all!" He howled at her. "He sees you!" He threw an arm out, spraying spittle. "He will come for you. Nothing can hide from him!"

Adina stared at the shrieking man in his body paint, scorched and bloody. It was all so… *abstract*, just patterns that moved in front of her.

"You can never defeat him! He speaks to the dead!" The raider spat at her, grimacing in agony.

"You think he speaks with the dead?" Adina stepped to him, glaring down at his mad expression. She didn't scream, she wasn't angry. She was beyond that now. "Now you'll know."

Adina brought the wrench down on his upraised arms. They weren't in the way after that. The image of the terrified girl filled Adina's mind, her helpless screams in Adina's ears as she brought the wrench down again. And again… and again. Adina kept pounding long after the raider stopped screaming. Until she couldn't lift her arms anymore.

Adina finally stumbled back and collapsed, heaving with exertion, the heavy wrench falling from her exhausted hands.

She suddenly couldn't breathe. She tore off her mask, the thick smell of the burning vehicle filling her nose as she retched hard, her belly cramping and pulling back into her spine. But nothing came up.

Adina wanted to throw up, to feel the physical assurance of casting out what she'd seen. But something inside robbed her of it. She dry-heaved until she lay on the hard ground, exhausted body, and soul, coughing and tasting dust with each breath.

Then the calm was suddenly gone. Agonizing, battering sobs crashed through her in a tempest of emotions too raw to process. The awful sound the wrench made when she brought it down on flesh and bone was everywhere, mixed with the girl's screams. The girl's wide-eyed terror twisted, becoming the raider's face as Adina crushed it with the weapon. Adina covered her face in her bloody hands and pulled herself into a fetal ball, trying to block out the awful sounds and images.

A scream ripped from Adina that felt like it might tear her soul from her body.

Adina screamed… and screamed… and screamed.

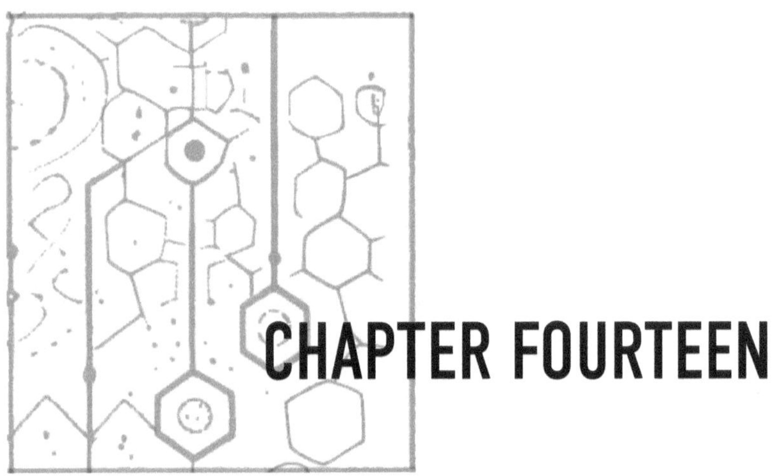

CHAPTER FOURTEEN

Adina rolled the bearcat to a stop on the outskirts of the slave camp. The brake pedal felt strangely heavy and hard under her foot as she stepped down to stop the big machine. Miles of dark, empty landscape sliding past the big truck's windows drifted through her mind. And there were the bearcat's tracks she'd followed to get back. Adina squinted, her eyes flicking between gauges in front of her as she tried to make sense of the muddy, undefined smear of events that were her trip back to camp. A glimmer was just starting on the horizon as she turned her attention to the abstract, sharp black silhouettes of tents and structures. More vague images of the trip back flicked by.

And then the terrified faces of the Ghost Eyes she'd killed were there again... everywhere she looked, wide-eyed, bloody, mangled faces stared back. She shifted the bearcat out of gear. It took what felt like all her strength to set the brakes. Idling there, she stared at the strangely orange light coming through the windshield. It painted bars in the dusty air of the interior.

The door was yanked open. Asher was suddenly there, pulling himself up the step to her level. "What were you thinking!" he snarled, his mask spattered with drying blood. Then he stopped. From the other side of the lenses, Adina watched his lapis blue eyes travel over her blood-stained clothes, sagging shoulders, and hollow-eyed expression. They moved to the passenger seat of the bearcat. Adina followed his gaze. The heavy wrench was propped there, the gory head resting on the seat, the long handle against the armored door.

"I…" Adina swallowed. She clutched the steering wheel trying to steady herself. The Ghost Eyes cries and howls of mad fury or agony mixed with the young woman's screams again. The moment one of them was going to rape her. The moment before Adina had plunged her knife into his neck. The body of the raider who'd been trapped in the burning car was there, arms thrown out of the vehicle's crushed window. Flames and smoke boiled around the corpse making him seem to move.

Adina felt like a poor puppeteer trying to make the unfamiliar marionette of her mouth work. "I killed them all."

Asher watched her for another moment, then pulled off his helmet and mask steadying himself in the open door. "It's alright." He reached across her, turned off the engine, then laid a gloved hand on her arm.

Even his touch felt strange, sort of *numb*. Adina didn't lean into him. She wanted to, but everything just felt so disconnected.

"You did the right thing." He held her arm for a moment, then pried her hands from the steering wheel. Her fingers snapped closed with the spasm of gripping it so tightly. He gently put her fists to her chest and enfolded her in his arms. "It's alright."

The light on the horizon had changed from a low line in the distance to a broad glow by the time a voice from outside pulled Asher's attention away. Adina couldn't make out who it was or what they'd said. It was just murky background noise. She felt Asher nod. He squeezed her tightly and descended a step, then stood and waited. When she finally turned to him, his eyes searched hers.

"We found Nat. He's here and he's okay."

Thoughts of Nat had fled completely from Adina's mind. Everything else had disappeared after the Ghost Eye Bulla had pulled the young woman screaming from the cage. Adina knew Asher's words were important, but they were lost in the fog holding everything hostage inside her. She nodded.

Asher watched her for another moment, then climbed down. Adina could see people moving in the camp, hear their voices, but they didn't seem connected to anything. When Asher reappeared at the foot of the step, Nat was clinging desperately to him. Asher looked at Nat's face and then pointed up.

"Look Nat, it's Adina."

Nat's little boy eyes were dark and haunted. His expression was terrible; bereft and vacant. His face was filthy, his dirty cheeks marked with long streaks from tears.

Pain like a hammer hit Adina in the chest when she saw the bright red chafe marks on his wrists. Everything inside Adina felt like it was suddenly breaking apart.

Asher boosted Nat up, then stepped up to steady him. "Do you want to hold onto him?" Asher ran a bloody, gloved hand over Nat's hair. "He's still pretty scared."

Adina pulled Nat into her arms. There hadn't been a thought. It was automatic, instinctive. And when Nat pressed himself against her, it was too much. Adina had no idea which of them started it, but they were both suddenly bawling. Nat clung to her desperately, shuddering with the force of his sobs. Adina felt Asher's eyes on them. After a moment, he stepped up so he could reach her and kissed her dirty, smoke-drenched hair.

Asher held his lips there. "I love you, Adina." The words she'd longed to hear him say were caught in the disconnected mist that seemed to shroud everything. She heard them, but they just didn't seem to touch her. He gave her another kiss, climbed down, and closed the door.

Adina blinked as the bright light of the sunrise seemed to suddenly stream in through the bearcat's windows. Maybe it was sudden; the sun just rising above the horizon, or maybe she only just noticed it. The sky looked like it was on fire, filled with glorious pinks, purples and oranges as the sun's warm rays fell across her.

And in the spreading sun, she could see people moving in groups outside. They appeared and disappeared like abstract phantoms between sunlit areas and long shadows.

Adina shaded her eyes. The fierce black woman who'd led the slaves in the fight was directing people, many of them working with purpose. Squinting against the brightness, Adina saw Asher. He was shepherding a group of slaves to one of the large shade structures.

And in one of the long, angular shadows, bodies were laid out in a row -- dead Ghost Eyes. Some were naked, others still clothed, everything useful stripped from them.

Nat had stopped crying. It was only when Adina noticed he'd stopped that she realized she'd stopped too. Seeing the work going on outside; something so familiar, so normal, the pain in Adina's chest eased like a muscle cramp letting go. A wave of calm rolled through her as she watched people go about the reassuringly simple tasks.

The intensity of Adina's rage, the fear and pain, all seemed to drain away, leaving her just feeling tired. Her hunched shoulders dropped, and she could finally take full breaths again.

Only now...

She looked into the rising sun, squinting against its brilliance, and taking in the colors that seemed so suddenly, shockingly bright.

Can't change what's happened. Don't know what will happen.

She looked down at Nat. He was still staring blankly into space.

There's only now.

Adina squeezed him and pointed to the sunrise. "It's pretty, isn't it?" It took her pointing a few more times before he turned and looked. He nodded mechanically. As she relaxed, she felt him relax too.

Adina squeezed Nat again. "There's work that needs to get done. Should we go and help?" Nat didn't say anything. He just clung to her. She shifted toward the door. "Okay, we're going to go help." Adina unlatched the door and looked down at him. "You're going to have to help me climb down, okay?" She canted her head to see his. "I'm not as strong as Asher. I can't climb down and carry you at the same time, okay?" Nat watched her eyes for a long moment, then finally released the death grip he'd had on her.

Adina caught up with Asher as he talked with the tall, fierce black woman. Nat was glued to her hip.

Asher's eyes traveled between them, then rested on hers for a moment before he gestured to the black woman. "Adina, this is Zara." Then he indicated her. "Zara, this is Adina." Zara looked her up and down with a hard, assessing gaze.

"You killed those men in the tent and then chased those others out into the desert by yourself last night." It wasn't a question, more an establishing of facts. Zara neither seemed impressed, nor disappointed. Her expression remained resolute and controlled. She pointed her chin out toward the wastes, her eyes never leaving Adina's face. "I hope you gave them the death they deserved."

Zara was taller than Adina, with intensely black skin and lighter brown eyes. Her hair was a mass of tight braids that must have taken hours to do at some point. They had gone toward dreadlocks from lack of maintenance, surrounding her face like a jet-black lion's mane. Zara's features were hard; deep creases under her cheekbones made her look even more severe. She might have been pretty if her expression wasn't cabled and carved the way it was. Zara's bare arms were muscular, but not big. She looked like a fighter but didn't have the battle scars Adina would have expected. Thin horizontal scarification lines just below her eyes stood out in the angled light with light-colored tattoos that curved across the dark skin of her arms and the right side of her neck. Adina had never seen such precise, light-colored tattoos before. Asher's tattoos were amazingly detailed, but the white tattoos against Zara's dark skin were striking.

Adina instinctively pulled herself up straighter at Zara's fierce, assessing gaze. She could see Asher watching their interaction out of the corner of her eye. "I did." Adina stuck out her hand. "I'm pleased to meet you, Zara."

Zara cocked her head. It was a hawkish sort of motion. Adina's impression was that Zara was used to people being cowed by her. Adina was done with being intimidated -- by anyone. Least of all someone whose life they had just saved. Zara watched her eyes, then took her hand. Zara's grip was firm, but there was no competition in the strength there. Zara nodded.

"And you."

"Ooh ooh!" a voice called in the way of a greeting and when Adina turned, she thought she was seeing some kind of psychedelic apparition. A tall, thin-framed man was approaching. He was wearing the most outrageous attire Adina could have imagined. It would have been striking anywhere, but with dead Ghost Eyes only a few yards away and surrounded by brutalized slaves, he looked like something that had fallen from another planet. Adina heard an unmistakably disdainful exhalation from Zara.

Asher turned to her again and gestured to the flamboyantly dressed man. "Adina this is Lew-Lew." He pointed from the astonishingly dressed man to her. "Lew-Lew, this is Adina."

The man flounced to her with the most unimaginable gait, crossing one foot in front of the other in a strange strut that made Adina's eyebrows climb up. Lew-Lew was as filthy as all the other slaves, but he walked like he was on a stage that no one else could see. He threw an arm up over his head, his wrist bent most decorously. "Here I am!" He was wearing what Adina could only think of as a tutu in an unnatural shade of pink with close fitting particolored trousers underneath it. He wore a vest in faded, and now torn bright yellow fabric with a short coat thrown over it. The coat was a shade of green that reminded Adina of warning signs for toxic chemicals.

And he was wearing makeup. There were dark circles around his eyes from where it had run and faded, and his cheeks were smeared with fading red. Adina had seen traveling storiers who were far less… *expressively* dressed. Seeing her obvious gawk, he stopped a few feet away and twirled. It was only then that she saw the gigantic, filthy blue bow that apparently tied the tutu around his waist. His pirouette finished; he threw his head to the side dramatically.

"Well, if you're going to stare darling, I thought I might as well give you the whole show!" He pointed skyward. "If they can't see how fabulous I am from orbit, why bother!"

Adina couldn't speak. She was so taken off guard by the wildly flamboyant man in the grim setting that she could only stare at him. Lew-Lew ignored her obvious derailment, stepped to Nat, and bent at the waist. "And how are you now? Feeling better?"

Adina looked from Lew-Lew to Nat and back again.

Asher pointed between them. "Lew-Lew was looking after Nat when we got here."

Nat still didn't say anything, but he nodded to Lew-Lew.

"Good!" Lew-Lew smiled and stood up, looking at Adina directly. "Have you recovered yet, Hun?" He stuck out his hand, once again with a most decorous bend in his wrist. "Say hi. You're just standing there."

Adina couldn't help the sudden grin that pulled her mouth wide. Lew-Lew was so… *unexpected* among everything else that it was the only expression her confused body seemed able to come up with. "You're… amazing," Adina stammered, taking his hand.

"Thank you, darling!" Lew-Lew cried effusively, putting his other hand on hers in an elegant gesture.

"What is it, Lew-Lew?" Zara demanded.

Lew-Lew threw his eyes skyward. "She's so gruff!" He let go of her hand, then turned to Zara and Asher. "We should have all the tentage we want down in the next two hours. We're separating usable scrap from what's not worth taking. It should be…" He made an elaborate gesture as if checking a pocket watch. "Three hours before we know what we have. And we have all the sick and injured under cover. Food and water are being distributed." He waved a hand. "We're not telling anyone what the food is of course." He turned and peered at Adina with a conspiratorial gaze. "They are hungry enough that it doesn't matter anyway. We are well stocked on water, at least ten days' worth without rationing."

Adina's head was spinning at the clash between how Lew-Lew looked and his certain and concise report about the goings on in the camp.

"We have thirteen vehicles," Lew-Lew continued. "One is being worked on. It may or may not be usable. We need to decide one way or the other in the next hour to give us time to strip what we can from it if we want to be gone by nightfall."

Lew-Lew flicked his eyes to Adina dramatically. "I know. I am so much more than just a pretty face!"

--

When Adina finally sat down in the open side door of the bearcat, the sun was halfway to its zenith. She took a long drink from her canteen. Nat wasn't physically attached to her anymore, but he was never more than a few feet away.

Everything in the camp was being stripped, even the slave cages were being broken down and loaded onto the remaining raider vehicles.

Asher approached the bearcat, Zara at his heel. "As soon as we've got everything useful loaded, we'll follow you," Zara announced, shading her eyes, and gesturing out into the desert.

Asher took the canteen Adina offered. "We need to get moving as soon as possible. We can't risk the Ghost Eyes finding us."

Adina offered Zara a separate water flask. Even though she and Asher had their masks off, they were still cautious about contamination.

Zara nodded a thank you and drank deeply. She handed the flask back and jerked her head out and away from the camp. "And you think these people at the Quarry will take us in?"

Asher shrugged. "I don't know. But if the Ghost Eyes razed your towns, what else are you going to do?"

Adina hadn't heard anything about where Zara and the rest had come from. It hadn't been a priority up to now. "You're taking them to the Quarry?"

Asher gave her a resigned nod. "Yes, the Quarry needs bodies. Zara and the rest of the survivors need someplace place to go." He turned back to Zara. "But I can't guarantee what they will say." He nodded to the slave cages that were being taken apart. "But if you bring them that much quality steel, it will certainly be an offer in your favor."

Zara's expression darkened. "And the injured?" She glanced back to the rest of the camp. "Some are too weak or wounded to make any kind of journey. But others… I don't know. They might survive."

Asher turned fully to her. His demeanor was sympathetic, even if the deep furrow between his eyebrows made him look severe. "That's your decision, Zara. I can't make it for you. The people in camp follow what you say. Whether you want it or not, that makes you their leader as far as I can tell. These are your people."

Zara's demeanor turned brusque and immediate. Adina had only known her for a few hours in an awful situation, but everything about Zara seemed hard. She wasn't someone Adina wanted to be on the wrong side of.

Zara blew out a breath. "I'll take care of it." She glanced at Asher. "You don't have anything that we could use to kill them painlessly, do you?"

Zara's all too direct statement felt like it knocked pins loose somewhere inside Adina. She knew as well as anyone that leaving people to die of dehydration, or worse, to be found by the Ghost Eyes would be cruel.

Ending their lives was the least cruel thing they could do. But Zara's directness was…. Unsettling.

Asher shook his head. "No, I wish we had something to help you. And we also can't spare bullets to help in that way either. I'm sorry, Zara." Asher's words were also direct. And while what they meant was harsh, unlike Zara, there was regret in his voice. Adina could feel his anguish, even if Zara couldn't.

Zara's hard features creased even deeper. "It is the wastes. We do what we have to." She turned back to the activity in the camp.

Nat pressed against Adina again and she put an arm around him. He hadn't said a word since Asher had put him into her arms in the bearcat.

Zara just watched the camp for a long moment and then walked away without another word. Asher settled down next to Adina on the step of the bearcat's open side door. He took another long drink from the canteen watching Zara's receding back. "I don't envy her." Then he turned to her. "Are you alright?"

Adina nodded and leaned against him. "I think so. I'm sorry I was so… out of it."

He put an arm around her and Nat, pulling them against him and gave her a kiss on the hair, then rested his cheek there. "It's alright. Last night was hard. You went through a lot."

Adina snuggled against him, feeling more herself. She relaxed more, reveling in the feeling of his security. "What are we going to do with them all? How many are there?" she finally asked, glancing at the work going on. Tents were being pulled down, shades rolled up, poles, posts and rigging being disassembled.

"Sixty give or take. It depends on how many Zara thinks can make the trip. We'll take them out in the desert, make it hard for our trail to be followed, maybe a day or two and make camp." He pushed her up so he could look her in the face. "Then you're going to take the bearcat back to the Quarry with Nat."

Adina's stomach crashed down inside her and she sat up fully. "What? Without you? What are you talking about?"

"I need to stay with them in case something happens." He glanced out at the camp again, speaking more quietly. "And make sure no one follows you." He indicated the camp with a sweeping point of his chin. "These people are desperate. We don't know what they might do. We can't risk them finding the Quarry until you talk to Priav and Rafi. They need to be ready if they are going to allow these people in."

"I can't talk on behalf of all these people!" Adina's heart was thumping madly in her chest again. "I wouldn't know where to start!"

Asher watched her eyes, his lapis eyes so assured. "Of course, you can. You know the situation here, Priav and Rafi trust you. I trust you." He nodded out into the camp. "These people need help -- a chance." He smiled and pushed a sweaty lock of hair out of her face. "And you can give it to them."

It was almost dark when the ragged caravan headed out into the wastes. Every vehicle was festooned with supplies and salvage. Several of them were so loaded that the passengers had to sit on top. As they pulled away, Adina looked back at the slave camp. It had only been a day since they'd first come upon it. And so much had happened since then. She'd killed her first person up close. With a knife. Then she'd killed a dozen more. The Adina that Asher had saved from the raiders was dead now too, as dead as the Ghost Eyes in the tent or strewn in the empty desert.

Adina tried not to think about the people who were left behind, or their friends. Zara had decided the swiftest, least cruel way to end their lives was by using guns taken from the Ghost Eyes. One bullet in each of their heads. The way she had killed the sleeping Ghost Eyes. But Zara's shots weren't silenced, and their sharp reports were surrounded by the cries of friends and families. Adina's heart felt like a rough piece of trail that had been driven over again and again. The rocks and stones had been driven deep. And some were left embedded that would fester for a long time.

But fifty-two people had survived, and they were moving now.

Hopefully out of danger at least. Maybe even to something better.

Adina tried to console herself with the good news, but it was hard. Lew-Lew had been cheering everyone on with seemingly limitless energy, cajoling and encouraging in equal measure, seeming immune to what was happening around him.

A huge dust cloud now followed them. The last vehicle in the caravan was dragging an assembly of pipes and chains that obscured their tracks as they wended this way and that doing everything they could to leave no trail for the Ghost Eyes to follow. They drove for hours into the night trying to put as much distance between themselves and the slave camp as possible before the sun came up. Nat sat in her lap, staring mute out into the darkness. Adina kept trying to get him to sleep, but he seemed immune; staring, saying nothing.

The moon was past its zenith, shining against the blanket of stars when Asher climbed the bearcat up an incline and stopped on top of the broad mesa.

"This is a pretty good spot, I think." He peered outside, then turned to her. "What do you think?"

The mesa was only one or two hundred feet taller than the surrounding desert but gave them a good vantage to watch the landscape around them. And there were large boulders and stones that would help hide the vehicle silhouettes.

Adina nodded. "Yeah, I think it's good." She turned and looked out the side window, scanning the wastes. "Probably the best we're going to find. Especially if they have to stay here for a few days."

Asher nodded. "Okay, I'll let everyone know." He moved the bearcat next to a large boulder. "Why don't you set up someplace for him to sleep." He leaned across the console and ran a hand over Nat's hair. "You're going to sleep in the bearcat with us tonight. Is that alright?"

Nat looked at him. Adina could see there was a spark of interest, but it was suffused under the blanket that seemed to lay over all his emotions.

--

It took more than an hour to get the caravan's vehicles settled and almost as long before Nat was finally asleep. He was exhausted but trying to calm him down enough for his exhaustion to overcome his anxiety took time. Now he was out, wrapped in a dirty blanket on top of piled tarps and canvas they'd salvaged from the camp.

Adina lay against Asher's side, leaning into the security of his strong arm. Each time she drifted toward sleep, dead Ghost Eyes were waiting, watching her. And when she opened her eyes, their ghostly white painted faces stared back at her from the shadows. Adina ran her fingers over Asher's scars, trying to forget the tactile memory of the wrench handle in her hands. But it was like she was wearing rough, sticky gloves that blunted the sensation of his skin.

Adina put her face against his neck. "I want you." She wasn't aroused yet but needed to feel him; his hard body against hers, inside her, to drive the images and sensations away. She stroked his cheek, pulling on his shoulder. As he turned to her, she pulled her shirt up over her head and wiggled out of her pants. He ran a hand over her naked hip and up her side. Everything inside Adina suddenly leapt into a tumult of confusion and arousal. The feeling that the dead Ghost Eyes were watching her set fire to a sudden, needy ache for him.

"Are you alrig…"

Adina kissed him. "Please."

When Asher pushed inside, Adina pulled herself hard against him, the storm inside her raging. She closed her eyes and bit her lip, holding back her body's desperate need to release. It was all she could do to wait until he was fully inside her before letting go. Her orgasm wasn't the violent, pitching, wild sort she so often had with him. It was a soul searing unleashing of tension. Adina grasped his back as everything inside her clamped onto his thick cock. She explored his scars with her fingers, but still could still only feel the rough, heavy handle of the wrench as she brought it down over and over on the Ghost Eye. She grasped at him trying to feel him. Adina started to cry.

"Adina?"

"Please…. Please don't stop," she begged, hooking her ankles around his strong hips, and pulling herself onto him, her body trembling as she wept, suddenly sweating. "I just want to feel you."

Adina clutched at him, biting him in frustration as the Ghost Eyes continued to watch her. "More," she begged and pushed on his shoulder to get him to roll onto his back. She kept her eyes closed, focusing on the feeling of him inside her and his hands on her as she plunged herself down onto his cock. The slapping of their bodies filled her ears and senses, his fingers or mouth on her breasts, rolling and sucking her nipples almost overwhelming as she rode him. But even as she panted, her belly trembling, she couldn't break the images. The Ghost Eyes were still there. "Get behind me." She grabbed the tin of boar grease and turned over, smearing the lubricant around the tight ring of her ass. Then she pushed back against his hardness. She guided his shaft over her vagina and up, until the head of his cock was against her slippery entrance. She pushed back.

"Are you sure?"

Adina didn't say anything, suddenly so aroused that all she could do was nod her head. Her breath caught as his penis pushed in, just a bit, her fingers reaching back and clawing at his hip. The pain was so exciting. He pulled back and ran his penis over her wet vagina again.

Everything was so slippery now as he played the head of his cock over her. She breathed, "Yes… Please…"

He pushed inside her again, the burning pain of him going deeper into her ass blasted everything else away. Her belly cramped with animal lust as she gripped the blanket. The feeling of the wrench in her hand was gone. All she could feel was her body stretching to accept him and pain that was so… Adina came again, hard this time, bucking and kicking. "Don't stop!" She bit the blankets, clawing at them as he pushed her down, his weight on her, plunging his penis further in. She filled her mouth with the blanket to stifle her screams. She reached down running her fingers over her hard, sensitive clit as he drove into her, pushing her hard into the mattress.

She could feel his arousal in the way he gripped her hips, making everything that much more intense as he pleasured himself on her. Adina pulled the blanket out of her mouth. "Fill me, Asher, I want to feel you cum!" She was close again, ready, but wanted to cum with him. She felt the whole length of him as he pulled back and filled her again, pounding fast and hard.

He stiffened and groaned. "I'm gonna cum!"

He rammed in deep, and Adina felt the hot explosion in her ass. And her body responded, thrashing, her legs kicking, held down helpless under him as he arched, pushing his cock in as far as he could. She was rigid for long seconds, trembling and frozen by the powerful orgasm before finally collapsing onto the blankets panting. A moment later his relaxed weight was on her, his breath on the back of her neck.

Asher's fingers lightly brushing her cheek brought Adina awake with a grin. She was tucked up against him under the blanket. It was still dark in the Bearcat. His fingers reminded her of how it had been after their first time together. The hot springs that felt like they were a lifetime ago.

"Are you alright?" he whispered in the darkness. She could feel his whiskers against her cheek.

She nodded. The faces of the dead Ghost Eyes were gone.

Adina woke to orange morning light streaming in through the bearcat's windows. She squinted and lifted her head. Asher's expression was relaxed. He was still asleep. Adina's heart thudded hard in her chest. He'd been so gentle with her last night -- so *careful* with her, even as their lovemaking turned hard... Adina's body suddenly remembered last night with a pang of pain.

She was sore; and in a way she'd never been before. She dropped her lips onto his chest, a grin pulling her cheeks wide as she remembered desperately grabbing at him behind her, biting the blanket as he filled her ass. And then her fiery orgasms. She kissed one of his scars, marveling at how the man she'd watched cut down Ghost Eyes with such relentless brutality and the man who'd been so gentle with her when she needed it most, both lived in the same body. Images of the fighting returned. Bodies moving, just silhouettes in the darkness, screams and... He knew what *she* was capable of. He'd seen it and had still been so gentle... "I love you." Adina kissed him. "I love you."

He opened his eyes and watched hers in the golden light. A corner of his mouth came up. But he didn't say anything. He just watched hers as if there was nothing else in the world. A red trail on his chest drew her eyes. It led to a red bite mark. Adina's eyes went wide.

"Did I do that?"

Asher glanced down and smirked. "You were very... *enthusiastic,* last night."

Adina covered her mouth with both hands, her eyes shifting from the bite mark to his face and back again.

His smirk forced a tickle in her belly, and she started to giggle. "Stop looking at me that way!"

His smirk widened, making his cheek dimple. "What way?"

Adina couldn't help the laugh that rolled up as she gingerly inspected the wound. It looked like she'd scraped the top layer of skin off, it wasn't deep. She grabbed the canteen and carefully wiped the blood away. "I was... I don't know -- scared, I think. I've never done anything like... that; what I did to the Ghost Eyes... before." He nodded, just listening. The scrape was already healing. Adina wiped away the blood, then met his eyes. "Thank you for being so gentle last night." She gave him a soft kiss.

He smiled back at her, taking the damp cloth and pointing at her chest. There was a streak of his dried blood. He wiped it away, drawing the cloth lightly over her skin. "One of us had to be." He smirked again and kissed her nipple. It sent electric shocks through her, and she hissed in arousal. Then he sat up. "Hold that thought." He slid a hand over her suddenly aching mound. "We have work to do." He closed his hand, squeezing and she curled around it, a lusty groan escaping. He grinned, watching her expression then let go and pulled on his shirt. "Let's go."

Adina narrowed her eyes at his playful expression, her body suddenly on fire again. "Bastard."

–

Hours had passed as Adina and Asher finalized the details of the plan with Zara, Lew-Lew and the other survivors. The rest of the camp was busy setting things up for their stay while Asher helped Adina prepare the bearcat for her solo journey.

Asher was working on something under the passenger side console, then rested his head on his burly bicep, just watching her. "You look very pretty this morning."

The simple statement couldn't have had more impact if he'd hit her over the head with the huge wrench which now sat clean in its normal bracket. Adina's face felt like it caught fire, then her chest, and other places she didn't want to think too much about for fear of being entirely derailed from the task ahead. She just grinned. The expression felt stupid, uncoordinated. Her facial muscles seemed as distracted as the rest of her by his all too tight undershirt.

"Uh, thanks." Adina pushed a strand of long, dark hair behind her ear. "You too. Not pretty… I mean…" she stammered and sucked in a breath. "You look… handsome…"

His eyes narrowed playfully, and his cheek dimpled again as he smiled. He pushed up, putting his face close to hers. "I had fun last night too." He gave her a kiss and when he leaned back, his expression was more serious, only slightly, but it was a sharp contrast to the moment before. "I was worried." He ran fingers over her temple and cheek.

Adina leaned into his hand, took it and kissed his palm. "I'm okay now." The natural smile that followed as she watched his eyes was easy, and not clumsy at all. He kissed her again. It was firm, but not hard, just holding their lips together for a long time, moving his over hers.

Adina smiled in the middle of it. "That's not fair! We're going to be apart for days."

He smiled back, his lips on hers. "I know. I just want to have this to hold onto while you're gone."

Adina held his head with both hands, kissing him deeply before pulling back. "Me too."

Adina's insides were a mess as she rolled away from the temporary camp. Fear mingled with the unmet lust that Asher had only continued to fan in the hours before she left. Worry meshed with pride at his confidence, his certainty in her abilities. He'd put all he owned, everything that would allow him to get him back home, into her hands, with nothing more than his certainty that she could bring them back to him. Adina looked back. In the harsh midday sun, everything was a stark contrast.

The vehicles were clumped together in various shades of cooler colors below the awnings strung between them, their upper surfaces blasted all but white by the blazing sun. Every face in the camp was watching her, hands raised to shade their eyes. Lew-Lew stood out, of course. The unbelievably bright colors of his outrageous attire were bleached by the light. Asher stood apart from everyone else. He just watched her. The pang in Adina's chest made her blink back tears. Then the camp vanished behind the edge of the mesa as she drove down onto the baked flats following the map Asher had given her.

Adina swallowed hard and looked to Nat, sitting in the passenger seat. He was watching behind them too. "Okay, Nat. We're on our way home." He turned and watched her uncertainly. Adina smiled at him. "A day or two and you'll see your mom again." Nat just pulled his knees up and turned away, staring out the passenger side window into the wastes.

__

Adina stood on top of the Bearcat scanning the horizon through the binoculars. It had been a day and a half since they'd left the makeshift encampment. Adina would never have considered going out into the wastes alone before meeting Asher. And even now, the idea of being without him was intimidating. But here she was, standing on top of the armored behemoth, armed, trained; and on her own. Adina shook her head thinking about what her life had been like a few weeks ago. What it would still be if the raiders hadn't razed her settlement. Adina squinted into the binoculars. A faint, dark line climbed upward near the horizon. *That's it...* She turned to Nat who was standing in the open cupola. "I think that's it. We're almost home, Nat." He still hadn't said anything. Adina gestured him to her, squatting and pointing. He squinted into the distance. "Right there." She held the binoculars for him and adjusted them. He looked through them then back to her. "I know, it's not much to see from here." She ran a reassuring hand down his back. "But we're nearly there." Nat looked through the binoculars again and watched for a long time. When he looked back at her, his expression seemed minutely more hopeful.

The booming voice of Omar, the big captain of the Quarry's defenses rumbled over the dry ground as Adina climbed down out of the Bearcat. "You're back!" His eyes searched beyond her and as soon as Nat appeared from the driver's side door, Omar bent over, hands on his knees and dropped his head. "Thank the sky!" Then he stood up and turned, booming back toward the rest of the camp. "Tell Devon…"

"*NAT!*" Devon's cry brought everyone's heads around. She was sprinting from the other side of the gate. As soon as Devon saw Nat step down off the ladder, she skidded to a halt, staring, frozen in place.

A long moment passed where no one moved or even seemed to breathe. Devon stared at her son and Nat just stood, his spirit seeming to have momentarily fled his body. Tears welled in Adina's eyes, and she swallowed hard to push down the lump in her throat. She gently put a hand on Nat's shoulder and bent to look him in the face.

"It's…" Adina had to clear her throat before she could get another word out. "It's okay, Nat. We're home." Adina took his hand and led him gently forward a few steps. Nat suddenly broke away from her and raced to Devon, colliding with her at nearly a dead run.

"MOM!"

Adina was suddenly sobbing. So were Devon and others who'd gathered. Omar stood, his burly arms crossed, sniffing defiantly against the tears brimming in his eyes.

Adina walked to him and put a hand on his thick forearm. "He's been through a lot." She wiped her tears with the back of her hand, watching Devon go between hugging Nat and looking him over for injuries. "I need to talk to Priav and Rafi." Adina heaved a breath to try and get her tears under control.

Her tone pulled Omar's eyes to her, and his tears subsided. He looked at the bearcat. "Where's Asher? He's not…" Omar didn't finish the thought. Adina could see the concern in his expression.

"No, he's fine. But Nat wasn't the only one we found. That's what I need to talk to Priav and Rafi about."

Omar craned his head back, understanding dawning on his thick features. "I'll let them know." A cry was already starting throughout the camp. Omar sighed. "Well, I guess they'll know everything before I get there." He nodded to the bearcat. "Bring it inside the perimeter and I'll tell them you're coming."

Adina held his eyes. "Fifty-two people, Omar. They need a safe place."

His eyes narrowed and his head cocked a few degrees as he scrutinized her for a long time. "And you think they belong here?"

Adina shook her head. "I don't know, Omar. But I think you need them as much as they need you."

CHAPTER FIFTEEN

Adina's heart felt like it struck rocky bottom as she listened to the Quarry council argue. Not so many minutes ago, she'd been filled with heady excitement. People had been cheering, crowding around the bearcat as she pulled in through the gates, celebrating her bringing Nat home safely. Now that excitement was gone, replaced by frustration, anger -- and fear.

Omar leaned on the table in the center of the council house and shook his head. "The risk is too high. I say no."

"You can't be serious!" Adina snapped.

Omar swiveled his head to her. His intense expression made his blue eyes stand out against his scruffy black hair and bushy beard. "This isn't your decision. You..."

"You need people here!" Adina interrupted, jabbing a finger out at him. "You said it yourself." Adina still wore her filthy clothes from the trek out into the wastes to find Nat, spattered with the remains of the battle with the slavers. She threw her arm out toward the empty desert beyond the camp's makeshift walls. "And they have nowhere else to go!" A stone felt like it had formed in Adina's chest. Images of what might have to happen if she and Asher had to leave the survivors to fend for themselves flashed through her mind. She could feel the weight of her rifle in her hands like a premonition. Adina pushed the awful images aside.

Omar turned to her, pulling himself up to his full height, half a foot taller than her. "There are two hundred and eighty-four of us here. With fifty-two people, they could overthrow us." His words weren't harsh, or weary, or *anything*. They were just cold — a statement of facts. And they made Adina's heart grind against the sharpness inside her.

"They're mostly women, girls, and boys like Nat! There are only a dozen men among them!" Adina's mind was instantly filled with the striking image of Lew-Lew parading among the ruined camp and dead bodies like he was on stage. "The slavers weren't interested in men!" She stared defiantly back into Omar's gruff, blue-eyed gaze. "You do the math!" The words struck Adina with comforting familiarity. It was Asher's figure of speech.

As she looked across the faces of the rest of the council, he filled her mind; so far away, alone, protecting the survivors.

In addition to Omar and Priav, Priav's husband Rafi sat silently on her left, his blind eyes staring into the center of the space, looking regal, serene, and wise, as always. He hadn't said anything. He just listened, his gnarled hands resting calmly on his walking stick. The other three people oversaw various elements of the camp's operation. A rail thin woman sat back with her arms crossed, her hair pulled back tightly, making her already gaunt, burnt tan face look even more severe. Her hair was mostly hidden under a brightly colored, block-printed scarf that did nothing to ease her appearance. She oversaw the farming effort, or something to do with the water.

"And how are we supposed to feed them?" the severe looking woman asked. "Almost another fifth our number? We're only just keeping a surplus as it is."

Priav held up a hand to quiet everyone and shifted the not quite red, not quite orange shawl around her shoulders, then stood up. Priav stepped close and put a hand on Adina's arm.

"Omar is right, Adina. We need to decide this. "They are not our people…"

"But…"

"We don't know them," Priav continued as if Adina hadn't interrupted her. Priav stuck her chin out at her and squeezed her arm. "*You*… don't know them." The words hung in the air for a moment. "You shared an experience which has made you close, but you don't *know* them."

"We didn't know you when we saved you either!" Adina glared at her. Her heart was suddenly hammering in her ears. Behind Priav, Adina could see the unsettled shift in the rest of the council at her words.

But Priav didn't react to what she'd said, or her glare.

Priav's tone and expression were conciliatory. "You've done something wonderful for us, Adina." Priav nodded over her shoulder to the rest of the council. "We have to talk about what you've told us." Priav patted her arm. "Go and rest, get clean."

"But if…"

Priav raised her hand. "We will celebrate you bringing Nat back to us tonight. But for now, let us talk."

Adina still wanted to fight, but the way Priav held her eyes… the kindness and quiet power there stole the fire from her. Adina nodded and dropped her head. She was suddenly so tired. And her clothes itched. She just felt filthy.

Adina felt Priav's wrinkled finger under her chin and lifted her head. Priav's eyes were filled with heartfelt intensity. "Thank you for bringing

Nat home to us, Adina." Priav tilted her head a few degrees. "*Few* would be so brave for people they don't know." And as Priav held her gaze, Adina had to blink back tears. She turned and left. She didn't want to see the rest of the council to see her cry.

--

The sun was hot across Adina's shoulders and neck where her black ponytail didn't cover as she kicked off her boots and dropped down into the shallow bathing area of the Quarry. Behind her breastbone, the stone that had formed after the council's cold response hung like a weight around her heart. But it was softened by Priav's gentle, powerful gratitude. Adina wasn't sure what she felt -- anger, frustration, fear, betrayal? It was all just a confusing mess inside her.

Further down in her belly, a knot of anxiety pulled.

Every eye in camp had been on her since she arrived. Without Asher there, all the attention was overwhelming. After the initial rush of the congratulations for bringing Nat home, Priav had told everyone to give her space.

They mostly did. But eyes followed her everywhere -- *men's* eyes. She could feel their interest like the heat of the sun on her skin. She squinted against the glare of the white stone walls as she squatted down in the water. A slick of dirt, sweat, and things she didn't want to think about expanded out from her. She watched the patterns it made in the water. Adina hadn't thought about how filthy she was until now. Or what all the filth meant. Not until the moment standing there with Priav. There were too many other thoughts, too many feelings. A little girl waved to her, a few yards from the edge of the water, grinning shyly. Adina's heart squeezed thinking about the girls among the survivors. What they'd been through in the slave camp… and what she and Asher might have to do if they couldn't bring them to the Quarry. Adina half walked; half paddled in the chest deep water to retrieve the soap from the rocks next to her boots. She gave the little girl a smile and waved back. Men watched her. Most were discrete about their interest. A tall, red-haired man that had shown his interest when she and Asher first arrived, stood in the sun, just watching. His boldness was a statement.

It was intimidating… and amidst all her other confusion, *exciting*. She could feel their arousal everywhere. No man could measure up to Asher in her feelings for him, how unbelievably handsome he was, or the things he made her feel when they made love. But fantasies about those men watching her flooded in. She ached for Asher, but he wasn't here.

Adina ran soap over her clothes and gave herself and her clothes an initial wash at the same time, the way she had in the rift so long ago. She took off her shirt and washed it thoroughly, keeping in shoulder deep water so that her breasts weren't on display through her undershirt. Then she stripped off her undershirt, feeling eyes searching to see more of her. She scrubbed the light fabric between her hands, feeling it flow around them under the water, watching more dirt float away. Her nipples felt like they were being pinched in her anxiety and arousal. She waded to the edge and tossed her shirts up onto the rocks, careful to keep herself down in the water. She made sure her towel was there so she could cover up when she was done. She took off her pants and underwear, washed them and threw them up on the rocks too.

Naked in the water, Adina's heart pounded as she washed herself. Everything was wildly sensitive when she washed between her legs. She could almost feel the erect penises around her, see the images in the men's minds of her underneath them, or being behind her, thrusting into her. She dunked down and scrubbed her hair, scratching her scalp with her fingernails. She stayed down, letting her hair flow out around her and closed her eyes, trying to drive the images and imagined feeling of hands on her away. But they just crowded in, more detailed, more explicit. She waded to where the ramp dropped off into deeper water and took a breath, then plunged down. She kicked downward pushing for the bottom of the next ramp, more than twenty feet below. The water pressed on her naked body, growing colder as she descended. She cleared her ears and kept kicking, willing the cold water and the pressure to dowse the fire in her. Adina reached the bottom and let out a stream of bubbles, watching them skitter and dash on their way to the surface. Then she just let herself hover in the cool, blue dimness. She was alone, no eyes on her, the cold seeping in. But the ache only intensified. The blue reminded her of Asher's eyes, the pressure on her like his body weight. It was so quiet. Just her heartbeat and the sounds her body made in response to the pressure. Her lungs started to burn, the need to breathe nagging at the peace of just floating there. She kicked lightly off the bottom and let her buoyancy draw her upward trying to relax. When Adina broke the surface, all her senses felt like they'd been set on fire. The way her heart pounded had little to do with the cold water. She paddled to the white stone edge and pulled her towel around her as she lifted herself up out of the water. She couldn't help but glance around. And as she saw men watching her, more fantasies crashed in.

At least Adina could blame her bright blush on the cold water. She could feel eyes on her bare legs, shoulders, and neck as she stepped into her boots, gathered her things, and clutched them to her chest. Adina nodded to people who smiled at her, replied in single words to hellos as she made her way back to the bearcat, suppressing the urge to run. At the bearcat, she climbed inside, slammed the hatch, and dropped her things, and fell onto the mattress. She put a hand on her mound. The touch made her curl up around her hand. Adina pressed. "Ohhh... Asher... where are you when I need you?"

CHAPTER SIXTEEN

Urgent banging on the side of the bearcat woke Adina with a start. "Adina!" someone yelled from outside.

"I'm here!" Adina answered groggily. "What's wrong?"

"Priav and Omar want you to come to the front gate, right now!"

Adina stopped with one leg in a fresh pair of pants. "What?"

"There's a storm coming. They want you at the front gate!"

At the word storm and the tone of his voice, Adina was wriggling into her pants as fast as she could. "What kind of storm?"

Storms in the open wastes could scour entire regions down to bare rock. She's seen the aftermath of a bad one when she was a girl. What had been dirt and scruffy green desert had been rendered into a lifeless rocky expanse for miles along the storm's path.

"A bad one!"

Adina yanked the door of the bearcat open pulling on her overshirt and stuffing her feet into her boots. She didn't need to know anything more than what her senses told her as soon as she was outside. The sky had a weird greenish tinge, and she could smell the change in the air. Asher had said the smell of storms was ozone in the atmosphere from static electricity.

If this kind of storm hit the survivors camp out in the open... Adina didn't want to think about that. She yanked the laces on her second boot. *Or it could permanently answer any question about the Quarry's survival.* She threw her gun belt over her shoulder, slammed the door of the bearcat, and followed him at a run. His name was Kerry, he was one of the men who worked on engineering around the camp. As Adina approached the gate, her run slowed.

As far as she could see in both directions, a massive black wall filled the horizon.

They come on legs of lightning, scouring, black and terrible... That's what the storiers said about storms like this. And as she stared at the oncoming monster, the lightning that cracked all along the front of it did look like legs. The storiers also told tales of the Lightning Men, and other creatures that supposedly lived in storms like this one.

Oh shit.

Adina finished buckling on her pistol belt and made for the crowd at the front gate.

"Get everything down that you can!" Omar was shouting. "Get everyone into rocks near the water and the wall. It's going to be safest!"

"But stay away from the water!" Priav hollered, standing right in the center of the churning crowd.

"What kind of storm is it?" Adina asked as soon as she was next to Priav.

"We don't know. This is the first big one we've had since we've been here. We were hoping that maybe we didn't get them." Adina could see the disappointment and concern in Priav's eyes.

Adina looked out into the looming tempest. Big storms tore up the ground. And depending on where they'd been, they could pull radioactive particles or toxins up into them. The resulting toxic or radioactive rain could render areas barren for years if not lifetimes. Toxins or radioactivity falling into the quarry could spell as certain a death for the community as it being scoured away by the savage winds.

Priav took her by the arm. "Adina, I would like to put the youngest children into your vehicle. We have no storm shelters yet." She nodded in the direction Adina had come from. "Your truck is the safest place I can think of."

Adina squeezed her arm and nodded. "Of course. As many as we can fit." She looked around. "I'll bring the bearcat up and then once were loaded, I'll move us to the back side of the bluff." She pointed to the massive white slab of stone at the far end of the Quarry. "Putting the bluff between us and the storm seems like the best idea." She looked from Priav to Omar.

Omar watched her for a moment then looked to the bluff. She could see the gears turning in his head. "She's right. It's the safest place we can be." He raised his burly arm. "Everyone! Move to the other side of the bluff.

We will shelter there. Bring coverings and tarps to protect yourselves!" He turned to Adina. "Thank you. Thank you for helping us."

Adina could feel Priav's smile without having to look at her.

"Of course. What else would I…" She stopped herself. The Adina who stood here now, who *could* help them, was only able to for one reason. "What do you think Asher would do?"

Omar nodded, then turned and boomed to the crowd. "Bring the children! We're going to put them into Adina's truck!"

Adina sang along with Devon in the dimness of the bearcat's interior as the howling storm raged outside.

What sounded like rocks pounded down on its metal skin as hailstones fell around them like artillery. Adina tried not to think about the people huddled against the stones outside with little more than tarps to protect them. Lightning crashed against the ground, shuddering the bearcat. Several of the eighteen children packed into every crevice of the bearcat screamed. After a moment's interruption Devon just sang louder, encouraging all the children to join her. Nat sat in a corner with his arms around a brother and sister, holding onto them tightly as they cried. He was singing too, but the flash of lightning showed his fearful expression as he sang.

Adina pulled the little boy she was holding tighter against her and wrapped her coat more fully around them. It was cold. The inside of the bearcat was filled with mist from all the small lungs breathing in the closed space, and the windows were running with condensation.

"Shhh... It's going to be okay. You're safe here," she whispered into the little boy's ear.

"Where's my mom!" he cried. Half a dozen women and older children were huddled in the relative safety provided under the bearcat, including his mother.

Adina set her head on his hair. "Shhh... She's alright," she lied. She couldn't imagine what it must be like outside with lightning crashing into the ground, hailstones raining down like gunfire, and winds that tore at the rocks and earth like claws.

Adina saw Asher in her mind's eye, sheltering in the flashing darkness, trying to protect the survivors, but powerless to do more than she was. Only he didn't have the safety of the bearcat to protect him.

There was a blinding flash and Adina was instantly deafened. The lighting strike lifted the bearcat up on the shock absorbers and abruptly dropped it again. She clamped the little boy against her again. "It's going to be okay... We're going to be okay..."

_

Adina eyes popped open. *I actually fell asleep?* The back of her neck burned with the intense feeling of someone or something watching her. The storm still raged outside. Everyone else in the bearcat was asleep. Adina's heart hammered in her ears, loud even over the storm's vicious howl. The storiers wild tales about things that lived in storms felt far too real as the crashing cataclysm clawed at the bearcat. Malevolent spirits were rumored to ride inside the storms or were awakened by their violence. Some people said they were spirits of the dead, left wandering after so many died in the ending of the world that used to be. Others said they were something else, birthed from the ruins afterward. But whatever they were, the stories said they stole people away or tore them apart during storms. As much as Adina always believed the stories were just made up to try and make sense of deaths and disappearances that happened during storms, her body was shrieking that something wasn't right. Something was out there. Adina was trembling violently as she turned to the truck's armored window. Fear or adrenaline, whichever, made her breathing come fast and shallow. Lightning flashed and she could make out vague shapes in the tempest outside; lumps among the rocks where people huddled under whatever they had, pressed against the rocks, trying to survive.

It's just a dream…

Then she saw movement. A silhouette moved from one rock to another, then vanished when the light did. Adina's chest tightened like there was an iron band around it.

It's just someone moving to check on the others. Probably Omar.

The darkness seemed to stretch on and on as she waited for the next lightning flash so she could see. The feeling that there would be a face right on the other side of the glass staring at her when the lightning came again stabbed Adina in the belly like a dull knife. She wanted to close her eyes, but she couldn't. Another flash came.

There was something out there.

It sidled low along the ground. It could have been part of a thick shelter cover caught in the wind. But it was dragging something behind it. Adina couldn't breathe, the air in her windpipe had turned to a solid object that wouldn't move. She felt her diaphragm push and pull, in rapid, panicked spasms, but no air moved.

Tears ran down her cheeks as whatever it was slid along the ground in fitful motions, appearing to struggle against what it was dragging. She could hear the whimpers that escaped her terrified lips, but she couldn't make a sound. And she couldn't move. Adina's hands shook violently.

Then it was black again. Her eyes hurt from the harsh transition and her terrified straining to see anything outside.

Adina jerked awake, her heart in her throat, her breaths coming in ragged, painful drags. The boy in her lap moved to get more comfortable. Everyone in the bearcat was asleep. Adina turned over her shoulder and waited for the next flash. When it came, there was nothing there.

It was just a nightmare.

But even as Adina thought it, she knew it was a lie.

--

It was light outside when Adina finally clambered down from the driver's side door of the bearcat. The storm had passed, but she could still feel the terror from the night before, like a shadowy hand gripping her shoulder. She'd told everyone to wait inside. All indications were that it was just a storm; no radiation registered on the bearcat's instruments, and there was no evidence of toxins. But Adina didn't want the children to see what her mind's eye had painted. Parents and people they knew scorched and bloody, scattered by the awful storm. Or evidence of what she'd seen the night before.

It was just a nightmare.

Adina went to where she'd seen it. There were fading marks in the sodden ground. They could have been drag marks. Or they could have been from a hundred other things. She searched quickly to see if there was any other evidence of it. Anger had been brewing inside her at her inability to move or do anything but sit there inside the bearcat like a terrified child.

What if it was real? And you just sat there and let it take someone?

Adina closed her eyes. Asher's voice was in her ear. "Don't put yourself between the hammer and stone because you're human. All of us fail sometimes. It's what happens after that matters."

It was just a nightmare, Adina tried to reassure herself again.

Not far off, she heard Omar shouting, "Fara! Has anyone seen Fara!" His voice was hoarse and tired. "Everyone! Try to find Fara!"

Adina made her way to him and to her surprise, there were dozens of people starting to move. She didn't see the scorched and battered corpses everywhere that she'd seen so clearly in her mind. But many of them were obviously injured.

"Omar! How bad is it?"

He leaned close to her and shouted, "What!?" Adina could see blood running from his right ear. "I'm kinda deaf this morning." He staggered and caught himself on a rock. Adina grabbed his burly shoulder to steady him.

"Where are Priav and Rafi?"

Omar nodded and slid down to the ground. His expression was pained, distant. "They're okay. Just wet." He grabbed her arm. "Thank you again for taking care of the children. It's… It was…" And the big man started to cry. He dropped his head and hid his face between his arms.

Adina fought to keep from crying herself as she watched him crumble before her eyes. She took a huge breath against the tearing pain in her chest and knelt, wrapping her arms around his burly shoulders, pulling herself against him. "You did good, Omar." Adina put her mouth right next to his ear and spoke loudly to make sure he heard her. "You did everything you could and probably saved a lot of lives last night." Omar just howled, his whole body shaking. Adina rocked him as best she could. "Shhh… I'll start looking for people." He didn't uncover his face. He just shook his head.

Fara… Adina shuddered at the image of something dragging someone away into the storm. She stood up and looked around in the new morning sun. That's when she saw the first body.

--

Adina stood in the damaged remains of the camp, looking at the line of bodies covered by multi-colored, salvaged sheets, tarps and shelter covers. Most everyone who stood there was injured. She, Devin, and the children who'd been crammed into the bearcat were the exception. Twenty people were too badly injured to walk. Five had died in the storm.

And three were missing.

They were just swept away by the storm… That's what everyone was saying. *It was just a nightmare.* Adina clenched her fists, trying to force herself to believe it.

The camp had survived much better than she'd thought it would. Adina's mind fled to Asher and the survivors.

Did the storm hit them?

"We have suffered a great loss," Priav called loudly in the bright, clean morning air.

Adina pulled her jacket closer around her. It was cool and humid

273

in the aftermath of the storm. The ground was still wet but would dry quickly once the heat of the day started.

"And we will grieve over it," Priav continued after letting her words hang for several long seconds. Rafi stood at her side, seeming as resolute as the white stone bluff above the quarry; serene and certain. Some people sobbed; others just stared vacantly into space. "But we have also been given new possibilities. Adina and the Myrmidon have rescued fifty-two people from the Ghost Eyes. And I have decided that we will see if they can become part of our family here."

There was a murmur throughout the crowd, people who had been staring suddenly came to life, many who were crying sniffled to a stop.

"We do not know them," Priav went on. "But we know her." Priav pointed to her, her eyes utterly certain.

Adina blinked back sudden tears under her unwavering gaze. "And the Myrmidon. We trust them. They brought me and many of you back after we were attacked. They brought Nat back to us." Priav looked to where Nat stood with Devon. "And last night, she saved many of our children." Priav looked across all the faces. "And what have they asked in return? Very little. And now, they ask us to help people we don't know. People who need help. Like we have needed help. Which they have *always* given." Tears rolled down Adina's cheeks as Priav gestured around the remains of the camp. "People we need." Priav let her words hang for several breaths again. "I will go with Adina and meet with the Myrmidon and the survivors. And we will see if we can give them a home here with us. Because what are we? One family. One family that can grow." Priav looked at her again. "I do not know these people." Priav inclined her head to her. "But I know Adina and Asher. And I trust them."

CHAPTER SEVENTEEN

Adina turned from the open side hatch of the bearcat at the sound of people approaching. She'd just finished stowing the last of the supplies for she and Priav's trip back to the survivors' camp.

Adina nodded at Devon's bright, "G'morning." Devon approached her, squinting in the sun, Nat at her side. "I know you're busy, but…" She ran a hand down Nat's back. "He… wanted to say goodbye before you left. He…" Devon's words seemed to run out. And after a moment of obvious struggle, she stepped forward and threw her arms around her. "Thank you," Devon breathed over her shoulder. Adina heard the quiver in her voice. "Thank you so much for…" Adina felt her gulp. "Bringing him home to me." Devon squeezed her.

Asher's words about contamination from close contact with others rattled through Adina's mind with how nonsensical they felt after having been spattered in blood and bodily fluids from the Ghost Eye's. She returned Devon's hug. "I'm just glad he's alright."

When they stepped apart, Devon couldn't meet her eyes and she was flushed. Devon wiped tears with the back of her hand. "Thank you," she mouthed again, but no words came out. Devon coaxed Nat to her, and Adina felt the weight of his eyes as he watched her with an uncertain, shy expression.

Adina's heart climbed into her throat. There were still lingering shadows under his eyes and the bruises around his wrists had gone to yellow. "I'm glad you're safe with your mom." Everything inside Adina was suddenly a storm. She pulled him into a reassuring embrace, holding him close for a long moment. When Adina finally released him, he met her gaze shyly.

"When I grow up, I want to be just like you and Asher."

Adina swallowed hard, blinking back tears at his heartbreaking earnestness. Devon's hand came to her mouth, and she started to cry watching them.

"You just be brave and strong. You were that before we got here." Adina pushed him back so she could look in his eyes. "And be *kind*." She ran a hand over the side of his face. "I've seen how kind you are with the other children. Remember, being kind isn't weakness. We came after you because we care, Nat. It's important that you care too. Be strong to protect the people you care about." Adina inclined her head to him. "Do you understand?"

Nat searched her eyes and thought for several seconds. "I think so."

Adina nodded and hugged him again. "Good."

_

Mile upon mile of empty wastes passed the windows as Adina drove the bearcat back along the course she'd taken from the survivor camp. Worry about what might be left after the storm pulled at her. And the image of the skittering shadow was there again. Adina's skin prickled, a chill running up her back.

"I… think I saw something in the storm," Adina finally said into the cab's dusty air. And as soon as she'd said it, she wished she hadn't. Uncertainty climbed up her back.

Priav had been staring out the passenger window, watching the wastes roll past, her usual, quiet contemplative self. Priav turned to her. Adina's uncertainty balled into a tight knot in her belly.

"What did you see?"

Adina turned back to what was ahead of them.

"There are all those stories of things living in the storms, or out in the wastes…" Adina shrugged, struggling to say what she really wanted. "And then three people were just *gone* after the storm…"

There was a long quiet. Adina could feel Priav's eyes on her.

"Derecho," Priav offered into the rumble of the bearcat's cabin. "I heard people call them a lot of things over the years. Ghasts, Windwalkers, Sand Devils and the like."

Adina glanced back at her.

Priav wasn't looking at her, but into empty space as if into the past. And when she continued it sounded like she was talking about a memory. "People dragged away during storms or in the night. Or being found torn apart with no way to explain it." Priav shook her head. "It's all bad business." When Priav finally turned back, her expression was intense. It was jarring compared to the easy, self-assurance that normally rested there. "And you think you saw one of them?" Priav's tone was neutral but struck Adina like an accusation.

"It was probably just a piece of tarp caught in the wind." But once again, as Adina said it, she didn't believe it. "Or I could have just been dreaming. Storms like that can make you think all kinds of things."

"They can," Priav answered. "But you don't believe it was a piece of cloth or a dream, do you?" Priav paused. "Adina, look at me." Her tone had become matronly again. "What did you see?" Priav just watched her, so open, undemanding. Just *there.*

Adina looked forward again, focusing on where she was driving, wrestling her suddenly churning emotions. It took a few steadying breaths before she could say anything.

"Something skittered along the ground, like a shadow, but it moved... weirdly. Sort of jerky and unnatural. Like I said, it was probably just a piece of one of the shade structures, caught in the wind."

When she looked back, Priav's eyebrows were pinched together, her eyes narrowed. "Like it was crawling with legs that... didn't seem like legs?"

Adina stepped on the brakes at Priav's expression, tone, and description, bringing the bearcat to a stop. "You *saw* it." Adina just stared at her, relief unspooling the hard knot at her center.

I'm not crazy and I wasn't dreaming!

Priav nodded to her. "I haven't told anyone. It would only create fear. I saw it take Fara away."

Adina's heart hammered madly in her ears now as new horror struck. Up to now, her fear had been that she might have seen something; something that may or may not have been there. But as what Priav said sank in, Adina imagined Fara's terror as she struggled and screamed in the pitch-black storm, helpless and alone as the creature dragged her away.

Adina groaned, "They're... *real?*" through sudden nausea.

Priav nodded again. "You doubt yourself too often Adina." Priav leaned against the door and pulled a foot up onto her seat, staring out into the scorched landscape. "Since I was a girl, people told the same stories you've probably heard." Priav nodded. "We both saw it."

I'm not crazy.

As the hot afternoon droned on into evening Adina told Priav every detail of what she'd seen during the storm and what had happened in the slave camp again. Adina talked just to fill in the empty quiet. When she didn't, the horror of Fara and the Derecho were waiting.

Adina's mind wandered to Asher and the survivors.

Will there even be anyone left to find? What if there was a Derecho? Adina pushed the thoughts aside, shook her head, and set her jaw. That's not helpful. She blew out a fierce breath. *He's okay. They're okay…*

Familiar rock formations suddenly peeked over the horizon and Adina's heart felt like it might leap out of her chest. The highest parts of the rise where the survivors' camp lay came into view slowly. Adina had been following thin, wisping lines of smoke along the horizon, praying they were the right ones. Now that she could see the mesa, everything inside Adina wrapped tight again. It was too high for her to see if the smoke was from campfires or devastation. *Please be okay… Please be alright…*

Circling the rise, she was rewarded by the silhouettes of people standing on the edge of the mesa. And they were waving.

Adina turned at Priav's hand on her arm. Priav's old eyes were smiling. "Breathe daughter…" Priav grinned, and Adina couldn't help but do the same. But as they pulled up the incline onto the mesa Adina's heart seized. Asher walked forward naked to the waist. He was covered in blood.

Oh no…

But as she got closer, she could see he was smiling, his bright white teeth standing out against his filthy face. He raised a burly arm, his tattoos showing from beneath all the red and brown as he waved to her. He wiped his hands on a cloth that was as filthy as he was.

Adina was climbing out the door of the bearcat before the engine had finished chugging. She never got to the ground. Asher scooped her off the steps, clamping her in a fierce embrace.

He smelled. Old blood, sweat and machine oil combined in a musty stink that filled her nose. And Adina just didn't care.

Adina hadn't realized she'd started to cry until she drew in a shuddering breath. "Earth and sky! I was so worried!"

Asher pulled her tight against him and she just let herself be squished. She felt the pressure of him kissing her head, his words filtering through her dark hair. "I was afraid you'd been caught in the storm."

Adina shook her head. She couldn't say anything.

She felt her feet touch down and his lips met hers. Everything inside her caught fire. She wrapped her arms around his neck and kissed him urgently. She tasted the blood and finally pulled back, her eyes roving up and down him. It had only been a few days, but she was amazed by how big and handsome he was, even filthy.

"What happened? What's all the blood?"

He smiled and nodded over his shoulder to the camp. "The storm drove a herd of boar onto the mesa." He peaked an eyebrow at her. Adina could nearly bathe in the fierce joy that poured off him. "After the initial… *surprise* of their arrival." He grinned with the same manic energy he'd had during the hunt that felt so long ago. "We were able to take most of the herd down."

He stopped and just stared at her like he was drinking her in. Everything about him seemed to quiet. Then it was like his brain restarted. "The ones we didn't get, ran themselves right off the edge on the west side." He held up his arms, showing off his filthy torso. "We've been making meat for two days." Then he glanced past her.

Adina followed his gaze. Priav was coming around the front of the bearcat. Adina saw the corner of his mouth come up. "Nice to see you, Priav."

Priav settled her lever action rifle in the crook of her arm squinting at the two of them, then nodded to Asher. "You look… unsurprising,

Myrmidon."

He chuckled. "And you're a sight for sore eyes, Priav."

Priav smiled, a wise and certain expression. "I know. I am a vision. Radiant and irresistible."

Asher's arm closed around Adina's ribs, and she looked up into his bright lapis-colored eyes. He smiled widely. "I knew you could do it." Adina's chest felt like a balloon that inflated at his sincere, certain confidence in her. He flicked his eyes back toward camp. "Lew-Lew thought fresh meat and hides might sweeten the deal with the Quarry." Then he stopped again, just watching her as if memorizing every detail. "I've missed you."

Adina's smile felt like it might break her face, the expression feeling lopsided and uncoordinated, like everything else inside her at that moment. "Me too."

She pulled him down for another kiss. Holding her lips against his, she smiled, trying to kiss him and talk at the same time. "Really bad!"

CHAPTER EIGHTEEN

Adina leaned back and blew out a breath as Zara and Priav verbally sparred in an open area of the survivor's camp. Zara sat on the ground, leaned forward, gesturing severely while Priav sat back in a chair someone had provided, just watching her. The mask of control and utter confidence was back. Priav was giving nothing away.

Lew-Lew had pushed the rest of the camp back to keep them at a discrete distance while the negotiations went on.

Why are they arguing?

When Zara finished her diatribe, Lew-Lew stood up. "Maybe we should take a break…"

"Shut up, Lew-Lew!" Zara snarled. "We need to get through this."

Adina felt Asher shift from where he was standing behind her. "Maybe Lew-Lew is right, Zara. I'm not…"

Priav held up a hand. "Shh… the women are speaking." She didn't look at Asher, but kept her attention fixed on Zara.

Adina flushed with anger at Priav's curt dismissal of Asher. She turned, glaring. "He's only trying to help."

Priav turned to her, the stern mask of her authority falling on her. "This is between Zara and I." Priav inclined her head toward Lew-Lew. "And Lew-Lew. You and the Myrmidon aren't part of this. Please leave us to work things out."

Fury boiled in Adina. She locked her eyes on Priav's.

"Adina…" Asher's voice held warning.

"Shh!" Adina darted her eyes at him. "Let me do this."

The edge of a smile lifted the corner of Asher's mouth at her fierceness. And there was… *pride?* in his expression as he watched her eyes. Adina's fury was suddenly jousting with confusion. Asher didn't seem the least bit offended by Priav's dismissal.

"I'll leave you to it, then." He turned so Priav, Zara and Lew-Lew couldn't see his face and leaned close. His smile widened to a secretive one. "Give 'em hell, Adie."

Now everything in Adina was just in disarray.

She was angry at Priav and confused by him -- again. Everything inside her heated up until there was nothing left but a churning mess of arousal and confusion.

His smile shifted to a more neutral expression when he turned back to Priav. "I hope all goes favorably for you." Then he turned to Zara. "And for you." He nodded to Lew-Lew. "Lew-Lew."

Lew-Lew threw his hand up, his wrist once again cocked at a decorous angle. "See you later."

Adina couldn't help but notice the way Lew-Lew watched Asher's receding backside. Then again, it would have been hard to miss Lew-Lew's obvious stare.

Part of Adina swelled with pride at Asher giving ground to her so publicly -- just because she'd asked him to. Him making certain she knew how confident he was in her abilities calmed the turmoil it had begun only a moment before. Adina pulled herself up tall and turned to face

Priav fully.

"We *are* involved." Adina raked Zara and Lew-Lew with her firm gaze. "We *do* have a say!" She inclined her head to Priav, fixing her eyes on the older woman. "You wouldn't be here to make a decision if he hadn't intervened!" She jabbed her finger out toward Asher. "And the only reason he did was because I begged him to!" She turned to Zara. "And until today -- this moment, you and the rest of the people with you, didn't have a future." Adina indicated the rest of the camp with a wide gesture. "Don't tell us we don't have a stake or say in this! We *made* this happen." Adina put her hands on her hips and nodded sharply at Priav. "Not you." Then she nodded at Zara. "And not you!"

Priav rose and approached her, laying a hand on her arm. Priav just stood for a moment watching her eyes. "Adina." Priav glanced to Zara and Lew-Lew, then adjusted so they couldn't see her face. Priav's expression softened. "Zara is a powerful, passionate woman. She has probably been talked down to or ignored by men her whole life. She's had to fight for everything. I'm giving her the opportunity show me, and everyone else, who she is. She needs to have her power and independence acknowledged." Priav just watched her eyes again.

Everything suddenly fell into place. Priav's entire demeanor had changed when they got to the camp.

Adina had thought it was Priav taking stock. Adina leaned close and whispered, "This is all for show?!"

Priav tilted her head and gave a conspiratorial nod toward Zara and Lew-Lew. "Not all. I still don't know them, Adina. I want to make sure they understand who is in charge at the Quarry. Dismissing Asher so publicly not only makes Zara feel powerful but sets a tone for the rest of our conversation -- strong women coming together to find a way forward."

Adina narrowed her eyes at Priav. She wasn't sure why she was surprised by Priav's canny strategy, but she was.

Priav's mouth turned up in a wan smile. "Besides, isn't there someplace you'd rather be while I keep everyone else busy?"

Adina felt blood rush up, her face and chest going suddenly hot. Everything inside her turned sort of awkward and lopsided again. She crinkled an eyebrow at Priav and grinned. "There is."

Priav pulled herself up straight and squeezed her arm. "See to it that your Myrmidon knows that we will talk once we are finished," Priav announced loudly for Zara and Lew-Lew to hear. Priav's eyes smiled at her, and the mask of authority descended over her face again. Priav turned back to Zara and Lew-Lew.

When Adina caught up with Asher, he'd just pulled open one of the armored side panels of the bearcat and was peering inside. He was cleaner than when they'd arrived. There wasn't extra water to bathe, but he'd scrubbed most of the blood off with sand and had rinsed his hands and face. He turned at the sound of her boots on the rocky, hard-baked ground. As his eyes walked up her appreciatively, Adina felt like each part of her heated up as his eyes touched them. He smiled and leaned against the hot metal skin of the bearcat. "I thought you were going to help with the negotiations."

Adina walked directly to him, put her hands on his bare torso, sliding them around to his back and pulled herself against him. "I had better things to do."

He grinned and gave her a quick kiss. "Oh, I agree." He tossed the wrench he was holding into the tool bag and scooped her up.

After a surprised squeak at his unexpected manhandling, Adina clamped her hands over her mouth to silence her laughter. He stepped up into the open side hatch and waited. "Wanna get the door?" She leaned for the handle and as soon as her hand was on it, she felt his lips on her neck. Adina's whole body curled up at the sensual touch. "Were you going to get the door?" he asked playfully as he continued to kiss her neck making it virtually impossible for her to do anything.

Adina concentrated, bit her lip and was finally able to slide the door closed.

Asher laid her on the mattress and just watched her. His bluest of blue eyes were mesmerizing, and when his fingers pushed her hair back and traced down her cheek, everything inside Adina came to life. It wasn't just that she wanted him *so* badly. It was like a part of her had been missing while they were apart. And that part was back in place again.

Adina put her lips to his, firm, but not hard, just holding her lips there before letting their kisses become more intense. She pulled back smiling, running her hands over his dirty face. He still smelled, but it didn't matter. Every nerve seemed to suddenly light up, her arousal now overshadowing everything else. Adina turned her back to Asher and pushed her butt back against him. "Pull my pants down, but not all the way."

Asher spooned up against her and Adina pushed back harder, feeling his bulge against her. She reached back and put one of his hands on her waistband, her other hand occupied holding onto the shelf. Adina wiggled her hips helping him push her pants down, then her underwear, leaving her ass exposed. The restriction of her pants holding her legs together made everything inside Adina suddenly pull tight. She looked back over her shoulder, past her naked ass and grabbed his belt, tugging it to unbuckle it, her heart racing. His hand suddenly slid up under her shirt and he cupped her breast. The thrill made Adina arch, jamming her bare ass back against him. As soon as he touched her stiff, sensitive nipple, she had to bite her lip to keep from crying out.

Then she felt his hard penis against her ass as he pushed his pants down.

"Yes, Asher… I want you so badly."

Adina groaned as he ran the head of his cock along her wet labia. And as always, he made a point of running it over her clit, bumping it, making her twitch.

Asher's fingers lightly rolled then pulled her sensitive nipple making her hiss with arousal. "Are you sure you want me?" he teased.

Adina reached back and grabbed his hip, pivoting hers to push his cock into position. "Bastard!" Her whole body was writhing with desire now as his fingers played on her breast and nipple and he taunted her vagina with his hard cock. She tried to force back onto it, but he withdrew, the head just teasing at her entrance. "Don't tease me! That's so mean!"

"You're sure, then?"

Adina nodded, breathing fast. "Yes!" she was able to get out. Then as she rocked back again, he met her and pushed forward, squeezing her breast, her nipple held between his fingers as his cock finally slid inside. Adina grabbed a handful of the blanket and shoved it into her mouth to stifle her ecstatic cry. She struggled against her pants, her legs wanting to open. The feeling of her pants holding her legs together as he penetrated deep inside was wildly erotic. She groaned into the blanket between her teeth, her ankles kicking in frustrated expression.

Slowly, maddeningly slowly, Asher pushed into her. "You feel so good, Adina." She nodded, chewing on the blanket. He lifted her shirt up and off, his hands running over her naked skin. His fingers lightly brushed her nipples as she turned onto her side. He pushed her ass cheek up to open her fully to him. One of his strong legs was against her back, the other against her legs as he filled her. The pace of his thrusts increased. Adina had her eyes squeezed shut fighting the urge to cry out. Each time she opened them, he was watching her expression or her body as she arched and writhed, her feet kicking with his movement.

Asher turned her fully onto her back and wrapped an arm around her legs, still trapped in her pants, using them to pull her onto his hard rod. His eyes watched her breasts as they bounced with each thrust, her expression as she groaned into the blanket, straining in ecstasy. It was too much. Adina yelped as the hot rush of her orgasm roared up through her. Asher held her firmly as her hips shuddered and she bucked under him.

"I love the way you cum, Adina." His words made everything inside Adina clench anew and she threw her head back, grabbing his hips and pulling herself hard onto him, wanting to feel every millimeter of him buried inside her. Her whole body locked into an arching, trembling spasm.

Adina finally collapsed onto the mattress, panting around the blanket that hung from her slack mouth. "Earth and sky…"

Asher pulled her pants off and opened her legs. He ran his still stiff cock over her sensitive labia and clit making her twitch again. "Do you want more?" he asked with a smirk. Adina could only nod, still in the afterglow of her first orgasm. When Asher entered her, her whole body felt relaxed, his shaft a perfect fit and completion of her. Her legs wrapped around him instinctively. She pulled the blanket from her mouth and sat up, kissing him long and deep. Adina arched her back throwing her breasts out to him, her hands on the blankets, lifting her hips and pushing down again as his strong fingers pressed into the skin of her hips. It was a slow, luxurious thing and Adina's body responded in relaxed rolls as the joy of being so intimately connected to him flowed through her. Then the inner fire caught again, and she tensed, her body moving more urgently trying to make him fill her even more. Asher pulled out.

"Noooo…" His lips fell on her neck, then down onto her breasts and he pushed her onto her back again, kissing down her stomach and finally onto her mound.

Adina opened her legs wide as his tongue played on her swollen clit. Asher pushed her legs up and sucked her clit into his mouth, rolling it with his tongue as he pushed two fingers inside her. Adina grabbed the blanket again, squeezing her eyes shut and moaning into the thick fabric, her hips quivering as he kissed, licked, and sucked. Suddenly Adina was shuddering again, her legs quaking. She grabbed his short hair, grinding her pussy onto his face. Everything crashed inside her and her back arched, her whole body spasming at the terrible, amazing torment. She screamed into the blanket as the fire of another orgasm raced through her. Asher held her legs firmly, keeping his tongue on her clit. Adina's abdominal muscles seized pulling her head and legs up, curling around Asher's tongue. Then she was lost. Nothing made sense as her body released into a twitching, uncoordinated mess on the mattress.

Asher kissed his way up her spasming body again. "That was nice."

Adina could only pant. For several minutes her stomach felt like it was yanked back to her spine as her climax slowly quieted and she could finally lay still.

When she came back to herself, Asher was lying next to her. Adina let her fingers run over his naked skin and watched his eyes. Then she kissed down his chest, to his belly and finally onto his phallus. She tasted herself on his shaft as she licked it and then pushed her mouth down onto it. Asher moaned in pleasure as she worked her mouth up and down on his cock. She got between his legs pumping her mouth, sucking hard and running her tongue against the underside of the head. He tasted so good and salty along with the lingering flavor of her own nectar. She kissed down the shaft and pulled one if his testicles into her mouth, rolling it with her tongue and sucking, stroking his cock with her hand. He moaned and his hips pumped. Adina sucked his other testicle, loving how he twitched as she did, his hips thrusting hard as she pushed his cock through her fingers. She pursed her lips, sucking up along his shaft, until she was at the head again, sucking in the cleft at the underside of the head. His hips trembled and then she gave him what he wanted, driving her mouth down over his cock, forcing all of it in. She moaned, cupping his balls so he knew how much she liked it. Then she pulled back again and sucked the top of his shaft, working the rest with her hand, his balls with her other. He was suddenly gasping, his hips pumping to meet her mouth.

Asher threw his hips forward hard and exploded in her mouth. Adina coughed at the rush of hot cum filling her mouth and throat. She choked but held herself down sucking and gulping. Asher's hips shook with each movement of her tongue as she tried to hold all of his cum in. When his hips finally eased down to the mattress, she kept her mouth on his cock not wanting to let anything escape. When he finally relaxed and she didn't taste any more of his semen, she pulled her mouth off and kissed his cock, then each testicle, then up his belly onto his heaving chest.

"Did you like that?" she asked between her own panting, looking up at his face. The crease between his eyebrows was gone.

He leaned down and kissed her, panting. "I loved it."

She returned his kiss and grinned up at him, laying her head on his scarred, tattooed chest. Everything inside her felt so relaxed now. "So did I. I love the way you look when you cum like that." She ran a hand over his smooth brow. "So much better." She just let her fingers trail over the skin of his forehead and between his brows where the crease normally was.

Adina woke to Asher shifting his arm under her and when she opened her eyes, he was watching her again.

She kissed one of the scars on his chest. "Tell me about Cosanti again. Tell me about the people there, how happy, and free they are. After seeing the slave camp, I want to know that there are better places in the world."

Asher was quiet for a while, his chest rising and falling against her head. She thought his expression was wistful, like he was looking through the top of the bearcat to someplace far away. "You can see it from miles away," he began. "Not a cloud of smoke on the horizon, but a glow, bright like the rising sun. From the south, it looks like two cities, a river splits it almost completely in half.

Many people who live there have never see it from far away." He looked down at her. "How beautiful it is."

She watched his eyes as he went on.

"No one goes hungry in Cosanti. The water is clean and the *food…*" his tone was longing. "Tastes and textures I can't wait for you to try, Adina." He smiled, his blue eyes on her face, a big finger running down the side of her face. "Beer, wine, tea, fruit juices, things you can't imagine." He raised his arm as if displaying a panorama above him. "From my balcony I can always see several of the wind generator balloons. They glow at night like floating flowers, and they have long tails, guidance fins that flow out behind them. There is a large market a few blocks from my home and the streets are lined with shops, apartments, and cafes." His eyes returned to her and the smile that followed was a peaceful thing. "When the wind is right, I can smell the spice market." Then he peaked an eyebrow. "When it's wrong, it get the smell from the dyers ward." He wrinkled his nose, grinning at her. "Phew!" He picked up his battered shirt. "There are newly manufactured clothes in soft fabrics and colors that you can't believe. People are happy, healthy. We have clinics and doctors and surgery. Things that normally kill people out here are solved with pills or simple injections."

Adina pushed up onto an elbow, feeling suddenly uncertain. "You're not making all this up, are you?" It all sounded so fantastical, like a dream, and sometimes she wondered if he was playing some elaborate joke. "It's really the way you say it is?"

He lifted his head so she could clearly see his eyes.

"You see the color of my eyes. It's the same as yours are turning after the inoculant. It's all real, Adina." He gave her a long kiss. She leaned into it and pulled herself partially on top of him to hold her lips to his.

"I can't wait to see it."

He pushed hair behind her ear. "I can't wait for you to." He smiled broadly. "I just want to watch your face when you see it all."

Adina nodded as if to things outside the bearcat. "Things like what happened to Nat and the survivors don't happen in Cosanti, do they?"

"No. Slavery is outlawed in Cosanti. By now, Nat would be in school, or maybe apprenticed to a tradesman if he was living there. His life would be..." He hesitated. "Easier."

Adina cocked here head at his hesitation and shift in his tone. "What?"

"I was going to say *better*. But that's not fair." He looked her in the eyes and the crease was back between his eyebrows again. "I don't ever want you to think I look down on you or anyone else who is able to survive out here. That's monumental hubris. Most of the people I know, even longhunters like me, would never have survived if we'd been born out here. A lot of people who live in the city states, who have never *seen* what life out here is like, feel like they are better than you or Priav, or Zara or Nat. And it just isn't true."

"Hubris?" Adina's heart thup-thupped in her chest.

He was just so *comfortable* to be around. Everything with him was easy. The shame she'd sometimes felt when she didn't know things just didn't exist with him.

"Sorry. Hubris is like pride but taken to an extreme. Someone who thinks they are better than other people and can't see what's in front of them or won't accept it -- that's hubris. Sometimes I fall into that trap too. I see how hard things are out here, how bad they can be, and I can't help but compare them to things back home." His expression closed incrementally, the crease in his brow deepening. "It just makes me want to do everything I can to make things better."

"And you do." Adina leaned up and kissed his furrowed brow, then relaxed, watching his eyes, her fingers playing in his beard. "You saved me. You saved Priav and the caravan, Nat, Zara and all the people with us now." She put an arm out as if to their makeshift camp.

"That was *you*." Asher nodded to her. "If you hadn't been with me, I wouldn't have intervened against the Ghost Eyes. Priav and the people in her caravan would probably be dead." His expression eased again and his eyes lingering on her face like he was making a map of it in his mind. "*You* saved those people, Adina. Not me."

His compliment made everything inside her warm again and she pulled herself tight against him. "I would never have been brave enough if it wasn't for you."

Asher kissed her hair. "I don't believe that for an instant."

CHAPTER NINETEEN

Hot sun burned across Adina's shoulders as she strained against the chain as the twenty-person team hauled the burnt-out wreck of an old truck up the Quarry's incline toward the bluff. She hissed and grunted, her boots scraping on the small rocks on top of the white stone as she fought for traction. She could hear the rest of the team pulling and grunting as well.

Even with the rough mat padding her shoulder, the chain dug painfully into her collarbone as she threw her weight against it like a beast of burden. Asher was in front of her, and her eyes were fixed on his bulging back muscles as he bulled forward. Omar and another large man were on each side of him. It had been six days since they'd arrived at the Quarry with the survivors and Adina could hear Zara growling in the traces behind her, hauling with everyone else, survivors and Quarry residents alike.

They finally reached the top of the wide lane that ran around the Quarry and the weight came off Adina's shoulders. From there it was a straight pull to the bluff.

The old truck was to become the engine and drive train of the stonecutting saw that Omar, Asher and the engineer had talked about. It would let them cut blocks from the Quarry's white stone, first for the camp's defensive wall, but eventually for buildings.

"Chock the wheels!" the foreman hollered. "Everyone take a break."

Adina collapsed onto the hot stone a few feet away and Asher flopped down next to her, his right shoulder bright red with evenly spaced darker, purple markings from the chain. He sat forward, a burly arm around his knee, his muscular abdomen pushing out and pulling in as he let his head hang, panting from effort.

Zara dropped down onto the burning white stones a few feet away, her skin almost black in contrast to the rock. "You said we'd work here…" Zara heaved a huge breath. "Not do slave labor!"

Since they'd arrived at the Quarry, Zara's harsh demeanor had eased a little with each passing day. She seemed like an entirely different person than the fierce woman who'd stared back at Adina from inside the slave cage. Zara was still hard as nails, but now she joked, and to everyone's surprise, especially Lew-Lew's, she even laughed. There was weary humor in Zara's complaint.

Asher nodded to her. "I wasn't exactly thinking of this either."

Adina laid a hand on Asher's heaving back. "You're the one who wanted to do this!" She let her fingers trail down over his scars as she fell fully onto her back, then threw her arms over her head, trying to breathe.

Asher's hand dropped onto her leg. "Would you have been able to just sit by and watch them struggle with that thing?" He threw his head toward the wheeled chassis.

Adina squinted at him. "Of course not, but this was still your idea."

Asher let himself collapse onto his back too. "Right."

Zara rolled her head toward them. "I could've sat in that shade right over there." She pointed. "And been more than happy to watch you all do this."

Asher chuckled and Adina lifted her head to see Zara past Asher's burly chest. "You are so full of it, Zara. You can barely let people cook without trying to put your hands in." Adina let her head fall again, breathing easier. "You can't help yourself."

Adina didn't have to see Zara's eyebrows rise; they were clear in her mind's eye with the way Zara's tone climbed up. "You've never seen me lazy." Zara pulled a knee up and hung her head. "I'm looking forward to showing you that."

It took all day to get the broken-down vehicle chassis into position at the base of the limestone wall. The sun was setting as Adina wearily walked back toward the rest of the camp with the rest of the hauling crew. Asher was a few feet away, talking with Omar and the engineer about ways to cut the stone.

Loud ululation brought Adina's head up. At the bottom of the ramp, a crowd was gathered with Priav, Rafi and Lew-Lew at its center. People carried trays of food and pitchers of drinks. Suddenly, Priav whooped and stamped her feet. Several people in the crowd broke into a stomping, circular dance.

"A hoe down!" Lew-Lew cheered in elation, throwing his hands skyward, spinning and dancing, showing off his newly made garish outfit. He was wearing a bright fluorescent pink sun hat, and was bare chested, showing off his lanky frame. He'd painted yellow flowers with pink centers across his chest. And he was wearing an outlandish skirt with strips and ribbons that flowed around him as he stomped and flounced, smiling as if he was trying to challenge the sun, dragging everyone into merriment with him.

Adina couldn't help but laugh. Part of it was joy, just watching Lew-Lew, but an equally large part was disbelief.

Where under all the burning sun did he come up with the material and paint for that?

Singing and celebrating broke out in a cheering, jostling chaos as the weary team reached them. Rafi held out a hand. "Asher!"

Adina was suddenly dragged forward, her hand clasped in Asher's as he pulled her with him. As soon as Rafi's hand was on Asher, Rafi pointed to the water. "Bathe! Cool yourselves, then we'll eat!" He looked past Asher, his blind eyes scanning back and forth in the direction of the other workers. "Come! You have worked hard on our new endeavor! Now let's celebrate!"

Before Adina could more than squeak, she was off her feet in Asher's arms. Then she was airborne.

She splashed down in the water. As she popped to the surface, there was a larger splash, Asher hitting the water right next to her. She was still sputtering when his arms wrapped around her from under the water and she was lifted up, shoulders out of the water and he pulled her into a kiss, his expression wide open and joyful.

Adina turned to the shouted, "Look out below!" Zara flung herself off the side of the Quarry seeming to try and make as large a splash as she could. There were more splashes, and the water was suddenly filled with bodies, shouting, and laughing as the singing grew from the shore.

--

Adina was laughing loudly as one of the young Quarry men did awful, drunken impressions of Priav, Rafi, Omar, and finally Asher. The young man appeared to be trying to educate the slave camp survivors about who was who locally. When it came to his impression of Asher, he puffed out his chest and threw his head back stomping around, stabbing at things with a stick as if it was a spear. Asher spat the sour tasting clear white liquor he was drinking, laughing at the young man's impression, then wiped the spittle from his beard. Asher was all white teeth and raised eyebrows, his dimpled expression joyful, without a hint of crease between his eyebrows.

Adina saw a gaggle of young women tittering among themselves, watching him and she grinned. She didn't feel threatened anymore by the attention that every woman with a pulse in camp seemed to lavish on him. Or the men. She also didn't feel the heat of eyes on her anymore. They were still there, men and women watching her, their interest clear, but she just didn't care. She grabbed one of Asher's big arms and gave him a kiss on the burly shoulder, drunk, grinning madly. He turned to her, the back of his hand still on his chin from wiping the spit drink away.

"What?"

"I'm just happy."

He leaned to her and gave her a kiss.

Out of the corner of her eye Adina saw Omar overbalanced near the water's edge. Her lips were still against Asher's when she nodded in Omar's direction.

Asher looked, and a breath later, Omar tumbled into the water with a huge splash. The culprit of his watery landing ran for cover, shrieking with joy; a boy about twelve from among the survivors. Adina laughed until she was crying hanging onto Asher as Omar hauled his bulk out of the water, then scanned the crowd, glowering theatrically looking for the child who'd pushed him in.

The child just giggled uncontrollably, half hiding behind a table.

CHAPTER TWENTY

It was well past midday as Adina packed the last overflow of non-perishable supplies into the tarp covered storage recesses on the top of the bearcat. They couldn't fit more supplies or equipment anywhere if they wanted to have a place they could sleep inside the bearcat.

People had been bringing them gifts all morning. Once word passed through the camp that they were leaving, there had been a nonstop stream of people coming to beg them to stay, and when that failed, to wish them well. Adina stopped, pulling the straps tight over the tarp, and looked around at the camp. She glanced at her bare arms, gleaming in the sun. She'd noticed how square her shoulders had become when she'd looked at her reflection in the bearcat's mirror this morning. It felt like the change had happened overnight. But she knew it hadn't. And she felt stronger too. She could see the quarry's gleaming water from the height of the bearcat.

She felt good. It wasn't just the well wishes, or what they'd done to help. There was a feeling like they were part of something. She glanced up into blazing sun and then out onto the bleak landscape past the camp's borders, her eyes landing on the cobbled together defensive walls. She thought about the stone from the bluff. The pace of construction on the wall had picked up with the arrival of the Quarry's new residents. But the wall still looked paper thin. Adina tried to put the worries out of her head.

There's nothing you can do about it now.

With the boar the survivors had brought with them from the mesa, no parties would have to leave camp for weeks. Hopefully, that would give them time to complete a basic wall before another group set out… *Hopefully.*

Adina climbed down and pushed past the bulging supply bags that filled every space inside, then hopped out of the bearcat's side hatch. Asher was talking with another pair of visitors and as Adina approached, the woman gave her a bright smile and held out a cloth wrapped bundle. "This is for you."

Adina took the bundle, watching the woman with her lapis and green-flecked hazel eyes. "Thank you." She saw Asher's glance. Adina opened the bundle. Inside were oily-looking blocks and round stones.

The woman pointed, grinning. "For your skin." She pointed at the bars. "It helps to keep your skin from drying." Then she pointed to the stones. "Those are so you can scrape away dry skin." The woman pointed at her own heels and elbows.

Adina lifted the bars to her nose; they had a subtle fragrance. "What is it?"

"It's a resin from some of the plants we've found." She gestured to the quarry. "They grow well near the water. Do you like them?"

Adina gave her a wide smile and stepped forward putting an arm around the woman. "I love them, thank you so much." When Adina released her, the woman was blushing.

"I'm so glad." The woman glanced at Asher and back to her. "I… hope we see you again." She was now flushed furiously red. The woman gathered the little girl who was following her and waved as she turned away.

The little girl continued to stare at Asher with wide brown eyes as the woman tugged her along behind her. The little girl finally gave a little wave and turned to follow her mother.

Asher's voice brought Adina's attention back to him. "It looks like I'm not the only one who's made an impression." A corner of his mouth crinkled up at her.

Adina stepped to him and held up the bars. "That was very kind. What do you think?"

He sniffed them. "Very nice." Asher pulled her against him. "You really like it here don't you."

Adina smelled the bars one more time and then closed the bundle again. "It reminds me of home. But more permanent. She shaded her eyes to look at his. "But we've got places we need to be." She grinned widely. "Don't we, Myrmidon?"

"We'll come back. His eyes lingered on the white bluff, now blazing in the afternoon sun. "They'll still be here."

In his certain tone she could hear his hope -- and his worry.

Priav and Rafi appeared from the other side of the bearcat. "I'm glad we were able to catch you before you left," Priav announced without preamble. Rafi walked confidently, his hand resting on Priav's arm. Priav stopped in front of them, and her old eyes spent a long time just looking at them, as if memorizing them. Then she stepped to Asher and lifted her arms, pulling him down into a hug. "You will be missed, Myrmidon." She gave him a kiss on the cheek then held his face in her hands, watching his eyes. "Don't worry about us." She gave his cheeks a squeeze. "We'll be alright. Thanks to you."

When she stepped to Adina, she didn't say anything but just gave her a long, lingering hug that ended with a firm squeeze. Priav whispered,

"Be safe pretty one. I miss you already," and gave her a kiss on the cheek.

Adina couldn't help the tears that suddenly rolled down her cheeks. Her voice was husky when she answered, "I miss you too."

When Priav pulled back, tears were leaking from her faded brown eyes as well. "Be well." Priav grinned at her. "Love well." She laid a hand gently on Adina's cheek, then stepped away.

Rafi gave each of them a hug in turn, then stepped back to Priav. "By the time you get back, our wall will be finished." He turned and pointed toward the bluff with his cane as if he could see it. "And it will be reinforced with stone." When he turned back, he looked supremely confident, and as always -- regal. "Thanks to you. And we will have fish and fresh crops to impress you with."

"I'll look forward to that," Asher answered. "Thank you so much for giving us such hospitality."

Priav waved a hand dismissively. "Bah! You saved our lives, brought us new people to strengthen us. You gave us far more than you received." Then she nodded toward the bluff. "And showed us this is our place. We belong here. Now go." She waved them away. "I don't want to cry anymore!"

Adina laughed and wiped her tears with the back of her hand, sniffling at Priav's dismissal. "Yes, Ma'am."

Asher closed the side hatch of the bearcat, then opened the passenger door for her. Everything in Adina's chest felt like it was flip-flopping as she climbed up, set the package inside, and sat down. She smiled down at Rafi and Priav as Asher disappeared around the front of the truck. It was a strange, awkward moment as she watched them. There was nothing left to say. And they seemed to feel it as profoundly as she did.

A moment later Asher's door slammed shut and the bearcat roared to life. Adina just watched them. She tried to say, "Thank you," but no sound came out.

Priav just smiled and raised a hand, tears rolling down her wrinkled cheeks.

Adina pulled her door closed and wiped her tears, taking large breaths to try and stem the sobs that wanted to burst forth. She returned waves as people gathered to watch them go.

Will they still be here when... IF we come back?

As they passed the patchwork wall, Devon stood with Nat. Devon's other children were tucked in between them. Devon's hand was over her mouth to hide her sobs, but she waved. The weight of Nat's gaze nearly broke Adina's hold on her tears. His expression didn't give anything away, but she could feel the emotion hiding behind it. He just waved to her.

As they pulled out into the barren expanse before them, everything suddenly became real. Adina turned back, watching the camp.

People waving turned to dots, then disappeared in their dust trail. Finally, even the bright white bluff vanished. Adina swallowed the stone in her chest. She felt Asher's eyes on her.

"Are you alright?"

Adina nodded. "I just... I don't know if we'll ever see them again." And strangely, by saying it, some of the tension suddenly fell off.

Asher nodded to her. "They are *good* people, Adina." He reached out and took her hand. "I worry for them and miss them too." He held her eyes for a moment before turning forward again. "And we wouldn't have met them if it hadn't been for you. Everything that happened with them, all the good we did, everything they did for each other. That was all you." He squeezed her hand and then let go, grasping the wheel again.

She leaned across and put a hand on his burly arm. "Thank you for saying that."

He smiled, much more playful than serious. "Well, it's the truth. You're hell to say no to."

She grinned. "I'm glad I'm with you."

Asher leaned over enough to pull her hand to his lips. "Me too."

Adina sat back and closed her eyes, letting a long slow breath escape before opening them again. The camp was behind them now. Everything that mattered was in front of them.

~ END ~

ABOUT THE AUTHOR

Marshal Hunter is an award-winning writer, filmmaker, and game designer whose passion is for world-building and storytelling. Marshal knows risk and adventure firsthand. Four years in the Navy took him more than halfway around the world, he's lived in a tent for months at an archaeological dig, is a living history expert, trained commercial diver, and has gone toe to toe with neo-Nazis and stood shoulder to shoulder with Sioux Water Protectors facing down oil company mercenaries in North Dakota.

Marshal explores themes that make our pulse race and that we all recognize; stepping into our own power, heroism, and what it means to be part of a family. Characters riding off into the sunset together may feel a long way from the grit and hard fighting along the way, but those moments are all the more satisfying because of the struggle to earn them.

Marshal believes that all fiction, regardless of genre, is character driven. If we aren't invested in the characters, what's the point? People want to feel the pinnacles of ecstasy and the crushing lows of defeat when we aren't sure how we'll ever be able to stand up again. That's what Marshal strives for in every paragraph he writes. He wants to feel. And he wants his audience to feel too.

Marshal lives on a beautiful farm in the Pacific Northwest with his wife and dog where he gardens poorly, makes art, and creates worlds to share.